Dark Thirty

Sticks and stones may break my bones
Words forever hurt me

T. Allen Winn

Pp
PROSEPRESS
www.prosepress.biz

Dark Thirty
Copyright © 2012
T. Allen Winn

Published by ProsePress
75 Red Maple Drive,
Pawleys Island,
South Carolina 29585
www.Prosepress.biz

Comments: Contact T. Allen Winn at
TALLENWINN@mail.com

Comments can also be found on
T. Allen Winn's Face Book

ISBN: 978-0-9851889-8-6

All characters in this book are fictional
Any resemblance to actual persons, living
or dead, is entirely coincidental.

Cover Design: OBD Art and Illustration
Contact: proseNcons@live.com

T. Allen Winn's Books In print / E book
Road Rage - Dark Thirty

Coming from T' Allen Winn in 2012
North of the Border
(Another Officer Trudy Wagner suspense thriller)

Jorge Cruz spots the stranded Mustang and the lady with her head buried in the steering wheel. He offers his assistance. He's no mechanic and unable to repair the broken vehicle, Jorge offers her a ride. She accepts. Without warning, the syringe penetrates his neck. How had he been so stupid? Detective Trudy Wagner and her crime investigators face a new challenge on the Grand Strand.

The Perfect Spook House

Abbeville, South Carolina, Halloween 1968, eleven 11th graders vent by exploring old deserted houses, something they've done countless times. Picking the wrong house on the Cedar Springs Road forever changes their lives. Nineteen years later, they're still searching for answers. Reminiscing is not for the weak hearted but the truth can set you free or can it? Sometimes it is best to leave the past where it belongs.

Foot

Mid eighteen hundreds, Washington State Mountains, trapper Bad Nose Ed Carlson leads a handful of hopefuls to a new life. The Spokane Tribe warns stay clear of the great northern woods. It is home of the S'cwene'y'ti, the giant hairy men. Patrons of the wagon train rival the unknown. Mountain men fear nothing. B. N. battles legend and his fellow man the only way he knows how, head on and he never looses but he had never met Big Foot.

ACKNOWLEDGEMENTS

Nothing is ever possible without the belief of family and friends who continue their support even after you have published your first novel. The real test will be determining if they are in it for seconds.

Winn Singleton, a camera, a few friends and the artistic juices flowing, staged and produced the perfect depiction of Dark Thirty for the cover.

Duncan Singleton, with his graphic expertise, the essence of the bully transformed.

Waccamaw Design produced the final imagery.

This could not be accomplished without the hard work of the proof readers; those volunteers who take the tales spun from my wild imagination and make it worthy of being read. Spelling checker does not reconcile wrong words. Use a semicolon or comma, who could have known? A name is but a name, except if it is spelled wrong or interchanged for the incorrect character. I'm glad I just write.

Bullies beware. You know who you are and so do we.

PREFACE

Breaking in new tormentors, not exactly how Dale Thomas Jackson had envisioned his sixteenth year. Worse still, the other existed to haunt his darkness and as always it would be waiting patiently for his arrival. Dale feared them for obvious reasons but feared it for reasons unknown. Meeting and greeting loomed two weeks from tomorrow but Dark Thirty dwelled on the fringes of twilight. Dale Thomas Jackson had no resistance for either, only submission.

Moving to a new high school in ones junior year isn't the most appealing venture for a sixteen year old, especially for a teenager with emotional baggage. Dale Thomas Jackson, pale skinned, slightly pimple faced, five foot ten, skinny as a toothpick, and introverted to boot, offered up a sure recipe for relentless peer pressure and hateful taunting or worse. Adapting to a new horde of disrespectful classmates could only spell new nightmares. He had just gotten accustomed to the last ones and had known just how far they would go, but now he would have to start all over again. He dreaded starting over and breaking in new bullies.

Dale, an only child, would have no sibling support or friends by his side to assist him in warding off evil doers, but such was his ranking in the food chain. Bottom feeders lived off the crumbs of life. He strived to be the best of the unworthy. Everyone had to be good at something.

In two short weeks his new prison sentence would commence with the first day of the school year. He had so little time to prepare. He had made a promise to himself. Take charge of his life this time and not let them get the upper hand. This would require confidence and strategic planning, neither of which existed in his arsenal. Who was he fooling? He had no arsenal.

Possibly he could remain in the shadows, fly under the radar into obscurity. This had never worked before. A new kid always stood out like a sore thumb for better or worse. There was no better ahead for him. They would seek him out. That's what they always did. Bullies despised people like him.

A bully's objectives never changed. They thrived on inflicting their peer pressure; making people like him do their biding. Being their cheap entertainment, through abuse and punishment, floated their boat. They were sadist, the devil's children, and he, their servant, a mere play thing, the crap from the bottom of their shoes. He held no significant rank in the pecking order. Why couldn't he just rebel, stand up to them, show them they couldn't treat him like crap? He always thought a good fight but cowards were not the defiant type. Avoid conflict, turn your head and maybe they would finally go away. No, they wouldn't. They never did.

Dale constantly reminded himself. Just survive two more years, through his junior and senior years then he would be an adult and no longer subjected to the prison system. Surely in the adult world he would no longer be their prey. In 1998, once he graduated, he could control his destiny and choose to live where he wanted, away from his parents and far away from them. Would the world suddenly transform just because he graduated? His tormentors would receive their diploma too and they would still be out there. Adults had choices. Right now he had none.

They would find him out there. They smelled fear from the pores of the insecure, fed on it, would seek it out. That's what the tormentors do. His inability to interact with people, his insecurities in a social world could not be disguised for long, not from them. So what did destiny really hold in store for him? Would he live the life of a reclusive, a hermit, like that crazy guy who lived in apartment 122?

Nope, who was he kidding? There would never be escape for poor little Dale Thomas Jackson. He had thought about the alternative; too many times in fact. He had even imagined the various ways he could end it. Suicidal tendencies were all too common to his kind. His kind; it sounded like some rare breed, his kind; a banished leper colony, so pathetic.

Two more weeks…

*"Bullies are always cowards at heart
and
may be credited with a pretty safe instinct
in scenting their prey."*

Anna Julia Cooper

1

Darby Jackson looked at the models in his room, his escape, a world of the supernatural and the unknown. Lon Chaney as the Wolf Man, Bella Lugosi as Count Dracula, Boris Karloff as The Frankenstein Monster, and The Creature from the Black Lagoon, each of the plastic assembled models drew him into their world and away from the real monsters of his own. He hated school and summer was almost over. He would be in junior high, a seventh grader. He should be excited but he wasn't. He had no reason to believe that 1964 would be any different than last year.

He would be the Lone Ranger, Tonto-less and horseless, a Masked Man traveling on foot into the desert with no hope of coming out alive. There would be no cavalry arriving to rescue him just in the nick of time. In his world the Calvary never arrived. The Indians and outlaws won every fight. Gunslingers ruled. Hostiles flourished. The good guys just got shot dead. He wasn't even sure he was one of the good guys.

The home room bell rang signaling the start of another day in hell. He sat straight up in bed, dripping wet with perspiration, and trembling uncontrollably. Crying out loud, he declared he was too sick to go to school today.

"Wake up, Darby. You're having another one of those nightmares and turn off that damn alarm clock before you wake the dead."

Fluttering his eyes and in a spastic jerky motion, Darby familiarized himself with his surroundings. Brenda, his beloved wife sat up in bed by his side. The digital alarm clock on the nightstand mimicked the start of school, but in this case it just warned him of Monday of another work day. He slapped the off switch.

"Sorry, guess I was having a nightmare at that." He kissed Brenda on the lips. "Turn back over dear. There's no need you getting up right now and I'm sure Dale Thomas didn't hear a thing. He sleeps like a rock."

Darby tumbled out of bed and stumbled toward the bathroom. He needed his morning shower to wash away the filth dredged up from years long passed. He didn't enjoy that part of his life the first time. Why would he wish to relive it now? Focus on the now, he told himself. The spray from the shower head conveniently masked his tears.

2

The moving van guys began unloading their belongings. Dale drew comfort knowing his things were concealed safely inside the cardboard boxes. They could not invade on his privacy, the boxes taped and secured. His life would not be stolen from him here but eventually they would crack the code and unlock his secrets. They always did and then his life would belong to them.

Dale recognized the load of uniquely marked corrugated boxes and led the movers to his room. Neither man spoke but he could sense they didn't like him. His black rim glasses marked him 100% geek. He knew it and he could see it in their eyes. They knew it too. Both were muscular, rugged yet handsome. Neither were his kind and yep, he could tell they had him pegged already. It has to be his glasses, a dead give away. They were adult versions of the spiteful species but because they were being paid for their services, they could not be tormentors, even though the stench from them said they were.

He pushed his glasses back up on his nose. Why did God allow both species to flourish, he wondered. Is this how the Lord tested his flock? He should know by now that sheep and wolf couldn't live side by side without grave consequences and sheep never came out on top. Someone had to be the wolf's whipping post he supposed. He had certainly paid his dues in his short life.

They were too cowardly to feed on one another. Bully law was never bully another bully. Wrestle a pig in the mud and the pig always wins. Throw a sheep in the mud and you had instant lamp chops. Sheep law was to avoid pig pens at all cost and never trust that wolf in sheep's clothing gimmick. Dale removed his glasses and rubbed his eyes. He should wear contacts. Who was he fooling? He knew what he was and so did the ones that preyed on his kind. Maybe if he had cool looking glasses or just maybe he should stop dwelling on what he couldn't change.

Gazing from his bedroom's second floor window he watched his parents directing the movers to their bedroom. He recognized their bedroom suit consisting of old, red mahogany, ugly furniture. He wondered how two normal looking parents could have possibly coupled and produced a mutant like him. His kind defied science. Darby and Brenda Jackson must have realized their mistake because he had no brothers or sisters. They must have decided not to tempt fate and bring another like him into the world.

He sighed. He had wallowed in self pity enough for one afternoon. He could check it off today's list of must do's; mission accomplished, out of my system until tomorrow when it would start all over again. Nothing would change the fact that he was nature's doormat, a place for their kind to wipe their dirty feet.

In two weeks the horror would begin. Bullies didn't really go by the calendar. They existed plain and simple. Time meant nothing in the land of tormentors but to their prey, every second was precious. Two more weeks…

3

Darby watched Dale Thomas standing at his new bedroom window. His heart ached. He understood what his son battled each and every day. He had walked in those shoes but had never shared his journey with Dale. He couldn't. His son looked up to him. How could he admit he had once been a loser? What sort of role model would he be to confess his sins now?

Popular kids made the rules and took charge of their lives and Dale thought good old dad was one of those people. He wasn't and Dale wasn't either and most likely never would be. Darby was ashamed of his decision to stay quiet but he feared worse consequences if Dale knew the truth about his old man.

Darby would do what a father should do. He would support his son and prop him up when he got knocked on his ass. Deceptive, yes, but Dale Thomas didn't need a wimp for a dad. He had been a wimp way too long.

His hope, Dale Thomas would find friends at the new school. He hadn't left any friends behind; that was for sure. Darby's job often kept him on the move. This was both a blessing and curse for his son. Just maybe he would find his kind here, ones he could relate to and could lean on. Sad Darby thought to always refer to them as their kind.

Darby reflected. Dale Thomas was no more a freak of nature than he had been at his age. The boy had feelings. Why couldn't they respect him for who he was or just leave him alone if they didn't. "They had never cut me any slack, so why would it be any different for my son. Turtles just frightened little turtles, first me and now Dale Thomas."

Why hadn't he taught Dale Thomas to be more self confident, a leader, or a lover, anything but a mirror image of himself? What was the old saying? You can't make potato salad out of shit. He hated thinking this way. Two more years and Dale might just have a chance in the adult world.

4

After Dale's furniture had been unloaded and placed in his bedroom, he began unpacking his personal belongings and customizing his new world. He rearranged the various models of The Wolf man, The Frankenstein Monster and The Creature from the Black Lagoon on his special shelve unit. These were not his creations. They had belonged to his dad. He had found them packed away and asked his dad if he could have them. His dad referred to them as his time capsule. For sure no one dabbled with models any more.

He shared a love of the old horror films and characters with his dad. Watching the old movies was one of the few things they did together. His dad called them the classics. Dale's version of the classics was reading Stephen King, Ann Rice and Stephen Koontz. His dad didn't share his love of reading. He read reports and news magazines.

He pulled out his laptop and placed it on charge. They didn't have wireless yet so no one could invade his world. Dale had learned to avoid the social network. Cyber bullies lurked there, seeking new victims. He had no Facebook account. Facebook was a magnet for their kind. They attacked and stalked people like him. Forget twitter and blogs; too much like blood in the water. Forget chat rooms or even e-mail. One might as well leave bread crumbs.

Dale Thomas used his laptop for research. He could Google any topic and become lost in the subject matter. He so enjoyed surfing the net, anonymously, with no fear of anyone finding or identifying him. Sure there were always risks like viruses or hackers but he had no fear of either of these foes. He hoped they got the cable service soon. It helped him pass the time. It was his world, his safe haven.

Dale decided he needed a little break from his strenuous work so reluctantly he ventured into the great outdoors, the front lawn, a new world and his new universe, the neighborhood. He didn't particularly love great frontier but it was a necessary evil. The first thing he noticed was every fourth house looked the same, a repeating pattern of three house styles. His was number two in the rotation, stucco, two story, large porch, tiny postage stamp front yard with a larger fenced in backyard.

Taking a deep breath, did he dare leave the safety of his new turf? He stepped onto the sidewalk. No trap door opened and engulfed him. No monsters rushed down the street to claim fresh meat. Doing a 360 he spotted no sign of life, people-less, pet-less, childless. He could have easily been in that classic Twilight Zone episode, certainly not a Mayberry moment. He saw none of their kind. He liked it.

Twelve houses later the street came to an end in a cul-de-sac. The sequence of the three enveloped the circle. His house appeared in the center. He stared at the front door expecting a Dale clone to appear. No doppelganger did. It would have been so cool if one had.

House three had a bicycle parked out front. The house, a single story dwelling, large bay window out front, small entranceway with unique roof angles, stood out to make pattern three unique. The bike had no middle bar. It belonged to a girl. Very lady like, the kick stand held it in place, not tossed on the yard like the boy's bikes in his last neighborhood. The purplish color looked feminine. Girls were such a predictable species.

Having seen what this stretch of neighborhood had to offer, Dale decided he had wondered far enough for one day and turned to head back to house design number two. He heard the sound of a door slamming shut behind him. What sort of beast had emerged and spotted prey, he wondered. Time to be initiated by one of them he feared. He quickened his pace.

A voice called out, "Hey, where you going?" It didn't sound threatening. Hesitating slightly, he flashed a quick look over his right shoulder. A girl stood by the once deserted purple bike. She waved to him. All of her teeth were bared but not in bite mode. She was actually smiling. Very strange, girls almost never smiled at him; laughed yes, smiled no.

He turned away, searched for another recipient of her smile and wave, but the side walk and street remained empty. This had to be the Twilight Zone. He heard a peculiar clicking sound approaching and whirled expecting to be blindsided. The clicking emitted from the bicycle's chain. The girl had closed the distance quickly to less than three yards. Sitting prim and proper on the slim seat, she pedaled, still smiling and coasted alongside him.

"Hi," she spoke with an enticing voice that sent a surge of pleasurable waves through his nervous system. He had never felt so tingly before from just a voice. "New to the neighborhood?" she asked.

Dale awkwardly, almost mechanically nodded yes.

"I thought so," she replied. Her face never changed expression, a mouth full of perfect teeth, smiling and accented by perfectly matching dimples. He had never noticed dimples before. "My name is Debra Floyd. What's yours?"

This completely unnerved him. He was not accustomed to peers asking him his name. Typically, none were interested in his name and would rather make up their own for him. Stupidly, he just stood there and remained speechless like some deaf and dumb lab mutation.

"I don't bite, at least not until I get to know you." She continued to smile flawlessly.

"Dale," he finally mustered. "Dale Thomas Jackson."

"Well, it's a pleasure to meet you Dale Thomas Jackson. Welcome to my neighborhood. Which house do you live in?"

"Number two," he replied holding up two fingers.

She stopped smiling and frowned for the first time. "Number two?"

"That style just next to your number three," he explained.

"Oh," she laughed. "Where is your number two?'

"Four cycles that way," he pointed.

"Got it and what shall I call you, Dale, Thomas or Mister Jackson or maybe just number two like on Star Trek?'

"Dale," he replied. It sure beat some of the names he had been called.

"Do you have a car?"

He shook his head no.

"I have my driver's license but since the accident my folks aren't so keen about me driving, so I settle for my bike right now. Do you have your license?"

He shook his head no.

"You got a bike? We can ride together some if you do."

Dale shook his head no again. He had never owned a bike. He had never wanted one. Where would he ever have ridden one anyway? He never had friends anywhere they had lived so a bike had been pretty useless. Their kind would have probably whipped his ass and taken it from him like he had seen them do to others. That's what they always did; stole his kind's stuff and never gave it back.

"No bike, no driver's license, that's so weird."

"I never had any place to go so I didn't need either."

"Here," she motioned. "You can ride mine."

"I've never ridden one."

"Never ridden a bike," she made that weird little frown again.

"No…and there's no need me riding one now."

"Here give mine a try. You might like it.'

"No thanks," he answered, fearing he would surely injure himself or at best make a complete ass of himself.

"Well, would you care to walk with me?"

"Walk where?"

"Anywhere, silly. What about to house number two?" She snickered, an almost snorting sound.

This wasn't the Twilight Zone. It had to be another planet all together. Girls didn't smile at him, talk to him and certainly didn't ask to walk him home. It had to be a trick to find out where he lived, and then she would call her gang to harass him. He feared it but certainly hoped he was wrong. The girl seemed too nice or maybe she was just that devious.

Dale finally answered, "Let's just walk wherever you want to walk."

"Okay, I was heading to the park. It's just a couple of blocks over. It has a pool, a tennis court, a nice lake and wonderful riding trails, or walking trails since you don't ride."

Dale nodded okay. She continued to jabber away, doing most of the talking. He never knew girls could talk so much but what did he really know about their species. Her tone had gotten less irritating and more soothing. It had a way of wearing a person down he supposed.

"So what grade are you in?"

"I start the eleventh in two weeks."

"Me too," she smiled. "Are you attending public or private school?"

"Whatever school is nearby…"

"Fantastic, that would be my school," she giggled. "Maybe, we'll have some of the same classes. The school is just three blocks away. We could walk together every morning if the weather isn't yucky. I don't like to ride the bus. Do you?'

"Walking sounds fine." No good had ever come out of him riding a bus. Too many of their kind rode the bus and lurked at the stops.

"I ride my bike but I could walk just as easily. If my folks give in, maybe I can drive us. Who am I kidding? They'll probably never allow me to drive a car again."

"Walking is fine," he repeated. He had never walked to school in his life. It was more dangerous than riding the bus. Their kind could too easily ambush him. His parents had always driven him to school but something prevented him from admitting this to the girl. He had surprised himself walking the twelve house distance alone.

"Do you have any brothers or sisters?"

Dale shook his head no.

"Me either. I guess we were so perfect our parents couldn't improve on perfection so they just stopped breeding."

He had never quite seen it that way before. It certainly beat his mutation theory. He had figured as preventive measures his mother had gone on the pill and his dad had a vasectomy for good measure. He liked the girl's style.

The girl, Debra Floyd, with her hazel colored eyes, petite little figure, tiny breast, auburn hair and a Samantha Stephens bewitched nose, had him mesmerized and a tad smitten. He had known her all of about twenty minutes. She even had his lily white complexion. They looked like a couple of vampires except vampires didn't come out in the broad daylight. Yep, some planet he had crash landed on for sure. She seemed too perfect. He had probably nodded off after unpacking. He'd wake up shortly.

"What sort of things do you like to do Dale Thomas Jackson?"

No one had ever asked him that question before. From vampire to zombie, he stood speechless, unable to articulate a coherent response. His armpits felt all sweaty. His mouth felt dry and turned wrong side outwards. Was he possessed or something?

"Do you have any hobbies;" she continued her one way conversation. "I'm sorry, I just chatter aimless don't I? My folks stay onto me about it. I'm surprised you haven't hauled tail and run away from me like most everyone else does. I never know when to shut up. I take medicine for it but it doesn't seem to be working so good right now, does it? My shrink says I could outgrow it. I say fat chance."

Shrink, Dale thought. He had never known anyone who saw a shrink. The girl was a piece of work.

"Nights are worse. I can't shut my brain down. I have medication I'm supposed to take about an hour before bed but it makes me have weird sex dreams. I wake up all hot and bothered. You ever dream about sex at night, Dale? Boys are supposed to get aroused, aren't they? Do you get aroused in the middle of night? What do you do about those feelings when you have them?"

Dale blushed big time. He had never talked sex to anyone before and now the girl was jabbering at him about erections, his and hers. He didn't know girls got them. She must have multiple personalities, or something he thought.

"I have crazy mood swings. I take medication for that too. I bet you're wishing you had never met me." She laughed that snorted laugh again.

Dale actually smiled for the first time since the beginning of Mister Toad's wild ride. He liked the girl. She was far more defective than him. Thank goodness he was on no medication. Maybe he should be. He finally spoke up. "How much further to this park or do we need to take medication to see it?"

"Next block," she snorted. "Why Dale Thomas Jackson I do believe you have a sarcastic sense of humor after all."

No one had ever told him he had any sort of sense of humor. Maybe the girl was smarter than he gave her credit.

5

Bobby Atkinson stood in line at Rocky's Pizza, his favorite fast food venue in the Four Seasons Mall. The aroma of the supreme he had chosen tantalized his nostrils and almost launched him into full fledge drooling. His stomach growled its approval. So enthralled and anticipating devouring every meaty and cheesy morsel he failed to see the ambush.

Jake Tyler and Austin 'Stoner' Wheeler snatched him from his place in line, each grabbing him by an elbow, almost lifting him completely off the floor. Only his one hundred eighty five pounds kept him on his tiptoes and grounded. Fast food had its perks and served his five foot five frame well right now.

"Lard Ass, what are you buying us?" asked Jake.

Bobby swallowed loudly and mustered up a wimpy reply, slightly above a whisper, "El Grande Supreme, loaded."

"Excellent selection, dickhead," spouted Stoner. "A '#2' will help expand that fat ass figure of yours."

Bobby said nothing. He looked to the small crowd for help but no one even gave him a hopeful glance. He had learned long ago it was best to just keep his mouth shut and let it run its course. The gang thrived on conflict and confrontation and could smell fear like a bloodhound. He faced facts. He would not be eating the '#2' but would be paying for it.

"Fork over your claim ticket," demanded Jake.

Bobby handed it to him without argument. Stoner held him firmly by his pants loops, almost creating a denim wedgie. Once Stoner released him he began making his hasty retreat.

"Not so fast," warned Jake. "We didn't dismiss you yet."

Bobby stopped dead in his tracks. He knew the routine and said nothing, just waited.

"Fork over your cash," ordered Stoner. "You didn't spend it all on the '#2' did you?"

Bobby fumbled in his pocket and removed his leather tri-fold wallet, a gift from his Aunt Martha last Christmas. Stoner snatched it from his palm before he could remove the cash. "Eight stinking bucks, that's it."

Bobby nodded then reached for the wallet but Stoner jerked it out of his reach. "Nice, said Stoner, we'll just keep this since you short changed us."

"But," then Bobby shushed up, figuring a wallet to spare an ass beating seemed like a fair trade.

Jake reached over and pinched him on his left nipple, bringing tears to his eyes. "You have some mighty fine tits for a boy. If times get tough, we might just invite you to one of our little parties. Now beat it."

Bobby blended into the mall pedestrians and rubbed his breast when he was out of sight. He had gotten off lightly this time and wasted no time putting some distance between him and Satan's offspring. He hadn't planned on having to deal with them until school started in at least a couple of more weeks.

He thought one of these days these bastards were going to pay for the crap that they dished out. Right, who was he kidding? Maybe they would be struck by a school bus or an eighteen wheeler. Evil never dies. Broke and hungry Bobby headed home.

6

Dale Thomas Jackson wandered through the park with the girl named Debra Floyd, an extraordinarily new experience to share alone time with an actual girl. She sure talked endlessly. He listened. He nodded and occasionally conjured up a smile. He had no previous experience with girls. Maybe all of them acted like this.

Two more weeks, he reminded himself. They would seek him out. That's what they always did. Seek and find the different ones; those that didn't fit in their self proclaimed society. Maybe with this girl as a friend he would blend into their world. Did he just think girlfriend? He surely assumed a lot. Why would she consider being his friend, much less girlfriend?

Yep, having an actual girlfriend could just work. Smoke and mirrors was new strategy. Possibly she would play along with his little charade if he asked her. Loners were such easy prey but numbers often spelled safety. Would they accept him for normal if he had the girl by his side? He would settle for them just leaving him alone. Would he put her in danger? This was almost overwhelming to contemplate.

The girl was sort of his kind so possibly deceiving them would be impossible. They wouldn't tolerate being scammed. He had too many questions and so few answers. His life was never easy. He didn't articulate questions so well and that wasn't good with girls so his lips remained locked tight.

Even while he thought, she jabbered away, speaking long sentences of nothingness. Could two wrongs make a right, he wondered? He had read somewhere that opposites were suppose to be attracted to one another but where were he and the girl on the opposite chart? Maybe they were too much the same so the formula was screwed up from the start.

"Would Dale Thomas Jackson like to ride my bike here in the park?" she asked, jolting him from his pity party.

He blurted out a response before really thinking, "I've never ridden one before. I might wreck it."

Surprised by his response, she replied, "It's easy. It's just like riding a bike, you never forget." She smiled at that stupid statement. "I guess that isn't the correct thing to say for a situation like this, is it?" She laughed out loud, that snorting sort of laugh again. He liked it. It sounded real, not put on.

Reluctantly he agreed to give it a try but dreaded it. She coached him through the process, holding the bike upright while he positioned himself on the seat. All he needed was training wheels and tassels and he would look the part. She directed him to place his lead foot on one of the peddles. How did she know which foot was his lead foot? He felt so stupid.

He gripped the handle bars and then pushed off. She held onto the handle bars and seat walking along beside him as if he were a mere child. This was embarrassing. His breathing became loud, labored and almost wheezy. He teetered on the verge of a panic attack, all because of this stupid bicycle.

"Are you okay?"

Nodding wasn't easy while concentrating so as not to fall. She gave him a push and yelled, "Start peddling! Keep the handle bars straight. Don't go too fast at first."

How am I supposed to remember all of that? She thinks I'm in control. I'm so not in control and she just turned me loose. Why did she do that? This was a bad idea.

"Press the opposite way on the peddles to use the brakes."

Dale subconsciously did just that and almost lost it. Wobbling he tried to regain his composure. This was not going well. There was a reason why he had never owned or ridden one of these things.

"Peddle slowly, one foot then the other."

Dale traveled three feet, then ten and soon he was well ahead of the girl and gaining confidence. He was one of the Wright Brothers at Kitty Hawk preparing to go airborne for the very first time. The grassy field offered no obstacles in his way. He was actually riding a bicycle by himself for the first time and at the young age of sixteen. How pathetic. Dale soon realized that thinking too much and riding for the first time equated to a bad formula.

The handle bars snapped quickly to his right and the ground got closer. The girl came to his rescue and pulled the bike off of him. He met her eyes, feeling so worthless. She laughed and snorted. He laughed out loud without the snort. His world felt safe with the girl by his side. She rattled off another barrage of endless chatter. He just sat there on the ground and smiled. Maybe there could be safety in numbers he surmised.

He must not forget the fact that school still loomed large just two weeks away. Arrive with a friend, fool them and walk away a winner. It sounded so easy. He should ask his parents for a bike. How silly. He could be driving an automobile. They had four wheels and stayed upright. He wondered if the girl could really drive. She had mentioned her parents revoking her driving privileges because of some sort of incident.

The girl said something about having to head back home and he nodded okay. Two more weeks…

7

Douglas walked home from his piano lessons. Miss Casey lived only two short blocks away from where his mom operated her florist shop. He helped his mom during the summer and after school putting up stock, taking out the trash and even made deliveries using the VW Super Bug all painted up in flowery advertisements. It put spending money in his pocket which in turn supported his video game habit. Next on his wish list would be his very own cell phone.

Douglas's mom sometimes even allowed him to help with the flower arrangements. She praised him for his creative talent and awesome designs. She said he had an artist's eye. He thought how funny since he wore these gosh awful quarter inch thick bifocals and was blind as a cave dwelling albino trout without them.

Those glasses advertised Geek. He wished he could wear contacts but they would probably have to be so thick he would look like some bug eyed freak. Without his seeing problem, he could have almost passed for normal. They came in handy when he was in the scouts. He could use them to start a fire anytime except at night. He earned a merit badge by not sharing the little secret with Mister Everett, the Scout Leader.

Doing flower arrangements wasn't what most guys did. Tack on playing the piano and he had gotten pegged as the resident queer. He liked girls and wished he had one for his very own. He wasn't queer by a long shot. Names and rumors tended to stick no matter how hard you tried to prove them wrong.

Screw them. He never allowed what others thought to consume him. He accepted who he was even if they didn't. This was a recipe for many violent confrontations with those who resented him. Unlike most of his cohorts, he didn't back away from a fight but rarely won one. He simply refused to let them run over him easily. In the end they always did just that. He had the battle scars to prove it, visually and emotionally.

Even though he received his fair share of abuse, most of them found much easier prey. He was usually the last resort or only a target when others weren't available. He tried to always surround himself with low hanging fruit. His friends never knew how much he used and abused them. If not for the stupid glasses he could have possibly passed for a jock, maybe a football player, even though he was too klutzy and clumsy to participate in any sport. Sports didn't really interest him at all but that didn't make him a queer.

His music bag tossed over his shoulder, he approached the last crossover where his mom's shop was located, just over a block further and around the corner. He spotted them before they saw him. Jake and Stoner were sitting on an apartment stoop munching on what appeared to be pizza. Douglas contemplated staying on this side of the street and passing safely by, then back tracking. Hell no, he thought. That just wasn't his style. He had just as much right to be here as them. They just didn't know it.

Taking them head on in broad daylight was his best option. If they saw him trying to sneak by it would be much worse. It would play right into their hands. Pushing the bag up on his shoulder, he took a deep breath, and then he crossed the street into the jaws of the beast. He would most likely regret this ploy.

Maintaining a brisk pace but not running, he quickly reached the stoop. Head down, he sighed relief after successfully passing unnoticed. Less than twenty more paces and he would cut the corner. Something snagged his book bag halting him in his tracks. Douglas spun to see what he had gotten it caught on and came face to face with Jake. Stoner halted to a stop on his skateboard, blocking his path. They looked none too happy, each still holding a slice of pizza. It smelled delicious; reminding him he hadn't eaten yet.

Jake Tyler was the leader of the local thugs. He wasn't particularly intimidating, average height and build, brown wavy hair and dark complexion, but he had the smarts and ability to charm a snake. He ruled by intimidation and shear numbers but could hold his own in an unfair fight. Jake's dad was in politics and his mom was some sort of lawyer. Jake didn't have to be such an ass.

Austin Wheeler was a true stoner, having earned his name honestly. He had stringy, dirty blonde, shoulder length hair, lazy eyes from smoking dope and a lanky body. His best asset was that everyone knew he was just plain crazy, always good for a dare. Douglas didn't know much about Stoner's parents. You never saw them at any school functions or Stoner with them in public. Stoner tended to do most anything he wanted.

"Damn inconsiderate, huh Stoner" snapped Jake sarcastically, whipping pizza from the corner of his mouth. "Big boy was just going to pass us by with not so much as saying a fine hello."

"Damn rude it was," replied Stoner with a mouth full of pizza, almost making his comment incoherent.

Jake pointed. "What's in that cute little bag?"

Douglas didn't flinch. He held his ground, standing there like a pillar of salt. He spoke precise and displayed no indication of being rattled. "They're my music books. I just finished my piano lessons." He saw no point in hiding them or lying about it.

"Faggots take piano lessons," remarked Stoner. "Are you a faggot?"

"You like sucking Johnson's," asked Jack, snatching the bag from his shoulder.

"Give that back, smartass," demanded Douglas, realizing the time it left his lips he had pushed it a tad too far.

Jake tossed it to Stoner. Douglas turned to face off with Stoner and Jack grabbed him from behind and in a choke hold. He had taken the bait. How stupid he thought.

"Asshole…" growled Jake, now twisting and pinning his right arm behind his back. "I really don't appreciate such language from the likes of you."

Douglas was unable to catch his breath. Jake now walked him down an alley then forced him to his knees. "Now that looks just too damned natural doesn't it, Stoner?

Why don't you let Mister Piano Boy tune up your organ for you?"

Stoner unzipped his pants, his crotch less than an inch from Douglas's face. Douglas squirmed but Jake tightened his hold on his throat and twisted his arm to the point it felt like he would break it. "Still too public," said Jake, jerking Douglas to his feet and guiding him deeper down the alley and behind a dumpster. "This is better."

Douglas could not escape the death grip. Jake had mastered the hold. He forced him back to his knees a second time. This time ripping his pants and skinning his left knee. "Open wide," commanded Jake as Stoner unzipped his pants again.

"I'm not going to do it and you can't make me," protested Douglas.

Stoner kicked him square in the stomach and he doubled over, falling face first onto the concrete when Jake released the hold. Jake propped his foot on his back preventing him from rising. Gasping for breath, he still struggled to right himself. Douglas heard the second zipper. These bastards intended to gang rape him or worse and he wasn't sure he would be able to stop then. He started to cry out but Jake shifted his foot to the back of neck, stifling the attempt. Douglas clinched one of his fists.

Warm liquid began splattering his head then his neck, burning his eyes. Piss, they were pissing on him. Jake removed his foot then kicked him in his side forcing him to roll over on his back. Stoner stood over him now; both of his assailants emptying their full bladders, guiding the streams and wetting him from head to foot. Stoner made sure he gave him a full shot in the face. For good measure, Stoner kicked him in the balls, ensuring he would remain there until they exited the ally. He did.

"Stoner, use your phone and snap a picture of this. If you breathe a word about what just happened, we share this with the world."

"Got it," laughed Stoner.

"Let's go, and remember what I said."

Finally the pain subsided and he made it to a sitting position and wiped his face with his shirt. His music books were shredded and drenched in urine. Tears formed in his eyes but he refused to allow them to escape. Instead he clinched his fists and vowed this would be the last time they pulled this crap with him. Who was he fooling? He was no hero. He wasn't really that brave but still, why not resist next time. Maybe they would tire of the attacks or maybe they would just do worse things. They had his photograph and they would use it. Douglas faced reality and headed to the flower shop.

8

Darby Jackson commuted toward work. In this traffic his office waited for him some forty minutes away, downtown, among the Charlotte skyscrapers. He despised the congestion, drivers cutting one another off and honking horns like wild animals. The drive had been much more peaceful at his previous location down in Greenville, South Carolina. He would make the best of it. Transfers were a part of his life. Job completed, Corporate always reassigned him. He had received a generous bonus by completing the project ahead of schedule.

Forty minutes gave him too much time to think. He didn't relish excessive thinking time. In forty minutes he could too easily descend into very dark places. Dwelling on this morning's nightmare, reliving every detail, he suddenly drifted back into a real life episode. He recalled that dreaded locker event.

He banged on that locker door until he bloodied his knuckles. He had developed his claustrophobia at an early age and still suffered from it to this day. He avoided any projects with confined spaces. Back then they had discovered how it scared him. That's all it had taken for them to wedge him in his locker and lock him inside. They had sealed him in his own locker using his lock.

He remembered those tears burning his cheeks, screaming for someone to let him out, sniffling like a little girl. Those ten minutes felt like an eternity. His tormentors had discreetly deserted their post. They had gone to class after banging on the locker door and harassing him.

He remembered while trapped thinking he had at least fared better than his best friend, Riley Thompson. Poor Riley had been forced into an even more shameful and compromising situation during PE class. Exiting the shower, the miserable horde had swarmed poor Riley and forced him outside onto the breezeway. Naked as the day he was born, he had no way back in except to enter the adjoining hallway reentering the gym via the main entrance way.

He had absolutely no way to hide his boyish attributes. Unfortunate for Riley, the girls PE class was still underway on the basketball court when he made his poorly planned, hasty grand entrance. The girls giggled and pointed. Poor ole Riley had been cursed with a tiny penis and now the entire school knew his secret.

Kids gave him hell for the remainder of the school year and probably forever. Names can truly hurt you. They taunted him with shouts of 'do you have to squat when you pee'? He wondered whatever happened to Riley Thompson. Thank goodness, there were no cell phones back then or computers for cyber abuse. Still, it was cruel just the same and quite effective.

Darby recalled that time his tormentors had jumped him and locked him inside his locker. After what seemed like an eternity, finally he had heard foot steps. He banged on the door with enough force to wake the dead. Through the vented slats he could make out a shadow now standing in front of the locker. He whined, "Please open the door and let me out."

A man's voice answered, "Do you know the combination?"

"Right 22, left 34, back right 44."

He could hear the tumblers being manipulated. Click, the lock was removed and the door opened. Standing over him, a crimson dressed Mister Grant asked, "Are you all right son?"

Mister Grant, named Lurch by the students, looked just like the Adams family's butler. No one would ever call him that to his face though. "Who did this to you son?"

"It was just an accident," Darby had told him.

"Son, you're telling me you accidentally climbed inside that locker and this lock clicked shut behind you. I don't think so."

"It just happened."

"We can put a stop to this sort of thing if you'll just tell me who did it."

"You don't get it. It would just make it worse."

"We can't stop the bullies if you don't tell us who they are."

Sure, Darby remembered thinking. They were Coach Grant's jocks, the ones from his track team. He would never discipline his own jocks for someone like him. "I've got to go to class, sir and I'm late. Fingering them would only make my life worse."

"Son you've been locked in that locker for God knows how long, so how can it possibly get any worse than that?"

"Trust me sir, you have no idea."

"Well, it looks to me you've been through enough so I won't report it this time."

"Thank you, sir."

A honking horn shocked Darby back to the present world. The driver was yelling a string of curses and giving him the finger. He didn't know why. He waved him off and maneuvered into the next lane. The two guys in the pickup truck looked like the ones from his school days. They probably thought the same about him. He was tempted to shoot them a bird but thought better of it. He had never challenged a bully before so why start now.

9

Brenda Jackson, unlike Darby, didn't suffer from any self esteem problems. Having won almost every beauty contest she had ever entered, she had few regrets except the ho-hum life she had become trapped in as a bored housewife. She needed more; much more. Each passing day devoured her like the worst cancer. She loved Darby but he wasn't enough to extinguish the fire blazing out of control.

Fearing time running out, Charlotte could just be her salvation, the perfect town for her to recapture the missing parts of the puzzle in her life. Still possessing her bodacious high school figure, a thick and flowing mane of red, luscious full lips and killer hazel eyes, she could still turn a head or two.

Brenda completely dominated this marriage, both in and out of bed. She was easily satisfied in either venue but a gamer, she could push the envelope and come out on top if she so desired. Yes she loved Darby and she had been with no other man but he couldn't always fulfill her needs, especially lately. She fantasized but didn't have the guts to take it any further. She was too devoted to her marriage and son.

No denying, Darby Jackson was a wonderful provider. She thanked her lucky stars for finding her soul mate. He had business savvy but behind every successful man stood a strong, and in this case, dominant woman. Poor Darby just lacked backbone. She ensured he made the correct decisions and stood his ground. She should work on commission.

Brenda was Darby's universe and he did her bidding. She wasn't overly persistent or pushy but she could effectively pull the strings. He allowed her. He hated any type of confrontation. Dale Thomas Jackson suffered from his father's disease. She knew at an early age that he was destined for tougher times and would surely follow down the Darby path if she stood by and allowed it. She would never let that happen.

Sixteen years old, he still had shown no interest in girls. He had never even tried for his driver's license, so un-teenager like. Most kids grew up wanting a bike, a skateboard, or scooter but not Dale. Stranger still, he never brought any friends home. She doubted he had any. She really had her work cut out to transform him into the furthest thing from his father.

Brenda for all her seemingly perfection was far from perfect. She had abused prescription drugs but had not considered it drug abuse. She had a fondness for adult beverages too, but refused to admit she verged on being an alcoholic. Mixing the two transformed her into something very unlady-like but she never saw herself in that light. Neither would ever catapult her into an affair no matter how badly she might think she needed it. She was too faithful to ever act on those fantasies.

10

Cassie Richards, with her buzz style haircut resembled more boy than girl. With breasts almost nonexistent and wide at the hips, looking the part of a girl became more challenging. Cassie, to her peers, was a broken human being, often taunted and called retarded. She was far from being retarded. She suffered from autism. When she spoke, and the time had to be just right, she did so with a raspy voice, almost sounding like a chronic smoker. Autism affected her ability to communicate and interact because of the restricted and repetitive behavior. She was no dummy.

Accused so often of being a lesbian, stereotyped as a butch, she was the furthest thing from it. She actually didn't think in sexual terms, had no sexual desires. She had not a tomboy bone in her body. She existed in a world that didn't accept her but she blundered on in life, mostly not impacted by any of it.

Her school girl peers had started a vicious rumor that Cassie had been caught in a most compromising position with a coke bottle. She didn't even like sodas. Kids can be so cruel. Unfazed by verbal abuse or physical attacks she would withdraw deeper, hum a no tune song until it was over.

Cassie sat on a park bench in the afternoon sun watching the squirrels. She so loved watching squirrels. In her lap rested a copy of *Dark Towers* written by Stephen King. She adored Stephen King but she couldn't read and watch squirrels at the same time. The sun warmed her back. It felt good. Cassie lived in a world of solitude. The squirrels shared this world for the moment.

Mack had been eyeing her from the video store across the street. Mack Stephenson, a senior member of Jake's so called gang, had a malicious side, much worse and darker than the other boys. He enjoyed torturing small animals and literally hated squirrels. If no animals were to be found, he could spend hours wreaking hell on the insect population. He was so demented and oozed pure evil, the Devil's offspring.

Mack had been a creation of rape. His mother's older brothers had sexually abused her until finally impregnating her. The act itself angered her father and he had kicked her out of the house, but not because he was ashamed of his daughter. He resented her for giving into her brothers. She had always belonged to him and him alone.

Just short of her sixteenth birthday she had given birth to Mack. An uncle and aunt had taken her in. His mom, resenting the pregnancy and birth of her bastard son, had ironically reciprocated the behavior inflicted on her by her father and siblings. She had taken liberties with her son, physically and sexually abusing Mack. She had created the monster that now watched Cassie. He had not yet tested his perversions on a human. He eyed Cassie and a plan developed.

Mack was two years older than the boys he ran with but was much smaller in stature. He had not fared so well in school and had failed two grades so far. He wasn't stupid, just lazy. Mack took the low road and blended in with the gang. He preferred not being a leader for now.

So focused, he didn't notice the arrival of a couple of his cohorts. "Mack, where the hell is your head, up your butt?" asked Buddy. "We've been yelling at you from the CVS." Buddy was pudgy and taller, had slicked back dark brown hair and not much of a neck resting on wide shoulders.

"Are you stoned?" asked Ray, standing directly behind him and giving him a playful push. Ray was wiry and red headed, wearing his hair cropped short. He was about the same height as Buddy, five ten but thinner.

Mack didn't like playful pushes. He didn't like being touched at all. He balled his fist and fought to hold back his anger. He counted from ten backwards in his head until the anger subsided.

"You lusting over the retard," chuckled Buddy.

"Not lusting but thinking," answered Mack with a wink and a smile. "I've never ever cared for that one but I bet she's never had any before."

"You're not seriously thinking about busting her are you?" asked Ray.

Mack smiled. "Can you say gang banger?"

"You're not serious," said Buddy.

"Think about it. She's probably ripe for the taking," Mack grinned, forming a hole with his thumb and index finger, fingering it with the middle finger of his other hand.

"You've got dog crap for brains," commented Ray. "She's a damned lesbian retard."

"If she is, she likes the same thing that we do," chuckled Mack, attempting to lighten the mood.

"Man, we would catch hell if anybody found out we done her," snapped Buddy.

"We'd catch hell if anyone knew we were even thinking about it," added Ray.

"We can do this," advised Mack. "She's too stupid to rat us out."

"Where are you getting this *we* crap?" asked Buddy.

"Yeah, my pecker is not going near that," boasted Ray.

"Yours hasn't even seen the inside of one so don't try to talk like you have," cautioned Mack.

"Man, if we get caught they'll toss our butts in jail," answered Buddy.

"You been planning this for a while haven't you?" asked Ray.

"Nope, just came up with the idea and thought you boys would be in for it."

"You're sick or wacko," snapped Ray.

Mack twirled around and grabbed Ray by his shirt and pushed him against a light pole. "Don't ever talk down to me like that again or I'll make you wish you hadn't."

"Can't you take a joke, man?"

Mack turned him loose and grinned, "Are you boys just going to jack off forever or are you going to bust your own cherries?"

"You better run this by Jake," advised Buddy.

"Jake is not here. Does he do all the thinking for you, limp dicks, or can't you make a decision on your own?"

"Hell no," spoke up Ray. "I do what I want."

"You're going to do it, aren't you," said Buddy, looking at Ray.

"Damn straight," answered Ray. "Are you in or not?"

Buddy took a deep breath. "I'm in but we better not get caught."

"Let's call this our little secret, our little initiation and if we all swear to keep our mouths shut then we can't get busted for doing the dirty. Everyone swear?"

Buddy and Ray responded, "I swear."

Buddy cut his eyes toward Ray and Ray diverted his look to his feet. If they rode this out, there would be no return. Keeping their mouths closed was a must and both knew it. It was still a very bad idea on all levels.

"I wish we could run it by Jake first," whined Buddy.

"We don't have time," replied Mack, pointing toward Cassie.

She was on the move. It was now or never. Cassie had seen the trio. Instead of walking home she switched directions and headed the opposite way. She sensed danger. Gifted, her sense of perception seldom let her down.

"Where's she going?" asked Ray.

It didn't take long for them to have their answer. She entered the county library. She had received a temporary reprieve. Cassie sat at a table and began reading her book, now oblivious to the dangers that had existed just mere minutes ago.

"We'll wait her out," advised Mack. "She can't stay inside forever."

"Let me go for Jake," said Buddy.

"Not enough for more than three," replied Mack. "It gets too sloppy after that."

Buddy gave up. Obviously he would be unable to change Mack's mind.

"Don't we need rubbers," said Ray.

"Not to worry," answered Mack. "Her kind can't get pregnant. Today everybody busts their cherry!"

11

Dale had returned to his island, his safety zone, his room in the house. Debra Floyd, nice name for a girl he thought. He smiled thinking he had just ridden his first bicycle. He wasn't so sure he should be that proud of it at age sixteen. He wondered if he could muster up the confidence to try for his driver's license. Would his folks even allow him to try?

He listened to his mom singing to the tune of *Afternoon Delight* from her Starland Vocal Band CD. She seemed to play that old seventies tune a lot lately. She had a wonderful singing voice. He couldn't sing a lick or at least he didn't think he could. He hadn't really ever tried. Music wasn't his thing.

Boxes, some empty, others still taped securely, were in every room. The house was still topsy-turvy from the move. Social disorder prevailed. He liked the chaotic state. Dale could easily become lost in the clutter. Society could be too organized for his taste. Perfection often attracted unwanted attention. He preferred maintaining a low profile, blending in and avoiding detection. This reduced the opportunities for belligerent assaults by them.

Glancing at the wall clock already secured in its new home, he realized that his dad should be arriving here soon from work. He knew the routine. They would eat as a family then he would return to his new room. There he would wait for the night time demon to seek him out in his new environment. Moving never threw it off his trail. It was a bloodhound and had his scent embedded in its brain like a memory stick.

Dark-Thirty would raise its ugly head soon enough. Sixteen years old and afraid of the dark, he still slept with all the lights on in his room. Darkness brought with it even darker secrets and fears. He didn't really give a hoot about his age. Evil lurked. It waited for an opportunity to take charge, to possess him. Bad things happened when it overpowered him. His mission, always stay a step ahead of it. So far he had been winning.

In the light of day he commanded control but the dark fed on him. It put horrible thoughts in his head and pumped evil into his bloodstream. Evil would love nothing better than to demand he did its bidding. It was so blood thirsty. It terrified him.

Only once had he allowed it to invade his world since turning sixteen. His bedside lamp had burned out during the night. He had awoken to pitch blackness when his bladder had urged him to visit the bathroom. If not for quick thinking and a flashlight within hands reach he could have been facing grave circumstances. Fortunately he had escaped unscathed but he could not risk such a close call again. Being older and stronger had definitely given him an advantage.

He often wondered if others were affected by Dark-Thirty. So far he had never met anyone that lived in fear of it like him. He hoped the girl didn't suffer from it. He really liked her. He hoped she liked him. She seemed to but what did he really know about girls.

Shadowy fingers began reaching though his bedroom window. He switched on the overhead ceiling fan light and they quickly retreated. Dale didn't drop his guard and remained watchful. Tomorrow he might just ask his folks for a bicycle, a red one with a headlight. Then again he would decide that tomorrow.

He had other things to worry about. The new school year in a brand school would begin in two weeks. He retrieved his laptop, switched it on and entered his password. Still they didn't have internet service so he accessed one of his research folders. He began perusing the information as he had done countless times before. He read the study conducted by ABC News. 1500 kids in grades four through eight had been surveyed asking them about bullying.

> 42% of kids have been bullied while online. One in four had it happen more than once.

35% of kids have been threatened online. Nearly one in five had it happen more than once.

21% of kids have received mean or threatening e-mails or other messages.

58% of kids admit someone has said mean or hurtful things to them online. More than four out of ten say it has happened more than once.

58% have not told their parents or an adult about something mean or hurtful that happened to them online.

Dale could have been any of these statistics. Dale skimmed through similar surveys from other study groups.

43% of US teens had experienced some form of cyber-bullying in the past year.

This was why Dale avoided Facebook and chat rooms. He refused to give them access to his privacy. More information just validated the wisdom in his decision.

23% of middle-schoolers surveyed had been bullied by e-mail

35% in chat rooms

41% by text messages on their cell phones

Fully 41% did not know the identity of the perpetrators.

This was a ritual Dale endured when preparing for a new school year. It was a bitter pill to swallow but it couldn't be sugar coated. Facing the reality helped him deal with the consequences. He hoped this year and the new school would skew the statistics but then again, who was he really fooling. The data never lies. Mere days separated him from the truth. Dale sighed and closed his laptop.

12

Darby Jackson worked his way through the Charlotte traffic, taking in the new landscape and city's skyline, having time to do both in snarled traffic. It crept along like a snail or came to abrupt halts. If you could block out the traffic woes, the big city wasn't so bad so far. Sure, it had its seedy side but all large cities did. In time he would learn how to avoid them. Today he would just keep the windows up and doors locked as he passed through the unsafe looking areas.

Darby had enjoyed the Greenville-Spartanburg area of South Carolina, especially those half and half plates at the Beacon. There was no beating those greasy hamburgers smothered in fries and onion rings. One plate could feed a family of three. An icon, it was tough to beat.

His work always required him to relocate so he tried hard to not become too attached to a particular location or home. Brenda and Dale Thomas always had a tougher time adjusting than he. Brenda had been no ray of sunshine this particular move. She had slipped into some sort of new funk. That wasn't really unusual for her but this time it seemed darker, more depressed and not her usual mere moodiness. He hated to think of her in terms of the "B" word but she could be quite bitchy under the worst of circumstances. While she seemed okay this morning, she had been taking on the "B" persona just last night. He loved her never the less.

Darby certainly hoped Dale Thomas had fared well today. His only son didn't adapt well to these moves with their new surroundings. He kept promising himself that he would spend more time with his son but he too often fell short on those promises. He found those father-son moments to be much too awkward. Darby didn't think he served as much of a role model. He was a good provider but that didn't translate to good father.

Dale Thomas should be driving now but had shown no interest in the right of passage for teenagers. He had never mentioned wanting to try for his license or a desire to drive, period. He was a chip off the old man's block. Darby had not driven his first automobile until he was nearly eighteen. This had not been entirely his choice. An unfortunate summer event had caused his folks to slam the door on his aspiration of driving. He quickly shifted his thoughts away from that episode. It's better to keep some things buried.

Nineteen years old and out of the nest; he wasn't sure if he left or they tossed him out. All was so fuzzy. He wondered how his folks were doing. He hadn't seen them since that day, twenty years ago. Brenda and Dale Thomas thought both were dead. At least that's what he had told them and as far as he was concerned, they were. They had never attempted to contact him nor had he them.

A kid deserved to have grandparents. Dale should know them and spend time with them. He quickly came to terms with that slip. His parents didn't deserve Dale. Thank goodness he had Brenda's parents to fill that void but Dale never showed much interest in spending time with them. They lived in Florida so that cramped the situation. Darby and Brenda had raised their son with little family support; more so because of his job and moving about.

He still couldn't believe how easy it had been to fabricate the tale about his parents. He had lied to Brenda about his past life and painted this sad story about both parents being killed by a drunk driver. He had found it easy to believe the story too. They were dead and buried. He had no regrets, no remorse. In his mind they were indeed deceased.

Darby still maneuvered through the city traffic and had not yet made it to interstate 85 where the real challenges of driving would begin. So deep in thought he failed to notice the half hidden stop sign, a box truck parked along the curb concealing it from view. The noise of the crunching metal and spinning blur jolted him from his day dreaming just seconds before all went dark.

13

Brenda picked up the phone on the third ring. "Yes, this is Brenda Jackson. Who may I ask is calling?"

Her face turned ashen. She dropped the cell phone to the tile floor; the compartment holding the battery shattering, sending the phone's battery careening under the table. Scampering up the stairs two steps at a time she didn't stop to knock on Dale's door as was their agreement. She instead flung the door open. It slammed against a dresser. Dale nearly leaped off the bed thinking their kind had invaded his inner sanctum.

"Dale, put on your shoes! We've got to go, now! There's been a terrible accident. Your father is in the hospital!"

Blinking nervously Dale mustered a response, "Is he dead?

"Hurry," screamed Brenda, exiting the doorway.

Dale took that as a no or possibly a maybe. He snatched up his shoes and quickly followed. "Welcome to Charlotte."

14

Cassie Richards eyed the large clock just above the librarian's checkout station. It would be getting dark in forty minutes so she had just enough time to complete her walk home in the daylight. Her chair made one of those loud squeaks, most turning their heads towards her displaying their annoyance and disapproval. The librarian shushed her.

Stopping by the desk, she checked out two additional novels, both authored by Stephen King. Standing just inside the safety of the glassed entrance way, she perused the outside and saw no signs of that Mack and his henchmen. She rationalized it to be safe to go home now. Descending the five steps she was on her way.

Upon reaching the sidewalk, Cassie surveyed the street in both directions. Other than an elderly lady walking her dog and another younger woman carrying an arm load of packages, the sidewalks were empty. Traffic zoomed by steadily, drivers oblivious to anyone.

Cassie's foot falls echoed as she passed store fronts. She had only one alleged spooky place to pass, an ancient cemetery. While others feared it, she had never found it scary. The graveyard bordered one city block of her walk, where she would make a right turn off the main boulevard and down a narrow side street. When Cassie made that turn she noticed that all of the street lights were out. Closer observation she realized they had been broken. Even though the last of the daylight made its final stand, twilight seemed to be winning the tug of war on this particular street lined with large oaks and elms. Shadows engulfed the sidewalk.

Clutching her books tightly to her tiny flat bosom, Cassie began her pass by the hallowed ground. She had often spent her afternoons exploring the 100 year old resting place, reading the inscriptions on the tombstones, fascinated by them. This time, head down, she maintained a steady pace with only one mission, arrive home safely.

She heard a twig snap or did she? Footsteps, she heard footsteps. Yes, footsteps; approaching from behind. Footsteps shouldn't alarm her. People should still be walking on the streets. It wasn't late. She stopped and turned to face the sound but saw no one. Footsteps were always caused by somebody so where was the owner?

Walking ever so cautiously backwards, she cocked her head and listened but heard no more steps nor saw anyone. Her heel caught an uneven section of sidewalk and she tumbled backwards. Unable to stop her fall she fell quite unladylike on her rear end, slamming the back of her head, unable to break her fall while clutching her books.

Woozy, she sat upright and rubbed her head after setting the books on the sidewalk beside her. Her head hurt but her pride hurt worse. Before she could right herself, they were on her. So many arms, she felt as if she was being attacked by an octopus. One hand covered her mouth while others lifted her off the walk. She recognized them. They were carrying her into the cemetery. This was something out of one the novels she had read except she wasn't enjoying the passage.

Casey made eye contact with Mack, clutching her ankles. He grinned and squeezed them. She had a sudden urge to kick him in the mouth but didn't. She was too worried about her Stephen King novels, *Salem's Lot* and *The Dark Tower*, both in hardback. She was aware of headstones towering to her left. She read the inscription on one as they passed. Hezekiah Woods, Born 1900, Died 1979, Loving Husband, Proud Father. She blocked out the world threatening her life. Where were her books?

15

Dale Thomas and his mother sat nervously in the emergency waiting room while Darby received the medical treatment hopefully saving his life. The driver of the dump truck that had t-boned his driver's side door miraculously escaped uninjured. Darby had not been so lucky. The fireman had used the Jaws of Life to cut him free of his vehicle.

Dale squirmed in his chair as if undergoing electrical shock from the seat. Brenda sat motionless, staring at the floral patterns on the wallpaper. Only one other person occupied the waiting room. An octogenarian held to a thread of hope that his wife of 53 years would survive her emergency cancer surgery. The doctors had not been very optimistic.

The emergency room door swung open and all eyes turned to face the doctor in surgical garb. He made eye contact and spoke softly, shaking his head as he spoke the words you never want to hear in this situation, "I'm sorry, we did everything we could."

The old man stood and shook the surgeon's hand and thanked him. A tear ran down his cheek. His wife was gone. She was with the angels now.

Brenda sighed loudly, relieved but sorry that the old man had received such heartbreaking news. Dale eyed his mother then the man. A strange thought overtook him. He wished he had known his grandparents, his dad's parents. He didn't know why he thought this and certainly had no clue that both were alive and well somewhere.

He and his mom resumed their vigil from hell. Brenda watched the second hand on the emergency room wall clock barely moving. She felt she had aged several years just waiting here. An eternity weighed heavy on her shoulders.

She needed a drink and her pills. She tried to rationalize, that by it taking so long, it might be a good sign. She couldn't really fathom why she thought that was good.

Almost three hours later the two Jacksons received their first news. The handsome young surgeon told them that Darby was in critical condition, unconscious, possibly in a coma. He had suffered severe head trauma. Most of his limbs were broken or battered. He had been placed on life support because he had no living will. The future looked bleak, recovery slim in Brenda's eyes.

The room closed in on her. She lost it. Incoherent, she blubbered, making no sense. She began screaming at the top of her lungs. Dale covered his ears and closed his eyes. The doctor called for assistance. An orderly and nurse showed up and the three tried to restrain Brenda but she resisted, clawing the orderly on his arms. She continued to scream and flail like a lunatic. Finally the doctor barked some sort of orders to the nurse. She departed then soon returned with a large syringe. The injection caused his mother to go limp in their arms.

They removed her from the waiting room then a few minutes later the nurse returned, assuring him that his mother would be all right. Dale figured they had given her one of those tranquilizers like they shoot at wild animals. The nurse said she was being admitted to the hospital for observation and then asked him who she could call. He had no one to call but he didn't tell her that. "I'll call my grandfather." He lied to her saying he had the phone number. He didn't know why he had lied to her, except possibly he had been too embarrassed to tell her he had no one to call.

She escorted him to a phone at the nurse's station and told him to take his time. She instructed him to press nine and then the area code and phone number. He fumbled with the phone then pretended to press the digits that would ring his grandfather's number. A stranger answered and Dale began talking. The stranger yelled a series of profanities and hung up. Dale continued to jabber nonsense at the dead line.

He finally hung up on his end and said, "He's meeting me out front in ten minutes."

The nurse assisted him to the elevator and bid him farewell after giving him a number he could use to reach the nurse's station directly. She told him he could come back and check on both parents tomorrow. She told him if they had any questions to have his grandfather call.

16

Dale, standing at the curb outside the hospital had no idea which way to go to return to the house they had just moved into yesterday. He regretted he didn't have his driver's license or even a bicycle. Worse still, Dark-Thirty was out there waiting for him. Only the well lit hospital perimeter offered him protection. He could see darkness on the horizon. Frozen, he could go no further. How could he possibly return to that third house and why would he?

He checked his pockets. He had four dollars and seventy three cents. How far could that take him in a cab? Where would he tell the driver to take him? He didn't remember his new address. If he got there, the house would be dark and dangerous. He sat down on the curbing. He had no plan. He counted the money again, still four dollars and seventy three cents. He returned it to his pocket. Maybe he would count it again later.

A gravely voice broke the silence. "Sonny, are you okay?" Dale leapt up from the curbing. "I remember you from the waiting room," said the old man. "How's your Pa?" He stood there solemn faced but mustering a smile.

Dale not one for making conversation and especially with a stranger, didn't answer. He just shrugged. He was trapped between the old gent and what lurked out there.

"I suspect your parents taught you not to speak to strangers didn't they young feller? That's a smart thing to remember. My name is Carl, Carl O'Conner. Now I'm no stranger. What might I call you?" Carl offered Dale his hand but Dale didn't take it.

"Dale Thomas Jackson and my father is in intensive care."

"Sorry to hear that. Who are you waiting here for?"

"My grandfather Jackson but he's dead."

Puzzled, Carl asked "Was he in your pa's car?"

"No, I never knew him. He's always been dead."

Scratching his head, Carl asked, "You don't have a way home do you?"

"I don't even know where my house is but it's the third in the sequence. We just moved here."

"What happened to your ma? Wasn't she up there in the waiting room with you?"

"She went loony tunes and they gave her a shot, locked her away. They told me to come back tomorrow."

"Is there anyone at your house?"

Dale shook his head no.

"Is there someone we can call?"

Another no shake…

"Do you have any friends near by?"

"The girl I just met today but I don't know her address or telephone number either."

"What are your folk's name?"

"Darby and Brenda Jackson…"

"We could go back in and get the information from a nurse."

"No," Dale answered instantly. "The nurse thinks my grandfather Jackson is picking me up."

Scratching his chin, Carl replied, "Then I reckon I'm your grandpa for the night. You can come home with me. I could use the company. My house would just be dark and lonely without her there."

Dale nodded okay, knowing this wasn't a very intelligent thing to do, to go home with a stranger. He could be a serial killer, a very old serial killer. Those serial killers that never got caught did grow old, didn't they? He didn't look like the serial killer type but did any of them? Maybe he was a sexual predator. He sure looked too old for that too. He really had no options. Dale decided to let him be his grandfather for one night.

"I can tell you're not so sure about this," smiled Carl. "It's your choice to make but I'll be leaving in about ten minutes. I have to get my truck from the parking garage. Be standing here when I get back if you want to go."

Ten minutes later Dale and the old man were driving away in an old Ford pick-up. The darkness closed in quickly, tapping at his passenger side window. He maintained his sanity by drawing comfort that he wasn't alone. Being alone after dark is not a good thing.

Thirty minutes later they pulled into the driveway. "Well, will this old place do for home tonight? It's not much but she always loved it."

Dale nodded it would. The small wood framed white house with black shutters looked just fine. It was a lot homier than the house he had just moved into.

"In the morning we'll figure out where it is that you live and I'll get you back to the hospital to check on your folks. Are you hungry?"

Dale just realized he was and nodded yes.

"Me too…I'll rustle us up something. I'm not the cook my wife is...was, but I can hold my own in the kitchen. I promise it will be edible."

Dale liked his new grandfather. Carl was what he dreamed Grandfather Jackson would have been like. He thought about his father and mother then stared out the kitchen window at the darkness, glad he was here with the old man. The things lurking there in the shadows were not nearly so intimidating when other people were around. He wondered what the girl was doing now.

After a modest meal of fried bologna, eggs and cheese toast, Carl introduced Dale to the spare bedroom. Dale figured two stories above ground level should keep Dark Thirty at bay. The bedroom had one window with blinds and the bathroom had none. Dale switched on every possible light in both rooms.

"If you need anything during the night, just make yourself at home. Feel welcome to raid the kitchen. There's some Oreos in the cookie jar and milk in the refrigerator. Good night, young man."

Dale mustered up a smile and nodded back. Taking a deep breath, he surveyed the room one more time. Nothing good happened after dark thirty. The illumination should keep him safe. Nothing bad ever happened in the light; except at school. He wished he had his laptop and internet. He hadn't seen any computers in any of the other rooms.

He slipped off his shoes and socks then stripped out of his jeans and shirt down to his jockey shorts. After making one last trip to the bathroom, he returned to the frilly bed and pulled the covers up to his nose. He really didn't expect to sleep a whole lot. He rarely ever did and didn't really require a lot of sleep. He was good to go on four hours of shut eye. A light sleeper, he heard every sound, his salvation and his curse. He had researched insomnia on the internet and had convinced himself that he suffered from it.

He lay there thinking about the old man. He seemed like a good grandfatherly type. His dad never spoke of his father. He really knew nothing about him except he was dead, same as his grandmother Jackson. They had died in some sort of automobile accident.

Dale eased the covers down to just below his chin. He scanned the room one more time then something strange occurred. He fell asleep, sound asleep. If he would have been awake he would have heard himself snoring for the first time.

Dale woke up smacking his lips. The smell of bacon caused his belly to growl loudly. He sat up, disoriented. A digital clock on the night stand displayed 8:11 AM. How was that possible? He last remembered it displaying 11:49 PM. He remembered the old man then he remembered his folks.

He eased out of bed and slipped on his same clothes, the only clothes he had. He urgently had the need to relieve his aching bladder. Standing over the john, the sounds of his forceful stream echoed off the bathroom walls, breaking the deadly silence. He looked in the mirror and Dale Thomas Jackson greeted him with a nod.

Opening the bedroom door, the aroma penetrated his nostrils, exciting his senses like breakfast had never done before. His stomach let out a yell, *feed me, now!* Cereal and milk never smelled this good. He padded his way down the hallway almost breaking his neck when his socks caused him to slide as if on ice. The hardwood floor apparently had been recently waxed. Dale has been accustomed to a life time on carpet.

The staircase was not any better, hardwood and slippery. He held firmly to the rail as he descended. The old man, his newly found grandfather Jackson-O'Conner stood with his back to him in the kitchen. He could hear the bacon sizzling in the frying pan on the stove and could see a cloud of haze rising above the old man's shoulders.

Seemingly equipped with radar the old man spoke without even turning around, "Sleep well young Jackson?"

Dale nodded then realized the old man could not see his response. He mustered up a "yes sir."

"A man needs a good night's sleep and a hardy breakfast to prepare him for the day ahead. Are you hungry?"

"Yes sir," he answered, thinking he sounded like a parrot.

"How do you like your eggs?"

No one had ever asked him that question before. Last night Carl had just cooked them without asking. He thought about it and answered, "Cooked."

"Fine way to have them," chuckled Carl. "How about I scramble them?"

"Okay," Dale responded.

"Have a seat at the table," Carl said with his back still to Dale. "Breakfast should be ready in less than two minutes. I've got bacon, grits, cheese toast and eggs, cooked my own secret way, scrambled."

Dale recognized eggs, bacon and cheese toast but what was grits?

"It was a mighty fine thing you did coming home with me last night. The house would have been empty without…are you ready to eat?"

"Yes sir." Dale assessed the kitchen. It felt good, warm and cozy. His kitchens had never felt any of those things. They had just felt like kitchens. He had never thought of rooms in this manner. He liked the way it felt. His stomach let out a thunderous roar.

"Best we get some food into you before that thing goes on the prowl," laughed Carl. "I'll bless it then we eat."

Confused, Dale said nothing. He had no idea how you blessed food but watched as the old man bowed his head and figured he was saying a prayer or something like that.

He finished thanking the Lord and wishing for a good day ahead. "Dig in."

This was another new experience, sitting at a table and eating. His family hardly ever ate together, much less at a table. His dad worked late most of the time. His mom served him meals on a tray and he ate them in front of the television. He wasn't sure when and where his mother ate.

"So tell me, young Jackson, should we plan to go by the hospital first or to your house to let you clean up and change clothes?"

No one had ever asked him what he wanted to do. He had never made a decision or had choices. He just nodded okay.

"I'm sorry. I have a tendency to ramble. Eat your breakfast and we'll figure it out later."

Dale stared at his plate. The white stuff he didn't recognize must be the grits. He tasted it but it really had no taste. He wondered why people ate it.

"Here, try this," Carl said as he added butter, a little salt and pepper and a slice of cheese. The old man apparently liked cheese on everything. He had to admit. It did taste better. Dale eventually cleaned his plate.

The old man smiled at him. He always smiled. His wife had just died but he kept smiling. He sure hoped the old man wasn't going crazy or something. He thought about those psycho movies. No, the old man was too nice to be a crazy murderer, wasn't he? But in the movies the ones that sliced and diced were the ones that looked normal and acted normal.

Carl broke the silence causing Dale to jump. "So tell me young Jackson, what do you like to do for fun?"

Dale shrugged. He asked as many questions as the girl did, almost. He sure liked to talk and smile. Dale didn't know what he liked to do. He had never given it much thought.

"I love to fish but I must admit I haven't wet a hook in way too long. Maybe you and me can go fishing, young Jackson?"

"I've never fished."

"Then it's about time you did. You'll enjoy it. I promise."

"I did ride a bicycle for the first time."

"Fishing is like riding a bicycle," grinned Carl. "Once you've done it, you don't forget how. I'm going to enjoy teaching you the art of fishing young Jackson, that I am. Sixteen years old, it's time for you to wet a hook and drown a worm or two."

Funny terms thought Dale but he surely did like this old man and couldn't wait to wet his first hook. Maybe they could take the girl with them. She probably already knew how to wet a hook. He wasn't sure about drowning worms.

"Tell you what. I'll drop you off at the hospital first. I've got some business to take care of, making some arrangements for my beloved. Then we'll find out where that house of yours is and I'll take you there. We'll work on a fishing date if it's okay with your folks."

Dale nodded.

"I'll put the dishes in the washer then we'll hit the road."

Dale nodded again.

Ten minutes later they were hitting the road. The old truck maneuvered amongst the heavy traffic on interstate 85, everything zooming by them and honking their horns. Hitting the road apparently wasn't done at very high speeds. Some of the drivers yelled not so nice things at the old man. He paid them no attention. He just hummed some unfamiliar tune. Dale liked the old man a lot.

17

Just past 10 AM, the truck pulled into the hospital parking lot. It looked like to Dale that most of the vehicles from the interstate had already parked there. Carl O'Connor circled the parking area forever before finally finding a vacant parking spot.

His new make believe grandfather accompanied him to the floor and ward where the desk had directed them to go. A nurse pointed down the corridor toward her room and told him he could go inside. Carl advised him he would return in awhile after he took care of business.

Dale pushed the door open and entered. He did not recognize the black woman in his mom's bed. He stepped closer as if expecting her to change color before his eyes but she didn't. Spotting a second bed just beyond the first, he slinked by the one occupied by the stranger. He could not make out the occupant of the second bed. The covers were pulled over the person's head. Something underneath stirred.

Just as he cleared the foot of the second bed, the black woman sat straight up and pointed at him with long fingers with red polished nails. In a shrill voice she proclaimed, "I see you, you little sneaky white boy. You're here to steal my money. I done fooled you though. My money is buried in a mason jar where you can't find it."

Dale stopped dead in his tracks, eyes wide open and swallowing like he had a golf ball stuck in his throat. The lady looked possessed. He expected her head to start spinning on her neck and for her to start spewing green puke.

Just as quickly as she had sprung to life, she fell backwards on her pillow. Her eyes rolled back in her head then she went silent. Taking advantage of her sudden mood swing he advanced quickly to the bedside of the phantom occupant. Standing between the bed and the outer wall he almost became claustrophobic.

The person under the sheets was now motionless. He hoped whoever was under there didn't spring to life like the black woman and accuse him of stealing buried money in a mason jar. He wasn't even sure what a mason jar was but he was positive it couldn't be buried in a tile floor.

He stepped closer to the head of the bed and reached for the covers. Taking a deep breath he began to slowly peel the sheet back. He sighed when he saw his mom's face underneath, but she still wasn't moving. He wasn't sure she was even breathing. He pulled the cover down to her waist. She wore a funny looking paper green bracelet on her wrist where she normally wore gold jewelry. He hoped she wouldn't think he had stolen the black woman's money. He was supposed to be innocent until proven guilty.

Speechless, not uncommon territory, Dale just stood there staring at Brenda Jackson. His mom said nothing. He said nothing. He decided to touch her arm. She stirred slightly but still didn't open her eyes. She was at least alive. He had this eerie feeling of being watched but her eyes remained closed. Slowly he turned. The black woman had her eyes open again and they were locked on him. She had two evil eyes capable of planting a curse on him like one of those voodoo women. He hoped she didn't leap from that bed again, dive across and grab him.

A blood curdling scream broke the silence. The black woman chimed in with a deafening scream. The first one had come from him after something grabbed him by the arm. It wasn't even dark thirty yet. He tried to break free but the grip held him tightly in its clutches. "Honey, everything is going to be okay," his mother said.

18

Douglas still hadn't gotten over the degrading episode of those two ruthless renegades peeing on him and his music books. He wished he had the courage to kill Mack and Stoner and that entire gang of thugs. They deserved to be dead, all of them. In his head he knew if he would have fought back harder he would have been the one that ended up dead. At least he would have died with honor and not pissed on. Now he was just pissed off.

Douglas stood outside the Cinema 12 reliving that awful moment. He waited impatiently for Randle to arrive. The new sci-fi flick was going to be the best of the Star Wars movies. If he had been Skywalker or Solo, he would kick their asses, no doubt. But like the fantasy on the screen, it remained a fantasy in his mind.

He spotted his buddy Randle from almost a block away. He recognized his screwed up stride. He was pigeon toed and his head looked too big for his body. His parents had just dropped him off at the entrance to the strip mall where the theaters were located. Randle sported a *May the Force Be with You* tee-shirt. Bobby waved and Randle waved back. He pretended to swing a laser sword as he approached.

"Crap," Douglas sighed, seeing Stoner, Jake and Mack closing in on Randle from behind. He started to yell and warn him but thought better. He didn't want to draw their attention to him. It got worse; others of the despicable gang, Buddy, Ray, David and Rich were laying a trap concealed in the doorway of the Dollar General Store. The entire horde was out in full force. This spelled bad news for their usual victims.

Douglas quickly handed his ticket to the lady at the entrance and left Randle to the wolves. He couldn't help him.

He was out numbered and there was no need in both of them getting their butts kicked. He hated doing this but was not guilt ridden by his decision to save himself. Sometimes sacrifices were necessary. How easily he has swept away the earlier degrading incident and returned to his cowardly ways.

Ahead at the Dollar Store entrance, the four demons from hell formed a human wall across the sidewalk. Jake and the other equally demonic entities closed the distance undetected. Randle spotted them but it was too late for him to veer in another direction. He slowed and thought maybe it wasn't too late to retreat. One glance over his shoulder dispelled the thoughts of an escape. He was surrounded.

Randle contemplated hauling ass across the parking lot but he could never outrun all of them. He was no sprinter. They'd be on him before he reached the first row of cars. He looked toward the theaters for help from Douglas but he was no longer standing out front. He didn't see him anywhere. Maybe he had gone for help he hoped. Out numbered seven to one, he was so screwed.

"Randy-Pansy," spoke up Jake. "I bet you're going to that fag riddled Star Wars flick."

"Leave me alone. I'm not bothering you, Jake."

"But you are. You live and breathe in my space. I don't like little deformed melon heads uglying up my world."

"Just leave me alone."

"Big talk from a little bitch like you," chimed in Mack.

"Where'd you get that fagot shirt?" asked Stoner tugging on one of the sleeves, almost yanking Randle off his feet.

"Please don't hurt me. Let me go."

"Please don't hurt me," mocked Rich.

"Leave me alone," repeated Buddy, mocking Randle too.

"I hate whiny little elephant eared fagot freaks," spewed Mack.

"I'm not a queer!" yelled Randle.

"I'm not a queer," mocked Rich. "All of you little geeks are."

"What you say we find out," said Jake, motioning for the others to encircle him.

They began poking him hard with their fingers. Stoner grabbed him by the forearm and spun him around. Mack spat on his shirt. Ray snatched him up by the back of his belt lifting him up on his tip toes and breathed hard on the back of his neck.

"You ever been in a circle jerk?" asked Jack.

"I bet you have, haven't you." whispered Mack. "We'll show you what we do in them."

Stoner yanked him tearing his shirt just below the collar. "Man, you wear such cheap clothes."

David snatched his wallet from his back pants pocket. "Thirteen lousy bucks, that's all you have?"

Randle rolled the dice and yelled at the top of his lungs, "Stop. Leave me the hell alone!"

A man wearing a camouflaged baseball cap and a Lynyrd Skynyrd tee-shirt approached from the parking lot. He spat a wad of tobacco on the sidewalk, splattering Mack's and Jake's shoes. Juice was lodged in his thick gnarly beard. He attempted to wipe it with the back of hand. "Just what the hell is going on here?" he demanded, clearly not fearful of the seven boys.

"Nothing, just messing around," answered a very pissed off Jake, but he toned down his response, not wanting to tangle with this guy.

"Well, nothing looks pretty damned suspicious to me. Do it someplace else and leave that kid alone if you catch my drift." He crossed his huge tattooed forearms, waiting for them to disperse.

Trying to remain cool and unshaken by the big redneck's threats, the seven parted, allowing Randle to escape. Mack gritted his teeth. He didn't like taking orders from anybody.

"I said scat!" commanded the man with arms the size of tree trunks. "Hold it there sonny," grabbing David by his shirt collar. "Fork over that wallet you lifted and the money."

David reluctantly gave him both.

"Hey kid, hold up," he yelled. "I believe these belong to you."

Randle paused and returned to retrieve his belongings. He said thanks then quickly headed back towards the theaters. He had dodged the big one.

"Now you bunch of hoodlums can get the hell out of here and best I don't see you hanging around here again or I might just completely forget my manners all together. You wouldn't like me when I'm really pissed, I assure you. Whupping up on a bunch of little snot nose brats gets my juices flowing." He disappeared inside the store next to the Dollar General Store.

Ray read the name, "Big Ed's Pawn and he must be Big Ed. He's certainly big enough."

Randle had already purchased his ticket and entered the movie theater entrance. He searched frantically for Douglas to give him what for. Douglas sat on the back row, center, so he could see the entire theater and thwart off any ambushes. He'd rather be sitting up close but he dared not given the circumstances.

He spotted Randle when he entered the aisle way. Randle's eyes hadn't become adjusted yet. The movie had just started. Douglas shouted and waved to get Randle's attention. The crowd shushed him, many giving him a go to hell look.

"What happened?" Douglas asked him, playing stupid and noticing his torn shirt.

"Lucky for me, nothing," replied Randle. "But I wouldn't count on it being over. It never is. They might just wait until we leave."

"Have some popcorn."

"What happened to you? Never mind, you're just a spineless chicken like me."

A lady in front turned around and starred them down. She shushed them, giving them that look that meant business.

"Pass me the popcorn, Doug. Let's hope we make it home afterwards."

"May the force be with us."

19

Dale sat at the chair pulled next to his mom's bed. Her speech was slightly slurred from the medication. She opened her eyes briefly and talked weird talk between dozing. A doctor came in the room and asked him to step outside while he examined her. The black woman said nothing but followed him with her eyes as he crossed the room.

Less than five minutes later the doctor had finished doing whatever doctors do and told him he could go back inside. He should have asked the doctor what was wrong with her. The doctor should have told him without him having to ask but he didn't. If the girl would have been here she would have asked him.

A girl in a red pinstriped uniform entered the room next. She looked too young to be a nurse. She stuck a thermometer in his mom's mouth, checked her heart and pulse, fumbled with the IV bag then left without muttering a word. She did smile at him. He blushed when she did. Why was no one telling him anything?

Two men dressed in white uniforms moved the black woman onto a cot on wheels and took her away. The voodoo woman was gone for good he hoped. School would start in less than two weeks. His world had fallen apart sooner that had been expected.

Meanwhile, in intensive care, Darby Jackson existed in a dark nothingness. He could hear distant voices and sensed stirring nearby but he could not see the source of either. He's eye lids were so heavy. His mouth felt parched but no words would form on his lips to ask for a drink. His world remained black as pitch.

He was no longer in the bright light or in the hallway of his school where he had drifted from time to time. He still didn't know where here was but it sure sounded like a busy place. He had no memory of coming to this place. Why couldn't he open his eyes or talk or something? Where were Brenda and Dale Thomas? Why didn't he feel something he wondered? His world was empty and lonely. He heard footsteps approaching. It sounded like they were very near.

Someone caressed his wrist. She put something cold in his mouth, a thermometer by the shape of it. A few seconds later he heard it beep. No one uttered a word even though he heard at least two more sets of footfalls. Just as quickly, he heard the steps leaving and all turned silent again. Where were Brenda and Dale?

Debra Floyd wondered the same thing. She knocked on Dale's front door for a third time in the past four hours with the same result. No one answered. She had really taken a liking to the skinny, pimply faced neighborhood newcomer. Dale was odd and quirky like her. She hoped he was okay, wondering where he might be.

He didn't talk very much but she probably talked too much. On average they were the perfect match. She sat patiently on the porch stoop wondering where they had all disappeared. How could a family move in then vanish? Tuesday wasn't a day you expected things like this to happen. It was just too eerie.

Debra sighed loudly, staring up the street then down; a little pouty expression worn on her face. Patience had soon worn out its welcome. She disengaged her bike's kickstand and peddled toward home. She took one more peek hoping to see activity at his house but it looked the same. She would try again later.

20

Dale's new make-believe grandfather Jackson returned to the hospital as promised to check on his newly adopted grandson. Walking into the hospital room he spotted young Dale Thomas sitting by his mother's bed. The look on his face told him things weren't going well but he asked the question any way. "How's she doing?"

Dale just shrugged then managed to say, "She's been asleep mostly."

"Did you see her doctor?"

Dale nodded.

"Did the doctor tell you what was wrong with her?"

"No sir."

"What about your father?"

"They won't let me see him. He's in ICU. What's ICU?"

"Intensive Care Unit...it just means that they're keeping a close watch over him," explained Carl O'Conner. "Let me see if I can dig up some dirt on what's going on."

"Okay."

"Have you eaten any vittles?"

"Vittles?"

"Food," clarified Carl, "You haven't eaten anything since breakfast?"

Dale shook his head no. Vittles, wetting a hook, drowning worms and grits, he was learning a new language.

"Nothing..."

Dale shook his head no again.

"We'll have to do something about that now won't we?"

Dale just shrugged. He had mastered the shrug and was quite accomplished at nodding. He could answer most any question with one or the other, except when he was on the phone.

Carl returned about ten minutes later and reported that Darby Jackson's condition had not changed much since the automobile accident. His condition was critical but stable. They were concerned with swelling around his brain. As for Brenda Jackson, her emotional state had become very fragile with the trauma of her husband's accident. She remained heavily sedated and under observation.

Carl decided there was nothing to do but bring young Dale Thomas Jackson home with him. He had already made the final arrangements for his wife. There would be a simple service at the chapel and a cremation. He really didn't want to be alone right now and figured God works things out. They both needed someone and had each other for the time being. Carl had no children. They had never been blessed with a child. Now he sort of adopted a grandson.

He had gotten the address, explaining to the authorities that he was a family friend caring for young Jackson. They would stop by Dale's home first and allow him to retrieve some clean clothes and secure the Jackson house hold. Dale made no objections to this plan. First they would drop by the Burger Barn for a couple of double cheese burgers, half and half fries and onion rings, and root beer floats. Carl had a weakness for root beer floats. His dear Massey always loved the onion rings. Both he and Dale wolfed down the meal as if they hadn't eaten in a week.

Pulling into the Jackson driveway, Dale scoped out the bicycle parked out front. He saw a familiar figure sitting on the porch steps. Carl looked over at Dale on the edge of his seat. "Is that her?"

Dale nodded yes.

"Well, it appears the young lassie is waiting on you young man. Don't disappoint her. Go talk to her."

Dale shrugged, pushing his glasses back up on his nose, a nervous habit he had and made worse by the girl. Chatty Kathy had not lost her touch. "Dale, where have you been? I've been just about frantic with worry. I bet I've been by here at least a hundred times. Where are your parents? Who's the old man in the truck? I'm glad you're all right. You are all right, aren't you?"

Dale overwhelmed by the bombardment of questions almost felt dizzy. She never stopped. To shut her up he said, "He's my grandfather, sort of."

"What do you mean sort of? That's just plain silly. How can he be sort of your grandfather? He either is or he isn't. Which one is it?"

"My father was in an automobile accident."

"Is he dead?"

"No, he's in ICU. That's Intensive Care Unit. He's in a coma."

"That's like being a zombie."

Dale shrugged.

"Is you mother with him at the hospital?"

"She's in the hospital, too."

"Was she hurt in the accident with him? That's just terrible, both of them."

"No, she had some sort of nervous breakdown and they've got her on medication."

"She went fruit loops. Man, a zombie dad and a fruit loop mom and a sort of grandfather. Your family is more screwed up than mine. Did they put her in a strait jacket or one of those padded cells?"

"No, just a hospital bed…"

"I had an uncle who went fruit loops and they locked him up and threw away the key. They said that it was for his own good. He swallowed his tongue and pulled out chunks of his own hair. How cool is that?"

"She just needs some rest is all."

After giving them a couple of alone time minutes, Carl exited the truck and said, "You must be that nice young lady Dale had been telling me about. Hi, I'm Carl O'Conner; pleasure to meet you."

"He's been talking about me. How long have you been his grandfather?"

"Since yesterday," Carl smiled.

"That's about how long I've known him too. I'm Debra Floyd. Do you know he rode my bicycle yesterday; first time?"

"So I've heard. Young Dale, why don't we go inside and check on things."

Dale and Carl joined Debra on the porch. The door was unlocked. Carl noticed boxes stacked here and there indicating they hadn't settled in yet. "Gather some of your things and we'll head back to my place."

"Why can't you just stay here, Dale, while your parents are in the hospital? I could help you with chores. I'm a good cook. You're sixteen and plenty old enough to stay by yourself. You don't need a babysitter."

Carl smiled. This one surely had it for young Jackson. Puppy love, an amazing thing Carl thought. "I would really feel better if you came home with me but Debra is entirely right. It's your choice."

Choices, here we go with choices. Why did he have to make a decision again? Trapped like a fly in a spider's web, if he said he didn't want to stay then the girl would be hurt and if he didn't go, the old man would be lonely tonight. He liked it much better when people just told him what they wanted him to do. He couldn't win this one.

Dark thirty, he couldn't stay here alone. The girl and old man would just think he was a big old baby if he admitted his fears. It would be here soon. How could he possibly stay here? They waited for his answer.

"If I stay here by myself, I would have no way to get to the hospital," he finally said and surprised himself with the response.

"If that's all you're worried about, I'll make sure you have transportation. If you would rather stay here, I understand and respect your decision. I can leave you my phone number."

This wasn't going the way he had envisioned it. He had hoped Carl would have insisted he go home with him. He didn't want to stay here alone. He couldn't tell them that.

"If you're staying, let's make sure you have provisions. We can do a grocery run if need be."

"Yeah and I can come along too. I'm an excellent shopper and I would know what stuff to pick up if I'm doing the cooking," said Debra in an excited tone. "And I can help you unpack and fix the place up."

This was going so very wrong. She was right though. Boxes were stacked everywhere. Dale eyed her then Carl. He was stuck. He didn't like the feeling of being stuck.

"You're quite a resourceful young lady aren't you Debra?"

"I'm not so sure my parents would want us unpacking their stuff or me staying here without them.'

"Nonsense, I bet you'd do your folks proud undertaking such a noble task," stated Carl.

Dale felt as if he was being double teamed and losing ground badly. "But…"

"But nothing," interrupted Debra. "This might be just what you need to take your mind off your parents. You can practice on my bike and we've still got over a week before school starts. I could even help you study for your driver's license. It would be almost like setting up house."

Yep, Dale thought, he was definitely loosing his footing, the ground crumbling underneath his feet. He couldn't think as fast as the girl. She had everything already figured out without his input. His sort of grandfather wasn't helping matters.

Carl eyed them under a new light with that setting up house comment. These two were sixteen years old with tons of hormones and staying here without adult supervision might not be such a great idea after all. He had no jurisdiction over them, no dog in the hunt and he had only known Dale less than a couple of days and Debra for less than ten minutes.

"Your decision, young Jackson," advised Carl O'Conner, figuring he must allow the boy to decide without additional pressure from him.

There he goes again with me and choices thought Dale. This definitely wasn't what he thought he wanted to do, was it? He wished he could just say hell no, I want to go but nothing like that would form on his lips. Stupidity did spew from his mouth, "Okay, I'll stay here." What a chicken he had been. He was a pathetically defeated man. He was convicted, guilty as charged and now subjected to eventual solitary confinement and at the mercy of Dark Thirty. He was doomed.

"Wonderful," Debra snorted. "Let's check out the pantry and make sure we have stuff for me to cook for you before Mister O'Conner leaves. We might just have to do that grocery run."

Well maybe not exactly solitary confinement Dale thought. He checked out the clock on the mantle, one of the few items unpacked and with new batteries. Three hours and ticking until Dark Thirty and less than twelve days before school would begin. He couldn't win for losing.

21

Jake and his band of recruited thugs watched patiently from the opposite end of the parking lot, waiting for the Red Neck in the GI Joe outfit to close his pawn shop. It had been quite a popular venue all afternoon. Customers were taking in some of the oddest items and exiting, counting their cash. Jake fumed. Teaching him a lesson for interfering in their business would be a pleasure.

"I thought the sign said that place closed at six," scoffed Mack.

"You don't think he's going to close long as the goods keep rolling in do you?" replied Stoner, droopy eyed and clinging to his skateboard.

"I need a business like that," stated David. "Just sit inside and wait for those hard luck farts to bring me their stuff and I pay them chicken scratch then sell it for a fortune."

"Most of it is probably stolen in the first place so those poor pitiful people don't come out so bad," explained Jake.

"And that's why we're going to steal his crap," added Mack.

"It's not going to be a piece of cake," explained Jake. "He has surveillance cameras and an alarm so we better wear our disguises and get in and out damn quick."

"And trash the place as much as possible," laughed Stoner.

"He probably has all sorts of guns in there," commented Mack.

"But I suspect he's got them locked up good," said Rich.

"That's why we have these," waved Mack, displaying heavy duty cutters from his uncle's machine shop. "These babies will chomp any chains."

"Way too cool," chuckled Rich.

"We should come up with a badass gang name, something that will scare the crap out of people. We have to leave our calling card," ranted Stoner.

"Nah, we can't afford to draw attention to us and create trouble with some of those real badass gangs out there. We don't need the cops looking for us. We best keep this quiet and just between us," warned Jake.

The Redneck appeared at the door and looked like he was finally closing up shop. It was still too daylight to make their move. Once darkness fell they would put their plan into motion. Jake and his gang would pad their resume with breaking and entering and stealing.

22

Carl had footed the bill for replenishing the kitchen for young Jackson's household, under the direction of Miss Debra Floyd of course. Apparently his parents had not been here long enough to set up house yet. He could collect payment later if he wished but he probably wouldn't. Helping the young lad did him good.

"All right young Jackson; I do believe this should hold you for a few days. Here's my number. Call me anytime, day or night. Let me know when you want to go back to the hospital. I'll come by and pick you up."

Dale nodded.

"And you, Miss Debra, you take good care of young Jackson here and make sure he stays out of trouble."

"I will take excellent care of him and thanks for the groceries Mister Sort of Dale's grandfather," she snorted that signature laugh of hers. "It was a pleasure to meet you Mister O'Conner. You make a fine grandfather."

Carl smiled at that remark and patted Debra on the head then offered a handshake to his new sort of grandson. Today had been a good day. He hoped tonight would hold more of the same. His nights lately had not gone well. He couldn't quite put a finger on it but something wasn't quite right. He had known it even before Massey's passing.

Dale watched as the old man climbed back into his truck and backed out of the drive. He liked Carl O'Conner and wished he was his real grandfather. Can you adopt a grandson, he wondered?

"Okay, what do you want to do first?" asked Debra.

He shrugged; more choices. He was much better at shrugging than making decisions. This new world of his required much adjustment yet.

"Are you hungry? I'm famished. I can cook us something if you're hungry too."

Dale nodded his head to confirm he was hungry too. He could nod almost as well as he could shrug and juggled them appropriately.

"Okay, sit back and I'll fix us something then."

Dark Thirty loomed an hour away. He asked Debra, "When do you have to go home?"

"Trying to get rid of me already? When do you want me to leave?"

"Your parents," Dale sputtered "I just…"

"Oh, they're fine. I called them on my cell while we were at the grocery store and I sort of explained the situation to them," she snorted again.

"Sort of…"

"I told them I was staying over at your house for a while but would be home by eleven. I didn't tell them about your parents. Sort of is your term, remember? I can't believe you don't have a cell phone."

Dale ignored the phone comment. "It will be dark then."

"It happens by eleven all the time but it will be dark long before then."

Dale fidgeted nervously. The girl noticed. She smiled. He smiled back, sort of.

"You don't like the dark either," she commented. "Can you not sleep at night? I can't shut my brain down. I'm just too wired at night."

He confirmed with a nod. Dale wasn't ready to confess how terrified he was of the dark. He had always been but didn't really know why. He had researched it many times on the internet and had found it wasn't so unusual to have a phobia. People were afraid of heights, bugs, confined spaces and all types of others. His just so happened to be the dark.

"I would offer you some of my medication but it's at home and it would probably give you those weird dreams like it does me. It makes me have sexual dreams. I bet you already wake up at night with those erections that boys get don't you? I've read about it. It sounds fascinating. I've studied the male anatomy on the internet and you're amazing creations let me tell you. "

Dale blushed. He could feel the heat sizzling on his face and neck. This girl not only talked none stop, she was capable of saying just about anything. Why was she so obsessed with sex? Were all girls like this or was she some sort of pervert? She caught his awkwardness about sex.

"Sex stuff doesn't embarrass you does it? I mean we're both sixteen and we're supposed to be sexually active and thinking about doing it. I know girls mature quicker than boys but you do think about it, don't you?"

"I'm hungry. Aren't you hungry?"

"Have you ever done it?" she abruptly asked him. "I mean with a girl?"

Dale gulped loudly, "Have you?"

"Not with a boy," she smiled. "Not yet anyway. What do you want me to fix you?"

Not with a boy, what was that supposed to mean Dale wondered, but he didn't have the guts to ask her. Had she done it with another girl? This was just too much to take in.

"What you say I just fix us a couple of sandwiches? What kind do you like?"

He shrugged. He hated making all these decisions. Freedom to choose wasn't that great. It just complicated his once uncomplicated life.

"I'll fix us a tuna and mayo sandwich. I just love chicken of the sea. Is that okay with you?"

He nodded. He didn't get why Star-Kist called tuna *chicken of the sea.*

"Do you ever masturbate? From what I've read, boys masturbate a lot when they discover their sexuality. How often do you do it? Does it make you feel all tingly when you do? It would be interesting to hear about it from your perspective. It would make it seem real; you know what I'm saying?"

Dale pushed his glasses up on his nose, adjusted them then pushed them again. This was bad on so many levels thought Dale. There were no good answers to these questions. If he said yes and picked a random number she might think he's some sort of pervert too. If he said no then she might think something was wrong with him. The answer was no. He wouldn't even know how to and had never felt motivated to do it. Did that confirm he was weird he wondered because she said she had read about it. It had obviously been researching the wrong subject matter on his laptop.

"Do you," he asked, not believing he had.

"That's what I meant earlier silly, when I said I had not done it with a boy yet." She snorted that laugh, "Like I said, it a scientific fact that girls do mature so much sooner, not that you're immature. We are aware of our sexuality at a much younger age. It happens soon after we have that first menstrual cycle. Period, most people just call it having your period or a slang for it is on the rag. I don't really like that term. We're sensitive afterwards, real sensitive. I guess that sounds a little yucky to you, doesn't it, talking about my period?"

Dale began patting his foot so loudly on the tile floor he sounded like a one legged tap dancer. He should have gone home with Carl O'Conner. He wondered if it was too late to call him.

"You're not so comfortable talking about sex are you? I know I talk too much but that's the way I learn things. I'm sorry. You must think I'm some sort of sex crazed predator don't you or maybe a slut?"

Dale shook his head no.

"Well I'm not a slut anyway," she snorted. "But don't worry; I'm not a rapist either. I can't deny it wouldn't be fun to fool around with a boy just to check things out."

Dale fired up his second foot and now he sounded like a full fledged dancer. He couldn't be still and he wondered what she would do to him here in the house alone. He wasn't prepared for this. He wasn't prepared by a long shot.

"Sorry, I'll can the sex talk for now. I don't want to be the one to be blamed for giving you leg cramps," she snorted, pointing to his feet.

"Just like riding a bike, I've never masturbated before," Dale said without knowing he was going to say it.

"Never?"

He shook his head no.

"Boy have you been missing out. It's good you have me for a friend to help you work though this. Here's your sandwich."

What did she mean by help me work through it? Momentarily he had forgotten about Dark Thirty. He had larger worries looming. His life was a mess and school hadn't even started.

23

Jake, discreetly as possible, walked the sidewalk just in front of the pawn shop. Stoner had already made a couple of passes on his skateboard. The remainder of the gang had parked themselves outside the video store four doors away. One of the movies had just let out and the crowd spilled into the parking lot like so many ants pouring from a mound. It was just past nine and other movies were still in progress.

Mack almost drooled with anticipation. He wanted to do this badly, to teach Redneck a lesson. Coming from more or less a broken home, he had learned to be a rebel at an early age. He never knew his father and his mother was somewhat of a closet drunk and whore. Mack pretty much did what he wanted when he wanted. Attending school kept him out of jail or at least it had up until now.

Jake, the self appointed leader was no more than a notch above those nerdy geeks that sent them into a feeding frenzy. Mack tolerated Jake. He allowed him to lead, figuring when things went wrong; the leader always took the fall. Jake made the perfect fall guy. He could be sacrificed in the blink of an eye once he had outlived his usefulness. Mack could play the role of flunky, follower, and henchman flawlessly. He remained content in those roles for now. He would pick his time to lead.

Jake never knew just how ruthless Mack could be or had been. In Mack's opinion, the rest of the boys were just a bunch of pathetic losers. Only Stoner had balls and only because he stayed wasted most of the time and oblivious to the real world around him. Stoner was the perfect puppet to do evil bidding and served as a lure to recruit other flunkies. Mack liked Stoner. In a twisted way, they could actually relate.

Mack enjoyed this life style. He needed it. Kicking ass, taking names and doing anything he wanted, pushing it to the limit and stealing from those who were not inclined to fight for what was theirs. He knew no boundaries, at least not yet. He lived by no rules and the consequences of his actions didn't really scare him. This made him extremely unpredictable and dangerous, but only he knew how dangerous and unpredictable he could really be.

Mack "The Knife" Stephenson, legend and myth rolled into one, garnished a buck knife, thus earning him his alias. He had never used the knife on a human, not yet; however, small animals had felt his wrath. He had career criminal written all over him. After the others had departed, leaving him in the cemetery, he had kicked it up a notch and crossed that line forever. There would be no returning to the ways of a kid. He had tasted blood. Like a vampire, he liked the taste.

Jake returned and reported he had spotted at least three surveillance cameras inside the pawn shop. He had seen the guns and they were secured as expected with a much thicker chain than they had anticipated. None of them had actually been inside the pawn shop so their plan was sketchy at best. Hard lessons lay ahead for those seeking revenge.

Jack announced they'd not make the actual attempt until after midnight, long after the last movie goers had emptied the parking lot and the chance of witnesses had diminished. Waiting here didn't make sense so Jack decided they would cut out for the time being. Mack smiled. The faithful leader had spoken and the little sheep followed aimlessly. There were all so pathetic. .

Rich and Ray announced they had to be home by 11:30 and could not stay. Five remained. Besides Mack and Stoner, Buddy and David would stick it out to the finale. The clock ticked, revenge loomed. Mack couldn't wait to get his hands on a gun of any caliber. With a loaded weapon, no one would ever mess with him again.

24

The first signs of blackness raised its ugly head, creeping toward the inevitable Dark Thirty and a rendezvous with Dale Thomas Jackson and his new side kick, the girl. Dale knew what lay ahead. The girl didn't. Dale peered out the window then glanced at the wall clock. He could almost hear the secondhand ticking like a heartbeat. Judgment time approached and Dale understood the verdict. This would be his first time alone without the support of either his mom or dad, excluding the rescue from Carol O'Connor at the hospital. He would have to depend on the girl instead tonight.

"Are you okay?" asked Debra Floyd, noticing how fidgety Dale had gotten in the past fifteen minutes.

He nodded but wasn't too convincing.

"There's more to this dark thing isn't there? It's not just being unable to sleep like me is it? Something out there scares you doesn't it? I can see it in your eyes. What is it? Can I help?"

The girl sure could rapid fire those questions. He tried to shrug them off but she would have nothing of it. Amazing, she had in only a couple of days wormed her way into his life. He still didn't understand it. He liked it but it made absolutely no sense.

"You can tell me," she spoke softly and sincerely, almost motherly.

Dale tried to ignore her request and began his ritual of switching on all the lamps and overhead lighting. Debra folded her arms and observed, ironically remaining quite. This boy had some deeply embedded emotional problems she surmised. He could definitely use her shrink. Completing his task, he sat down on the couch with sweat on his forehead and above his upper lip.

She sat down beside him, placed her hand on his knee and asked, "Have you ever been to a shrink about this? They can really help."

"I'm not crazy!" blurted out Dale as he began patting his foot to her touch.

"I'm not either but I have a shrink."

"I didn't mean to bite your head off."

"Hey," she said, placing her hand on top of his. "I'm much better than I used to be. You should have seen me before I saw Doctor Guy and started taking my meds. I would have probably scared the crap out of you. You would have thought I was possessed. *Linda Blair* had nothing on me."

Her hand felt so soft thought Dale. Her touch sent tingles where he didn't know he could be tingled. His face flushed. His foot began tapping faster. He couldn't speak. The room had gotten suddenly hot. He reached for his glasses.

"Doctors can help people like us, really. Sure, it comes with side affects like the medicine that makes me crave sex and have those wild erotic dreams, but like I said, I've always acted older than I look."

Dale said nothing. His patting feet said it all.

"I've never had a close friend to tell this sort of stuff to, until you," she confessed.

The second foot joined his first, taping up a storm. He couldn't control or stop them. Neither of his feet had rhythm. His armpits felt wet.

"Boy, just mention sex and you go into a tizzy don't you. We need to put this to music," she said, squeezing his hand tenderly.

Dale sprang to his feet and rushed toward the kitchen. He needed something cold to drink. Debra followed like a little puppy. She watched as he guzzled a glass of water.

"I'm sorry. I didn't mean to upset you. From the brain to the mouth, I can't help it. I'm cursed that way. I know I talk too much and probably say all the wrong things."

Dale retrieved a soda from the refrigerator and handed her one, popping her top then his. "When do you have to go home?"

"Do you want me to leave? I said I was sorry. I'll drop the subject. I promise."

He shook his head no. She smiled and Dale even mustered up a smile back. He could now see pitch blackness through the living room bay window. Dark Thirty had arrived. This was bad, so very bad. The lights at least kept it in check. It couldn't invade his world as long as all the lights remained on.

"How long do you think your folks will be in the hospital?" she asked attempting to change the subject, but it actually made things much worse because now Dale had to think long term staying here alone.

He did manage a reply. "Don't know."

"Your sort of grandfather, Mister O'Connor, seems like a nice enough man and it's certainly a shame he lost his wife."

Dale nodded his agreement. His labored breathing was a little better but he still wasn't out of the woods yet.

"You know," she said without cracking a smile, "You're really talking my ears off so I really wish you would shut up for a while."

Dale actually managed a laugh. "You ought to be a shrink."

"Doctor Floyd at your service, you'll love my bedside manner. I'm here to tuck you in, beddy-bye. I know some real good bedtime stories but they might just keep you up all night."

He smiled through another foot tapping episode. Taping one's foot, while standing and holding a soda is an art form. Why had his world turned upside down?

25

Banging on the locker, he screamed for help, begged for someone to set him free. School had been dismissed. He heard no foot steps in the hallway. He should have fought them. He should have never allowed them to force him inside his own locker. Hindsight, it didn't matter now. What mattered was how to get out.

He banged and rattled the door lever but his combination lock imprisoned him. They used his lock, can you believe that, he thought. Without help there would be no escape. He wondered if he would die in here, starve to death. It was Friday after all and no one would be back until Monday. Could you die from lack of food or water in three days he wondered.

How long had he been in here? Maybe thirty minutes he guessed. His bladder ached. He had to take a whiz really bad. He couldn't hold it for three days. His teeth hurt from having to pee. He couldn't concentrate. He felt the warm liquid fill his underwear and trickle down his legs. In the confined space the urine almost burned his eyes. What would he do when he had the urge to do number two?

Screaming again, he thought he heard something. How embarrassing, to be trapped in your own locker and having peed in your pants. He almost dreaded being set free. There would be consequences if he snitched on those that put him here. Loser, loser, loser they chanted inside his head.

He heard footsteps approaching. His first thought, they were coming back. What else could they do to him in here he wondered, plenty. Should he yell or not he contemplated. He had nothing to lose so he yelled and banged like his life depended on it. It did.

"Kid, you all right in there?" asked a deep husky voice he recognized. It was the janitor, Laney Kinsey.

"How'd you get in there?"

"By accident. Can you just get me out of here?"

"Is this your lock?" he asked jiggling it.

"Yes, it's mine."

"Do you know the combination?"

"It's mine, sure I know it. Get me out of here!"

"Call it out."

The tumblers were deafening and took an eternity to set him free. Finally the locker door opened. Greeting him outside were the very same ones that had locked him inside. They held a bucket of tar and a torn pillow case.

Darby woke up again screaming except he heard no screams and saw only darkness. In a comatose state, he really couldn't yell, move nor open his eyes. He existed in pitch black darkness. He had dreamed this nightmare so many times in the past and had always awaked terrified and in a cold sweat. Reliving the reality of that incident had forever haunted him. Brenda had always calmed him but where was she now? Where was he?

Brenda lived her own nightmare two floors below and her journey had only just begun. Dale Thomas Jackson faced Dark Thirty, without them, but unlike his parents, he had the girl with him, at least until she had to go home. The Jackson family was in shambles.

26

The five future criminals of America returned to the scene of the crime that would soon be perpetrated. The bank's large clock displayed ten minutes before midnight. The parking lot was finally empty. Jack saw no human activity. Cars still whizzed down the highway but the view was slightly obstructed by a hedge row near the entrance way to the strip mall.

"Let's do it," he commanded.

Mack tossed a brick through the entrance door window shattering the glass. The alarm signaled they had breached entry. David, bug eyed, covered his ears then panicked and hauled ass. Buddy watched him retreat then looked back at the broken glass and thought about doing the same.

Mack gave him a hateful look to warn him to stay put. He shook his head no and chickened out too. "Spineless, both of you," yelled Mack, then he kicked in the remainder of the jagged glass around the doorway.

Stoner entered, still holding his skateboard, followed by Mack. Jake hesitated but brought up the rear. All wore full face stocking masks and gloves. Mack thought what a leader, slinking in last.

Mack didn't hesitate. He went straight for the guns. Even though the heavy duty bolt cutters fit comfortably over the chains that secured them, he lacked the strength to cut through the metal links.

Stoner zeroed in on two cool electric guitars and a set of amplifiers. He laid claim to them. He even took time to pretend he was rocking and rolling to sounds of the blaring alarm. He had burned one before entering so the stage had been set.

Jake surveyed the shop for something personal that belonged to the Redneck. He wanted to really tick him off. He saw what he was looking for behind the cash register and on the wall. It was an enlarged photo of Redneck and a group of his buddies posed with the late Dale Earnhardt. All framed, dated and autographed by the NASCAR driver several years before he had died in that crash. They were all dressed in camouflage and posed behind a gigantic dead grizzly bear. "Boy this will get him," whispered Jake.

Mack gave up on cutting free the assortment of shotguns and rifles. He had moved on to a display cabinet with Rambo sized hunting knives and several pistols. He used the cutters like a sledge hammer and shattered the display case glass.

He snatched up a huge knife but then discarded it for a pearl handled Colt 45. He also grabbed a smaller gun and shoved it in his belt. He liked its compact size. He saw no ammo. A gun was almost worthless without bullets.

Flashing blue lights reflected inside the pawn shop. The cops had arrived in the parking lot. There would be no exiting the way they had entered. Stoner, guitar and amplifiers in tow, bolted for the rear of the shop. He had discarded his prized skateboard. Jake followed, almost busting his ass over a stack of weed eaters. Mack still searching for any signs of ammo was not far behind.

"Crap," yelled Stoner, pointing toward the barred and padlocked back door. "We're screwed. There's no way out!"

"What now?" screamed a panic stricken Jake. He cringed, thinking about being caught by the cops. His parents would kill him.

Mack ignored the whiner after laying his eyes on the cabinet labeled ammunition. Of course it was locked too. He put the cutters to use again and slammed them into the door, once, twice then a third time before finally breaking the handle and lock from the cabinet. He saw a box of bullets for the Colt but wasn't sure of the smaller gun's caliber.

"What the hell you going to do with that gun?" asked Jake.

"Shoot our way out, what else," answered Mack, waving the Colt in the air, having not loaded it yet.

"Super," shouted Stoner. "We'll be like Butch and Sundance, plus one."

"You're both crazy," yelled Jake.

"Hey fellers, over here," shouted Stoner. "There's some sort of chute and I think it's big enough for us."

Sure enough, Stoner had found a trash chute in the back of the store. He shoved his guitar and amplifiers inside and heard them slide through and crash somewhere outside. He slid inside head first and belly down then disappeared. Buddy was too terrified to want anything from the pawn shop except to get out. He followed Stoner.

Jake tossed the autographed photo through the opening and bellied through. The chute sent him down at lightening speed and into a huge metal trash bin landing on top the others. Mack stuffed the Colt in his belt along side the other pistol and shoved the box of bullets inside his shirt and joined the other two, crashing on top of them too.

"Shush," warned Stoner, finger to his lips.

Footfalls passed. The cops had circled around the corner to the back exit. A few minutes passed and they heard nothing. Stoner peeked over the edge of the bin, saw no one. "Coast is clear, let's get the hell out of here before they figure out how we escaped."

Jake huddled at the bottom of the bin until Mack pushed him and pointed to Stoner, now climbing out. Two blocks later they had cleared the commotion. Several police cars raced by them. They hid then immerged from the shadows each time they heard them pass. They had committed the perfect crime, thought Mack. He was two for two, first Cassie and now this.

"Man, what a rush," yelled Stoner, firing up another joint.

"I still can't believe you wanted to shoot your way out," fussed Jake.

"Like Stoner said, Butch and Sundance, all the way," yelled Mack, retrieving the Colt from his belt and loading it.

"You're insane, man," said Jake, regretting almost immediately he had spoken the words, seeing Mack's reaction. Mack now had a gun. The game had changed and Jake knew it.

27

Almost midnight and Dale had remained cool and collected while the girl chatted up a storm. She announced she would have to be home before midnight and his foot tapping fired back up once again. What could he say? I'm scared. I don't want to be alone. Don't go. No such words would form on his lips but his foot worked just fine. He did what he always did and nodded. Dread sunk in, realizing he was mere minutes from being in the house alone.

She removed his glasses then kissed him on the cheek and said, "I'll be over first thing in the morning to make you breakfast. If I had my pills with me, I would give you one but then you might just go into a sexual frenzy and I wouldn't be here to help." She snorted that laugh and slid his glasses back over his ears and nose.

Dale instinctively touched the bridge of his nose and pushed up the frame then he nodded and tried to smile. He didn't want her to go. Why couldn't he say the words, *please stay with me.*

She kissed him again for good measure, this time square on his lips. Foot number two tried to keep pace with the tapping of foot number one. He had to stand up to get them under control. She waved as she exited through the doorway. The house echoed nothingness quite loudly in her absence.

The silence overwhelmed him. He had not heard it since the girl arrived and it terrified the crap out of him. He completed a sweeping 360 in the kitchen then snailed his way from the kitchen into the den. Every possible light burned brightly. He eventually reached the bottom of the stairs. The steps disappeared into a dark cavity at the top. He had forgotten to switch on any lights on the second floor.

Trapped on the first floor, Dark Thirty occupied the second level and surrounded the house outside. Dale had a death grip on the handle of the lantern style flashlight, his security blanket. Two more flashlights rested on a table within hands reach.

Dale sat with his back to a corner, watching all the entrances to the den, kitchen and stairway. Tears formed and soon trickled down his cheeks. There would be no sleeping in this house tonight for darkness was not his friend, even though he kept it at bay with the lighting. There was no such thing as too much light. This was no time to be frugal. His parents weren't here to make him switch them off.

He missed Debra. Her constant jabbering soothed him. He thought about phoning Carl O'Conner but instead he shrunk deeper into the corner, almost blending into the wallpaper. The light helped him maintain his sanity but only barely. He wondered if his parents would get well. He thought about school; anything to occupy his mind. What new breed of bully would be waiting for him there?

The darkness taunted him. He swung a flashlight about, mimicking Luke Skywalker. Darth Vader probably lurked out there somewhere beckoning him to do battle. He vowed to hold his ground. He thought he heard noises upstairs, possibly footsteps, and hunkered down for the duration. Being alone had not been his choice.

28

Debra Floyd lay awake too, darkness not her friend either. Her brain cells in overdrive, she recapped the events from the last couple of days, processing and reprocessing. She really liked Dale Thomas Jackson and stared at Facebook on her computer screen, contemplating whether she should tell cyber world how she felt. He was so like her, lost, misunderstood with a tad of weirdness, just trying to muddle through life the best he could. Could he be her soul mate she wondered?

She typed her thoughts. Her finger hovered above the Enter key. If she pressed it, it would be there for anyone to read. Did she really want anyone to know something this personal? It might make Dale hate her. She didn't mention his name but still, two and two equaled four. She pressed the *Backspace* key and then logged out of her account. She remembered stories she had researched about other kids being tormented to the point they committed suicide. Cyber bullying was all too real. Be patient.

Life, like running a continuous obstacle course, had offered her little relief. Persistence, she oozed it but she wasn't sure about Dale. Something so very demonic and forbidding haunted him and it had something to do with the darkness. She had to pry this out of him before she could help him conquer it. He wasn't a sharer. She would change that too.

She typed in *fear of the dark* on her computer. From *Wikipedia*, the free encyclopedia, she read: *The **fear of the dark** is a common fear among children and to a varying degree is observed in adults. Fear of the dark is usually not fear of the darkness itself, but fear of possible or imagined dangers concealed by the darkness.* Now she was getting somewhere. It said that some researchers, beginning with *Sigmund Freud*, consider the fear of the dark as a manifestation of separation anxiety disorder.

Debra perused some other websites, jotting down notes. One said *fear of the dark phobia or Nyctophobia is common among young children who often fear that something catastrophic may happen to them in the night*. Dale wasn't that young. Possibly he had just lived a sheltered life. After all, he had never ridden a bike before. She turned off her computer. He had *Nyctophobia*. Doctor Guy could probably help him.

She fingered her night pill on the bed side table, rolling it back and forth, contemplating whether she should take it or not this late. She certainly didn't need it tonight to enhance her sexual awareness and that's what it always seemed to do even though that wasn't listed as a side effect. She could still taste his lips on hers.

"The pill is supposed to make me relax," she whispered, "and help me shut down this stupid brain of mine, but it just makes me horny."

Those crazy dreams, it came with a price. And those enhanced sensations just made her stroll down memory lane. She had never shared this with her shrink. Maybe she feared he would change the medication so she kept this little dirty secret. Side effects weren't always bad. She decided to pass on the pill tonight. Staying awake might just be more rewarding. She slid below the sheets and smiled reliving the kiss.

29

Ed Bravo walked through his pawn shop, cursing those who had dared do this to him. He pointed to where the items had been to the young officer. Assessing the broken display case, he informed the officer that seven pistols were missing and at least as many collectable knives. He lied, figuring he may as well cash in with the insurance. He assured the officer he would provide a complete inventory list.

Stopping where the guitar and amplifiers had been, he reeled off almost ten instruments that had been stolen by these bastards. The list went on and on as he surveyed the shop. He smelled cash cow.

"This had to be a professional job," Ed told the officer.

"How did they get all this stuff out of here?" asked the officer. "We had the front covered and all the back exits were locked. We were here within minutes so it is tough to fathom how they escaped with this many items so quickly."

"Professionals, they're damn good," he assured the officer. "They have it timed to the last little nanosecond."

Ed spotted the wall and realized his autographed photograph was gone. He went ballistic. They had taken #3, the intimidator, his possession.

He explained to the officer that his priceless souvenir had been lifted. "They knew what they were doing. You better catch them because if I get my hands on them first."

"Let's take a look at your surveillance video Maybe we can learn something from it."

Ed had forgotten about the video. It might show more than he wanted the officer to see. "I'll make a copy and bring it to you along with the inventory list.

"That's not necessary," replied the officer. "We can review it now and if it turns up anything, I'll just take the original with me. You do want to nail them don't you?"

Ed took a deep breath and pressed the rewind button on the VCR. When it clicked to a stop he pressed the play button. After a couple of uneventful minutes the officer pressed the fast forward button until he saw the masked figures on the screen. Ed rolled his eyes as the scene unfolded. After about eight minutes of viewing the officer stopped the tape and pressed the eject button.

"I believe we've seen enough," he advised Ed. "Professionals, huh?"

Ed, speechless and busted, stared at the floor.

"So much for your long list of stolen goods," commented the officer. "And now we know how they escaped. I think it's best you accompany me to the station but not before I read you your rights. You lied to us Mister Bravo. You were planning to dupe the insurance company weren't you? You do realize that is fraud."

"So maybe I was wrong about what they may have taken," scrambled Ed. "I told you I would give you an actual inventory list."

"Are you sure this wasn't staged?" asked the officer. "You too eagerly listed all those alleged stolen items."

"I need to call my lawyer."

"I think you do."

A second officer entered the shop. "Mister Bravo will be coming with us to the station. Cuff him. He has a lot of explaining to do to us and possibly his insurance company. It looks like a bunch of kids did this from best I can tell. I hope they weren't in on it with him."

The young officer watched Ed Bravo with disgust as his partner escorted him to the cruiser. The video had looked like a bunch of kids and only kids could have cleared that chute. Worse still, the kids had guns now and ammunition. The sooner they found them the better thought the officer. The disguises would make this difficult. The autographed photo might be the key if they tried to sell it. Or it could be just another one of the numerous daily robberies that would never be solved. He'd not lose sleep over it either way. Ed Bravo would not sleep well for perpetrating fraud.

30

The first of the dawn's early light appeared like a laser through warped slats in the blinds. Dale held his ground in the corner. If anyone had been present they would have sworn he must be deranged. Wild eyed and definitely fatigued, he didn't move from his defensive position.

More light filtered in and finally he blinked. Insanity dwindled. His arms were still wrapped around his legs in an upright fetal position. He surveyed his surroundings as if seeing the den for the very first time. He released his knees and wiggled his finger, attempting to restore the circulation.

Standing up on shaky legs, he yawned and stretched. He had actually survived alone in the house. The thunderous knocking at the side door almost caused him to release an already aching bladder. Had the demon waited in the shadows to catch him off guard?

A familiar voice spoke his name. "Dale Thomas Jackson, are you awake in there?" She rapped harder. "Are you okay? Let me in. I'm here to cook you a manly breakfast."

Dale opened the door. She stood there smiling like an angel, the sun silhouetting her frame. Dressed in a long tee and short shorts and sandals, she took his breath away. She was beautiful. He had never thought in these terms before so what was happening to him he wondered.

"Did you sleep with your clothes on? You look all wrinkled. Men just have no sense of hygiene or fashion."

"I didn't sleep."

"You didn't sleep. Then what were you doing all night?"

She looked refreshed and almost glowing. She had changed clothes, unlike him. He felt like crap. He tried to focus and respond but didn't. He maintained his zombie persona.

"Why didn't you sleep? You know my history but I don't know yours. My brain doesn't shut down at night. I didn't sleep a whole lot either. I was thinking about you. Were you thinking about me?"

Before thinking it through, he shook his head no. Her smile dissolved instantly. He had obviously head popped the incorrect response. He should have selected a shrug but that would have probably been just as bad.

Sighing she said, "Okay, I'll bite. What were you thinking about that kept you up all night? Is there someone else you haven't told me about?"

Dale couldn't muster up the words to respond coherently. He had already screwed up his answers and hadn't really muttered a word. He didn't wish to plant both feet in his mouth. Against his better judgment he gambled on the shrug and knew instantly by her reaction that he still hadn't chosen wisely.

"Fine, then don't tell me. You've really got to find a way to loosen up. I'm a good listener. If you think our relationship has a prayer, you're going to have to learn to trust me and talk to me."

Relationship, when had this blossomed into a relationship? Was this how the girl-boy thing worked? He had so much to learn and she apparently wanted to be his mentor.

"Are you hungry? I'm just raring to whip you up something. Trust me you'll feel better after you have sampled my cooking. What would you like?"

Questions, she always talked in questions. She cornered him constantly with questions. Verbal interaction wasn't his forte. He had certainly mastered nodding and shrugging but even those got him too deeply into trouble.

"Breakfast, that would be good I suppose," he said, actually compiling a sentence. "You choose."

Smiling she said, "He speaks. Now that wasn't so difficult was it?"

Dale shrugged and she snorted that laugh. Moving like greased lighting she was in the kitchen to the sounds of clanging pots and pans. Bacon, eggs and toast were soon being prepared by the master chef.."

Are you going to the hospital today to check on your parents? Is that nice sort of your grandfather coming by to take you?"

Dale first shrugged then added a verbal response, "I haven't decided."

"You haven't decided you're going or you haven't decided if you're going to call him?"

"Do you always have to ask so many questions?"

She snorted that laugh. "I've worn you down. Now you're rebutting with a question. Tell you what, why don't you go shower and throw on some fresh clothes while I finish breakfast. You're a little gamey."

Now the girl sounded like his mother but with a much sweeter voice. He nodded okay and headed up the stairs for the first time since yesterday. He smelled his shirt and under his arms. He smelled all right to him.

Dale rummaged through one of the boxes he hadn't unpacked and retrieved clean underwear, a black Aliens tee-shirt and pair of denim shorts that made his legs look like sticks when he wore them. He didn't like wearing shorts but it was too hot to wear jeans. After removing his glasses and placing them on the vanity, Dale adjusted the water valve until the temperature felt just right then stripped down and settled in under the spray.

Standing with his back to the shower and lathering up, he realized he had to pee, having not relieved himself during his night's vigil. The warm water and soapy hand felt good as he washed his privates. He shouldn't pee in the shower. It wasn't sanitary.

"Oh, I forgot to ask you how you like your…eggs," said Debra, from the open bathroom door, eyeing Dale in the buff for the first time through the clear shower door.

Dale, startled, made eye contact with her but she wasn't looking at his eyes. She was staring much lower. No cloth, no hiding place, just a bar of soap and his hand holding his semi-rigid pecker. He twirled to face the back of the shower, now exposing his bony butt to her.

"I should just hold the eggs and join you in there Dale Thomas Jackson. Were you thinking about me?"

He started to nod no but then thought better of it and nodded yes, glancing over his shoulder for her reaction. She was taking a step in his direction. She was going to get in the shower with him it appeared. They were separated by less than four feet and the shower door. His bladder unleashed, warm yellow urine ran down his legs and between his toes. He blushed as he lost his battle with gravity and was ashamed for peeing in the shower.

"You know you don't have to hide it from me. I think it's beautiful," she smiled.

"You should really go now."

"Guess you don't need anyone to wash your back then. Come on down when you've got that thing under control and I'll serve you breakfast but I'll be thinking dessert."

After the girl had gone back downstairs, Dale continued soaping up and the erection returned. This time he was thinking about her. It refused to go away and hurt like a toothache, only much better. He faced the shower and continued to rub it hoping the swelling would subside but it didn't. Without warning his toes began to curl and he felt like he was transforming into the hunchback man. He was gritting his teeth. Something happened.

It scared the hell out of him. He felt like he was suffering from some sort of convulsion. Sixteen years old and he had just experienced his very first ejaculation. He felt elated and confused by the new experience. He smiled and exited the shower.

In the past three days he had met the girl, rode a bicycle and experienced the most wonderful feeling while showering but he couldn't lick Dark Thirty or stand up to bullies. Take one thing at a time he reassured himself. He could smell breakfast before he descended the stairs. His belly rumbled loudly. He felt his crotch to make sure it was still asleep and by touching it, it stirred. He immediately removed his hand.

"What took you so long? You've already confessed that you don't masturbate."

He smiled and she caught his drift. "You have arrived Dale Thomas Jackson! Tell me it was wonderful!"

He nodded to confirm and she stood up from the table and applauded. He bowed and sat down quickly to conceal his excitement. She had certainly prepared a manly breakfast and he was famished. He devoured everything on his plate as if he hadn't eaten in days. He liked her. She made things seem right even if she did talk nonstop.

31

Mack admired his mini arsenal. He only had ammo for one of his prized possessions but that didn't really matter. He was now packing. He would be a force to be reckoned with if anyone dared mess with him. He pondered whether he would allow Jake to continue to be the leader. His old argument won outright. Allow him to remain leader and take the fall when it happened. Sooner or later it would. His money was on sooner.

Mack had watched the local morning news and had seen no mention of the pawn shop break-in or the other incident. Best he lay low just in case. He thought about the upcoming school year and how his being there served no purpose. Mack was destined for greater things. School just cramped his style.

Mack craved attention and thrived on chaos. He desired to be notorious, to make his mark in history. Notoriety could be gained in many ways. A legend is a legend, good, bad or ugly. This made him an extremely dangerous teenager.

He fondled the Colt. He placed it in his belt and practiced drawing it. Mack wanted badly to discharge it, to smell the powder, and feel its power. Power, it oozed such power. It made him powerful, invincible, unstoppable and deadly. He wished he had that Redneck store owner in his sight this very minute. He smiled and placed it back in his belt.

He was the man now. He could do anything. He could even shoot his mom if she dared cross him or ever tried to crawl in bed with him again. He nodded his head and fingered the trigger thinking how he could blow away one of those boyfriends of hers. Yep, old Mack was in charge now, in control and ready for anything.

32

The two larger kids had him pinned against the gym mats suspended from the wall behind the basketball goal. Two others taunted him. The gang's leader, a slick haired older boy held back the first mat and motioned for them to send him through the gauntlet.

He didn't want to do this. Why did they have to make him do it? He had been forced to do it too many times and he knew the outcome. He dared not defy them. It would only make things worse. Onlookers not involved directly in the incident watched. The boys and girls could put an end to this if they just stood up to them. How could he expect them to do something he wasn't willing to do?

A kid kicked him square in the seat of his britches and yelled for him to go. Two more began chanting. Trying to catch them off guard he sprinted through the mat's opening into the belly of the whale. Once underneath the mat, all bets were off and the punishment began. One after the other they slammed their bodies against the mat pinning him. He was again in sandwich hell from their pounding. He could advance very little from their relentless charges. The ordeal lasted less than a minute before he reached the other end.

Aching from his waist to his shoulders, he just hoped they wouldn't send him through a second time. His classmates stared, some laughed while others whispered. To add injury to insult, one of his attackers snuck up from behind and jerked down his gym shorts to his ankles, exposing his jockstrap to the world, boys and girls alike. He snatched them back up and ran for the exit but the damage had been done. He had been humiliated again. Their laughs echoed in the background.

Darby wanted to wake again from one of those awful nightmares like he had done so many times with Brenda reassuring him that it was just a dream. His comatose state offered him no escape. He could not wake from the darkness, the nothingness not of his own making, a prisoner just the same.

He could still hear those faint beeping sounds. He thought he heard voices. He couldn't decipher the origin of either. They seemed so far away. He missed Brenda and Dale Thomas. He hoped he could find his way back to them but where were they? Where was he?

Darby thought about how he so hated being in school. The bullies would never leave him alone there. They held him captive in this damn time warp. Darkness prevailed. He remained trapped. A life without purpose was no life. He needed purpose in the worse way.

Carl O'Conner had phoned Dale and asked if he wished to visit the hospital but Dale had passed. He decided to remain at home today. Carl did not press the issue. He could relate to young Jackson's sorrow. After all, it wasn't any of his business, but he had connected with the young lad. He probably needed his company more than the youngster needed him. He would call again tomorrow if he remembered to do so.

Debra and Dale had sat around much of the afternoon watching television. She had assisted her new companion in stashing away his clothes that had been packed in the cardboard boxes. All of his stuff was neatly folded in his dresser drawers now. She had enjoyed seeing every single article of his attire. She had imagined him not wearing any of them, flashbacks to the shower dancing in her head.

It was late afternoon, almost six, the summer days still long in August. Several hours remained before darkness paid another visit. The girl couldn't stay with him forever so Dale had to develop a better strategy for the approaching night. Dark Thirty waited for no one. He would have to begin his preparation by gathering flashlights, checking batteries and switching on the upstairs lights in her presence. Accomplishing this might be difficult to explain to her.

His corner fortress last night had served him well but he preferred being upstairs in his bedroom tonight. A smaller space was much easier to defend. Customized surroundings made him feel secure. Bravery wasn't part of the game and to Dale it wasn't a game - not by a long shot.

Debra had noticed the change in Dale again. The transformation while gradual had increased as the afternoon wore on. She couldn't quite put her finger on it but was sure it had something do with the approaching night. "Are you all right?" she asked. "You're sort of drifting away from me just like you did last night. Do you want me to ask if I can sleep over?"

Sleepover Dale thought. No parent would allow their daughter to sleep over with a sixteen year old boy with no adult supervision in the house would they? What a crazy notion she had, to sleep over here. The thought, absolutely impossible, she couldn't stay here, not that he didn't want her to. Where would she sleep? What would she wear?

"Well," she asked, standing there with her arms crossed and weight shifted to one foot, tapping that foot impatiently. "Not even a shrug, so should I take that as a possible yes?"

He sputtered out a, "Your parents aren't going to let you stay here all night with me alone!"

"They don't have to know I'm staying here," she replied. "I'm spending the night with my friend Rachel tonight."

"Does Rachel know you're not staying with her?" asked a confused Dale.

"She doesn't even know I'm planning to stay with her silly boy. It's sort of a white lie. You know, it's your term, *sort of.*"

"Okay," Dale spoke still not comfortable with making all these choices.

"That was the biggest decision I've ever seen you make and vocally," she snorted her laugh. "You are progressing nicely."

Dale shrugged. Backsliding to old ways came natural.

"Okay, I'll drop back by home and lay the groundwork and will be back here before dark."

"Yeah, before dark," he repeated to make it sound real.

Just minutes after her departure the walls closed in on Dale and it wasn't even Dark Thirty yet. The girl had this knack for calming the situation. She made things seem so right. He missed her already but then his thoughts abruptly shifted to school starting in less than eleven days. That certainly dampened his mood. She better be back before dark or he was in trouble.

33

Jake admired the autographed photograph of Dale Earnhardt, the Redneck and a bunch of strangers. With an ink pen he poked a hole through the head of the pawn shop owner, smiling at his actions. He wished he knew voodoo and by doing this the real Redneck's head would explode. He had no idea of the net worth of the diseased Earnhardt's autograph.

Stoner sat in the corner playing some outrageous unknown tune on his newly acquired guitar. Having just fired up a joint, he had passed it to the others. Buddy, Roy David and Rich passed it from one to the other. Stoner was their personal pusher man.

David, after taking a toke, coughed out, "Did you see the news? They reported that Cassie retard is missing. They think she may have been kidnapped or run away or something like that."

"No way," commented Ray.

"She probably wandered off somewhere," stated Jake. "She's not all there you know."

"Damaged goods and wasn't that good anyway,' whispered Buddy nudging Ray.

Mack said nothing. He just replayed the episode in his head, every little detail. He fondled the Colt inside his jacket pocket and decided to leave well enough alone for now. Jack walked out back to take a piss. Stoner joined him outside the deserted building to burn one.

Ray waited until they were gone then said, "I'm glad she kept her mouth shut like we warned her to do." He poked at Buddy, attempting to get a reaction from him. "Mack, why didn't you some? It was your idea."

"I don't do sloppy leftovers," answered Mack. "Watching you boys get your ten seconds of fame was a hoot. I don't think she was the only one getting it for the first time."

"Screw you," answered the rapist duo.

Mack just winked and grinned. Sex didn't interest him. His mother's abuse had ruined it for him. He drew his satisfaction from far worse acts.

"You're not a fag are you?"

With lighting speed, Mack pulled the Colt and had it resting against Ray's forehead. "What did you say?"

"Man, I was just messing with you," whined Ray. "Can't you take a joke?"

Mack laughed withdrawing the Colt. "Can't you?"

Jake returned, seeing Mack waving around the Colt. "Quit horsing around with that piece, Mack, before you hurt somebody. What are you planning on doing with it any way?"

"Anything I want to," he smiled and winked, pointed the Colt and pretended to shoot Jake.

Mack had a past he wasn't proud of, one nobody else knew about. His mom had moved them to Charlotte a year before he turned eleven. Besides being small for his age and despite the abuse he had received from his mom, he also battled a number of conditions. He suffered from ADHD and other disorders that went undiagnosed for years. He suffered from double depression, which apparently ran in his family. It's a condition described as a chronic depressed mood that lasts at least two years and is sometimes referred to *as veil of sadness*.

Probably his biggest secret, he had been on the receiving end of bullying when he was in middle school before they relocated to Charlotte. Once a larger kid had forced Mack's head into his crotch area and had teased him about it while another boy had taken a photo with a cell phone, not unlike how he and the gang treated others now. This had been a turning point in Mack's young life.

He vowed then that it would never happen again. His mother stayed out of it, saying her involvement only made things worse for him and it did. She told him he must learn to stand up to them, which he also did.

Mack began writing dark thoughts in a journal. He wrote of getting a gun and taking it to the bus stop and shooting all of the bullies. He also talked of turning the gun to his head and ending it all in front of those same bullying students. He wrote, 'It's a strange thing to know you might be going to die and you might take others with you.'

He scribbled a passage from Martin Luther King Jr. in the back of his journal. It read 'You shouldn't fight violence with more violence. That's how a war starts.' Under that passage written in red, 'Let the war begin.' Soon afterwards he attacked the bully who had forced his face in his crotch. He ambushed him from behind with a baseball bat. The kid never knew who had attacked him. He had almost died from his injuries. Afterwards, Mack burned his journal. No one had successfully bullied him since.

34

The phone rang. Dale answered, recognizing the girl's voice. "Houston we have a problem. My folks are hauling me to some sort of family thing tonight for my dear old Aunt Ida and said I've got to go, no back talk. The sleep over has been nixed. Sorry, I think we're spending the night at her place in Greensboro."

Dale couldn't effectively nod over the phone so he choked out an okay.

"We leave in thirty minutes. Will you be all right without me?"

"Yeah," he lied, not knowing what else to say.

"Talking my ears off," she snorted. "I've got to run. I have to pack my PJs. I'll see you when we get back. I'll miss you." Her thoughts drifted to what she had researched, *Nyctophobia,* and she wondered if she should have mentioned it to him and if it would have helped.

"Bye," Dale said, already missing her and dreading what lay ahead.

It was time to reinforce his bedroom fortress so he began accumulating life's necessities for his bedroom defense. Switching on all the lights, both floors, had become first priority. Dark Thirty would be here before he knew it.

Meanwhile, Carl O'Conner sat in his old wooden rocker, inventorying his room. He didn't recognize all the items that surrounded him. Restlessness transformed to full blown panic as the darkness began to smother him. He couldn't comprehend the feeling that now choked the life out of him. He had been suffering from episodes of dementia but Carl didn't know the term or the symptoms of the illness that beckoned him. He didn't even realize he was sick.

Carl began to mumble, "I've got to get a grip on things. She would never forgive me if I went insane." The trauma and heartbreak brought on by his wife's death had seemingly accelerated the process. Right now he could not even remember her name but he saw her angelic face, her face before cancer ravished her.

Rocking faster and faster, he finally launched from the chair and hit the floor and began pacing frantically. He needed some fresh air. He rummaged in his pocket and found his keys. His chest felt tight. He was struggling to breathe.

He had to get out of the house now. Fumbling with the door he made his way to the street. Without thinking he opened the truck door and slid under the steering wheel. He wasn't sure where he was going but he had to think and driving always helped him think. The engine startled him as it sputtered to life.

Concentrating, he placed one hand on the steering wheel and fumbled with a lever until it clicked on D. Luckily he had backed into the drive or he would have crashed through the garage door. His feet found the petals and soon he had stormed down the street. Carl just drove and drove and drove; reaching speeds of almost sixty miles an hour, much faster than he normally drove. He sweated profusely. The pain in his chess became unbearable. Unintentionally, he floored the gas peddle.

Dale Thomas Jackson had completed his fortification of his room sanctuary. He had barricaded his bedroom door with a nightstand and a chair. Three lamps and an overhead ceiling light burned brightly as were the bathroom lights. Three flash lights with fresh batteries were strategically placed.

He had a Playmate cooler filled with ice and sodas, and a ham and cheese sandwich. A battery operated radio sat next to the telephone on another night stand. His small television provided welcome noise playing some sort of detective show. He was primed and ready for Dark Thirty, much more prepared than last night.

He wished he could remember why the darkness terrified him so. He strained to recall any information from the deep reaches of his mind but drew blanks. He missed the girl. He wondered if his parents were all right. Funny to be thinking about them now when he had passed on the opportunity to visit them in the hospital.

He placed his hand on the phone and stared at the number scribbled on the paper. Dale contemplated calling Carl O'Conner but dismissed the thought. No one could really help him now. It was too late. He eased over to the window and bent the blind slat just enough to peek outside. He hoped nothing peeked back from the outside. Nothing did but Dark Thirty was just precious minutes away.

35

Brenda Jackson lay in her hospital bed, covers pulled up to her nose. The bed next to her was now occupied by a rather obese elderly woman. The old lady farted periodically filling the room with an awful stench, a smell of rotten death. She snored loudly, much too loudly. Brenda could not escape the smells or the sounds.

She tried to focus on someone besides herself but the waves of panic attacks ravished her thought patterns. She had never felt so lost and helpless and feared for her ability to return to the normal world. Brenda Jackson almost didn't have the will to live. The medication helped. She needed more, much more than they would administer.

She should ask to see Darby or at least ask if her husband was still alive but she couldn't, fearing the worse. And her son, where was Dale? Was he all right? Who was seeing about him? She should insist someone tell her the truth but she wasn't sure she could handle the truth. What a terrible wife and mother she had become. This was her punishment for considering being unfaithful.

She had been the rock of the family not so long ago. She had been the driving force behind Darby's success. She had given up so much for her family. Look at her now. This was beyond pathetic.

The nurse entered the room, first checking on the bellowing whale in the bed next to her, and then walking over to her bedside. "How are you feeling Mrs. Jackson?"

Without pulling down the covers she responded, "I need more medicine."

"The doctor did leave you something to help you rest. I will administer it to you shortly."

"My husband, is he all right?"

"Mr. Jackson is still in ICU."

"And my son…"

"I do believe he's with his grandfather," the nurse smiled then exited the room.

Brenda had not remembered seeing her parents here. Had they arrived from Florida? Who had contacted them? Who knew to contact them?

The nurse returned with a syringe and before Brenda could ask those very questions, the miracle drug delivered results. Sleep arrived. Dale and Darby were no more. She drifted back into the land of the lost.

Dale listened to every creak and thud the house made. He had one of his father's golf clubs under the covers with him. The metal wood would serve as the perfect club. It even said so engraved on the shaft, *The Perfect Club*. He had never witnessed his father using it and hoped he would know how to use it if the time called for it. He wasn't a sports person himself so he hoped swinging it wasn't that difficult.

He wondered what his handicap would be. He had often heard his father discussing handicaps. He hoped it didn't handicap him if he had to use it to beat something to death. What a pathetic existence for a sixteen year old he thought. It should be time for him to grow up. That's big talk for a wimp. His world continued to crumble.

His father remained comatose and his mother, what had happened to her? Carl had come along and saved the day. The girl was a real friend he could count on but she wasn't here. School lurked not much over a week away. He tried to think of something good but Dark Thirty probably waited for him to drop his guard. His nemesis was alive and well out there just looking for weakness in his armor.

Who was he fooling? He was no warrior, not even close. He couldn't face the dark. He couldn't stand up to their kind either. Bullies were just as bad as what he was now facing. One advantage, he could see them. What did the girl find so interesting about him, a pimply faced, skinny ass coward? He hoped he would survive the night to find out.

36

Mack sat on the edge of his bed fondling his prize possession, the Colt. He felt like *Dirty Harry* except Clint Eastwood's Magnum was much larger. He still envisioned himself saying *go ahead punk*; *make my day* to one of those worthless jack-offs at school. Dirty Harry movies were so boss.

He wished he could have found bullets for the other pistol but the cops had left him little time to search. He had been lucky to spot the ammo for the Colt. He switched on his TV and caught the last segment of the news, still reporting Cassie missing. Her parents were on screen pleading for her safe return. "Good luck," he muttered, switching channels to MTV.

He flopped backwards on his bed, now visualizing his next brutal attack and already had a victim in mind from his many school mates. School, he hated the thoughts of its arrival. He tolerated Jake and the others. They represented the lesser of the evils he supposed. Mack really needed no one but couldn't deny he craved attention. He struggled with keeping a low profile and staying out of the center ring, where he belonged.

The Colt was going to pave the way for him. He could do anything he wanted now. The Colt commanded respect. Even the bullet-less pistol could do the trick under the right circumstances. He should spur off from Jake and form his own gang, one to be reckoned with. He just might do that very thing. Yep, he owned the world.

37

Dale snapped to attention when he heard the radio DJ announcing the time, seven AM. He had survived another night on Jackson Island. Feeling it safe to peep through the blinds this time, he saw the first beams of sunshine. Stretching, he prepared for another day. He retrieved a soda from his Playmate and washed away the night's cotton mouth.

Cautiously he descended the stairs. He switched off the lights along his path, no longer requiring their protection. The day belonged to him. He beamed at his accomplishment. Exhausted, he had beaten Dark Thirty a second night.

He wondered when she would return. He felt like bragging to her about his conquest but how silly to brag about surviving the dark. He figured he should probably call Carl O'Conner and arrange to visit his parents in the hospital. Thinking had never been an issue. Making decisions and acting on them was the problem. He faced new challenges.

Procrastination won out. He decided to wait and allow Carl to make the first move and call him. He might even allow Carl to tell him when he would take him. That seemed like a much better plan. He would not have to choose and it might just minimize the conversation.

Noon passed quickly. The house remained silent. The phone had not rung. The girl had not returned. He had made no new decisions and remained inside, alone. He once thought he liked being alone. Now he wasn't so sure. His laptop seemed so useless without internet connection. He could have really used Time Warner about now.

Drowsy from standing guard all night, his eyes had become heavy. He curled up on the inviting den couch to watch a little television. He flipped channels not finding anything particularly good to watch. In less than ten minutes he had fallen asleep. He missed the late breaking news segment.

A Ford Pick-up had just been pulled from Lake Wylie. A man's body had been found inside but they were withholding his name until the next of kin had been contacted. No foul play was suspected. It appeared the truck had left the highway before reaching the bridge and plunged into the lake. No skid marks were detected. The man could have suffered a heart attack or some sort of seizure.

A fisherman had witnessed the truck leaving the road at an incredible speed and had located it in the water by the headlights still burning twenty feet deep. Carl O'Conner had joined his beloved wife in heaven. Dale's sort of grandfather had exited his life.

Dale woke to pitch blackness. Disoriented he sat up, twirled then landed on his feet on the carpeted floor. His heart thundered loudly, breaking the deadly silence. Frozen in fear, Dark Thirty had him firmly in its grasp. He had never allowed it to catch him off guard. Too late, he was snared in its deadly hold. He would have to face it on its terms and in its world. Petrified and plan-less he began to whimper and whine like some deranged animal.

He had no covers, no hiding place. His flashlights were in his bedroom upstairs. The wall switch seemed miles away. He shook convulsively. He pissed in his pants. The warmness ran down both pant's legs, between his bare toes and in a puddle silently on the carpet. He should have called Carl O'Conner. Where was the girl? Why wasn't she here? What was he supposed to do now? He wasn't prepared for this. He had never encountered Dark Thirty so up close and personal.

Gradually his eyes began adjusting to the darkness. This only worsened his situation. Now every shadow took shape. He could hear evil breathing close by; could feel its hot breath. It had come for him. He was at its mercy.

Knees folded underneath his chin, arms locked around his knees, he assumed an upright fetal position on the couch. He locked his eyes closed and began to rock and hum. He could not imagine death being any worse than his present predicament. It was worse than any medieval torture chamber. Tears flowed freely even from eyes clamped shut.

The phone, if only he could reach the phone. But if he could reach the phone, he could reach the light switch. Both were somewhere out there in the darkness. It would never allow him to do either. He knew it was just waiting for him to do something stupid. He would not fall blindly into its trap.

He took a quick peek, looking for a clock but saw nothing but darkness. He had no idea how long the darkness would last and if he could possibly survive it. He cried out loud, begging for it to leave him alone. It didn't answer but he knew it was there, feasting on his fear.

He managed to dislodge the couch cushion he wasn't sitting on and positioned it over him making a lean-to. With his head now buried in the arm rest he made his last stand. He began repeating the Lord's Prayer out loud. If he only had holy water and a crucifix he may be in business. Did he think Dark Thirty was a vampire? Regardless, this world belonged to Dark Thirty and he was smack dab in the middle of its kingdom.

He cried then screamed then cried some more. He had been so careless. This was the moment it had waited for, him to screw up. His conquest from last night had been short lived. "Help me, someone please help me," Dale pleaded, teetering on the edge of insanity.

Debra, still away with her parents, missed Dale Thomas Jackson. She stared out the window into the darkness. She wondered how he was doing by himself with the phobia she was convinced he suffered from and wished she was there. She had hinted to her parents about calling him but they would not allow her to use their precious cell phone's minutes on a kid back in Charlotte. They hadn't totally got over her driving fiasco. She would have to suffer through the night and hoped he made it okay without her.

38

Jake, Stoner and Ray stood just outside the video store, concealed by a parked box truck making deliveries to the pizza place next door. They passed the cigarette around, wary of any adults that might spot and know them and tell their parents.

"I heard they still haven't found that little twit, Cassie yet," mumbled Stoner, having smoked a left handed cigarette earlier.

"Crazy people like her are sort of unpredictable," added Ray, admitting nothing.

"She is a strange one. Who knows what could have happened," said Jake, not really interested one way or the other.

"Oh well, who really gives a rat's ass," scoffed Stoner. "She was pretty damned worthless on all levels."

"Look, here comes Albert," pointed Ray. "It looks like he's returning some videos."

"Good old Albert," smiled Jake. "He's always good for a little fun. Let's check out those movies and see what he's been watching."

Just as Albert arrived at the door, the three figures stepped into his view, cutting him off and leaving him nowhere to go. "Here take them," he offered the tapes, no questions asked.

Jack smiled, "We have them trained so well don't we. I wonder what other tricks little Albert can perform?"

Albert Grubb, half and half, as they liked to call them, had a white mother and black father. That alone put him on the target list. Dark complexion but not black, and if not for the kinky curls, he could have probably passed for white. Jake hated half breeds of any kind. He especially despised

Albert Grubb. While Albert equaled his attackers in size, he lacked the poise and confidence to challenge them.

Albert would have been quite handsome if not for the huge pinkish birthmark covering the left side of his face over his eye, across his cheek and just past his ear. Jake thought this made him look like a mutant and often called him *The Mutated Grubb Worm*.

Stoner and Ray forced Albert behind the box truck. Albert neither protested nor resisted. Jake poked him in the chest and asked, "So Grub Worm, you carrying any cash?"

Albert went through the process of emptying all his pockets. Jake counted three bucks and thirty five cents. Jake shook his head in disgust. "That's it?"

"I'll have more Friday when I receive my allowance."

"So are you going to write us an IOU?" asked Jake.

"Yes, if you want one."

"Priceless," commented Jake. "What's on the tapes, Stoner?"

"You're going to just love this. We have *Revenge of the Nerds I, II and III.*"

Jake put his finger hard against Albert's nose. "Mutant, are you and your buddies planning some revenge?"

"No, I just like movies. They're funny. We would never try anything like that. We're not insane."

Ray began pulling the ribbon tape from one of the VCR tapes. "Oops, that's going to cost you." He dropped the other two to the asphalt and crushed them under foot. Albert never changed his stone like expression and said nothing. He had learned long ago to just let it run its course and live to see another day.

Ray punched Albert in the arm. "Guess what nerd. Your membership is now history."

"It's my dad's membership," remarked Albert, shifting his weight from one foot to the other.

Two adults passed by but neither paid any attention to Albert and his unfortunate predicament. Albert should have yelled but what good would it have done. If he escaped them this time, there would just be another. He decided best to take it now and get it over with.

"Tell you what Grub Worm," explained Jake. "We'll meet you here next Friday, same time and you can share your allowance with us. Hell, we can do this every week if you want to. What you say about that?"

"Friday, same time, every week," repeated Albert Grubb, almost too mechanical.

"Now get the hell out of here before we remember just how much you piss us off," growled Jake as Stoner kicked Albert square in the butt.

Albert quickly disappeared around the corner and stopped only when he had crossed the street almost two blocks away. "Butt wipes," he murmured, looking around almost expecting the boogeyman to appear out of nowhere and make him pay for the remark.

Forming his hands into fists he questioned why he couldn't stand up to them. His answer came almost immediately, because I want to live. He had never actually heard anything about them killing anyone but he certainly didn't want to be their first. Dead boys tell no tales.

39

Dale Thomas Jackson remained burrowed underneath the sofa cushion, eyes closed so tightly that they twitched and hurt. Every muscle cramped. His clothing almost suffocated him from the stench of sweat and urine. His stomach ached from a need to perform a bowel movement. He felt the thing closing around him. If he opened his eyes and Dark Thirty caught him in its gaze, it would be all over. He would be sucked into hell's pit.

The night had lasted at least a week. The room had actually lightened but in his pathetic state he had failed to witness dawn's arrival. Dark Thirty, an over powering foe had him where it wanted him. It had never ever gotten this close to him before and he vowed he could never allow it to happen again, if he could just survive this time.

The phone rang, sending his safety cushion launching into the air like a misguided missile. Dale scrambled to reclaim his shelter but too late, it was out of reach. The evidence of light in the room offered him the first hint that Dark Thirty had retreated. On the third ring Dale attempted to muster up the energy to set a foot onto the carpet. Neither of his feet was tap dancing right now nor did they immediately beckon his command. He felt around until he located his glasses.

First step, his foot asleep, he stumbled and fell, his head barely missing the corner of the coffee table. By the forth ring the answering machine kicked in. He heard his dad, Darby, greeting the caller then he heard her voice, the girl's. Finally Debra was home and checking on him.

"Hey Dale Thomas Jackson, we're still in Greensboro. Hopefully we'll be home later this afternoon. My aunt had a weak moment and let me make this call. Where are you?

Why aren't you answering the phone? I hope this doesn't mean something terrible has happened to your folks. I should be there with you. You should own a cell phone. I used to have one but my folks took it after my incident with the car. Dog gone it! I wish you would pick up. I'll…Beep." The time had expired.

The girl talks way too much. Dale felt worse than warmed over crap and smelled about as bad. The trauma inflicted by Dark Thirty the past couple of nights had taken its toll. He needed a bathroom break and a shower. He took care of both in that order.

Clean and feeling better in the light of day, Dale grabbed a chunk of extra sharp cheese and three slices of bologna from the refrigerator and gobbled it down like there would be no tomorrow. He washed it down with a glass of orange juice. He still couldn't wrap his mind around the events of the last few days. His life had gone to hell in a hand basket as his dad would say if he were here.

He exited the front door, unsure why and where he might be headed. He just needed to be outside of that house. Twenty minutes later he had arrived in the park. Spotting a bench, he sat down and buried his head in his arms against the back of the bench. The sun warmed his back and felt simply wonderful. He closed his eyes, exhausted from Dark Thirty's inflicted insomnia and somehow fell asleep.

He woke to some one kicking the side of his foot. He scrambled to a defensive position, secretly hoping the kick was from the girl. It wasn't. He didn't recognize the boy standing over him and expected nothing but the worst. He had dropped his guard again and deserved the punishment about to be dished out due to his carelessness.

"Are you one of those homeless kids?"

Dale had to contemplate that question. He certainly felt like an orphan, or at least for the last few days but he lived in a house. He finally shook his head no. The kid was maybe forty pounds heavier than him, red hair and a zillion reddish freckles. He almost looked like *Opie* on the Andy Griffith show.

"I suppose you do look too clean to be homeless and you don't smell like the ones that hang out near the soup kitchen."

Dale sat up and stretched then rubbed his eyes and let out a loud yawn. The boy was still standing there. What the heck did he want?

"I've never seen you around before. Did you just move here?"

Dale nodded yes, not that he owed him any sort of explanation. A nod really wasn't too much information.

"Are you mute? I guess you can either read lips or can hear. Can you talk or are you one of those deaf and dumb kids?"

"I can talk and I'm not stupid."

"Are you deaf?"

"No and I'm not blind. Why don't you mind your own business and leave me alone?"

"Nope, you don't sound dumb but you do sound angry."

Dale shuddered. This kid had to be one of them. They had a knack for finding him where ever they moved. "Okay, get it over with. Hit me. Kick me. Cuss me out or something. I don't have any money on me so just get it over with how about it?"

"Are you one of those crazies who like to be tortured?"

"Stop playing games. Just do it and finish it. I'll take it like I always do."

"Now I'm quite honored. You think I'm one of Jake's goons."

"Jake…goons...who is Jake?"

"Jake is the alpha bully. I'm one of the good guys. I wear a white hat. Well, I would if I wore a hat. My name is Ted Parker." He extended is hand.

"Dale Jackson...I live in the second house in the sequence." Dale cautiously shook it.

"What?"

"Nothing, never mind…"

"Did you sleep here in the park all night?"

"Does everyone who lives here ask so many stupid questions?"

"You just asked a question, so I reckon you fit in too," laughed Ted.

"Okay, you got me there."

"You sure do look like crap. You should sleep in a bed, not on a park bench."

"It matches how I feel. For the record, I didn't sleep at all last night."

"They say it's not healthy to not sleep. You're supposed to get at least eight hours every night. You got any brothers or sisters?"

Dale thought this Parker guy was all over the place just like the girl. "I'm the middle child," grinned Dale, finding it easy to talk to this Ted Parker.

Ted didn't get the joke. "So, which do you have, brothers or sisters?"

"Neither, I'm it."

"But you said…oh I get it, you were yanking my chain. I've got three sisters. What a pain. They're all older than me. How old are you?"

"Sixteen…"

"Me too, just last week so I guess we'll be classmates this year if you do live in the neighborhood."

"I do and I guess we will."

"What do you like to do?"

There he goes, just like her. Why was he so important to everyone here? "Right now I would like to sleep."

"A park bench is a funny place to do it unless you're homeless."

"I'm not homeless I told you. I just don't want to go home right now."

"Oh, your parents are ticked off at you. What did you do?"

"My parents are not at home and they're not angry at me. I just don't want to go home right now. Is there a law that you have to sleep at home?"

"Now it sounds like you're ticked off at me again."

"Look, I just want some peace and quiet so I can sleep for awhile. That's all."

"Okay, I know a place. It's a private spot, a secret place where no one will bother you if you don't want to sleep at home. Sure is strange you wouldn't want to sleep at home though."

"Where is this place?"

He pointed toward the woods. "In there and I can stand watch while you sleep."

"If it is so private and secret, then why do you need to stand watch?"

"Jake Tyler and his goons might show up and you wouldn't want them to find you here alone and asleep. That would spell bad news for you."

"I've known Jakes everywhere I have lived. None have ever killed me."

"Suit yourself then. Follow me."

Dale couldn't believe he was following a stranger into uncharted territory. He didn't perceive this Ted Parker as a threat. Someone could pound him while he slept but for whatever reason he felt compelled to trust him. Charlotte was certainly different so far from any of the places they had previously resided. Kids were drawn to him and not for bad reasons.

"See, the perfect hideout," boasted Ted Parker, pointing to the small clearing nestled between a briar thicket and thick stand of cedar trees. "Stretch out and enjoy. The clover is cool and soft."

"I should probably check on my parents," Dale admitted loudly.

"I thought you said they weren't at home."

"They're not," responded Dale, amazed how openly he talked to this strange kid. "They're both in the hospital."

"Sorry to hear. You didn't do it, did you?"

"Do what?"

"Do something to cause them being there?"

"Do something, like what?"

"I don't know…maybe attack them with a baseball bat or something. You're not a whacko are you?"

"Why in the world would you say something like that?"

"Hey, I'm not the one sleeping in the woods while my parents are in hospital."

"You do argue a good case but no, I didn't attack them."

"Lots of kids do. You see it on the news all the time. Kids go off the deep end and kill their parents or grandparents. They just snap. I'm glad you're not one of them."

"Me too…"

"So why are both of them in the hospital?"

"My dad was in a car accident and my mom had some sort of nervous breakdown worrying about him."

"Bummer, so that's why you're alone and no adults are at your house right now… cool. We can hang out at your place. How long will they be in the hospital?"

Dale figured there either must be something in the water here or the mother ship dumped all the alien morons in one place. He talked almost as much as the girl. Dale figured he must be infected too because he had begun to act like them, sort of.

"I don't know. My dad is in some sort of comatose state and mom is zoned out on drugs."

"This could really work out for us. Your house could be our bachelor pad, our main hang out. How cool is this?"

Another sign thought Dale. This state of mind made those infected smile a lot. The girl smiled and laughed a lot. He missed that crazy snorting of hers. He hoped he didn't start smiling all the time too.

"I can invite some friends over and we can have one of those house warming parties. Do you have any booze at your house?"

"Do you drink?"

"Don't you?"

"I really do need some sleep."

"Kick back. Consider me your personal alarm clock. What time do you want me to wake you?"

"At least three or four hours before it gets dark and I do mean what I say."

"Got it, buddy. I'll be here around five and I will contact the other guys."

"No party tonight, please, Ted," Dale said as he lay back on the ground and closed his eyes to the warm summer sun.

40

Debra Floyd was eager to get home. She had already played way too much nice-nice with her aunt and relatives. All of them wanted to pinch her on her cheeks, pat her head or give her a hug. Too many of them either suffocated her with their perfume or overwhelmed her with other strange body odors. She had had enough. Besides, she missed Dale Thomas Jackson and had only just met him.

"For heaven's sake, I'm going on seventeen years old, I don't need this baby crap," she whispered. Not having big boobs certainly didn't help her cause. She looked twelve. "Man, when will I ever grow breasts," she sighed only loud enough for the little white poodle to hear her. She hated that poodle with the bows on its ears and tail. It was spoiled rotten. People acted like it was human. It was just a stupid fluffy dog.

Her aunt's grandfather clock chimed, signaling 10 AM. That aggravating clock had kept her awake every hour on the hour. Her bed, a fold out hideaway couch in the den, with the loud ticking, chiming clock had tormented her all night. Didn't they think even a sixteen year needed her beauty sleep. Probably the lack of sleep had inhibited her boob growth or maybe it was caused by her prescribed medication. She should read the warning label; may cause headaches, diarrhea, stomach cramps, night sweats, crazy horny dreams and stunt breast growth.

She placed her hands on her breasts. Hadn't she read somewhere that more than a mouthful was just a waste? If so, bring a spoon for hers. Why was she so worried? No one had ever seen or touched hers anyway. Maybe Dale Thomas Jackson would have first dibs.

Her folks were ambling their way toward her. Could this be a sign? Another relative, Uncle Billy, ambushed and sidetracked them. There was no end to this family madness. She hoped Dale Thomas Jackson was faring well without her. She doubted it. He looked to be one that would require a lot of maintenance and she would provide the service for his needs. Uncle Billy looked at her and smiled. He was a cheek pincher. She hoped he didn't come her way.

The poodle began yapping. She stifled an urge to kick it. Yep, Uncle Billy had her in his sights and was coming this way. She rubbed her cheeks preparing for the inevitable. Her cousin, Julie made the mistake of walking by and Uncle Billy grabbed her by the arm and began jabbering and smiling at her instead. Debra took advantage of the diversion and exited the room.

"Get me out of here," she sighed. "I'm needed back in Charlotte." The poodle had followed her and barked and had ratted her out. Uncle Billy appeared and now pinched her left check, babbling stuff about how big she had gotten since the last time he had seen her. *Everything but my boobs…*she smiled and hugged him. He smelled like cigarette smoke. *Gag a maggot.*

Her mom was motioning for her. Another bunch of relatives were hovering about her mom, all looking in her direction. Was there no end to all this hugging and kissing and just plain nonsense? "When are we going home?" To her surprise, her mom said they were about to leave. Avoiding as many people as she could, she made her way to her parents' car and waited patiently.

"I'll be there before you know it my sweetheart," she giggled loudly at the mere thought.

The drive home seemed endless. Traffic was stop and go as they got close to Charlotte. Interstate 85 could often become a parking lot if you hit it the wrong time of the day. Unfortunately they had done just that. It gave her too much time to think. Thinking about Dale Thomas Jackson was a dangerous thing for Debra to do. She should probably not admit to him she could be dangerous if she expected their relationship to blossom and grow. First she must convince him they were in a relationship. Finally traffic began moving again.

After forever they finally arrived home. Debra Floyd tossed her bag in her room then rushed back through the house and out the front door. She mounted her bike and peddled like a maniac with one destination in mind. She arrived on Dale's front lawn in world record breaking time. She knocked on the door and called out to Dale but he didn't reply. She knocked again then tried the knob. The door opened.

Entering, she called out Dale's name but still received no answer. Exploring the house room by room she found no Dale Thomas Jackson. She sensed something dreadfully wrong with the scenario. She hoped she was wrong. Maybe he had gone to the hospital. She wished she knew the *sort of* grandfather's phone number. She thought about calling the hospital but what would they tell a stranger.

"Oh well," she sighed. "I'll just wait here." She glanced at the wall clock. It was almost six in the afternoon. He should be home soon.

Dale lay on the grassy patch of clover heaven secluded among the thick hardwoods and a hedge row of small cedar, bordered by the thicket. He slept deeply, snored loudly and had not a care in the world. He dreamed he sat by his mom's side surrounded by bright yellow couch cushions. His dad lay in the bed beside his mom. Both wore vampire looking costumes and their arms were folded across their chests. They looked so peaceful, like angels but angels didn't look like vampires. They must be angels. They had glowing halos.

Dale drew such comfort from just being in the same room with his parents. They would protect him from the evil Dark Thirty. But if they were vampires, would they not be the legion of Dark Thirty? Angels, they glowed too much like angels but he saw no heavenly wings.

The door swung open and a nurse entered carrying a silver tray. Her face was fuzzy. He could not make out her features. She hummed a familiar tune, one of those *deep down in the south* songs, somewhere in the land of cotton. She removed an ominous syringe from the tray and squirted a yellowish stream into the air. Yellow drops landed on his dad's face. The nurse spun to face his mom. Her face came into focus. It was the crazy black woman that had accused him of stealing her money from that Mason jar.

"Don't worry honey child," she told him in a Gone with the Wind slave accent. "Her be out of her miseries shortly."

Dale had to stop her but he discovered he was being restrained, strapped to his chair. "Dad, stop her!"

Darby rose to a sitting position, canine fangs exposed. He was no angel. The crazy black nurse planted a kung-fu style foot directly to the side of his dad's face and sent him reeling. The huge syringe transformed into a wooden stake and she plunged it through his chest. He crumbled to dust.

She turned to face Dale now, her mouth full of oversized teeth. Grinning she warned, "Mess with my money young Mister Jackson and see what I does to you." She held a foot long needle.

Dale screamed for help, rocking his chair back and forth. He saw Carl O'Conner pass by the doorway in the hall. He called out to him. The old man turned and waved then joined an equally old woman and disappeared. She had to be his dead wife. Yelling at the top of his lungs, his eyes were filled with twilight. Dark Thirty approached.

He sat up. He was on the grass, in the woods, in the park and Dark Thirty was already approaching. Ted Parker had failed to wake him up as he had promised. Never trust a stranger.

Life and death situation, he must now outrun Dark Thirty and arrive at home before it did. He sprang to his feet and ran like the wind, exploding through the brush almost running over an approaching Ted Parker. He said nothing to his defective alarm clock, held fast to his mission to reach home before Dark Thirty beat him there. He sprinted across the openness of the park.

Ted, losing ground quickly, attempted to follow. "Dog gone it, he's a fast one. He must run track or something."

The shadows closed in on Dale. He thought about evasive maneuvers like zigzagging but wasn't sure it would improve his chances. It probably only worked against submarines. Shortest way, a straight line; run in a straight line toward home he reminded himself.

He could see house #2 ahead. The street lights began to flicker on, waking up to the approaching nightfall. He would never survive another night like last night and three in a row would be the death of him. Dark Thirty was wearing him down. That was its plan. It must thrive much stronger in Charlotte, North Carolina.

Huffing and puffing he charged through the front door, flipping on wall switches as he passed them. After completely illuminating the den, he bent over, hands on his knees, attempting to catch his breath.

"Are you all right?"

Dale almost stained his underwear. The recognizable voice jolted him back from the dead. An angel spoke to him. The girl was back. There stood Debra Floyd.

"No, I'm not all right. Do I look all right? What took you so long?"

"Did you brush up on speech while I was gone? That actually sounded like you were talking. Three sentences, back to back to back, I'm impressed."

"Shut up and help me turn on the rest of the lights," Dale ordered quite rudely.

"And assertive to boot, you have been studying while I've been away. I like this new you." Puzzled by his strange request, she did what he had asked. A couple of minutes later they stood face to face and Debra told Dale, "You look like crap but you probably know that already don't you?"

Before he could answer, the doorbell rang. He leapt into her arms before giving it a thought. His heart pounded like a frightened animal. She held him tightly against her. It felt good. She must have liked it too.

"I really like all these changes, especially this one but don't you think we should see who's at the door?"

He broke her hug, reached down and grabbed her by the hand then led her to the door. He opened it just a crack and peeked outside. Surely Dark Thirty would not have rung the bell.

"Man, are you going to go out for the track team? You should. You'd be the fastest one on the team. I bet you could win every ribbon and medal single handed."

"Ted," said Debra. "What are you doing here?"

"You were supposed to wake me up!"

"Wake you?" asked Debra. "You and Ted are sleeping together?"

Both boys replied, "No!"

"I don't sleep with guys," shouted Dale, adjusting his glasses.

"I'm glad because that would mean you've lied to me about being a virgin."

"A virgin?" remarked Ted. "Hey Deb, what are you doing here? You got Dale in your sights. Is he your boyfriend? Are you going to un-virgin him?"

"Ted, that's none of your business if we do or we don't."

"Hey, I'm right here," Dale reminded them. "Am I not part of this conversation?"

"And now you're so talkative you're butting into other people's conversations," she said arms crossed and raising an eyebrow. "You continue to amaze me, Dale Thomas Jackson. Does that mean you do or you don't?"

Dale threw his hands in the air, rolled his eyes then gave her his answer. He shrugged.

"Are you going to make me stand out here forever?" asked Ted, still peering through the door crack.

Dale opened the door and Ted said, "I found him asleep on a park bench this afternoon. This dude has some serious issues, much worse than ours, Deb. I guess that's why I like him."

"Me too," replied Debra with a wink.

Dale had forgotten about Dark Thirty and drew comfort from them being here. Maybe they were just what the doctor ordered. He would have to put up with their constant chatter and persistent questioning but that's the price you pay, he supposed.

41

"The body was found inside an old mausoleum by the cemetery's caretaker," quoted the reporter on the local nightly news. "The deceased has not been identified but our sources say this could very well be that of the missing young girl, Cassie Richards. More details are expected from the chief of police within the hour. We will cover the news conference so stay tuned. Now we return you to your local programming."

Mack was unmoved by the news. He switched off the television and lay back on his bed. Buddy on the other hand was shocked. A blubbering mess, he feared the worse. He looked over at the cool and calm Mack, still unemotional and unconcerned. Cassie had been alive when he, Ray and Mack had left her there in the cemetery.

Ray saw the fear in Buddy's facial expression. He encouraged him to stay calm and everything would be all right. Mack warned him to simply keep his mouth shut.

"Maybe she just committed suicide," spoke up Ray, but he somewhat doubted it and refused to vocalize his real suspicions about her death; best not to end up the same way.

Mack eyed his two accomplices and sat up abruptly and issued a warning. "She was alive just like Ray said. You saw her there when we left. What happened to her afterwards is not our concern."

"But…" Buddy attempted to say before being cut off by Mack.

"She was alive, right, Ray?"

"Yeah," replied Ray. "But what we did to her…"

"She brought that on herself," interrupted Mack.

"How, just by walking down the street?" asked Buddy.

"There's no place for girls like her around here," proclaimed Mack. "She's better off. She was broken and no good to anybody. The world is a better place with her gone. Just keep your mouths shut and it'll be fine." His warning was understood loud and clear. Mack stood, clutching the Colt in his belt.

"But what if the police come around?" asked Buddy. "They have ways of uncovering things at crime scenes."

"Who said it was a crime scene?" asked Mack.

"But we…" Again Mack cut him off. "We did nothing. Stick to that story and we'll be fine."

42

"All set," said Debra. "My mom thinks I'm sleeping over at Carol's tonight. I'm good to go and can stay here with you tonight if you want me to."

Dale smiled and nodded his approval.

"Hold on," spoke up Ted. "You're not doing this without me. Give me about an hour and I'll be right back."

"You don't even know the concept of time," snapped Dale.

"Ouch," answered Ted. "You're still ticked off about that? I told you the circumstances were out of my control."

"What happened to three's a crowd," Debra threw in her two cents worth, expecting to spend the night alone with Dale Thomas Jackson.

"Hey, I'm coming back to protect Dale from you," smiled Ted.

"What makes you think he wants your protection?"

"It doesn't matter. I'm in and there's no talking me out of it."

"There you two go talking like I'm not here. Hurry back Ted."

Debra looked over at Dale and gave him an ugly frown. She felt so cheated. Her plans had been sabotaged. Ted was ruining everything.

After Ted departed, Dale thought briefly of the darkness outside but quickly dismissed his concerns once the girl began chattering away again. He watched as she stuck a frozen pizza in the oven then opened them both a soda. She seemed too mature for a sixteen year old. He wondered if all girls were like her.

Out of the blue she said, "So tell me why you're so terrified of the dark."

That one caught him off guard. His best defense was a shrug.

"That's no answer. That's a cop out. You need to get this off your chest."

"I really don't know. I just am and always have been. Can we drop it?"

"No, I think we need to explore this phenomenon or phobia and do what we can to get you beyond your fears."

"Is that how your shrink talks?"

"Exactly," she snorted. "We must analyze it and break it down so we can understand it."

"I'm not so sure he has helped you a whole lot."

"That's a sense of humor, a good sign," she snorted again. "See…we're making progress already. Just continue to relax on the couch."

"Another shrink trick you've picked up I suppose."

"Not really," her tone changed. "I just thought it would be nice to join you there."

"Ted better hurry up," blurted out Dale. "I need him more than ever now."

"Two sentences, another breakthrough," she winked. "Are you sure you don't want to explore your enter fears. I have been researching it. Maybe I can help."

"Drink your soda," Dale said handing it to her. "I'll turn on the TV."

"Shucks, I thought you might just try turning me on."

"I think you already are."

"Now you're talking my language," she answered in her most seductive sixteen year old voice.

Dale's leg began patting the floor and he accelerated his channel surfing. He wasn't familiar with the cable channel lineup yet but it really didn't matter.

"Channel 373 is a wonderful music channel if you have expanded basic," she instructed him.

Dale surfed and opted for a deer hunting channel instead. Debra took control of the remote keyed in 373 and easy listening music filled the room. "Soothes me, how about you?"

Dale shrugged and gave in to her. He really had no choice after she slipped the remote behind her back. She patted the spot next to her and motioned for him to slide closer. He wasn't so sure about this but did what she had asked.

"I'm not going to bite, at least not for a while," she let out a toned down version of her snort laugh. "Now let's figure out this night time trauma of yours."

"Good luck…"

"When did it start?"

"I told you already. It's always been like this."

"Always is a long time. You don't know why it scares you so?"

"I don't remember ever not being bothered by it."

"It looks far worse than a bother."

"Look, I don't remember."

"Let's try a new approach."

"So you know hypnosis."

"No silly," she smiled. "Why does it terrify you?"

"I don't know."

"You must feel something?"

"It closes in on me. It suffocates me. It's out there trying to take me away."

"It, what is it?"

"I don't know."

"Were you ever buried alive?"

"That's a stupid question. Have you been buried alive?"

"The mind blocks out events like that."

"So I was buried alive and don't remember it?"

"See, we've made some headway. When were you buried alive?"

"You tell me. I don't remember it."

"I thought you said you did?"

"This is crazy," said Dale, throwing up his hands. "I don't remember anything."

"There's got to be an assignable cause, some trigger that makes this happen to you."

"So everything I don't remember could be the cause?"

"Could be…"

"I don't think that shrink is helping you a whole lot."

"That's why I take medication. Maybe you should too and if you did you would be more sexually aroused and dream those crazy dreams like me. Maybe you need a bath to calm you down. I could scrub your back." She smiled that sparkly smile, reliving the scene in the bathroom.

Dale blushed. "This is going nowhere."

"You've got to relax."

"You got any of those magic pills?"

"Like I said, you would just have sexual fantasies like me if I gave you one."

"Something tells me you would have those without the pills."

"Not if I don't go to sleep but you might still have that that little problem I saw you have in the shower that guys get. I do read a lot."

"Not after I take a leak I wouldn't. Pee doesn't mean I'm sexually aroused. It just means I have to pee."

"That's such a waste of one of God's little miracles. Would you like to have sex with me, Dale Thomas Jackson? W could share the first time together."

"I haven't had one of those pills and don't have to pee."

"I think I can fix that," she answered, placing her hand on his thigh and kissing him square on the lips.

She certainly knew how to push his buttons because he could feel the stir in his pants and heat rising around his shoulders and neck. The knock jolted them both to attention. Dale became wild eyed. Debra patted his hand then said, "Ease up. The boogie man doesn't knock. He snatches you up when you least expect it."

She opened the door. Ted Parker stood there smiling, holding a sleeping bag. "I'm in for the sleepover."

"Ted, I told you three's a damn crowd," muttered Debra.

"I smell pizza. I'm back just in time."

"Yep, just in time," mumbled Dale, wiping sweat from his brow.

"I'm starving," said Ted, heading towards the kitchen.

"Me too," added Debra, locking eyes with Dale.

"I'll get the sodas," stated Dale, leaping from the couch.

"Hey did you hear" asked Ted. "They think they may have found Cassie Richards."

"What do you mean? Who thinks what?" asked Debra.

"Who's Cassie Richards?"

"A missing classmate of ours," replied Debra. "She lives just a couple of streets over. She's a real sweet girl. Like you, she doesn't talk much. She has autism, unlike you."

"So what happened?"

"They found a body in the cemetery but they're not saying officially that it's her."

"That's so sad," exclaimed Debra.

"I've never known a real live dead person before," stated Ted.

"That comment doesn't even make sense," said Debra.

"What doesn't?"

"Never mind," she responded. "Let's eat our pizza."

Dead girl in the neighborhood thought Dale. Could this possibly be the work of Dark Thirty? "What do they think happened to her?"

"She got dead. Who knows? Like Deb said, she had problems."

"I didn't say she had problems. I said she was autistic. It's not a disease. It's a condition, something she couldn't help or control. She got picked on because of it. She was actually very intelligent. She just couldn't express it very well. She read a lot of books. Autism is an interesting condition."

"I guess you read about that too."

"As a matter of a fact I did. I bet her folks are frantic about this news."

"I don't think we've ever had a dead classmate before," mumbled Ted.

"Shouldn't you go home, Ted?"

"Nope, like I said, I'm in. My folks were glad to be rid of me. What are we going to do first?"

Debra glanced over at Dale, fluttering her eyes. Dale's foot began tapping. She wished she could be rid of Ted Parker

43

Jake phoned Stoner. "Did you hear they think they've found Cassie?"

"Freaky, right here in the cemetery," replied Stoner. "Might be some sort of serial killer…cool, you think?"

"Stoner, we need more than one body for it to have been a serial killer and nobody else is dead or missing."

"It would still be cool if it was a serial killer though, wouldn't it?"

"That's pretty damn lame even for you. Why would you want it to be a serial killer, one that kills teenage girls?"

"Think about it," Stoner replied as only he could. "A teenage killer that only hits girl retards…that would be freaky."

"Better be glad you're a male then," snickered Jake.

Stoner missed the jab. "You want to meet somewhere and burn one? I've got some bad stuff."

"Nah, not tonight…it's getting late and my folks would crap a brick if I left the house. They're both camped out downstairs. The old man is in one of his moods and they're both freaking out over this Cassie thing. I don't think they'll let me go anywhere tonight."

"It's not that late, man," replied Stoner, looking at his radio clock, its digital display glowing eleven fifteen.

"It's not going to happen. They feel like they're protecting me from the evil out there. They have now friggin clue. See you tomorrow," said Jake, ending the call on his cell. He must remember to text Stoner next time. Cassie is dead, he mumbled. Who in the hell would have killed the little zombie? I guess she would have been easy if blood and guts was your thing he figured. Oh well, not his concern.

44

Brenda Jackson sat up in her hospital bed, pillows resting against her back. Everything seemed so far away. She struggled to focus. The voices from the hallway echoed in her head. She held a plastic cup in her hand and sipped the cold water though a straw. The top combined with the crinkly straw made it look like some sort of giant sippy-cup.

A conglomeration of wires and tubes were attached to her. She was aware of various beeps and clicks. She hoped none were life support. She didn't feel that close to death's door.

A person in the other bed snored loudly making sputtering sounds like one of those automatic firing weapons. On second thought it sounded more like a piece of cardboard clicking in bicycle spokes. She wondered why she was still here. She no longer felt anxious or panic stricken but instead, mellow and laid back.

A young man entered the room in green hospital garb. His dark complexion and jet black curly hair complimented by a gorgeous smile, made him seem much too boyish to be a doctor. He had a stethoscope hanging around his neck and clipboard in hand so he must have a medical degree. He could certainly fulfill her fantasies if she was into cradle robbing. She quickly dismissed that thought.

"Mrs. Jackson, you're awake…fantastic. How do you feel?" His voice sounded more mature than his looks.

"I am. Is that a good thing? I guess I'm okay."

"Very good," he replied, sporting a mouth full of pearly whites.

"So what's wrong with me?"

"Nothing more than stress," he replied. "Shock induced likely by your husband's unfortunate accident unless there are other issues going on that you would like to discuss."

"Nothing that I know of…"

"Do you drink, Mrs. Jackson?"

"I'm no lush I can assure you," she responded, insulted by the question.

"I didn't mean to imply that you are. I apologize. However, depression sometimes is associated with frequent alcohol use."

"So you think I'm a depressed alcoholic?"

"Sorry, these are routine questions and are not a personal attack."

"I have an occasional drink. That's all."

"Once, twice, three or four times a week?"

"I don't maintain any records." She didn't like his bedside manner.

"Your blood alcohol content was extremely high when you were admitted, Mrs. Jackson. How many drinks had you consumed before your arrival?"

"I said I didn't count them."

"How often do you consume alcohol?"

"As often as I want to young man. Would you like to confirm my age. I haven't been ID-ed lately. How often do you drink?"

He smiled. "Have you been mixing prescription medication with alcohol?"

"You tell me. You seem to have all the answers and the test results."

"I shouldn't have to warn you that mixing the two can pose deadly consequences."

"I'm not a drunk or a drug abuser, and I certainly don't appreciate your condescending lecturing."

"I'm just doing my job."

"When can I go home?"

"There's no reason you can't go home in the morning."

Brenda nodded her approval. "How's my husband?"

"I'm not at liberty to say. He's not my patient but I will ask Doctor Lawson to drop by when he completes his rounds. He's your husband's physician."

"And my son Dale," she asked.

"Is he in the hospital too?"

"No, doctor…it seems to me I remember someone saying he was picked up here by his grandparents. My parents are the only grandparents he has and they reside in Florida. I was surprised to hear they had already arrived."

"I'm sorry. I have seen no young boy here nor am I aware of any arrangements with your parents. I'll ask the night nurse to drop by. Maybe she can shed some light on it. How old is your son?"

"Sixteen and his name is Dale. He's a wonderful boy but he has never stayed at home alone so I hope my parents are with him."

"I'll see what I can find out for you. Do you require anything else?" Sixteen and never been alone, interesting thought the doctor.

"No, I'm just ready to go home."

Puzzling, how would anyone have known to phone her parents in Florida? She didn't remember telling the staff. Maybe Dale did. She didn't think he knew their Fort Myers phone number or address. Possibly she didn't give him enough credit.

The woman under the covers in the other bed turned her back to Brenda. She grunted like a pig then farted loudly. The stench from her bowels sent Brenda scrambling underneath her own covers. It overtook the room like a tidal wave. She continued to rapid fire in Brenda's direction.

Brenda had to come out of the covers and fumble for her bedpan certain she would vomit. She fought off the urge and held the covers against her mouth and nose. The door opened. An elderly looking doctor entered. He never flinched or acknowledged the awful smell or sounds erupting from the other bed. In a monotone voice he introduced himself as Doctor Lawson, her husband's doctor.

"How is he," she asked, without removing the linens from her face.

"Excuse me," he asked, unable to understand her muffled question.

She eased the sheets below her mouth and repeated the question.

"Your husband is an extremely lucky man, Mrs. Jackson, but I'm afraid he remains unconscious. He's in a comatose state due to swelling around his brain and extreme bodily injuries. He requires time to heal."

"Then he's going to be all right."

"He has a long battle ahead of him," answered the kindly older gentleman.

"Will he recover from all his injuries?"

"Only time will tell. First thing first, we must diminish the swelling."

"Can I see him?"

"I see no reason why not, if your doctor says you can."

"Have you seen my parents or my son, Dale?"

"Not during any of my rounds."

"Thank you, Doctor Lawson."

"Please get some rest, my dear. He will require you at hundred percent. This could be a long journey for all of you, both physically and mentally."

Thirty minutes later a young candy striper arrived with a wheelchair. She affixed the IV to the side, disconnected the monitors and wheeled her down the hallway. Three floors separated Darby from her. Parked by his bed, she stared at her husband and could hardly recognize him because of his injuries and the bandages.

She put her hand on his and began to cry. He deserved better than this she thought. He was a good husband, father and provider. A wave of guilt overwhelmed her. How could she have ever thought of being unfaithful? She had a good life.

Darby could feel the warmth of her coupled hand around his. He recognized the angelic voice of his wife but it sounded so far away. He strained to understand the muffled words. Why could he not hear her clearly?

"Darby, I'm so sorry. This is my fault. It's my punishment. I should have been content, happy with my life with you and I really am. I just...I just thought I needed more. Please forgive me."

Darby could sense distress in her but could not comprehend what she was saying. He so needed to comfort her and assure her that he would be all right. He still had no idea where he was and what had caused him to be here. Was he dead he wondered or was she?

"I'm so weak. I thought I could recapture my lost youth. How stupid to think an affair would do that for me. I had never been with anyone but you and longed to know how it would be with someone else. What a horrible mistake I made. I confess my sins to you now and hope you forgive me for those elicit thoughts."

Did she just admit to having an affair? Darby had made out sorry and affair from the jumbled dialogue. Not his Brenda, his beautiful wife, an affair…

"See, God has punished me by taking you away from me. I should have been the one to have had an accident, not you. I suppose this was his way of knocking some sense into my lustful heart and hard head before I crossed the line. It worked. I have repented."

So she didn't have an affair sighed Darby from his dark world. Her voice had suddenly become clear. He could hear every word now.

"I love you Darby. I only wish for you to be well."

I love you too, but what happened to me? Where am I? Why can't I see you?

"I think my parents have Dale. I should be able to go home in the morning. They're releasing me tomorrow."

Go home…release you from where? This doesn't make any sense? Are we in the hospital? Did we have some sort of accident? Are you all right, my sweet Brenda?

"The doctor says you have a lot of mending to do yet but there's hope you'll recuperate fine and hopefully live a normal life. You rest. Rest is the best thing for you right now."

I'll live a normal life. Tell me what happened, Brenda. Darby screamed but no one heard him.

"I'll check on you in the morning before I go home."

Darby felt her warm lips touch his. He so badly wanted to hold her and tell her everything would be just fine. The darkness enveloped him. He remained silent and motionless, listening to her fading foot steps. What was happening?

45

Dale miraculously experienced a wonderful night at his house and had actually slept. He and his new found companions had chatted for much of the night before giving into slumber. He had never stayed up and chatted with anyone before. This move had been filled with firsts. Feelings bloomed, ones he had never experienced before. Debra and Ted were his friends.   He had never had real friends.

Only briefly had he thought about Dark Thirty and the darkness that engulfed his world. He felt safe, protected in their presence. In the wee hours around three or so, Ted had given in to the tugs of sleep first. He and Debra had lasted another hour before each crashed, she on the sofa and he in a chair. Debra did not take her medicine, saying she didn't need it and hadn't taken it since meeting him.

Daylight had been lurking outside for a couple of hours before the first of them stirred. Dale woke last to the smell of breakfast. After a quick bathroom break, he located Debra in the kitchen. Ted sat at the bar drinking orange juice. The three of them made the perfect dysfunctional family. It hit him like a runaway eighteen-wheeler that his parents were still in the hospital. He must check on them.

Locating the phone number that Carl O'Conner had given him, he quickly keyed in the digits. The phone rang four times before the answering machine greeted him. Dale experienced another first. He actually left Carl a voice message asking him to please come by and pick him up and drive him to the hospital.

Hearing his voice, Debra entered the den with a glass of juice in her hand. She smiled, offering it to him. He took a deep breath and took it from her hand. Their fingers touched. He swore he saw sparks and felt heat, almost making him woozy. He chuckled. It had been static electricity from her shoes on the carpet.

Elsewhere, Mack Stevenson lay in bed pretending to be asleep until his mother closed the door. She seldom came into his room anymore except when she had been drinking. When she did, she craved companionship and incest resulted. Mack knew better than to refuse her advances. She could become violent if he resisted. Playing possum was his best defense. She was coming in from another late night. Soon she would be asleep then he would get up and out.

He wasn't exactly sure what his mother did for a living. She never said. He never asked. He had his suspicions. She always had ample cash on hand. She dressed like a slut when she went out, day or night. She smelled loud of perfume. He suspected she was either a prostitute or drug dealer. She didn't keep normal working hours so it had to be something illegal.

Mack's life had been anything but normal. The only stability he had experienced came from his grandfather, just a stint of a couple of years when he was much younger. He had been dead now for too many years to count and had been replaced by an endless string of his mother's men. Some were nice to him. Others had abused him even worse than his mother. As he had grown older and wiser, he realized his mother had been selling him like meat on a platter to the worst of them.

He no longer allowed them to take liberties with his body. He had stood his ground with her and she had at least ceased that practice, except when drunk out of her mind. He had the Colt now and would use it if she or any of them ever tried again. A part of him hoped they would try. Blowing them away would feel good.

Fondling the loaded pistol, he contemplated using it on his mother. He could feel the power it gave him. He envisioned placing the Colt to her head and pulling the trigger. A much more evil and darker Mack began to emerge. He personally liked the transformation, fearless and defiant and oh so deadly.

46

Brenda Jackson had changed back into the only clothes she had. She opted to go without underwear rather than wash them in the basin. She almost felt liberated by doing this. She thought about those days when women burned their bras and couldn't help but smile. She still didn't understand why she hadn't heard from her folks or Dale.

She waved off the supposedly mandatory wheel chair ride and visited Darby a second time. He looked exactly the same as last night. His injuries were so severe. She spoke to him, touched the one cheek that wasn't bandaged. "I love you. I'm going home now to check on our son. I'll return tonight." She kissed him on his cracked lips.

Wait, Darby screamed. Don't leave me yet! Don't leave me here in the dark alone! Please Brenda, stay with me. I need you. Please explain what's happening. How did I get here?

Brenda Jackson could not hear her husband's pleas. No one could. If she had, she would have stayed by his side. She still couldn't believe this had happened to him and to her. She promised God again that she would make it right.

I love you, Brenda. Tell our son I love him too. Darby willed his eyes to open, a finger to move, something to make her understand he could hear her but nothing responded to his commands. Darkness held him captive. He heard those strange beeping noises as her footsteps faded.

Brenda had plenty of time to reflect driving home. She was excited about restoring her life and becoming the perfect mom and a role model wife. She hummed a little tune, maneuvering through the morning traffic. Things will be just fine.

Debra Floyd had not lost her gift. She talked none stop to either one of them that would listen. She talked even if neither acknowledged it or answered her. While Dale loved the soothing tone of her voice, he grew tired of her constant jabbering. He learned to tune her out and resorted to nodding and shrugging.

Why hadn't Carl O'Conner called or come by he wondered. While he enjoyed this new freedom, he missed both of his parents. He began to slowly withdraw into his world before the girl had come into his life. He didn't wish to purposely return there but it tugged at him, almost as powerful as Dark Thirty.

All three heard the jiggling of keys and the door creaking open. Debra was taken by the beautiful woman entering the den. Even without makeup she looked like a cover model. She smiled and the lady returned a perplexed smile.

"Mom," yelled Dale.

Brenda ran to her son and held him tightly to her bosom. She rubbed her fingers through his hair and kissed him on the forehead. "Are you all right?"

He nodded yes.

"Where are my parents?"

"Florida," answered Dale, "Unless they've moved."

"I thought they were here with you. The nurse said you had left with your grandfather."

"Sort of," snorted Debra.

"That was Carl O'Conner," explained Dale. "I met him at the hospital."

"You left with a stranger," she gasped.

"He's a nice man. His wife just died."

"I hope he didn't kill her!"

"Mom, I wouldn't leave with a murderer."

"Who are these kids? I'm sorry, that didn't sound very nice."

"My friends, Debra Floyd and Ted Parker and they stayed here with me last night. Debra cooked us breakfast."

"You have a hard floor," commented Ted. "Even with a sleeping bag. My back hurts like a..."

"Nice to meet you Mrs. Jackson," Debra butted in.

Brenda nodded and smiled back at her and Ted. She should be thankful that Dale had made friends. He usually stayed to himself. This was different. She liked the change.

"Yep, you're his mom all right. He's got your nod," snorted Debra.

"Young man, after I shower and change, you have some serious explaining to do." She then whispered, "By the way, I like your new friends, especially the young lady."

"Did you see Dad?"

"I did and the doctor says it will take him a while to completely recover. We can go visit him tonight if you'd like?"

Dale nodded then said, "Sure. That would be great."

After she went upstairs Debra told Dale, "She's so pretty. She could be a movie star. I like her."

Dale shrugged, never having given it much thought. He was just glad to have her back home. He wondered why he had not heard from Carl O'Conner. He then responded, "She likes you too."

"What are we going to do now?" asked Ted, rubbing his back.

Dale shrugged. He was fading fast and didn't know why. He almost felt like he did when Dark Thirty approached but it was daylight.

"We should give Dale and his mother some alone time," suggested Debra.

"We'll meet you in the park when you've finished your alone time," added Ted, rolling up his sleeping bag.

Dale nodded, returning to his speechless ways, almost as if induced by his mom's return.

Debra came over and kissed him on the cheek. Dale couldn't believe she had just done that in front of Ted. What was she thinking?

"Yep, you're lucky I was here last night," snickered Ted.

Debra shot him the look, that look only a female can express. "See you later."

47

Jake, Stoner and Rich had just finished inhaling Hardee's ham biscuits and slurping the bottom of their cokes when Mack and David arrived. Ray and Buddy were the only two missing or all the merry gang would have been present and accounted for.

"Guess you heard they found Cassie dead in the cemetery," said Jake.

"Yeah, do they know what happened?" asked Mack, playing dumb.

"Nah, they're not saying. I guess they have to do that CSI stuff and an autopsy first."

"They're so damn good now at this DNA stuff," added Stoner. "All they need is a hair or a piece of skin or threads or something and they can name the killer."

Mack had not thought about that. Those investigators were sharp for sure. He subconsciously placed his hand on his head wondering if any of his was missing. It wasn't possible to leave any finger prints on flesh was it? At least he hadn't screwed the retard. Those other two had so it would be their sperm the police would find, not his. They'd take the fall. He would be free and clear. Nothing linked him to her murder. He had the Colt to ensure that neither of them ratted him out.

"Has anybody seen Ray or Buddy?" asked Jake.

"Not since the pawn shop," answered David.

"Weird, those two love ham and biscuits," replied Jake.

"They've been acting a little strange," Mack attempted to paint the picture and set them up just in case. "I think they're up to their asses in something."

Jake shrugged. "Let's head over to the park."

"I've got a couple of joints we can fire up," added Stoner.

Five desperados trekked toward the park destined for a head-on collision. Mack brought up the rear. He didn't like the fact that the other two were missing in action. What could they be up to he wondered. They better keep their mouths shut.

A much calmer scene played out at the Jackson home but the day was early yet; much too early.

"So tell me more about this Mister O'Conner," encouraged Brenda Jackson.

"Like I said, I met him in the hospital waiting room. He took me to his place. I spent one night there and two here while you were sick."

"I'm sorry to have left you alone. I was so upset about your father's condition…"

"You flipped out, didn't you? Are you going to end up in one of those asylums for crazy people?"

"No, and they don't have a monogrammed straight jacket for me either. Do you have Mister O'Conner's phone number? I would like to invite him over for dinner and thank him."

Dale handed her the crumpled piece of paper. "I tried to call him but got his answering machine. I did leave him a message."

Brenda was impressed. "I'll give him another try." She did and she also got the answering machine. She left a message too. "Where did you meet Debra and Ted?"

"In the neighborhood…they live here."

"They both seem nice enough. It pleases me for you to make and have friends." A girlfriend at that she thought.

"How old are they?"

"My age, sixteen…"

"So you'll all be attending the same school then?"

"I'm supposed to join them in the park if it's all right with you."

"Certainly, go ahead but remember we'll go to the hospital around five so please be back then."

He nodded okay. "I hope dad gets better."

"Me too," she replied, taken by Dale's new found persona.

Walking to the park helped clear his head. The glorious sunshine warmed his back and recharged his batteries. He wished it would remain daylight forever. He smiled, thinking how he resembled a mutated Vampire, fearing the night and thriving during the day.

He could see the park's vast lawn but did not see his friends. He did spot a group of strangers congregated near the bathroom, young men about his age. Puffs of smoke indicated they must be passing a cigarette between them. One looked his way. He dropped his head and kept walking. The wooded oasis lay ahead. He decided to check out the secret place where Ted had taken him.

He relived the horror of waking up there in the almost dark. He wasn't convinced Ted was the dependable type. He had sure failed royally in waking him.

Picking up his pace he cut the distance in half. One of the boys yelled something. He turned and they were pointing towards him. He couldn't hear exactly what they were saying but they were now heading his way. A second one yelled. It sounded like he had asked him to stop. Instinct told him to ignore them and to speed up instead. He was quite accomplished at outrunning tormentors.

They moved like one and were on course to overtake and cut him off before he could reach the wood line. He walked as fast as he could without breaking into a terrified run. Running always made things worse, especially if they caught you. Thirty yards from him reaching the woods they had all but cut him off. A human wall lay in his path. He veered to go around them but they blocked his maneuver.

"Where did you come from, narrow ass?" one shouted.

Dale sighed. Now it begins. His suspicions were confirmed. It was them. He was about to have his first encounter with their kind, the Charlotte version of bullies. He had hoped this wouldn't happen until school started, if it happened at all but it looked like he would face it sooner than later. It always happened eventually. He might as well get it over with now. At least he could gauge what he would be up against when school started and strategize a contingency plan.

"I asked you a question, dipwad! Where did you come from?" the same voice remarked.

Without thinking he said, "Second house." He smiled, surprised by his bold reply.

"Second house?"

"Second house, repeated pattern," he replied, almost proud of smarting off to them.

"Are you another one of those retards, four eyes?" asked a second voice.

Dale just took a deep breath and braced for the worse. He almost removed his glasses and stuck them in his pocket. The five encircled and closed in on him. He found himself in an all too familiar spot. Their tactics don't really vary that much. Names and places do but not the usual abuse tactics.

"What's your name?" asked another one, holding a funny smelling cigarette. He recognized it as a joint. The kid was on drugs. This spelled bad news.

"Dale Thomas Jackson…"

"Well Jackson-hole, are you carrying any cash?" asked another one.

He shook his head no.

The leader motioned to the others and two grabbed him, one by each arm while a third checked all his pant's pockets, leaving them turned inside out.

"Nothing but lint," announced the searcher.

"Not good," said the apparent leader. "It cost good money to be here in our park."

"Your park?" questioned Dale before thinking, knowing it is an unwritten law, never question one of them.

"We have ourselves a little smartass here and you know how I hate smartasses," snapped the leader again, motioning to the others.

The boys holding his arms twisted them painfully behind his back. He thought they would snap any minute. The searcher planted a fist to his stomach, knocking the wind out of him and making him retch. The leader grabbed him by the chin and held his head up spouting, "This is how we treat trespassers." He removed Dale's glasses and tossed them aside.

"I…" Dale started to say something but thought better of it. Another rule of engagement, don't engage.

Too late, the leader kicked him square in the nuts. He would have easily collapsed or doubled over if the two others hadn't held him firmly in place.

"Strip him," ordered the leader. "Let's give him the royal welcome."

The one holding what he had recognized as a marijuana joint jerked his shirt up over his head, assisted by the two holding him. Just like that he stood shirtless. His pants were yanked to his ankles leaving him standing their in his white jockey Fruit of the Looms.

"You're all skin and bones, aren't you," said the leader, eyeing him head to foot.

"Hey, what the hell are you doing Jake?" yelled Debra, stepping from the brush near the wood line. "Stoner, leave him be."

Startled, Jake didn't immediately respond. Mack did. "Out of here bitch…this is none of your business." Mack then moved to cut off her approach.

"Leave him alone," Debra demanded, Ted standing behind her, hands by his side and saying nothing.

"Get the hell out of here, both of you," shouted Mack.

"I'm just trying to save your worthless butts," she exclaimed.

So embarrassed, Dale really wanted to pull up his pants but they held him like a vise. He wondered just exactly what the girl was up to. Surely she didn't think they would abide by her wishes and she certainly couldn't take them on, clearly out numbered and over matched. He hoped they didn't do the same to her and Ted.

"Save us from what…you two," laughed Mack.

"His father is a police detective, one of those special bad ass units," she lied, hoping it would work. "I don't think he would take kindly to you doing this to his son."

This definitely got Mack's attention and he fell silent. Jake held eye contact, trying to detect a bluff. She didn't flinch. He turned and nodded for them to set him free. Stoner crushed the smoldering joint between his fingers and stuffed it his pocket.

"We don't want any trouble with the cops, kid. Let's just forget about this…all right," encouraged Jake, pissed about having to admit defeat.

Dale nodded and gathered up his clothes. The girl had saved his butt from their kind. She was quite remarkable, a good talker and bluffer.

Mack clutched the Colt in his pocket. He didn't like this but had no desire to tangle with the police right now. Things were much too hot for that; with them still looking for Cassie's killers and after the pawn shop break in.

"We were just initiating the new kid," explained Jake, trying to laugh it off.

What a worthless little twat thought Mack. She would one day get hers and he was just the one to deliver that promise. He had done it once. There was nothing to it. Now just was not that time.

Dale pulled up his pants and slipped his shirt back on as he eyed the five attackers. Jake, Mack and Stoner stuck in his brain. He didn't know the names of the other two but he wouldn't forget those three.

"Are we square on things now?" asked Debra.

"Just keep your mouth shut and we're square," answered Jake then he whispered, "Let's get out of here. This isn't over by a long shot." Mack couldn't agree more.

Debra walked over and tried to assist Dale in righting his attire. "I thought I was going to get a second peek," she snorted.

"Second, did I miss something last night?" Ted handed him his glasses.

It was Debra's turn to shrug, and then both she and Dale burst out laughing.

48

Brenda Jackson attempted to phone Carl O'Conner a third time. She didn't leave a message this time. She had already left two. Flipping through the phonebook she located a Carl and Mattie O'Conner and wrote down the address, opposite side of town it appeared. She still wanted to meet this man.

She had been home just over an hour and her world felt as if it was collapsing around her. There was nothing particular that should make her feel like this but being alone in the house with Darby in the hospital nibbled away at her. She craved the drug induced state from the hospital and the calm it had brought. How dare the doctor insinuate that she might be depressed and abusing alcohol or prescription drugs? Stressed, yes, but she wasn't depressed. There was a distinctive difference.

Brenda eyed the decanters on the bar. Surely one drink couldn't possibly hurt. It would help calm her nerves. She absolutely wasn't an alcoholic, regardless of what that doctor had tried to imply. One drink and she would settle back for a little rest before returning to check on Darby. One drink did not make her an alcoholic.

A half bottle and two prescription pills later she had regained control of her life. She glanced at the wall clock. It glared 3:39 in the afternoon. She and Dale would head to the hospital at 5. She poured another drink, waiting for him to return from the park. She really liked that girl, Debra. It was good to see him with a girl. She curled up on the love seat with her bottle, downed the shot and poured another. It wasn't happy hour yet but she felt quite happy. This family will pull together and we will overcome this diversity. We are Jackson's and that is what we do.

Dale had allowed time to slip up on him. Actually he had forgotten about it all together. Debra and Ted posed too much of a distraction. After the park ordeal, they had gone over to her house for lunch. He had now met her mother, a very nice lady and just like Debra, she talked a lot too. She looked just like an older version of her. Where had he heard it? You should always look at a girl's mother so you would know what she would look like grown? What did he even know about these sorts of things?

Ted had headed home about an hour ago. Dale and Debra had watched a remake of The War of the Worlds. He had liked the original version better. It had scared him badly the first time he had watched it. He enjoyed most of the older versions better because they had less blood and gore. Today's movies were so predictable with a deranged maniac running around killing stupid high school kids. It was the same old boring plot.

Content, he had reared back with his hands folded behind his head. He had taken in every single minute with the girl by his side. He suddenly noticed twilight through the den window. He sprang from the sofa, announcing to her he had to go and out the door he ran. She sat speechless for the first time, watching him disappear. That dark thing again she thought. She would have to get to the bottom of that mystery.

Dale had almost waited too late but he did manage to barely make it home before dark. He checked the time. It was after 8. He noticed his mother curled up on the couch and saw the glass and empty bottle on the table. She didn't hear him enter the house and he was anything but quiet. There would be no hospital visit tonight.

He clicked on all the lights except those near her and then covered her with a throw. He retired to his room, drawing comfort that she was here with him. Dark Thirty would be no threat tonight.

Brenda awoke from her stupor around 2 AM and stumbled up the stairs. She looked in on Dale and found him sleeping soundly. She regretted botching up the hospital visit and took full blame for it. She would never know that Dale had gotten home too late anyway. Tomorrow they would visit Darby.

Darby Jackson's day or night held no discernable difference. He remained in his pitch black suspended animation. This was the best description he could come up with to describe his world. He now heard every sound clearly. He recognized voices and what they were saying. He didn't know the names of the various visitors but he recognized each of them and basically knew what to expect when they arrived.

He could feel. He knew when he was being touched, turned, poked and prodded. He could not respond and that drove him crazy. He was aware that Brenda had not returned even though he had no real sense of time. He wondered when she would be back. He needed her more than ever.

For now he…he just what? He didn't know what he was or wasn't doing. Was he awake or asleep? He believed he was still alive or somewhere in-between alive and dead. Could death be worse than this?

He heard footsteps and voices. He didn't recognize either of the voices as being Brenda's. This one was a new one. Someone shoved a pencil sized object in his mouth and felt his wrist. A thermometer, someone was checking his temperature and pulse. I'm okay. Can't you tell? Please help me. I need to open my eyes. Please…open them for me. A beep, then the person removed the thermometer. Footsteps faded. He was alone again. He didn't like being alone.

Over the next week Dale watched his mother ride her wild roller coaster. She had so many ups and downs he lost track of her many mood swings. She drank a lot and took pills even more. She never justified their use or apologized for the abuse. She reminded him she was the adult and he was not. Twice they had visited the hospital, only twice. There had been no major changes in his father's condition. His mom seemed indifferent about it. This was beginning to scare him.

He spent more time with Debra and Ted than with his mother. She didn't seem to notice. The three of them had quickly become almost inseparable. His mother didn't seem to care if he was there or not except when it was time to go to the hospital and that was almost never.

Debra had made no more asserted efforts to seduce him but he figured Ted being around all the time had cramped her style. He wasn't sure how he felt about it. He just liked spending time with her without any sex involved. Sex scared him worse than his mom's moodiness.

There had been no more run-ins with Jake and his gang. They had given them wide berth fearing his make-believe cop dad would haul them to jail. He wasn't sure how long that would last but he basked in the glory for now. Debra had given him the low down on all of them. They were the worst of the worst. This school year wasn't going to be easy. His new tormentors were professionals. He was not nearly on their level. This was going to be a problem.

Dale was still puzzled what had become of Carl O'Conner, his *sort of* grandfather. He had just as quickly exited his life as he had entered it. He had no idea if he was dead and buried or had just moved on after losing his wife. He wished he could have met her. They had stopped trying to call him. His mother had said maybe he had gone to visit relatives while grieving for his dead wife. Maybe she was right but he didn't exactly trust her instinct right now either.

Dale had not had a serious encounter with Dark Thirty since his mother had returned home and the talkative girl had re-entered his world. He had it back under control...for now. School would begin Monday. Only the weekend separated the inevitable. It was so ironic. He had overcome one phobia just to have to face another.

He had informed his mother that he would like to try for his driver's license. She had gotten him a copy of the driver's manual and seemed thrilled about his decision but then just as quickly her excitement and coaching had faded. Yes, he was now making decisions. The butterfly had emerged from its cocoon but could he spread his wings and actually fly?

Debra was still on probation and not allowed to drive. She still hadn't divulged what she had done to warrant this punishment. He figured it must have been something awful because she was not the type to do anything halfway. He decided he really didn't want to know.

Investigators had not found the perpetrator of Cassie Richards' murder. Authorities had confirmed she had been raped before being brutally killed. Police were looking for matches to at least two DNA samples. More than one had raped her and they had not used a condom. The police apparently had no suspects yet. Maybe the killer had moved on to a new hunting ground thought Dale.

The new house was slowly emerging as a home. Debra and Ted had sped up this process by helping him unpack and arrange things. His mother, with her deteriorating new life style, had participated very little in making this a happy home He really needed his father back. In some ways his life was screwed up worse than ever but in other ways was better than it had ever been.

Three more days…school…hell on earth had not yet begun.

49

Darby Jackson had been removed from intensive care and placed in a private room. He was no longer on life support, breathing on his own. He had not regained consciousness. Cat scans and an MRI indicated he was not brain dead. His broken and battered body was on the mend. His physical wounds were definitely healing.

The physicians had no concrete diagnosis for his mental state. It was a crap shoot if he would regain motor skills or speech or even wake up. He might come out of it any minute or never. If and when he did, what would he be? What would he be able to do? It was anyone's guess. These types of cases often defied medicine.

So far Darby's insurance had taken care of his needs and those of his family. It was early yet. The financial strain could easily gain ground if this stretched out over months.

Darby still had no concept of time in his dark world. He never slept or he didn't think he did. He heard and experienced everything. He still could not speak except in his mind. The bullies no longer tormented him. He had ceased dreaming. He missed being able to see and talk to his family but anxiously awaited their visits. He still didn't understand how he lived in this nothingness place.

Determined to return to a world of daylight he spent his time willing movement. He attempted to make his lips form words. He strained to open the lids of his eyes. All had failed so far but it just made him try harder. He wondered if all people in his situation experienced what he did. He should write a book about it some day.

50

Saturday, the three amigos decided to take in a movie matinee. Dale had talked them into going to see the new John Carpenter movie. He had actually talked them into it, who would have thought…him talking someone into doing anything…him talking period.

Mack had seen them enter the theater. He had clinched his fist and gritted his teeth at the mere sight of them buying their tickets. He hated the freaky girl the worst. Still, he had no use for that Parker mutant or the skinny anemic looking cop's son. He caressed the Colt. He seldom went anywhere without it now. Some day he thought.

He eyed her bike chained out front. It wouldn't be much but it would quench his need to do something destructive. Those three tested his frustration level. He figured it time to do something about it. His buck knife would do the trick. He nonchalantly slashed both bike tires. He then snapped a link in the chain and loosened the seat and handlebars. Proud of his handiwork, he headed home satisfied that he had demolished her ride for good.

Earlier he had rendezvoused with Buddy and Ray. He had brandished the Colt just to ensure they both understood to keep their mouths shut about that Cassie retard. Ray had the balls to ask him if he had been the one to go back there and kill her. He smiled then winked. He confessed nothing. He did mention to them that the funny thing about killers, once they had killed, they wouldn't hesitate to do it again. That certainly grabbed their attention. He saw the fear in their eyes. He loved it.

So far the investigators had not come knocking at their doors but he had seen an influx of policeman in and around the cemetery. They had uncovered no witnesses, no motives and no suspects. No one suspected such a grisly crime would be one that teenagers would commit. There was no history of such heinous behavior. That's where Mack was sadly wrong. The sperm had been associated with that of youths. Mack's sperm could not be connected to the crime because he had not participated in the rape.

He arrived home just in time to see the new man leaving his house. His mom half dressed stood in the doorway. Neither saw him. He triggered the Colt and thought how easily he could waste both of them. Now was not the time for that either. He opted to go elsewhere. He didn't want to go home right now while his mom smelled too fresh of sex and whisky. At least she wouldn't be slinking into his room tonight. She would live another day.

51

The remaining couple of days dropped from the calendar with a thud. School started tomorrow. While comfortable with his two new friends, Dale dreaded entering the lion's den. They would be there. Their kind was always lurking, blood thirsty and had the last laugh at his expense. He expected they would have at it once they figured out his father was not a hot shot policeman. Instead he was more like a vegetable on their dinner plate. A Brussels sprout wouldn't intimidate them.

Dale had received terrible news this morning, His mother had found out that Carl O'Conner had been killed in an automobile accident over a week ago. Now he knew why he had not returned any of their calls. His *sort of* grandfather had joined his wife, the sort of grandmother he never knew. He was probably in a happy place now.

He heard the chattering in the background and turned his attention to the girl. Debra asked, "What you say we meet at the park in the morning? We can walk to school together."

"Yeah, I'm not riding the bus no matter how bad the weather is," added Ted. "Bad things happen on the bus. It's a death trap."

"You don't have permission to drive yet?" asked Dale.

"Nah, but I'm wearing them down. Besides, they wouldn't let me take the car to school anyway. Bike's still busted so walking it is."

"You still don't want to tell us why they won't let you drive."

"You ask too many questions, Dale Thomas Jackson. I liked you better when you just nodded and shook your head," she snorted.

"You must have really pulled something bone headed," commented Ted.

"You are going to walk with us aren't you, Dale?" She asked, quickly changing the subject.

"You'd be one stooge short if I didn't."

"Sarcasm, we've created a monster," she snorted loudly.

"Never open Pandora's Box if you're not ready for what lurks inside," he warned her. She mocked him with a shrug.

"It's safer if we stick together as much as possible," advised Ted. "Safety in numbers and remember, your dad is a badass cop if anyone asks."

"Have they caught that Cassie girl's killer yet?"

"No and thank goodness we don't have to walk by that cemetery."

"What makes you think the killer only stalks the cemetery? The killer could be anywhere or anybody."

"Yeah, but I like our chances better by staying away from there."

"If the murderer had returned to the scene of the crime, the police would have probably already caught him."

"So what do you guys want to do with what we have left of Sunday?" asked Ted.

"Something real good since this is our last day of freedom," answered Debra.

"Let's go to the cemetery," said Dale.

"Are you crazy or do you just have a death wish?" asked Debra.

"Going there so ain't right," added Ted.

"I'm serious. It would be cool to visit the scene of the crime don't you think?"

"And this coming from someone who is afraid of the dark," Debra reminded him.

"I didn't say I would go there in the dark."

"Why go there at all?" asked Ted.

"Think of the rush. We'd be tempting fate, defying the evil doers and we might just solve the crime."

"Where was all this bravado the other night?"

"That's different so please just drop it."

"So what if we agree to do this, what then?" asked Ted.

"Like I said, maybe we can figure out who did it."

Debra reminded him, "We're not crime scene investigators and your dad really isn't a cop."

"Sometimes things like this just need a fresh pair of eyes."

"I'm no hero," added Ted.

"So are you in or out?" asked Dale.

"You've got your mind made up, haven't you," said Debra.

He nodded.

"All right I'll humor you. I'll go."

"Well, it's my job, Dale. I've still got to protect you from Debra so I can't leave her alone with you, but I'm not going there without weapons."

"So choose your weapons," advised Dale.

"I have pointy shoes and one hell of a kick. That's all I need," boasted Debra.

"I'll go home and get my aluminum baseball bat. I flunked at baseball but I bet I could hit a murderer."

"What about you, Rambo?" asked Debra looking at Dale.

"Wits," he smiled. "I'll out think them if we encounter anyone."

"That worked so well with Jake and his thugs, didn't it?" Debra reminded him.

"It would have if you wouldn't have interfered. Stripped down, I would have been much faster than them," he smiled while tapping the side of his head, indicating wit.

"Right!" she said, arms crossed over her breast and shaking her head in disbelief.

"Okay then, I'll go home and retrieve the fire poker. I can hit or impale them with it."

"Or throw it and haul ass with us," snickered Ted. "But knowing you, you would freeze up and let them get you."

"Nope, I would just have to outrun one of you."

"Yep, we were much better off when you were the silent type," snorted Debra.

"Let's meet at the cemetery in thirty minutes," stated Dale.

"You're bluffing…in front of the cemetery," exclaimed Ted.

"All right, inside the cemetery," Dale challenged them feeling just a tad too Froggy. "That is if you have the balls."

"No fair,' spoke up Debra. "I don't have any balls.'

"Don't shortchange yourself," snickered Dale. "You have more balls than any girl I've ever met."

"In the cemetery it is then," she confirmed. "I'll go get my hockey stick."

"Thirty minutes," Dale reminded them. "You play hockey?"

She smiled. "There's a lot you don't know about me yet."

"Yeah, like why you got banished from driving," he countered.

52

Jake and his boys gathered outside the Kangaroo quick stop. They mulled over their last conquest, the pawn shop. All were accounted for except for Buddy, whereabouts unknown. Buddy had been missing in action lately for some reason. Ray confirmed he had not talked with him. Ray acted a little strangely too, thought Jake.

Mack noticed Ray's nervousness and shot him a warning look. Ray received the message loud and clear. Buddy had been the smart one, surmised Ray. Cutting ties with Mack and the others could be a life saver.

"Last day," announced Jake. "Our prison term starts tomorrow."

That comment definitely rattled Ray's cage. Mack positioned himself next to him and poked the Colt into his ribs and winked. "Yep, nothing like school to get the old adrenalin flowing."

"I hope we're not going to rob anymore stores for awhile," added Rich.

"Nah, I think the redneck learned his lesson," bragged Jake.

"Why don't we just find someone's butt to kick?" asked Mack. "That always makes us feel better."

"Yeah, we haven't done enough of that lately," chimed in Stoner.

Ray started to say something but Mack nudged him with the concealed Colt. He fell silent. He hated Mack's guts and didn't trust him at all since he had acquired the gun.

"How about that skinny ass kid," asked Jake, "Has anyone seen him since the park?"

"He's still hanging out with that little prick, Parker," stated David.

"And that motor mouth, Debra," added Stoner.

"Too bad his old man's a cop," sighed Jake. "We don't need that heat right now."

Ray blurted out, "You got that right." Mack couldn't believe he had said that.

"Stifle it, Ray," Mack warned.

"Who put a bug up your ass?" asked Stoner, looking over at Mack.

"What I mean is we can't have those three grunts ruining our reputation. Word gets out that we backed down and before you know it, they will all get these bravery streaks and try to rebel or something, just like in one of those Nerd movies."

"We do have a reputation," agreed Jake. "Let him go until the time is right but the other two are fair game."

"Yeah, we'll nail him soon enough," grunted Stoner.

"Let's fan out and see if we can find Parker or Floyd and have a little pre-school fun."

"I forgot to tell you. I've got my brother's car next week while he's out of town," spoke up Rich.

"Perfect," smiled Jake. "We'll ride to school in style."

Fear no evil, especially when evil is nowhere to be seen. Dale arrived at the cemetery first. He had faked them off with talk about retrieving the poker and came straight to the graveyard. He didn't want to chance an encounter with his mother. She continued to weird him out with the drinking and pills and it would only lead to a confrontation if she was awake.

Entering the graveyard, he ran his hand along the top of one of the older tomb stones. The dates were from the early 1800's; Franklin T. Woods born 1829, died 1875. He walked deeper into the hallowed ground examining the various stones as he strolled along. He visualized ghouls exploding from the gravesites. He spotted a mausoleum ahead and thought about vampires. This was the perfect home for flesh eating zombies and floating ghosts. This was his type of place...in the daytime.

He saw yellow streamers blowing in the wind near the mausoleum entrance. Upon closer observation, the tape revealed it was crime scene tape. It marked the area where

Cassie Richards had been found. Curiosity drove him to investigate. He could hardly contain himself. This was like a movie set and he was the super sleuth.

Stepping over the yellow tape, he stood at the entrance. Good stuff, he thought, as he touched the doorway. He had never been close to a murder scene before and it intrigued him. He pushed on the old wooden door. It creaked loudly but moved. The metal latch was set to open. This was simply fantastic, exceeding his wildest dreams.

Light filtered inside. He pushed it again and it noisily moved until he had it standing wide open. He stepped inside and paused until his eyes adjusted to the change. Once it had, he could see the inside pretty well. It wasn't really dark with the door wide open. Another step and he got a whiff of the musty, moldy dampness just like he would expect it to smell. Vampires would just thrive here.

Just inside and to the left he saw it, a chalked outline of Cassie Richards. How cool was this. On the floor he could make out dark stains. It had to be her blood. He should feel some remorse but he had never met the deceased. Squatting, he rubbed his fingers over the chalk and even touched one of the dark spots. He tingled all over from the excitement of being there.

He stood up and eyed the entire crime scene, pretending to be looking for clues. He really wasn't sure what he expected to see. The CSI team would have already removed any evidence. Maybe they had missed something and he would find it and break the case wide open. A hero, no one would dare mess with him then.

He tried to visualize the attack. Had it happened here or somewhere else and then they had dumped her body in here. Had there been any witnesses or had they killed them to tidy up loose ends? Engrossed in the experience he failed to hear the footsteps outside.

The door creaked loudly as it closed. Some one had slipped up on him and had pulled it shut. He heard the latch as someone engaged it, sliding the bolt into place. The thought entered his head. They always return to the scene of the crime. Worse still, he now stood in the pitch blackness. Dark Thirty had arrived well ahead of schedule and had enveloped him. He was trapped inside. His nemesis was present.

Dale called out, hoping it was just the caretaker or the police. The thought crossed his mind that it might be Debra and Ted. He screamed to whoever stood on the opposite side of the door to please let him out. This wasn't funny. No one answered. No one opened the door. Panic set in. He wished he had that fire poker now and his flash lights.

He began slamming his fists against the door as the darkness devoured him alive. Tears ran down his cheeks. He screamed again but no one came to his rescue. The darkness strangled him, sucked the life out of him, and crushed him like an insect. He could do nothing to defend himself. He finally cowered in a corner screaming at the top of his lungs and pounding his fists against the stone wall. All remained silent and too dark.

Debra Floyd and Ted Parker stood on the sidewalk at the entrance gate to the cemetery. They waited patiently for Dale Thomas Jackson to arrive. It had been forty minutes since they had left to retrieve their weapons and had met here.

"What do you think is taking him so long?" asked Ted.

"Who knows," she shrugged. "Could be that his mom needed something. She hasn't been feeling so good lately from what he's told me."

"Drinks like a fish, you mean," Ted filled in the blanks.

"It could just be her medication," Debra attempted to defend her. "Mine has a lot of side affects."

"Yeah, especially if you take them by the butt loads like she does. Everybody knows you're not supposed to mix drugs with booze."

"She's been under a lot of stress with her husband in that comatose state."

"She's a parent. She's supposed to set an example for us. Haven't you heard of role models?"

"I got it already," said Debra rolling her eyes.

"So how long are we supposed to wait here for him?"

"Let's give it a little while longer. He seemed so excited about coming."

"I hope he doesn't show. I really didn't want to go in there anyway. It creeps me out knowing they killed Cassie in there."

"Me either but he was so serious about it."

"Maybe he was just jerking our chain and never intended to come back. He's been acting like a smartass. I think you're a bad influence on him, Deb."

"I bring out the best in everybody. Look at you." she snorted. "Just a little longer, please."

"What if the police see us hanging out here? They might think we're the killers."

"Be honest, Ted. Do we really look like murderers?"

"You could pass for one, I suppose. Killers don't always look like killers. Besides we're standing here with a baseball bat and hockey stick. If I were a cop I would ask what kind of new sport were we playing?"

"Then it could be you. You could be deranged, a closet maniac with a bat."

"Cut the closet crap. I don't think he's coming. We should probably go to his house. I bet he's there."

"Just a few minutes longer, he'll show. I know he will."

"Have you and he done it?"

"That's none of your business, Ted Parker, and I can't believe you're even asking."

"You have, haven't you? I knew it."

"You don't know squat, Ted Parker."

"I know he's not going to show.

53

"Yep, that's where I saw them, Jake, standing in front of the graveyard," confirmed Stoner.

"That's where the police found the retard's body," said Jake. "Wonder what they're up to?"

"We better not mess with them there. Police might be watching," warned Ray.

"Good idea," replied Jake.

Mack joined them. He had heard most of the conversation. "He's got a point. That place is probably staked out. If we do something to them, they may think we're the ones that done Cassie."

"Okay, we go covert and wait for them to leave and then we'll nail their butts," stated Jake. "Did you see Jackson-hole?"

"No, just them two," replied Stoner.

"I just remembered," spoke up Mack. "I told the old lady that I would come home and run an errand for her."

"Run home to your mommy then, if you're too chicken to nail the little weasels," laughed Jake.

Mack fondled the Colt. He could blow Jake's brains out so easily. Instead he gave him the finger and cursed him under his breath. It was still too early to knock off old Jake. Besides, he wanted to return to the graveyard and check on things. He arrived fifteen minutes later. A couple of Mexicans were operating a weed eater and clearing brush with a bush ax near the mausoleum. The door remained closed and latched. He watched and waited.

Inside Dale could just vaguely hear the sounds outside. He had covered his ears, mumbled incoherently and rocked back and forth, oblivious to everything but the darkness. Every shadow tugged at him, wanted him, sucked life's essence from him. He remained between two large marble vaults, the markings indicating that those resting there had been there for over ninety years. The husband and wife apparently had died three days apart. Dead bodies didn't concern him right now. Dark Thirty did and it reeled him in. Soon he would belong to it forever.

"Okay, he's not coming," stated Ted.

"I concede," answered Debra.

Stoner, Jake, Rich, David and Ray watched and waited for the two to depart. Finally it appeared they were ready to leave. "Next block, we've got them," stated Jake.

"What you want to do to them?" asked Stoner.

"I say we see what she looks like naked," snickered Rich.

"And what about Parker?" asked David.

"Naked, I don't want to see him naked," stated Stoner.

"Let's make them swap underwear and run down the street," added Rich. "And video it and post it on You Tube."

Ray didn't mutter a word. This sort of thing just didn't appeal to him anymore. He should have stayed in hiding like Buddy. He now had no graceful way out. He had to think fast. "If we do that, the police may think we're the ones that did Cassie."

"We make them do that all the time," Stoner reminded him. "That's our signature move but I really don't want to see Parker naked. I mean it."

"We're not planning to rape them," stated Jake. "And I'm certainly not going to kill either one of them. You've really lost your mind, Ray?"

"I'm just saying we should do something different, something that doesn't resemble a sexual assault, that's all.'

"So what do you have in mind?" asked Stoner.

"I'm not sure but haven't you guys noticed that she has a hockey stick and he has a baseball bat. This might be some sort of set-up," warned Ray.

"I don't think either one of them excels in sports," spoke up Jake. "You've turned chicken on us too, haven't you, Ray?"

Ray said nothing else. They had their minds made up and he knew there was no stopping them. He wished he were home.

"Well, time to show them their place on the food chain," added David.

"Let's do it," grinned Stoner.

"I can't believe Mack is missing out on this," stated Jake. "He loves this sort of crap."

"Look, they're crossing the street," pointed Stoner. "We can snatch them at that vacant building."

The cruiser's light lit up the street and short bursts from the siren got everyone's attention. The police car pulled to a stop adjacent to Debra and Ted. Two officers stepped out. Jake and his horde blended into the background.

The older, heavier cop with a bushy grey mustache spoke first. "What you two kids up to?"

"Just heading home," answered Debra.

"What's with the hockey stick and the baseball bat?" asked the younger black cop. "Funny sport you're playing?"

Ted looked at Debra and mouthed, "I told you."

"Protection," replied Debra. "This is a bad neighborhood, especially since our friend was murdered back there."

"What's your name missy?" asked the older cop.

"Debra Floyd…"

"And you sonny?" asked the other cop.

Ted felt like his tongue was too large for his mouth and had a tough time forming the words. Eyes bugged he just became extremely fidgety.

"He's Ted Parker."

"So you say you knew the girl that was murdered?" asked the older cop.

"She had a name," replied Debra. "Cassie Richards…she was autistic."

"So why are you wandering around here if it's so dangerous?" asked the young cop.

"We were waiting on our friend Dale but he never showed up. He's usually quite punctual. We were supposed to meet him back there in front of the cemetery," Ted spilled his guts.

"Your friend's full name…" asked the older cop.

"Dale Thomas Jackson," answered Ted.

Stupid, stupid, stupid thought Debra then she asked, "Don't you have to read us our rights and let us phone our lawyer?"

"Cute," smiled the young cop. "You're not under arrest unless you know something we don't. Would you like to confess anything?"

"So why were you meeting the Jackson kid in front of the cemetery?" asked the older cop.

"We were just hanging out. It's our last day of freedom before school starts," answered Debra.

"So what do you think happened to your friend?" asked the young cop.

"Aren't you supposed to do the good cop-bad cop routine?" asked Debra.

"It's tough to fool anyone when we're both good cops," grinned the older cop.

"So you knew the victim?" asked the younger cop.

"What, you trying to pin this on us now?" asked Debra. "We know you're looking for two killers but check it out. I don't have a penis. I couldn't have raped her."

Ted looked at her funny then back at the two policemen. "I'm a guy and I wouldn't even know how to rape a girl with mine."

Both cops laughed. "Kids, get your butts on home and stay away from this area, you hear me?" said the older cop.

"Are you ever going to solve this crime or is it going cold case?" asked Debra.

"I assure you the detectives are following all leads," answered the young cop.

"So what are you two doing besides harassing innocent children?" asked Debra.

"Kids, go home, please. Here, take my card. Let me know if you hear anything," stated the older cop.

"I guess you boys sense the *hot light* is on don't you?" asked Debra.

"Donuts, I smell donuts," chuckled the younger cop as he got back in the car. "Please be careful kids."

"That went well, don't you think?" Debra asked Ted.

"Let's go find Dale."

"Yeah, I don't enjoy being a blue light special."

Jake and the gang watched them disappear around the corner. Today was not a good time to mess with them. "You were right, Ray," said Jake. "Police must be really watching this area. Let's go."

Dale had become wild eyed but in the pitch black darkness his frightful appearance really made no visual impact on his desperate situation. Rocking back and forth, arms wrapped around his knees, the dark world squeezed the life out of him like a gigantic vise. Dark Thirty had never been so terrifying and to think, he thought he had finally licked it.

Releasing his knees he began slamming his fists against one of the marble tombs as if trying to wake the corpse inside. A low guttural growl emitted from his throat. It would have sounded remarkably primal if anyone would have been there to hear it. He covered his ears with his bloody hands to block out new screams. The screams were coming from him. Dale pulled at his hair and cried. He was just an eyelash away from requiring a straight jacket. Dark Thirty was winning the game and the game clock wasn't ticking in his favor.

The scene combined with the sounds had the earmarks of a monster movie set. A poor soul trapped inside a mausoleum, buried alive and no one around to rescue him. Dale, taken by horror flicks, could have probably appreciated the setting if he wasn't the protagonist in the show. Dark Thirty, a worthy adversary, proved to be the antagonist from hell and had the hero down for the count.

This was by far his worse ever episode and his most terrifying encounter with Dark Thirty. In less than an hour, Dale had almost transformed into something inhuman. He clawed at the side of the crypt like a feral animal. He had bitten his tongue and lips more than once. Blood dripped down his chin. In the daylight he would have passed for the perfect graveyard ghoul. All he needed was a corpse to dine on and the scene would have been complete.

With each tick of the clock he drifted further away from reality. If the madhouse continued, chances were he'd never find his way back. What a fitting end to his family heritage;

father in a coma, mother in a drunken, narcotic induced abyss, and now him going completely Looney Tunes. They took dysfunctional to a new level, an all time low. Dale dug his fingernails into his hands as he clinched his fists closed. This had to be over and it had to be over soon. Dark Thirty tightened its grip around his throat. Suffocating now, Dale felt his life force slipping away. His will had been broken. He was on the brink of no return.

The latch bolt clicked. The door moved slightly and a ray of light, of hope, pierced the darkness zeroing in on Dale's right eye. He blinked, attempted to focus on the beam, a life preserver being tossed in his direction. The door creaked and opened wider. Sunlight exposed his face to the outside world.

Dale stood then bolted toward the doorway. His frail and skinny body shot through the slight opening as if he had been fired from a cannon. He tripped and fell face first into the dirt, mouth scooping up an acre of ground like a steam shovel.

The older officer, still standing, yelled, "Stay down, don't move!"

The younger policeman regained his footing after having been knocked backwards when Dale charged through the door. In one swift move he had Dale's arm pinned behind him and one cuff already on his wrist. He stopped when he saw the kid's bloody condition, realizing he was no threat and most likely the victim here.

"Are you Dale Jackson?" asked the older cop.

Dale didn't respond, not even a nod. He blinked wildly, almost spastically, taking in his surroundings. His breathing became less labored as the sunlight quenched his fears.

"Son, are you all right? What happened? Who locked you in there?" asked the older cop.

Dale tried to focus, looked the cop dead in the eyes. He managed a shrug then looked over at the younger policeman. He heard the click as the young cop removed the handcuff.

"Call an ambulance," requested the older cop.

"No," spoke up Dale. "I'm Dale Jackson and I'm okay."

"You don't look okay," commented the younger cop. "You require medical treatment."

"Make the call," ordered the older cop. "How did you get locked in there? You do realize this is a crime scene, don't you? Didn't you see the tape?"

Dale nodded he had. Questions, everyone here had nothing but tons of questions.

"Son, tell me what happened," asked the older cop.

"I was curious," he spoke softly. "I've never seen a crime scene before so I came inside. Somebody locked me in and wouldn't let me out."

"Did they attack you first?" asked the younger cop pointing to his bloody hands and lip.

"No," Dale answered. "I was scared and tried to get out."

"You really screwed yourself up doing that," commented the younger cop.

"Your friends, a Debra Floyd and Ted Parker, were looking for you earlier. You can thank them that we came in here to check things out," advised the older cop.

"Did you know the victim, Cassie Richards?" asked the young cop.

Dale shook his head no. "We just moved here."

"Where do you live?" asked the young cop.

"Second house..." then Dale told them his actual address.

"Are your parents at home?" asked the older cop.

"My mother is home. My father is in the hospital."

"All right, once the medics get here and fix you up, we'll take you home," advised the older cop. "Fredericks, comb the area and see if anyone else is here. Somebody bolted that latch. Maybe it's connected to the murder."

"You think the killers are that stupid," commented Fredericks.

"You've heard those dumb crook segments. There's one born every day."

Mack watched from behind another crypt. He had heard the entire interrogation. The kid's old man was not a cop after all and was in the hospital. Debra Floyd had snookered them. This changed everything. Better still; the skinny little new kid was scared of the dark. I hope he makes it to school tomorrow. "We'll have the welcome wagon waiting," he whispered.

He ducked as the young cop passed by his location. He held onto the Colt under his shirt thinking he would use it on a policeman if push came to shove. He wasn't sure but it felt good in his hand.

54

Debra and Ted were less than a block from Dale's house when the police cruiser passed them and parked out front. They ran full throttle and arrived as the officers retrieved Dale from the backseat. The fresh bandages on his hands and split lip indicated something wasn't right. He had apparently been in a fight and had been on the wrong end of it from the looks of his condition. Debra elbowed Ted as the officers escorted Dale to his front door. At least he wasn't hand cuffed thought Ted.

After what seemed like an eternity to Debra, the policemen exited the house and drove away. Debra motioned for Ted to follow and they stepped up to the door and rang the bell. The lovely Mrs. Jackson greeted them. Her demeanor tipped them off that she had most likely been throwing back a few. Debra wondered if the policeman had noticed the same thing. Apparently they hadn't because they had left Dale in her custody.

"Is everything all right?" Debra asked Mrs. Jackson.

"Yes dear. He's a little shaken up but has no serious injuries from his ordeal."

"Ordeal? Just what exactly happened to Dale?"

"Someone locked him inside a mausoleum in that dreadful cemetery," answered Brenda. "People can be so cruel."

"Did they beat him up?" asked Ted.

"No, he did that to himself trying to get free. He'll be just fine. He's in his room if you'd like to see him for a couple of minutes. It would probably do him good having his friends here."

"We would like that," replied Debra, "if it's really okay with him."

"I'm sure he wouldn't mind. Go on up, dear."

Debra glanced back as they reached the stairs. Mrs. Jackson was pouring a drink. Debra figured she was zoned out of her mind and figured she was better suited to tend to Dale Thomas's needs right now. She elbowed Ted and he nodded.

"Just like we thought," he whispered. "Boy did you smell her breath?"

She knocked on his door, saw Dale curled up on his bed, his back to them. He didn't move so she knocked a little louder. Still he lay motionless. She spoke up. "Dale Thomas, can we come in?"

He turned over recognizing her voice. "I thought you were my mother. I have enough to deal with right down. I don't need a drunk meddling in my business."

"She's worried about you."

"You look like crap," stated Ted.

"Thanks for noticing…"

"So spill it. What happened?" asked Debra.

"I saw the crime scene and decided to go inside that crypt where they found her and the door closed behind me."

"Maybe it was the wind?" suggested Debra.

"The wind doesn't lock doors."

"Maybe it was Cassie's ghost," said Ted.

"Ghosts don't have fingers and walk loudly."

"You don't think it was us, do you?" asked Ted.

"Was it?"

"Absolutely not," snapped Debra. "We wouldn't horse around with you like that. We know you don't like the dark."

"Maybe it was the killers," suggested Ted.

Or Dark Thirty, thought Dale.

"The police didn't find anyone when they searched."

"How did you get so messed up?" asked Ted.

"I panicked and tried to get out."

"That didn't work so well," commented Debra. "The dark got you, didn't it?"

Dale sheepishly shrugged. He wasn't quite ready to admit just how badly he feared Dark Thirty right now, not in front of Ted, even though he figured they knew. He actually didn't remember inflicting most of the damage to himself.

"What really happened in there?" asked Debra. "You can tell us."

"I honestly don't know. All is sort of blank after the door closed."

"Weird, don't you think?" asked Ted.

"The next thing I remember was being cuffed by the policeman."

"They handcuffed you?" asked Ted. "Cool!"

He nodded. "I saw her blood on the floor and the chalked outline of her body."

"You weren't afraid?"

"Not until that door closed…"

"Do they hurt?" asked Debra pointing to his hands.

"A little but I'll be all right," he smiled, sporting his bitten lip. "It was a bad idea, wasn't it?"

"We tried to tell you that," answered Ted. "Why didn't you use the fire poker to pry open the door?"

"I didn't have it with me. I didn't return home."

"See, I told you he needed protection."

"You said he needed it from me," she reminded Ted.

"And still does," winked Ted.

"Will you be able to go to school in the morning?" asked Debra.

"What waits for me there can't be any worse than staying here with my mother."

"Sorry your life is so miserable," said Debra, giving him a hug.

"I have friends now so it's not all bad."

"Group hug," shouted Ted, joining in.

School morning arrived early. Dale crawled like a snail from bed, one never to be very excited about attending, and so beaten and battered, it didn't really concern him. He never had high expectations and was never disappointed by the outcome. He was used to it happening at school though. The swelling had gone down in his hands and his wounds had scabbed over but his ego remained tarnished from the ordeal.

After relieving his aching bladder, he dressed and tiptoed down the hallway. He could hear his mother snoring soundly, still in her drunken stupor. Breakfast would be left up to him if he chose to fix it. He opted not to and peeped outside. The street lights were still on; darkness had not yet given way to the dawn. He waited patiently for the first signs of light. He didn't have to meet the others for at least another thirty minutes. It should be plenty light by then.

He dwelled on what had happened yesterday, at least what he could remember. "Why am I prisoner of the dark?" he asked out loud. "Debra's right. There has to be a reason, a trigger, something."

He questioned whether he should heed her advice and visit a shrink. Could one help him overcome his fears? He wondered why his parents had never suggested sending him to one. Did they think one couldn't help him, or did they not want to spend the money? Maybe they were just too embarrassed by his affliction.

He sorely needed his father. His dad would know the right thing to do. His world had turned upside down in his father's absence. His dad would have prepared breakfast for him and would have taken him to school. He wondered if his father would recover from his coma. How much more could he endure with his mother drinking like there was no tomorrow but then maybe there was no tomorrow.

She hadn't visited his father in the past three days. Had she given up on him and them? She stayed in her room most of the time or crashed on the sofa. In such a short time she was not as beautiful as he had remembered. Her looks had become haggard. She didn't seem to care if she wore make-up or even changed from her nightgown. He felt like little orphan Dale. He feared social services would put him in foster care, but at age sixteen didn't he have the right to refuse, go out on his own?

He peeped through the blinds and yelled out loud. His worse nightmare had finally come true. Another pair of eyes stared back at him. He risked a second peek. A hand raised and greeted him. He recognized her smile. Debra stood on the other side of the window mouthing something at him. She could even talk when he couldn't hear her. He motioned for her to go to the front door.

"I couldn't sleep and couldn't wait. I had to see you. How are you feeling?"

"I'm okay. Where's Ted?"

"He'll meet us at the park. You look better than you did last night."

"Warmed over crap…" he smiled.

"Have you had any breakfast?"

"No, but I'm good."

"I thought so," she said handing him a cinnamon roll. "Do you have the first day jitters?"

He shrugged. "I hate school, always have. First day or last day, feels the same to me."

"You have me and Ted this go round to help you."

"Who's going to help you two? You have targets on your backs just as big as mine."

"We'll be fine. We do this all the time. It will have its challenges I'm sure, but we're smarter and faster most of the time."

"Jake?"

"Oh yeah, we'll catch our share of hell from him and his crew but so will others with similar problems as ours."

"That's what their kind does. Every school has a Jake or two."

"And all *Jakes* seek us out," she added. "Hey we're sixteen and still alive so we must be doing something right."

"Something tells me we might be hedging our bet this time."

"Maybe you'll be better at love," she snorted, giving him a quick kiss on the lips.

Feeling his face flush, he quickly shoved the cinnamon roll in his mouth. "Good," he mumbled.

"The roll or me?"

Dale nodded yes.

"What you say we go meet Ted?"

"But it's still dark out there…"

She grabbed him by the hand. "You're with me. No boogey man will get you as long I have something to do with it."

Dale nodded. Dark Thirty didn't seem to be an equal opponent of hers. He followed her out the door like a dog on a leash, another first.

"See, not so painful after all," she smiled, squeezing his hand.

55

Rich had made all the stops, picking up the guys in his brother's sporty Mustang; everyone but Buddy. His mom had said he was sick. Close quarters but the six managed to cram inside the car, two in the front seat, and four in the back. Jake sat in the front passenger's seat. Mack had called one shotgun in the back while Stoner had laid claim to the other window seat. Ray and David were sandwiched between them.

"So what's up with Buddy?" asked Stoner.

"Who knows," spoke up Mack. "It appears he no longer has any use for us."

"Screw him," shouted Jake.

"This is cool," remarked Stoner, hanging his head out the window like a dog.

"Beats the hell out of riding the bus," added Mack, feeling naked without his Colt. He knew better than to bring it to school. "We're nailing that skinny new kid today, right?"

"If what you said it true, his dad's not really a cop," replied Jake.

"It's true all right. I heard it from a reliable source. His old man is nothing more than a carrot. He's been like a vegetable since a car wreck several weeks ago. I heard his mom is a lush, too."

"You're just full of late breaking news today, aren't you," commented Rich.

"Yep, a big ass dump truck creamed him is what I heard," added Mack having researched the accident. "Found out they moved here from Spartanburg and I know where he lives."

"You've been busy," stated Jake. "I've never seen you want somebody like this before."

"I had time yesterday afternoon to do some snooping."

"You really do have it bad for him, don't you," said Stoner.

"All three of them," answered Mack.

"The chatty Cathy is mine," spoke up Jake.

Mack didn't like the sound of that. He wanted her too. *Sometimes you don't get everything you want, big man,* thought Mack. *Who died and made you the sheriff?*

"We might want to take it easy," advised Ray. "We don't want to get suspended the very first day, do we?"

"Yeah, you're right," agreed Jake. "We have all school year. Where can they hide? We know where they live."

"Just as long as we nail them," added Mack.

"You really get into this, don't you?" commented Jake.

"And you don't?"

"I don't make it my number one priority but its fun to torment the crap out of them."

"Maybe you're like Buddy, losing your touch," ragged Mack.

Jake let that one slide. He had seen a change in Mack lately and didn't want to cross him. Something told him that Mack was ready to pull rank and lead. He wasn't ready to relinquish that role quite yet.

"Mister News Hound, any late breaking news on Cassie?" asked Jake.

"Still looking for the killers," Mack replied. "Anyone here want to donate any sperm for a DNA match?" Mack eyed Ray.

Ray rung his hands nervously and then said "Yeah, we could do a circle jerk for them, best man wins."

They all broke out in laughter; all except for Mack. He didn't appreciate being mocked by Ray. He added him to his list.

"All right girls, we're here," announced Rich, braking to stop in front of the school.

"Another freaking day in paradise," yelled Stoner.

"Two more years and we're out of this hole," added Jake.

"You just had to say that," grimaced David. "Two more years..."

Dale, Debra and Ted hoofed it on foot and were almost at the main entrance when Ted pointed them out. "Well, there they are, all the likely suspects."

Mack saw them too and pretended to be firing a gun at them with his finger. He mocked blowing smoke from his finger tip. He wished he had his Colt.

"You know Mack came from a real screwed up home. I've heard my parents talking about his situation. He's off the scale when it comes to being totally messed up," Debra told them.

"It almost sounds like you feel sorry for him," stated Dale.

"Almost, but he knows what he is doing when he messes with us so, nope, no sympathy from me."

Both boys chuckled.

"Hold on to that sense of humor. You're going to need it."

"Don't ruin my reputation," replied Dale. "I have no sense of humor…remember."

"Hey I haven't even started yet with helping you develop a reputation," she winked.

"Protection, my job is never done," added Ted.

56

Brenda Jackson, waking from her deep slumber, panicked when she saw the time. She threw on her robe and sprinted down the hallway to Dale's room. The door was open and he was already up and gone. She had missed his first day at the new school. She had never done that before. She sat on the edge of his bed and cried.

After about five minutes of bawling and wallowing in self pity, she mustered up the strength to shower and dress. Redemption, she decided she would go visit Darby. That should be an uplifting experience she imagined, then she felt guilty for thinking such terrible thoughts. God should strike her down for thinking this way but she admitted it was true.

She may as well be the one in a coma for all the good she was doing. She regretted that thought, too. Her life was just filled with regrets and *what if's*. Just for good measure she popped a couple of her magic pills, washing them down with a Bloody Mary. She chased it with a gargle of mouth wash.

When she returned to the den, her cell phone was beeping. She hadn't remembered hearing it ring. Whoever called may have left a message. Three messages were in the phone's folder, all from yesterday. She pressed the message number then entered her password but before she could listen to the first message, the display blinked off. She had not recharged the battery lately. She sat on the sofa, placed her face in her hands and cried a second time.

She seemed to be too good at this crying. Now she would have to freshen up her make-up. She decided to have another Bloody Mary first. She had already forgotten about recharging her cell phone. Brenda ascended the stairs, resembling an eighty year old. Once she arrived at her bedroom too exhausted to deal with her makeup she downed the drink and curled up on the bed.

Her plans to visit Darby had been nixed. She would go tomorrow when, hopefully, she'd feel better. She would get up in time to have Dale a hot meal when he returned from his first day at school. Right now she needed a power nap. She would be fine after a little sleep. She thought about setting the alarm clock but didn't. Seconds later she sputtered into dreamland.

57

"Welcome students," Miss Agnes Talbert greeted the class. "You will be attending my homeroom and I teach Social Studies."

Her class would be one of three classes that Dale, Debra and Ted shared. After those, he faced the new hell alone. Bullies would be waiting for his arrival.

"I do hope each and every one of you had a wonderful summer vacation," she spoke in a much too syrupy voice, thought Dale. She sported her silver streaked hair in one of those tight little buns in back and wore a dress that almost reached her ankles. In her forties, looking more like seventies, she had never been married and lived with her mother.

Dale thought she looked like some sort of time traveler from decades long gone or maybe a librarian, keeper of the national archives. Sliding her thick bifocal glasses down over the lower portion of her nose, she began calling the role. She almost sang the names and her nose whistled when she inhaled. She was most entertaining.

The worst of the worst shared the first class with them. Jake, Stoner and Mack were huddled in the back where they could eyeball the entire room. Dale chanced a peek and all three gave him the proverbial look that their kind was noted for. They intended to kick his skinny butt for sure. Welcome to another wonderful school year.

Debra reached over and touched his arm. His skin tingled. Debra managed a quick look at the three in the back of the room. Mack flicked his tongue in a very crude sexual gesture then winked. She quickly averted her attention back to Dale. Dale turned and looked at Mack. He completed the same gesture at Dale and smiled. Ted stayed focused on Miss Talbert, lesser of the evils in his book.

Stoner's eyelids were heavy, almost to the point of closing. He had burned one in the parking lot then stashed his Ziploc and rolling paper under a loose brick. He knew better than to get caught on school grounds with reefer.

Dale's new sense of humor kicked in. He scribbled a note and passed it to Debra when Miss Talbert's attention was diverted to another section of the class. He had not anticipated Debra snorting out her loud laugh when she saw his antisocial caption with stick figures of Jake, Stoner and Make.

Miss Talbert gave Debra the look and asked, "Do you have anything you'd like to share with the rest of the glass, Debra?"

"Some one farted," she answered, scrambling for a diversion.

"Watch your language in my class, young lady."

"Sorry, that was un-lady like. I should have said pooted."

"Debra," snapped Miss Talbert.

"Passed the gas, cut the cheese, choked a frog…what?"

"Enough," she demanded as the class roared.

"What was all that about?" whispered Dale.

"Diversionary tactics," she clarified.

"It worked, sort of."

The second bell rang signaling the end of homeroom and the beginning of antisocial studies. The first class ended uneventfully but the three amigos knew terror could lurk in the hallways as they tried to make the next one. A quick glance by Dale to the back of the room confirmed that fear. Mack gave him the slit throat sign with his finger. Jake winked and nodded. Stoner slept, oblivious that the bell had just rung.

Dale, Debra and Ted moved as one, practicing safety in numbers, the ultimate buddy system. One problem thwarted their plan. None of them shared the next class. They would have to split up and swim in shark infested waters. The others looked like they already smelled the blood in the water. They eyed their prey, deciding which one to take if they decided to take any of them. Sometimes scare tactics were just as much fun to their kind.

Coach Rob Elliott, a mountain of a man, topping six feet, three inches, had drawn hall monitoring duty. This provided a temporary reprieve. All three made it to their next class unscathed. Jack shared Dale's English class so he wasn't quite out of the woods yet.

Everett Graham watched Mack Stevenson as he changed classes. He blended in with a group of students near a stairway, becoming a chameleon as he avoided contact with the ruthless one. Everett had caught his fare share of crap from Jake and his marauding band of ass wipes and figured maintaining a low profile might work for a while.

Everett almost jumped out of skin when the finger tapped him on the shoulder. "It's just me," responded Kit Argo, the poster child for geeks. "Any encounters?"

"Negative," responded Everett.

"Same," reported Kit.

"The others?" asked Everett.

"One…Butch had his locker super clued. No one saw the culprit."

"First day isn't over yet."

"Ronnie and Greg have PE after lunch," advised Kit. "Mack, Jake and Rich will be there."

"Deaf Con 4?" asked Everett.

"Standing at 2 right now," clarified Kit.

"Rendezvous at 1700…"

"Zone one…" confirmed Kit giving him a secret hand shake.

"Eventual total annihilation…"

"Affirmative…"

"Butch, Chris?"

"Chemistry II, no bogeys spotted," confirmed Kit.

"Recruits?" asked Everett.

"One on my watch…"

"Two on mine," added Everett. "Later."

"Later…"

Everett wished they were allowed to carry their cell phones but school rules required them to leave them in their lockers. Failure to comply could lead to expulsion. In a world of texting, they were useless in the lockers.

58

Darby Jackson remained in his dark tomb, his own personal black hole. He heard things, understood most conversations. He felt, he smelled, he tasted but he couldn't move, see or speak. Time was endless as was the constant darkness. He remembered everything except what got him here. He had received no recent visits from his family. It would have felt like an eternity if he had any sense of time.

Darby had willed his eyes open a million times, his hands to move a zillion more times but he hadn't even caused a simple eye flutter or finger movement. This frustrated him beyond comprehension. He could think. Why couldn't he will everything else to work?

He heard footsteps. Someone had entered his room. He recognized the perfume. She turned him over on his side, positioned a pillow between his knees, fluffed his head pillow, felt his cheeks and emptied his catheter. He heard his urine being poured in the toilet. She hummed while she did her chores and never complained. He missed standing and peeing.

Doctors had no idea what people like him could experience. He aspired to some day document his ordeal in a how to manual for the medical field. He just needed that first eye flutter, some sort of attention getting movement, and then he could let them know he knew everything going on about him. Where was Brenda? Had she given up on him? Why can't God just let me scream?

59

Lunchtime, five short minutes away, would serve as their next hurdle. The trio reunited in the hallway, stuck to their plan, safety in numbers. Making their way to the cafeteria and through the lunch line, they picked a table in the center of the room, close to a table full of teachers.

Jake passed close, brushing against Debra's back with his tray. Mack took a more deliberate approach and circled the table once, making an obscene gesture. Ted kept his head down, fork in hand. Debra defied them and maintained eye contact. Dale took in the scene, watching the antics from both sides. The game had changed. His pals were not taking it; at least Debra wasn't.

Two tables away, the entire horde took their seats. Talking loudly and making ominous threats, they taunted the three for the next twenty minutes. Mack nudged Jake and nodded toward the exit. Ronny Templeton emptied his tray and then made his worst mistake. He left the cafeteria alone, milk carton in hand. The pack moved quickly and had taken poor Ronny before he reached his locker. Stoner tripped him and he fell, landing on his milk carton, exploding it like a grenade underneath him.

This did not go unnoticed. Kit saw them but made no attempt to interfere. Outnumbered six to one, he could not help Ronny. Mack looked his way and Kit quickly disappeared around the corner.

"Clumsy little snot, aren't you?" said Mack as he helped Ronny to his feet.

The front of Ronny's clothes was stained with milk. He was now bleeding from a hole ripped in his pants knee. He swallowed, expecting more punishment.

"You've got to learn to be more careful," said Jake, pretending to dust him off and straighten up his ruffled clothing. "We'll see you later, Ronny."

"What was that all about?" asked Mack as they walked down the hall.

"Vice Principal Manley at five o'clock,' whispered Jake.

Ronny looked down and he had a huge wet and white stain directly on his crotch. Laughter erupted from several guys a few lockers away. Two girls booed the exiting Jake and his gang. Vice Principal Chuck Manley sheepishly turned and walked in the opposite direction. He too had been bullied as a kid. Even as an empowered adult he reeked of fear, programmed to avoid conflict.

Kit joined Ronny. "What a mess!"

"Game's on," replied Ronny.

"Game's on," repeated Kit. "You better go clean up before your next class."

Mistake #2, he visited the bathroom alone. Mack was standing at the urinal and greeted him by turning and pissing on his pants. Zipping up, he wiped his hands on Ronny's shirt before leaving. Ronny did nothing. He washed up as quickly as possible and exited, hoping his turn had ended.

The final bell rang signaling day one was history. Dale, Debra and Ted, still traveling in their small herd, migrated homeward. They had thwarted the nemesis and survived to see another day. Successfully avoiding several near misses, they were content with the results.

"Well…should we celebrate?" asked Ted.

"Celebrate what?" asked Dale.

"Defeating the enemy…"

"Not quite yet," chimed in Debra, pointing to where their adversarial force filed into Rich's automobile.

The three stepped behind a leisure van parked conveniently on the opposite side of the street. Like turtles they strained their necks to peer at them until the Mustang's tail lights passed them by and cut the next block. A sigh of relief emitted from Ted.

"We really shouldn't have to live this way, you know," stated Debra, standing with her arms crossed and tapping her right foot.

"It's the way it's been since the beginning of time," explained Dale. "We're at the bottom of the food chain and their kind feed on us."

"I don't think they eat their young or they would be extinct by now," chuckled Ted.

"Shouldn't evolution have kicked in by now and made us a stronger species?" asked Debra.

"Maybe in another few thousand years," smiled Dale.

"It's them against us," remarked Ted. "And we never win."

"There's a difference," said Dale. "We have each other."

"Right, we're a force to be reckoned with…NOT!" said Debra. "We've never really stood up to them. We just try to avoid them or make sure we have enough witnesses to fend off the worst of their violence."

"Hey, you stood up to them for me in the park," Dale reminded her.

"I lied my ass off."

"It worked so we must learn to always out think them, out maneuver them and avoid putting ourselves in compromising positions."

"That was quite a mouthful for you, Dale Thomas Jackson."

"Friends for life," chanted Ted.

"My first real ones," added Dale.

"How sweet," smiled Debra, high fiving them.

"The three Musketeers," quoted Ted, placing his hand out for the others.

They placed one hand over the other and shouted, "One for all and all for one."

"That was sort of cheesy, wasn't it, even by our standards," snorted Debra.

"We're pathetic at best," commented Dale.

"See you tomorrow," waved Ted, cutting down his street.

"Same time, same place," answered Dale.

"Will you be okay without me by your side tonight?" asked Debra, kissing him on the cheek.

Blushing, he replied, "Mother dearest will be there, but yes, I will miss you."

"Appropriate answer, Dale Thomas Jackson…I'll see you in the morning and if you get lonely, you have my number."

He nodded and waved, heading towards his house. She glanced over her shoulder to look at him one last time. "Not much meat on those bones," she whispered, "but I like the wrapping paper."

Dale thought how he really liked the girl. She had brought so many firsts out of him. He liked living here better than any other place they had ever moved. It was incredible to finally have friends.

Entering the house, he found it too deathly quiet. He smelled no dinner cooking so that signaled worse things ahead. Tipping up the stairs, he stood at his mother's bedroom door and peered inside. Somewhere under the wadded and jumbled bedding lay his mother. Discreetly closing the door, he returned downstairs to prepare his dinner, a toasted cheese sandwich. Unfortunately he found no bread or cheese and settled for a slice of three day old pepperoni pizza. .

Having no homework, he opted to watch television. Channel surfing, he located a rerun of the old sitcom, *Lost in Space*. The Robot with its flexible arms raised announced *"Warning Will Robinson, Danger!"* Doctor Smith was up to no good as usual and young Will was being conned to do his bidding. Will Robinson fell for it every time but was smart, a winner. He'd take on their kind full throttle. The Robot would be his back up; so much for fantasy land.

The late August summer days were still nice and long. Dark Thirty would not officially arrive for at least another four or five hours. Dale could accomplish plenty with that much time if he had anything specific to do. He didn't. He sure missed his friends. He especially missed the girl. They should have planned to meet in the park or do something.

After the *Lost in Space* episode ended with its usual cliff hanger, Dale clicked off the TV. Antsy, he had to find something to do. Switching on the interior and exterior lights as a precautionary measure, he set out walking with no particular destination in mind. The orphan image penetrated his thoughts. Basically he envisioned himself parentless for all practical purposes. He visualized being cast aside and becoming a homeless street person. Foolish thoughts he knew but he felt so alienated.

Enough gloom and doom he decided. He breathed in deeply and took in the glorious sunny afternoon. The summer heat soon had him perspiring profusely. He didn't seem to mind. Apparently he had been on auto-pilot. He had ended up at the neighborhood park. Quickly he scanned the perimeter in search of their kind. He spotted an elderly couple walking hand in hand, chatting and enjoying one another's company.

Sitting on a bench ahead he saw a rather attractive woman wearing a low cut blouse and short-shorts, nose buried in a book. Even from this distance he could tell she was braless, her nipples were pushing against the fabric. He had not really noticed such things before the girl had come into his life. He wondered what Debra's breasts looked like. They seemed so tiny in comparison to this woman's. Dale experienced other first, seeing things in a whole new light.

Walking along the shores of the small lake, he reached down and scooped up a couple of small stones and skipped them across the water. Tiring quickly of this, he flopped down on the grass, lay back on his back and took in the rays. He heard a loud honking sound and sat up. Shadowing his eyes with his hands he watched a flock of Canadian geese landing on the lake's surface. Smaller Mallards swam along the shoreline. Nature was all about him. It had been all along but now he experienced its wonders.

He lay back and closed his eyes, drifted on the edge of sleep. He embraced the solitude and peacefulness of his surroundings. He had never felt so content and at ease. He wondered what would come along and destroy it for him. He didn't have long to wait for an answer.

A shadow elongated over his face, blocking out the sun's rays. He sensed the presence of someone standing over him. This reminded him of peeking out those window blinds. He wasn't sure if he really wanted to see who watched over him.

"Can I join you?"

He didn't recognize the voice. He opened his eyes and saw a girl standing directly behind him. It wasn't *the* girl. She was a different one, not Debra. They seem to be falling out of the sky here. This one had much bigger breast than Debra, wore thick glasses and had long red hair, the color of Ted's and a similar freckly face from what he could see, almost looking at her from upside down. She had a strange looking brownish birthmark above her upper lip, about the size of an oblong quarter.

Standing with hands on her hips, she said, "Hi, I'm Chris Herndon. I'm in your Algebra class."

Dale vaguely remembered the name but hadn't actually been that observant in any of his classes, except for perusing them, looking for Jake and his gang. He sat up as she repositioned herself in front of him.

"You're new here, aren't you?" she continued the one way conversation. "Dale Jackson, I do believe."

He nodded, having fallen back into old habits.

"So how did you enjoy your first day at school?"

Dale sat their dumbfounded. Words would not form on his lips. He finally just shrugged.

"Mind if I have a seat?"

Dale swallowed and said, "My grass is your grass." How stupid was that, he thought.

"How cute," she smiled. "I like that." She sat down beside him, her thigh touching his.

He had gone girlfriend-less his entire life. How had he suddenly transformed into a chick magnet? His skinny self wasn't much to look at, so why would any girl be interested in sitting beside him on the grass where anyone could see them?

"So really, how was your first day?"

"I suspect no different than tomorrow."

"Did you have any trouble?"

Now why would she make such a comment, Dale wondered. She was fishing for something. "You mean with Algebra?"

"No, silly," she grinned, placing her hand on his arm. "I mean with our local bully brigade."

"You mean Jake and the others…"

"So you know them?"

"Let's just say I've met the welcome wagon."

"They have a tendency to target new kids to show them who rules the roost. Their kind is at every school."

"So how do you handle them?"

"I don't. I just try to avoid them and we travel in a group."

"We?" she pretended to not know what he was talking about.

"My friends…"

"You sure made friends quickly." She acted surprised.

"I met them before school started…Debra Floyd and Ted Parker."

"Yes, I know them. She's a little strange; talks non stop and can ask a lot of questions."

"That's her. She's a regular little motor mouth."

"So when did you first meet Jake and the others?"

"Right here, a few days ago…"

"Did they harm you?"

"They would have but Debra rescued me," he blurted out, regretting he had just admitted to her just how wimpy he was that a girl had to save his sorry butt.

"So how did she pull that off?"

"You're really not much different than her. You ask a lot of questions too."

"Sorry. I find the best way to get to know someone is to ask. So how did she save you?"

"She lied to them. She told them my father was a policeman."

"So, I take it, he isn't."

"Afraid not, but they don't know it."

"I'll have to remember that one," she responded, caressing his arm.

Her touch aroused him. Funny, he had never noticed those feelings before but then again no girl had ever given him the time of day. His eyes shifted to her huge breasts. He couldn't prevent it. He had never been attracted to them before but now he realized they existed. When he looked back up, she was smiling. Busted; she had seen him looking at them. He blushed then ironically looked again. She patted his arm as to say it's all right to look.

"I get picked on a lot too," she confessed. "They have had their fun at my expense more times than I can count. I have the loser target on my back, I suppose."

Assessing her features, the way she dressed and her mannerisms, Dale could see why she was in the same boat with him. She had a much deeper voice than most girls and had a slight stutter. Yep, she fit the stereotype perfectly.

"What do you do when they pick on you?"

"I let them get away with it," she replied in a bitter tone. "We shouldn't do that, should we?"

"But we do."

"Have you ever fought back?"

"Never…"

"Have you ever thought about it?"

"Every time it happens…"

"What about revenge?"

"Mine or theirs?"

"Yours…"

"Why waste my time; they wouldn't let me get away with it."

"What if there was a way to ensure they didn't?

"Didn't what?"

"People like Jake didn't or couldn't get away with or ever hurt you again."

"What you going to do, kill all of them?"

She smiled a most devious smile. "I've got to go. I'll see you tomorrow in Algebra class or before." Her hand followed his arm to his shoulder where she rubbed it then squeezed it like she was more than just a new acquaintance.

Dale thought what a strange encounter that had been. She almost sounded like she was proposing that they organize some sort of task force. Revenge of the Nerds only succeeded in the movies. He'd just stick with their original plan, safety in numbers. Utilize the buddy system. Right, he thought. Get beat up with a buddy. That sounded like an effective plan. No sooner had he laid back on the grass and closed his eyes again, a second shadow blocked out the sun. Had she come back or was he about to be pounded into the sod?

"So Romeo, how art thou?"

He did recognize that voice, even with the hint of sarcasm.

"I see you met the resident nerdy slut," snapped Debra.

"So we have sluts among us?" asked Dale, "And coming from one with all the wild sexual fantasies."

"Sluts exist in all species. Are you calling me a slut?"

He didn't answer that one.

"Did she proposition you?"

"Why would she be interested in a skinny pimply faced geek like me? Why would anyone?"

"She knows quality merchandise when she sees it."

"You women, we're just merchandise to you. If that's what I am, then you can probably find me on the discount rack marked *60% off*."

Debra crashed on top of Dale and kissed him on the lips and beyond. Another first; he had never been French kissed before and didn't know she had so much tongue. He wasn't sure what to do with it. She had to have tickled his tonsils. Excitement erupted between them. She could feel his arousal pressing against her and wanted to just grab it but she didn't. Dale could feel it too and his face reddened.

"You sure are possessive," he told her after she removed her tongue from his throat so he could talk.

"I like to think of it as protective."

"I thought that was Ted's job."

"Ted's not here right now and apparently you don't have a built-in slut warning system."

"Shouldn't most sixteen year old boys be thrilled to meet a slut?"

"You're not most and you're still a virgin. I'm not going to allow someone like her to steal your virginity from me."

"What's that supposed to mean?"

"Your cherry belongs to me whether you like it or not," she half way snorted but still meant business. "I am the protector of the treasure."

"And just how long have you been in the protecting business?"

"About two weeks but I only have one client right now."

"I suppose I should be honored that you have rescued me from her evil slut infected clutches."

"You certainly needed it."

"I...needed it?"

"See, you just admitted it."

"Are all girls like this?"

"Like what?"

"So protective?"

"The slut isn't."

"So what should I do if Chris comes around again?"

"Nothing if you know what's good for you."

"That doesn't sound like a protective thing to say. It sounded more like a threat."

"Maybe it was but you can do better."

"Got anyone in mind?"

"Horniness is such a terrible thing to waste."

"You want an ice cream? I want an ice cream. Let's go get an ice cream," Dale said as he rolled her over and leapt to his feet.

"I suppose I could lick a cone about now and I'm buying."

"Is this part of your protection policy?"

"I refer to it as bribery."

"I feel so dirty and cheap."

"So who's the slut now?"

"Let's have the ice cream on you," Dale quickly changed the subject.

"On me; now I like the sound of that."

"Slut," Dale said with a laugh.

"Your slut," she replied, kissing him on the cheek and grabbing him by the hand.

Ted Parker had pounded on Dale's door but to no avail. Even Brenda slept though the banging. He walked to Debra's house where her mother had informed him she had gone to the park. Back tracking, Ted now headed in that direction. Neither had mentioned to him that they intended to go to the park this afternoon.

Taking a shortcut through an alley way between two deserted cotton mill buildings would cut a few precious moments off his trip. Jake and Rich stepped from behind a trash bin, proving that his decision had been a bad one. He still had time to make a hasty retreat and twirled to do just that. Mack and Stoner stood at the opposite end of the alley blocking that maneuver.

"Where are the others?" asked Jake, having closed the distance.

Ted searched frantically for another escape route but saw none. Trapped like a rat, he prepared to face his punishment.

"Got any cash?" asked Stoner.

Ted quickly retrieved the five dollar bill from his pocket and forked it over to Stoner, hoping it would be enough to buy his way out of it.

"That's it?" asked Jake, plucking the five spot from Stoner's palm.

Ted nodded. "Can I go now?"

"You don't like our company?" asked Mack.

"I've done nothing to any of you. Why can't you just let me go?"

"You've insulted us with this little token," exclaimed Jake.

"That's all I had…" whimpered Ted.

"They're all such pathetic whiners," scoffed Mack.

"What do you think we should do with you, Teddy?" asked Jake.

"How about letting me go?"

Making a game show buzzer sound, Jake said, "Wrong answer!"

"Please, I promise I won't say anything."

"What is there to say?" asked Jake. "Friends met in the alley and one lent the others a five."

Ted nodded.

"And you know what we do to snitches," Stoner reminded him.

"Just get it over with," whined Ted, closing his eyes, expecting the worse.

"What?" asked Jake.

"Whatever it is you plan to do to me."

"Rude and crude, aren't we?"

"Insulting," snapped Mack.

"I gave you all I had."

"Sometimes that's just not enough," smiled Jake.

"I know the drill," replied Ted as he began to unbutton his shirt. "You want me to take off all my clothes and run home naked."

"They're so trainable," snickered Stoner.

"We've seen you naked before and it's no big thing," laughed Rich. "Once is enough."

"I've got it," Jake snapped his fingers. "Let's keep this fresh so it isn't so predictable. Come with us Parker unless you have a better offer."

Ted sighed and re-buttoned his shirt. Mack gave him a hard push from behind. "You heard him. Let's go."

Ted didn't like the sounds of this and thought about taking his chances running. He was not a good runner like Dale. They would easily catch him. He didn't want to piss them off. He would take his punishment like he always did and just pray that they didn't physically hurt him. Shortcuts, how stupid had this been.

"Good strawberry shake," announced Debra. "

"Thanks for treating me. Next time I'll buy."

"I must admit. You've come a long way in the past couple of weeks."

Dale's eyes widened as he stared past Debra and out the ice cream shop window. She turned to see what had caught his attention. Her jaw dropped open. Ted stood just outside, on the sidewalk and he appeared to be covered in blood. Debra stifled a scream as she and Dale rushed to meet him.

"Are you hurt?" asked Debra.

"It's not mine," Ted advised them.

"Not yours?" asked Dale.

"The blood…it's not mine. I'm not bleeding."

Ted was drenched from head to toe with the gooey red substance.

"You look like you're bleeding," said a rattled Debra Floyd.

"It's just paint…buckets of paint. They found it in a tool shed near the park. They caught me when I was heading to find you guys."

"Thank heavens you're not bleeding," sighed Debra, touching him on his shoulder.

"You're going to have a heck of time getting that off," advised Dale.

"They don't make anything easy. At least they didn't make me strip then pour it on me."

"How can you act so calm?" asked Debra.

"Easy…they did this and only took my five bucks. I got off easy. I didn't even have to run naked down the street this time and they didn't pound me. They said you were next."

"Me…why do they have it in for me?" asked Dale.

"Actually, they said they were gunning for both of you."

"Who did it?" asked Dale, figuring he knew the answer.

"Jake, Stoner, Mack and Rich…I should have kicked their asses." Ted managed to muster a smile.

Debra snorted. Dale smiled and said, "Guess you thought you needed a paint job instead."

"Why us?" asked Debra. "What did we do to deserve the extra attention? We're no threat to them."

"When have their kind ever needed a reason? Maybe we are sort of a threat. We're typically smarter than them. Besides, society will not allow them to threaten the popular kids. Those jocks would kick their butts. And they don't attack their own kind so that leaves us, the unworthy in their eyes."

Debra nodded. "We don't fight back. We're easy targets. We hardly ever snitch but I agree, we're way smarter than that bunch of Neanderthals and I think they're jealous."

"Get off your high horses. Remember the park. They know your dad is not a cop and they know you lied to them about it, Deb. They told me to tell you."

"Crap-ola," she replied.

"I've got to see if I can get this paint off me."

"And if you can't, what will you tell your parents?" asked Dale.

"I'm clumsy as hell. I'm always having accidents. They'll believe anything I tell them."

Dale thought about his parents. At least Ted could talk to his. Maybe they would adopt him. He could be Ted's brother.

Kit Argo sipped on a root beer float at an outside table and took in the conversation. He had clearly heard the names of the perpetrators and now witnessed the aftermath of their evil doings. This further justified their case but much work still lay ahead. He texted the others, filling them in on what he had observed.

60

Brenda Jackson drained the bottle of wine and watched the last drops splash into her glass. She had done all but wring it out to squeeze out the very last of it. Sadly, it was the last alcoholic beverage in the house. She now faced venturing out to purchase more. Groceries were just as scarce. She figured to kill two birds and replenish the depleted cupboard and refrigerator. She should optimize the trip and stop by and check on Darby. That thought so depressed her even though she had lost track of her last visit. Dale no longer asked to go see him so she decided she really wasn't under any pressure to go.

Sipping the sweet red wine, not her favorite by a long shot, she passed by the full length mirror in the hallway. The reflection did not resemble the beauty queen she had once been. She stared at the stranger in the ratty discolored terry cloth house robe with hair that looked like she had been caught in the worst wind storm. She had a wild woman look, or possibly she resembled Medusa with all those snakes on her head. Dark blotches rested under the woman's eyes and it wasn't eye shadow. It looked more like that black shadow on a football player's cheeks. Her skin was pale but it could have been from the lack of makeup and sun. This woman in the mirror required an extreme make-over for sure.

Parting the robe she peeked at the body underneath. It didn't look so bad, did it? She held up her glass and toasted "Bite my big old butt. Who would you pretty up yourself for anyway?"

A fleeting thought, I should have had that brief affair before it came to this. I look like a cheap drunken prostitute after a bad night on the streets. She laughed out loud then tossed the empty glass at the mirror. Even from three feet away she missed it and it shattered on the wall.

She opened her robe with both hands as if flashing the person in the mirror. "I have plenty of good years left." Her underarms had about a weeks' worth of growth as did her legs. "All I need is a shave, a shower and good powdering and I'd have them falling at my feet." She held her finger under her nose like a mustache. "I look like a Russian." She laughed and saluted the woman staring back at her.

She stumbled up the stairs to her bathroom and into the shower. She skipped her shave, again, leaving legs with briars and slightly hairy arm pits. She indeed resembled a Russian or one of those other nationalities that never shaved.

Darby Jackson, still unable to open his eyes or speak, had worked somewhat of a miracle. He had managed to open his right index finger and close it. He had pulled off the feat twice in the last thirty minutes. Unfortunately no one had seen the movement.

Still, confidence blossomed. Just maybe he was on the road home. He strained to open an eye; either one would do but nothing happened. Baby steps, he would settle for baby steps. He still required an audience to make this worth while. He hoped when the perfume smelling nurse returned he could dazzle her with his magic. He wondered where Brenda had disappeared. He needed to show her too.

This would be another chapter for his *how to* manual. Doctors, they think they know everything. Living and experiencing this from the other side gave him a new respect for those thought to be brain dead. Oh the stories he would be able to share. He would rock the medical world with his discoveries. He listened for footsteps but only heard the usual beeps and clicks.

Lessons learned; never ever give up from either side. He wished he could scream out loud. Brenda, my dear Brenda, where are you? I love you so. I'm here in my dark abyss but I promise you, I'm coming home. Dale Thomas, I so understand your fear of the dark now but together we'll lick the demons that haunt you, I promise. He wiggled a thumb and smiled from the inside out. Please, somebody, come see what I can do! He heard no footsteps but waited patiently. He had nothing better to do with his time.

61

Over the next several days, Dale, Debra and Ted managed to avoid any additional assaults. Traveling as one and remaining in the view of others had proved to be effective strategy. While they escaped the wrath, others were less fortunate. Their kind could always find someone to torment. They fed on those fears just like a vampire requiring the nourishment of human blood, so primal.

David had been busted once, caught in the act and placed in detention. Others of the gang had close calls but without snitches, allegations wouldn't stick. Their kind seemed so untouchable until they eventually pushed the envelope too far, inflicting critical injuries on the helpless. Parents of those would then step forth and demand retribution, sometimes even as those affected begged them not to.

An underground movement of sorts watched, kept score and documented each and every case. Numbers still small, they selectively recruited. Reckoning day loomed. Vengeance would be theirs. Patience, they practiced patience, keeping in mind the meek would one day inherit the earth. Texting and e-mailing made communicating a breeze.

Chris Herndon also shared study hall with Dale. She took advantage of Debra Floyd and Ted Parker's absence. She had Dale to herself and worked it. On this particular day she pulled her desk up next to his and melted him with her smile. She could tell he liked her. She actually liked him more than she would publicly acknowledge. She pretended to do her sworn duty for the better of all.

"What are you studying?" she asked Dale.

"Actually, I'm not. I'm just reading this Ann Rice novel about vampires."

"What are you doing after school?'

Dale just couldn't wrap his brain around why everyone was so interested in him, his business, his likes and dislikes, flirting with him, wanting to be his friend and such. Where had all these people been the first fifteen years of his life? What did he have to offer them? He had never had to maintain an itinerary before but might have to learn to do it soon. He finally answered, "No plans."

"Good," she smiled, touching him on the arm again, rubbing then squeezing it.

She certainly liked to touch him. He liked her to touch him too. Boy how things have changed.

"Can you meet me at the mall, the food court?"

"I guess so."

Nipping it in the bud she said, "Wonderful and please do come alone."

Being alone with her smelled of trouble but only if Debra found out. Listen to me, he thought. I'm worried about two girls; another first. Living in Charlotte had been like crossing over into an alternate universe. Maybe all the kids here are *Stepford* children; all except their kind. They do smile a lot and just by them showing interest in me makes me think they're androids or something. Maybe this is some sort of governmental experiment. I hope they didn't plan to replace me with a robotic Dale Thomas Jackson.

The bell rang. Study hall was over. One more class remained, history and Debra would be in that one. Jake, Stoner and Mack would be there too. He faced his biggest challenge. How could he ditch all of them? History class, he thought. He could certainly *be* history if he doesn't do this thing right. A worse development; Debra had seen him exiting study hall with Chris with her arm around his. This wasn't going to be good, wasn't going to be good at all.

Debra stood arms crossed at his locker. No smile accented her face. He would just about rather face Mack now instead of her. There was nothing left to do but go take his medicine. He had to retrieve his history book. Pretending that all was well, he greeted her as if he was oblivious to her mood.

"Hey, one more class then we are home free." Her expression didn't change. She hadn't bought it or didn't care or both.

"Well, what were you two talking about all snuggled up back there?"

"Did you actually see my mouth moving?" He asked, surprising himself with his boldness.

"I know your body language, Dale Thomas Jackson, and it oozed horniness."

"Remember, I'm a virgin. I don't know horny. We've got to get to history class."

"I'd better be your first, Dale Thomas Jackson."

He smiled.

"I promise you I'll be the last. Once you've had the best, you'll forget the rest. I've been practicing for this moment all my life."

Dale wondered how you practiced for it but knew better than to ask. He had already heard her masturbation stories. Too much sexual talk before history was way too uncomfortable. School had certainly become complicated.

During class he kept his head buried in his book and eye contact to a minimum. Mister Chuck Manley wasn't the most pleasant sight to focus on with his funny Hitler looking mustache, a bad comb over, and portly shape. Dale smiled thinking 'he's one of us'. His monotone voice could put you into a vicious series of nods.

The few times he looked over at Debra and she met his eyes passionately. It was tough being a sex symbol. Two weeks ago he had just been a geek with no girls giving him the time of day. He still didn't understand what had changed. He liked it but just didn't get it. He smiled just thinking about it and received an elbow in his ribs.

"You better be thinking about me."

"Fishing," Dale whispered. "I was thinking about wetting my hook." He regretted that Carl, his *sort of* grandfather would never be able to teach him how to fish.

Debra threw up her hands in dismay. Mister Manly saw the antics and asked, "Debra, do you have something to share with the class?"

Why did all the teachers think she had something important to share with the class? Red faced she asked, "Have you ever wet your hook, sir?" The class roared in laughter.

"I'll expect to see you after class, young lady," he told her.

"Are we going fishing, sir?" Mister Manley didn't appreciate her humor.

One down and three more to go, thought Dale. Jake, Mack and Stoner watched his every move. Ted would be waiting to walk home with them. He had plenty of questions but didn't have all the answers yet.

Surveying the class, he made the mistake of making eye contact with Mack. There was no passion in those dark eyes. His resembled those of a great white shark. He grinned and his teeth resembled Jaws. Jake's movement caught his eye so he glanced in his direction. Jake just nodded and clinched a fist on his desk.

Safety had been ensured in numbers but he was about to abandon that strategy for what, to meet the new girl in the mall. Females made him do stupid things. He had to avoid Jake and the gang and ditch Ted. Life had been much less complicated before he had arrived here. At least Dark Thirty was no threat this early in the day.

The bell rang. Show time had arrived. His classmates began pouring into the hallway. Dale watched Jake and his cronies exit the room. Before Debra could say anything he scooped up his books and followed. Once in the hallway he became fair game. Neither Jake nor the others were anywhere to be seen. Dale thought ambush.

He hastily headed toward the exit door. He spotted Mack at the water fountain, pretending to take a drink. Stoner stood further down the corridor, partially concealed by an open locker door. Jake, arms crossed defiantly, waited directly in front of the door.

Shadows appeared, flanking him and grabbing him by both arms. "You're Dale Jackson, right?" asked one of the figures. "I'm Butch Harmon. This is Greg Rollins and that's Ronny Templeton. Care if we walk out with you?"

Dale nodded his approval.

The four passed by the others; safety in numbers. It didn't hurt when the coach stepped into the hallway.

"Where are you heading?" asked Butch.

"The mall…"

"What a coincidence, so are we," replied Greg.

Ted had not been so lucky. Frustrated, the trio saw him as he tried to flag Dale down. The pack closed in. Paint was not on the agenda this time. Ted reached in his pockets and pulled out the only two dollars he had. They weren't interested.

The mall was over six blocks away in the opposite direction of home. Dale, surrounded by his self-appointed body guards left the school in their wake. This could not have turned out any better. Butch, Greg and Ronny appeared to be his kind, all having nerdy or geeky attributes, misfits for one reason or another. He felt comfortable in their presence. They, too, had discovered the value of traveling in a herd.

Very little conversation passed between them on the walk and that suited Dale just fine. His kind didn't typically chat that much, except for the girl species, and Ted. The mall loomed less than a block away. Traffic and people activity had increased three fold. This one looked to be several levels high. It even boasted an ice skating rink and this was August for goodness sake.

Entering through the food court access, the noise level became deafening. Kids scurried around like ants. This mall was the parental dumping ground, the ultimate baby sitter. Dale had arrived at the premier social event. Here he could easily blend in and be forgotten. He wasn't sure where he was supposed to meet girl number two. She had just said the mall food court. This might be difficult, he thought.

The trio appeared to be steering him through the human maze as if they knew the final destination. Suddenly there she was, sitting at a table in the window front of Barnes and Noble, sipping on a Starbucks. She somehow picked them out of the crowd and waved. He waved back.

Delayed reaction or somewhat choreographed, Butch announced, "There's Chris."

Chris Herndon, girl number two motioned for them to join her. They did.

"Hey guys, I see you've met Dale," she said with a smile that almost rivaled Debra's.

Dale smelled set-up. This looked too staged. What did they have in mind for him, he wondered? He didn't feel threatened by them but his senses were on high alert. They wanted or expected something from him. Everybody in this town did.

"Too crowded in here, Chris," spoke up Butch. "Why don't we head outside to that table, back of J.C. Penny's?"

"Super," she replied, standing and grabbing Dale by the arm as if he was her personal escort or she his.

Just what were they up to Dale wondered. He felt much too uncomfortable in this new popularity tug of war. Why had he become such a hot commodity? This definitely stank but he wasn't sure why. He decided to play along. What other choice did he really have?

Once outside and perched on a table at what Dale perceived to be an employee smoking area, they were joined by others of the not so blessed kind. Kit Argo and Everett Graham suddenly materialized. Yep, this was planned for sure, he thought.

"How are you adjusting to our school?" asked Everett.

True to form, the questions started. Did everyone in this town want to know his business, likes and dislikes, how he had adjusted. What next, would they want to know his astrological sign?

"All right, I suppose. Is this some sort of inquisition? If so, I'll nip it early. I'm not a witch or warlock."

Spontaneous laughter erupted. It didn't appear to be choreographed. "Certainly not," replied Everett, the apparent leader of the nerds. "We're here to simply offer our friendship. We understand how difficult it can often be, adjusting to a new school and the surroundings."

"You really mean Jake and his merry little band, don't you? What are you, the local protection agency?"

"You've very perceptive. That's why we picked you."

"Perceptive or just a nerdy geek like the rest of you..."

"That too," replied Everett, still doing all of the talking for all of them.

"So why am I really here?"

"We've all experienced difficulties with those you've mentioned," spoke up Chris. "We've decided to organize and deter and disrupt their aggressive behavioral patterns."

"Traveling in numbers is a start. Debra, Ted and I have implemented that technique and it has worked so far."

"See," pointed out Chris, "Perfect reason for joining us."

Dale figured Chris had been the bait to get him here. She really had no interest in him. That should make Debra happy.

"Take it from one who knows. This school has nothing on every other one I've attended. They all have a Jake or two and we are the targets of their aggressions. Their kind feed on us like we're their next meal."

"That's where you're wrong," advised Everett. "We're no longer standing down and if I can be so blunt, putting up with their crap!"

"So you're taking them on. What, are you starting a gang war?"

Everett smiled, "Trust me, there will be no war."

"You can't beat them. Their kind has existed since the beginning of time. We were put here like domestic cattle to serve their every whim."

"You're so cynical," commented Kit.

"Not hardly. Experience is a good teacher."

"Dale, we're offering you the opportunity to join us."

"So are you telling me that by joining you, it prevents me from being attacked?"

"There are no guarantees in life."

"What does this alliance buy me, a sudden death? What are you really up to?"

"We cannot share that information with you until you commit to our cause."

"Does this come with a decoder ring and secret hand shake?"

"That was uncalled for," spoke up Chris. "We are your friends.

"Friends with a catch...I've never been much of a joiner."

"Please think about it," said Chris, caressing his arm and pouring on the smile.

"We're providing you with the opportunity to be part of the solution, not the problem," advised Everett.

"So if I don't join, you'll consider me the enemy. I assure you, I'm not one of them."

"No one is accusing you of being like them," said Chris.

"You are one of us," spoke up Butch.

"I'm not so sure. I don't know what you are yet. I like just being me."

"When the time is right, you will. We request that you keep this conversation confidential."

"That means don't tell your friends," clarified Kit.

"I'm not even a registered member of your little elite club and you're trying to tell me what to do. I like this less and less."

"Please," beckoned Chris. "Give us your word."

"Yes," added Everett. "Can we trust you not to speak of this?"

Questions, everyone asked too many questions. They all wanted his opinions. Now they wanted his soul. Just what was this new breed of challenger?

"I don't know about this. I'm certainly not sure about any of you."

"Give it a couple of days and we will speak again," advised Everett.

"We can't prevent you from talking," stated Chris. "This is a free country but we trust you will do the right thing. People's lives are in jeopardy if the wrong ones find out about us."

"You mean Jake and the others?" She talked his language. She nodded.

"Two days," spoke up Everett. "Keep it to yourself for two days and we'll meet with you for your final decision."

Dale conceded and nodded okay.

"How about we buy you dinner," suggested Everett.

"Bribery…"

"Fellowship…"

"Thanks but I better head home."

"I'll walk with you if you don't mind," offered Chris.

Dale nodded okay, still suspicious about her role in this but he had a long walk and company would be good. After they departed, for their protection, Everett had instructed Kit and Butch to follow just in case, but to not let him know he was being tailed.

The return walk had taken over an hour. The girl had chatted up a storm the entire way. She could probably hold her own in a talk-off with Debra. This had to be a girl trait. She had not disclosed any additional information about their little secret society. Their group appeared to be well structured and disciplined. Just what they were up to remained the million dollar question. She stopped a couple of times and responded to a text. She was reporting in to them.

Even with all the mystery, Dale was warming up to her. She ran a close second to Debra but then again, he only knew two girls. Possibly he just liked girls in general now. Boy had he been missing a lot. Turning down his street, trouble brewed ahead. Debra and Ted sat on his front door steps. She wasn't smiling and Ted looked peculiar. Chris saw them too and bowed out, telling him she would leave him to his friends. They appeared none too friendly right now. To make matters worse, she planted a kiss on his cheek just to stir the pot. The pot didn't need more stirring.

Before he reached the lawn's walkway, Debra had already stood. She had those arms folded and hip thrown out to one side. These were all bad signs. Ted remained seated and appeared to be clutching his ribs. He had a blooded upper lip and looked to have been dragged through a mud puddle.

Diverting eye contact away from Debra, Dale asked, "Ted, Are you all right?"

"Does he look all right?" snapped Debra.

Dale had no choice but to look at her since she had taken charge of the conversation. He shook his head no. She looked furious. He had really messed up and he knew it.

"They got me again. They wanted you but settled for me. It's not paint this time."

"Where were you all afternoon?" asked Debra. "I thought we agreed to stick together. Oh, never mind. I think we know that answer, don't we?"

"I can..." but Debra cut him off before he could finish his sentence, which suited him just fine because he didn't really have a sound explanation.

"Explain," she snapped. "Explain to Ted how you allowed him to get his butt kicked while you traipsed off with her. Explain why you left me without saying a word about where you were going. I'm lucky I'm not in the same shape as Ted or worse."

Dale could say nothing. She was right. He had let both of them down. It was entirely his fault. Making decisions wasn't one of his strengths.

"I thought we were friends," said Ted, "The three Musketeers."

"I hope she was worth it. Are you still a virgin? Never mind, I really don't care."

"But…"

"But your bony, narrow ass; why don't you save it for someone who gives a rat's ass? I'm going home." She stormed off.

"Ted…"

"Not interested," he interrupted. "You screwed us. I watched you leave with her. I yelled at you and you ducked out. I know you saw and heard me. That's so messed up." Ted turned and walked away too.

Things didn't get any better when he went inside. He located his mother still in bed. The room smelled liked a distillery. He saw the empty glass and an empty bottle of gin on the bedside table. A bottle of pills were spilled on the table beside the bottle. He hesitated, wondering if she was still breathing then he got his answer when she let out a series of snores. Just drunk again, her normal pattern…

He didn't attempt waking her and returned downstairs to find something to eat. He really wasn't hungry but it gave him something to do. He settled for a can of chicken noodle soup and Cheez-its. He thought about calling Debra but didn't know what he could say to smooth over the mess he had gotten himself into, so he opted to turn on the television instead.

He bided his time waiting for Dark Thirty, no more than an hour away. He began his ritual of turning on all the interior lights preparing for its arrival. Even though he would eventually retire to his room, he didn't wish to leave it to chance, just in case he had to venture to any other parts of the house. Having his mother in the house offered little comfort, given her current condition. Preparation and survival rested squarely on his shoulders.

Worse fears loomed. School tomorrow took on a whole new meaning. He would be a force of one unless after a good night's sleep, Ted and Debra reconsidered their stance. He didn't hold his breath. He thought how badly his world sucked right now and to kill time, he jotted down a list of all the tragic events hoping that by doing so, he could come up with solutions to them.

   1. Father in a coma – solution none
   2. Mother, a pill taking drunk - solution none
   3. Carl O'Conner, dead – water under the bridge
   4. Debra Floyd, pissed and no longer a friend – apologize?
   5. Ditto, Ted Parker – ditto!
   6. Dark Thirty still out there - solution none
   7. Jake and his gang – figure it out or prepare to take my medicine
   8. Chris Herndon, the other girl - confused
   9. Mystery of the Secret Society - confused

Assessing what he had just written, he had learned nothing. He would be better off wetting his hook than being here. He again wished Carl O'Conner had taught him how.

62

Dale woke up to the tune of Man on the Run blaring on his clock radio alarm. It seemed appropriate. He had showered before going to bed so after relieving himself, he slipped on fresh clothes. He tipped down the hallway and checked on his mother. She was still asleep or passed out. He wished either Carl or Debra was here. They would have already prepared him a wonderful breakfast.

Searching the kitchen, he located cereal and no milk, bologna and no bread, and an empty Pop-tart box. He laid out a slice of bologna on a plate, sprinkled on Cheerios and rolled it up like a Burrito. It was crunchy and not half bad. He washed it down with tap water. He scribbled a message on bright orange sticky note paper and pasted it to an empty Gin bottle he had retrieved from the trash can. It read ***NEED GROCERIES –WILL WORK FOR FOOD***.

He had choices. Go to school or stay at home. Get my butt kicked or live to see another day. Face Debra and Ted or Mother. None were very appealing options. He decided to risk school and take his lumps. He really needed a plan. He had extra time so he began to strategize.

After the lonely walk, he arrived to homeroom, untouched by those wishing to do him bodily harm. He received ice cold shoulders. Neither Debra nor Ted acknowledged his existence. He had not mustered up an appropriate apology for either of them. He wasn't sure if either of them would forgive or forget during his life span.

Dale had managed to skirt disaster and many close calls throughout the day. He faced his final challenge, how to escape after the final bell. Jake, Mack and Stoner shared history with him and would have had him yesterday if not for

Butch and the other's intervention. He wasn't sure he could count on a repeat.

Fifteen minutes before class ended he requested permission to use the restroom. He left his books behind to ensure the others thought he would be returning. This would give him a head start home. Obviously this particular plan could only be used once. He would have to think of something else tomorrow.

Arriving home safely, he dreaded going inside. He stood for a few seconds, overcoming the inevitable and preparing for the scene ahead. Entering he noticed something different. He smelled food cooking. Clanging of pots and pans emitted from the kitchen. Could Dark Thirty be baiting him with some new trick to capture his life force? Surely not, he thought. It wasn't dark by a long shot. Had Debra beat him here and this was her way of making piece. No, she had still been in class when he had excused himself.

Cautiously he entered the kitchen, peeking around the door. To his surprise, there stood his mother. She was standing in front of the oven, busy and oblivious to his presence. He wasn't sure what to make of this transformation. Apparently his note had hit its mark and had quilted her into cooking. Whatever works, he thought.

Turning to retrieve something from the refrigerator, she screamed and dropped a large stirring spoon, startled by him standing in the doorway. "You're home early!" How did she know that? She had never been awake when he departed or returned from this particular school. Dale drew pleasure from having startled her. She had it coming.

"How was school?" she asked, like she really cared one way or the other.

"Same as it's been for forever," he smarted back.

"Unwind a little then wash up. We'll be eating in about thirty minutes."

He saw her familiar insulated mug on the counter and realized she had not been cooking alone. Why complain, he figured. Any food on the table was an improvement, regardless of what assistance she needed. She was standing upright and awake. That in itself was a first for her lately. He would give her thirty minutes of redemption time.

Dale went upstairs, washed up and flopped across his bed, attempting to absorb what he had just witnessed. Possibly he could cross her off his problem list. Boy, how that one mall excursion had really screwed up things. He would have to work on Debra and Ted next. His life had never been so complicated. He wished he knew their e-mails. He wished they had internet hook up so he could e-mail. He had no phone so he couldn't text.

Over the next twenty minutes Dale contemplated what he should do about his friends, his foes and the secret society. Something wasn't right. His eyes were watering and he had a peculiar twinge in his nostrils. Breathing in deeply, he caught the distinct odor of food burning. Bounding down the stairs, he saw smoke bellowing from the kitchen.

Flames shot from a frying pan, its contents unrecognizable. Remaining calm and recounting a page out of his Boy Scout training, he first switched off the stove eye, smothered the pan with a lid conveniently resting on the counter, then using a pot holder, he removed it from the eye. He didn't see his mother in the kitchen. Satisfied that the fire had been extinguished, he doubled back through the house, fanning smoke as he walked. He located his mother sprawled on the sofa, clutching her mug. The Gin bottle sat on the end table. He decided it was too early to remove her from his list.

Dale foraged through the other pots on the stove and scrounged up some edible food. He cleaned up the aftermath as best he could then he prepared for Dark Thirty's scheduled arrival. He checked on his mother one more time before returning to his room. She snored loudly but otherwise had not moved.

63

Debra sat on the ground near the lake pondering the previous twenty four hours. She missed Dale Thomas Jackson but stubbornness had her firm in its clutches. She wasn't ready to forgive him. She had never had a boyfriend before so wasn't sure how to handle the situation. She wasn't even sure if Dale considered himself her boyfriend. While he was definitely a boy, he may have thought they were just friends. She wasn't sure he had connected the dots. She hadn't been one hundred percent sure either until Chris Herndon had entered the picture. That had sealed the deal for her.

"Not so safe being out here alone," said Ted, startling her from behind.

"I didn't hear you come up."

"I rest my case."

"How's the wounded warrior feeling?"

"More of a wounded Piñata," he smiled. "I'm alive so that alone is a step in the right direction."

"Have you seen Jake or any of them?"

"Not since they beat the crap out of me," he answered, still favoring his ribs. "Do you think we were too hard on Dale?"

"Look at you, what do you think?"

"Forget me. You're still ticked off about Chris, aren't you?"

"Madder than a wet hornet…"

"I think that's a wet hen."

"Hen, hornet…I'm still madder than hell."

"So what do we do about it?"

"I'm not sure. That's what I've been trying to decide."

"Do you think one day of punishment for him is enough? I do miss him."

"I suppose so. I miss him too but we can't let him off too easy. We've got to lay down the law."

"You mean tell him to stay away from Chris."

"And stick to our original game plan." She shrugged off the Chris comment.

"Come on, I'll walk you home."

"You go ahead. I haven't finished my thinking and potential punishment for Mister Dale Thomas Jackson."

"It'll be dark soon. You get your butt home before then."

"Yes, Daddy. I'm not afraid of the dark or the boogeyman like you know who."

"Jake and Mack are worse than any boogeyman. How about in the morning, are we walking together?"

"You and me for sure but we'll have too see how it pans out with our third wheel."

"Okay, meet you at our usual spot," he said, leaving her to her thoughts.

Mack watched from the men's restroom. He fondled his Colt and even aimed it towards Ted as he passed by. He then turned his attention to her, sprawled on the grassy lawn and ripe for the picking. She wasn't a retard like Cassie but defective all the same. Mack didn't consider himself defective but he was probably in worse need of repairs than all the others combined.

Dale, in an extremely somber mood, lay back on his bed, staring up at the Star Trek Enterprise suspended from the ceiling. He wished desperately that he could turn back the calendar and have a re-do. Where was a good time machine when you needed one? Could one actually change the past if given the opportunity? An age old question still remained unsolved.

If he actually could turn back the clock, he would go back far enough to prevent his father from having the accident and he would save Carl O'Conner. He could possibly dig up his past and determine why he feared the dark. He thought how selfish to think this way when the world needed fixing.

The sun's rays were fading. Dark Thirty had begun reclaiming the night. He switched on his bedroom and bathroom lights then completed his ritual of testing all the flashlight batteries. He made sure he had extra batteries strategically placed. The phone rang. He jumped to his feet. If he would have been a cat, he would have just lost eight lives.

Third ring and it was obvious that his mother either didn't hear it or wasn't going to answer it. He didn't personally like talking on the phone because nodding and shaking his head was very ineffective, but on the off chance it might be Debra, he answered it.

"Yes, this is the Jackson residence. No, she is not available right now. Yes, yes, I understand. I will make sure she gets this message. Yes, we will be there as quickly as possible."

The hospital had just informed him that his father had taken a turn for the worse and suggested that they come as soon as possible. Sprinting down the stairs he arrived by the sofa and began shaking her. She mumbled incoherently and swatted the air with her hands. He shook her again but more of the same. He ran to the kitchen and returned with a glass of water. He dreaded doing this but had no other choice. He dipped his fingers in and splashed her face. It wasn't working. He poured the contents on her head and face.

She sat up spitting and gurgling as if she had just resurfaced from a dive. Wild eyed, she looked around the room, searching for answers. Dale grabbed her by the hand. "Mom, we've got to go to the hospital."

"Are you sick, honey?" She slurred, blinking and trying to focus on her two sons standing there at the foot of the couch.

"No ma'am, I'm fine."

"Am I sick?" she asked, not feeling so well.

"That's debatable," Dale answered. "It's dad. The hospital said we need to come now. Something is wrong. The hospital called it an emergency."

Brenda attempted twice to stand but each time fell backwards. A third try and she stayed upright for three seconds before she almost fell forward. She sat back down.

"I'm sorry, honey, I don't know why I'm so dizzy all of a sudden. I must have tried to stand up too quickly."

Dale wanted to scream you're drunk as a skunk but he didn't. He tugged on her until he got her upright on her wobbly feet. He assisted her to the downstairs half bath to freshen up. She sat on the John and just moaned and swayed. This wasn't working.

"Mom, we've got to go. He needs us. You've really got to do this."

"We don't have to go right now, honey, not this very second, do we?" She realized that she was sitting on the commode and was peeing in front of her two sons. Closing one eye, the second son disappeared.

Dale pulled her to her feet and thought about trying to help make her a little more presentable then opted for plan B and led her towards the garage. He scooped up her keys from the counter as they passed. "Mom, you have to drive us to the hospital...now...it's an emergency."

"I'm still a little under the weather. You'll have to drive." She handed the keys back to Dale.

"I don't have a driver's license. That would be illegal." How stupid he thought. Her driving drunk was even worse. He pushed her into the passenger's side.

"It's easy. Remember your manual. I'll talk you through it." She was slurring even worse now and barely able to keep her eyelids from closing.

Dale pressed the garage door opener then turned the key in the ignition switch. The garage door opening revealed Dark Thirty waiting for him outside. It was okay...just fine...he could deal with the darkness as long as he wasn't alone. In her present state he wasn't sure if he was really safe from his demon.

Debra sat up as twilight approached. She had decided to give Dale another chance but there would be new rules. Pining for him seemed more like her punishment than his. She would reconcile it at the meeting spot in the morning if she could wait that long. She might just call him when she arrived home or just go by his house.

Righting herself she strolled toward the street. The lights were just flickering on. She decided to take a potty break first. She didn't particularly like using public restrooms but it was either there or squat behind the bushes. She entered the bathroom and checked each of the three stalls, choosing the cleanest of the three. While finishing up her business, she heard the bathroom door open and then footsteps. She wasn't alone. It wasn't unusual for joggers or walkers to use the facilities. She wiped and flushed, then opened the stall door. Mack greeted her on the other side.

"Sort of late to be out here all alone, isn't it? It's not a very safe place. Things can happen. Fear not, you're no longer alone. I'm your knight in shining armor."

"What makes you think I'm alone?"

"Do I look stupid?"

"Do you really want me to answer that?"

"Parker is gone and I haven't seen your skinny little boyfriend. You know the one I'm talking about...the cop's son."

"What do you want, Mack? I'm broke. I don't have a cent on me."

"You have plenty to bargain with," he told her while caressing the Colt inside his shirt.

"That's an all time low even for you," she smarted back showing no fear. "When are you guys going to grow up and stop pulling your silly ass pranks and bullying?"

"So you're ready for something grown up," he smiled, fondling the gun then his crotch.

Debra prepared to plant a foot in his grownup place once he removed his hand. She was ready to go home and had grown tired of this foolishness. Mack was just a boy, a runt of a boy at that. She could handle him with the others around. She could handle anybody.

Mack was pissed by her defiant attitude. He suddenly stepped closer, now too close for her to kick him. He could smell her perfume. He fingered the Colt's trigger still concealed inside his pocket.

Debra could smell his breath too. It smelled like he had been eating dog crap. He really needed a breath mint and wished she had one she could offer him. When he grinned she could see particles of food lodged between his yellow teeth. Did he ever brush she wondered. She despised people with poor hygiene.

Mack grabbed her by the arm then pushed her backwards toward the stall. She caught the side of the stall preventing him from successfully maneuvering her inside the confined space. Debra took a half step forward and bumped against his chest.

"You've had your fun. Now I'm going home." She tried to push by him but he held her arm in a vise like grip.

"This is going to be tougher than the retard," he blurted out getting her attention.

"Cassie," whispered Debra. "It was you."

Mack clutched her firmly by the throat then spun her around and against the concrete wall outside the stall area. Before she could kick or even claw out at him, he had tripped her and pinned her to the cold tile floor, temporarily knocking the breath out of her. Straddling her chest, her arms pinned underneath his legs, he retrieved the Colt and held it against her forehead.

She started to scream but he pulled back the hammer and warned her to remain silent. She did. She hadn't counted on this. Where had he gotten a gun?

"What are you planning on doing?'

"Anything I want to do," he smiled. "This is my ticket. I can pull the trigger and end it if you want me to. It really doesn't matter to me."

"You raped and murdered Cassie, didn't you?"

"I didn't rape anyone but I've been looking forward to this."

64

Dale had managed to start the car and had shifted the stick to reverse. Pressing the gas peddle the car lurched from the garage. One foot on the gas and the other on the brake made for a lot of whiplash opportunities. The brake was winning. He should have read that manual and tried driving before now.

"Take your foot off the brake, sweetie," slurred Brenda. "It'll drive better."

He did and because he still pressed the gas with his other foot, the car launched from the garage. Dale pressed the brake and removed his foot from the gas peddle, bringing the car to a screeching stop on the curb on the opposite side of the street. The car rested against a Slow Children sign. Luckily no vehicles were traveling on the street at the time of his little maneuver, no children were either.

Sixteen years old and I can't drive a car. I can wreck a bike and maybe a car next. "This isn't going to work, mother. You'll have to drive."

"Turn the wheel to the left and remove your foot from the brake. Now, press the gas slowly." She tried to regain her composure but she was still so messed up from her drinking binge she was losing the battle.

He nervously adjusted his black rim glasses. Perspiration beaded on Dale's forehead and upper lip. His back was soaked. Surprisingly, this maneuver had worked. He glanced over at his mom and her eyes were about to close. "Mom, wake up…now what?"

His voice jolted her to attention like an electrical shock. "Stay on your side of the street. Don't cross that center line and let's go to the hospital." Brenda saw two center lines then covered one eye with her hand to make one of them go away.

Dale thought four wheels would be easier than two wheels but it came with new challenges. With his mother fading in and out and at speeds almost reaching forty five miles an hour, they pressed onward. Between learning to drive and keeping his mother upright, awake and not puking, he had no time to think about Dark Thirty. Almost an hour after surviving near misses, honking horns, obscene gestures and his mother's babblings, he finally saw a sign stating the hospital was just one mile ahead.

Dale smiled. He was very proud of his accomplishment, regardless of the road rage he had caused from those sharing the streets. He looked over to receive a warm congratulation from his mother, but instead found her passed out with her face pressed against the passenger side window, drool evident on her chin and the glass. Her seatbelt and shoulder harness held her upright. "Wake up," Dale said, poking her on the arm.

Brenda mumbled something but never opened her eyes. Dale couldn't worry about her now, being so close to the golden ring, the hospital. One mile and they would be home free. He could actually do this. Suddenly the car began to sputter and cough. He pressed harder on the gas peddle and it died, eventually rolling to a complete stop. He turned the ignition but nothing happened. He placed it in park and tried again but the engine refused to fire. He was no mechanic so he wasn't sure what had just happened.

He poked his mother again but she didn't even grunt. Taking a deep breath he began surveying the numerous gauges. The headlights were still burning so he figured it must not be the battery. He checked each display until he found it, out of gas. The display indicated empty. What to do, less than a mile from the hospital. Obviously his mother would not be able to walk that distance. He couldn't carry or drag her. There was no gas station in sight.

The darkness struck him like a thunderbolt. It enveloped him. The headlight's beams disappeared ahead into oblivion. Dale began ringing his hands. He searched the door pockets and glove department for a flashlight but found none. He had switched on the interior lights and drew comfort from the illumination. He wasn't alone. He tried to build on that fact.

Surveying the street ahead, the spaced out street lights offered hope. While Dark Thirty invaded the street between light poles, it wasn't pitch dark anywhere. He opened the door. The key in the switch, a warning bell sounded almost causing him to piss his pants. He quickly slid out and stood on the asphalt before he lost his nerve. "I can do this," he whispered out loud. "I can do this."

He had a plan. He would go to the hospital, check on his dad and ask for help for his mom. Taking a deep breath, he took a step, then a second and a third, closing the door behind him. He bolted and ran like the wind. He was after all, one heck of a sprinter. "Plenty of light," he whispered, attempting to reassure himself.

He covered the first block quickly and had not been attacked by anything from the outer boundaries of darkness. Gaining confidence, he quickened his pace. Cutting the corner he could see the hospital in the distance. He smiled as he maintained his stride.

Brenda had been jarred by the slamming door. She blinked and attempted to focus. She wasn't sure where she was or how she had gotten here. Instinctively she unfastened her seat belt and with much effort slid across the seat until she could use the steering wheel to pull herself over. Now sitting behind the wheel, she turned the key in the ignition but nothing happened. She instinctively tried to fasten her seatbelt around her torso but that just wasn't working either.

She slumped against the wheel, head hitting the horn. She jerked to attention, looking around wildly, wondering where that noise had come from, and then laughed out loud. She started grabbing at the dash board and switched on the radio. With volume way too high, it began blasting the lyrics of *Born to be Wild*. Brenda flailing away, engaged the wipers, the emergency blinkers and the defroster, anything she could press or flip.

Blue lights reflected in the mirror. The police car had pulled to a stop directly behind her. The officer approached cautiously, standing well behind the driver's side door as he tapped on the driver's side window. "Ma'am, are you all right? Do you need help?"

Brenda reached for the door, opened it and almost fell out. "I'm not sure, officer. My car is broken. Can you fix it?"

The woman reeked of alcohol. "Ma'am, your driver's license and registration please."

Brenda lost her balance attempting to step out of the car and fell into the policeman's arms. "Have you seen Dale and Darby? They really need me. I'm their foundation."

"Ma'am, how much have you had to drink?" He propped her against her vehicle.

"I told that doctor I do not have a drinking problem. I was fixing dinner. I really was. You should have seen the menu. I had to stop and take a break. Cooking can be a challenge sometimes. You know what I mean?"

"Ma'am, you are parked in the middle of the street."

"Where's my kitchen? Hey, you're parked here too! You are as much at fault as me, officer. What are you going to do about that?"

"And you were not wearing your seat belt."

"You're not wearing yours," she giggled, poking him in the chest. "I've got to pee." And then she did.

The policemen radioed for back-up then cuffed Brenda and sat her down on the curb. Brenda just tried to stay awake. She felt nauseated but not humiliated. The policeman prepared the breathalyzer and just shook his head, wondering where these people come from. Brenda smiled then vomited on his shoes.

"Why me?" exclaimed the officer. "Welcome to Charlotte."

Brenda looked at the officer, trying to focus but instead puked a second time. The officer snatched her by the cuffs and managed to sidestep the second endless stream. The stench smelled like something had died inside her. The officer choked back a gag.

"Lady, let me know when you're done. I'm not loading you in my backseat while you're doing this."

Brenda looked up at the twin officers and sat hard on her ass, landing in the slime she had deposited on the asphalt. The beauty queen had sunk to a new low. A jail cell now awaited her arrival.

65

Dale had successfully maneuvered the streets, staying in the light from the street lamps and away from the shadowed perimeters. Now standing at the entrance to the hospital, he took a deep breath, drawing pride from his accomplishment. Entering the automatic doors, he approached the desk centered in the large lobby. He actually asked the attendant for Darby Jackson's room number unsure if the ICU had room numbers. The attendant looked up the information on a ledger and told him where he could find his father. He was no longer in ICU. She treated him like an actual person of importance and didn't ask him a lot of unnecessary questions.

He pressed the elevator number. Three people entered along with him, one black man with flowers, an elderly woman with a cane and the third, a nurse. Everyone pressed their desired floor numbers. No one spoke. Dale exited the elevator third. He ambled down the hallway, searching for his father's room number. He had forgotten that the doctor expected his mother, not him alone.

Entering the room, he immediately faced his worst fear. There stood the doctor by his father's bedside. The doctor turned when he heard the door open. "Young man, where is your mother?" asked Doctor Fitzgerald, recognizing him.

Dale hesitated. He didn't think it wise to shrug and a nod or head shake would be pointless. He couldn't divulge he had left his dear mother passed out in their automobile a mile from the hospital. Facing choices, again, he must make the right decision, so before the doctor could question him, Dale took charge.

"She was unable to come, sir. She's in bed sick. She sent me in her place."

"Very unusual circumstances I must admit," stated Doctor Fitzgerald. "And son, I do not mean to insult your mother or you with my comment, but when do you think she will be able to come to the hospital?"

"I can't say. She's very sick. She's been throwing up in a trash can. How's my dad?"

"How old are you, son?"

"Sixteen…is my dad okay?"

"Very well," replied the doctor, reluctant to unleash bad news on the juvenile. "His vitals had plummeted earlier."

"Is he going to die?"

"I can't deny his situation is critical right now, son," explained the doctor, attempting to choose his words correctly. "We have stabilized him. I think he is presently out of harm's way."

"Can I see him?" asked Dale, unable to actually see him behind the curtain where the doctor now stood. "I've seen him before. I know he can't talk or move if you're worried about me freaking out, sir."

"Please come with me, young man," motioned the doctor. "I think that is an excellent request." The boy had spunk. He admired his tenacity and bravery under these extraordinary circumstances.

Rounding the curtain, Dale stood at the foot of Darby Jackson's bed. He looked no different than the last time he had seen him. He remembered standing by his mother's bed. It sure seemed he was doing this a lot lately. He stepped to his dad's bedside and reached over, touched him on the hand. He had read on the internet that people in a coma were said to be able to hear you so Dale decided to speak, something he had sort of gotten better at lately.

"Hey dad, it's Dale. Mom couldn't come right now so I came when they called." Darby did not respond. He lay lifeless except for the very shallow breathing. The doctor had been taken by the young teenager's boldness and tenderness.

"I've started school. I have two new friends but I hurt their feelings when I made a bad decision. They're mad at me right now and I'm not sure if I can make it right." Nothing, Darby Jackson looked as if he was chiseled in stone.

"You'll be all right. I just know it. We sure do miss you, Dad. We need you at home." Even Dale was surprised by his long winded dialogue. The doctor sensed this was not the ordinary.

Darby's little finger twitched and machines connected to him reacted. No one had seen his movement. Doctor Fitzgerald began monitoring his dad's vital signs.

"Is something wrong?"

"Please keep talking to your father, son. I do believe that he's responding."

"Dad, I did something that I've never done. I drove the car today. I drove it here. I can't wait to try for my license."

Darby's hand moved. His fingers closed then opened. Both witnessed it this time. That last comment had disturbed Doctor Fitzgerald. The young man had apparently driven to the hospital in the family car with no driver's license. He had gumption but he would make sure someone drove him home if his mother didn't arrive.

Darby's eyed twitched as did his mouth. His body rippled with spasms. "Ask him another question, son. Mister Jackson, squeeze his hand if you understand."

"Dad, can you hear me?"

Darby squeezed his hand. Doctor Fitzgerald smiled. "Good work, son. Are you in any pain? Squeeze your son's hand twice if you are." Darby squeezed once. Dale confirmed he indicated he wasn't.

"Remarkable," nodded the doctor. "You're the perfect medicine."

"Is he going to be all right?"

Darby responded instead by squeezing once. Dale smiled conveying to the doctor his dad's response.

"Excellent," commented Doctor Fitzgerald. "Let's allow him to rest. You have been the perfect medicine indeed." Darby squeezed his son's hand agreeing.

Doctor Fitzgerald asked a young intern to drive Dale Jackson home. They passed the location where Dale had run out of gas. Both the car and his mother were gone. He didn't mention this to the intern figuring she had somehow gotten the car started and had gone back home.

Arriving home, Dale remembered he had switched on the interior lights before they had departed for the hospital. Thanking the intern, he entered the house expecting to see his mother. After searching the house and not finding her, he checked the garage. The car wasn't inside. What had happened to her? Where had she gone? The tank had been on empty. There was nothing he could do about it tonight. She was the adult and he was the kid. She was supposed to know how to take care of herself.

He made a sandwich and washed it down with a glass of milk. He climbed the stairs and settled into his room, exhausted from the ordeal. It had been a miraculous day indeed. Good news is always offset by bad news. He hoped his mother was all right. His dad was getting better. He had lost his only two friends. His mother was a hopeless lush. He had no energy to worry about Dark Thirty. Tomorrow would be another school day.

Brenda Jackson opened her eyes. She sat on a bunk in a jail cell occupied by six other women. She felt like crap. Still woozy, she didn't remember how she had gotten there. She eyed her cellmates and realized she had nothing in common with these derelicts. They eyed her thinking the same thing.

Wasn't she supposed to get a phone call or something? She didn't remember whether she had or not. She recalled little of the events leading to her incarceration. She last remembered cooking and Dale arriving home from school. She didn't know her automobile had been impounded nor did she remember being fingerprinted and photographed. Her clothes were wet and smelled of urine. She wasn't sure how they had gotten like this.

She didn't remember that Dale had been driving them to the hospital. She tried to stand but lost her balance and sat back down. She was insulted by her surroundings and these people whoever they were.

"You're some kind of screwed up," laughed one of the women.

She blinked and tried to focus on the voice but wasn't sure which one had spoken. If she hadn't already made her call, she figured she should do that now. She dreaded facing the consequences of her actions. Brenda didn't want to embarrass her family.

She had to use the bathroom very badly but this required her doing it in the open on a toilet in the corner of the cell in front of all these other women. Suddenly she vaguely remembered peeing in her pants in the policemen's presence. She didn't remember the arresting officer's name.

She folded her legs tightly attempting to repress the urge to pee. She strained to remember what else had happened but only drew blanks. Brenda began to sob quite loudly. This didn't set well with her cellmates. One particular cocaine abuser vocalized her irritation.

"Shut your mouth, lady," she demanded, but Brenda continued to cry. "I said shut up!"

"You heard her, Princess," chimed in a second one. "Don't make us shut you up."

Brenda blinked her eyes trying to clear the tears but couldn't stop sobbing. Her cellmates closed in on her, determined to make her understand their demands.

66

The alarm clock ringing in his ears reminded Dale that another school day had arrived. Still dark outside, he took his time rising from bed, allowing the clock to tick precious minutes to dispel Dark Thirty's foothold. He waited patiently for dawn to arrive.

Finally seeing dawn's early light peeking through the blinds, he slipped out of bed and tiptoed down the hallway expecting to see his mother in her bed. She wasn't. He wondered if she was too drunk to make it home or could she be dead. He couldn't solve the mystery so he dressed then descended the stairs to the kitchen where he found cereal in the cupboard and milk in the refrigerator. She had at least bought groceries yesterday.

Dale would have felt abandoned and desolate if not for what he had witnessed last night at the hospital. His dad was getting well. This had been the toughest relocation they had ever done. Daylight continued to force the dark back into its lair. It washed away his fears of Dark Thirty but within, Jake and those others stirred new fears. He and those other bullies would be waiting for him at school. Maybe he shouldn't go. His parents weren't here to make him attend.

No, he had to find Debra and Ted. He had to make things right. Dale wondered if they would be waiting for him at their morning meeting place, all forgiven and forgotten. He doubted it. No need postponing the suspense so he set off to find out.

Dale soon received his answer. They weren't there. He surely missed them. Cautiously he completed the trek to school alone. He didn't encounter any of the dreaded tormentors and sighed relief, safely making it to homeroom.

Ted sat at his usual spot, squirming very nervously, but avoiding any eye contact with Dale. Debra's seat was empty. Dale stared at Ted until brief eye contact was made. Something was wrong. He could see it in Ted's eyes. Ted reciprocated the concern in Dale's eyes. The last bell had not rung yet so Ted slipped out of his seat and walked over to Dale.

"Have you heard?"

"Heard what?"

"Debra is missing."

"What do you mean she is missing?" His heart pounded in his chest. He removed his glasses and rubbed his eyes before putting them back on.

"She didn't come home last night. I was the last one to see her. I had to tell the police I left her in the park. I don't know if they believed me. I might be a suspect."

"A suspect…a suspect in what?"

"In her disappearance…"

"Disappearance," repeated Dale.

"In thin air, just like Cassie…I think it was the serial killer."

"Serial killer," repeated Dale like a parrot.

"Yep, I had it pegged dead on but you and Debra didn't want to believe it and see what happened."

"No…not Debra, she can't be missing."

"She can and she is."

"I hope you don't think I'm a suspect too."

"Are you?"

"No, I'm not. At least I don't think I am. The police might think differently."

"Then who did it?"

"The serial killer…haven't you been listening?"

"So who's this serial killer?"

"Do I look like a detective to you?"

"We've got to find her."

"If the police can't find her, what makes you think we can?"

"It's my fault."

"You're the serial killer."

"No, I'm not a serial killer. I screwed up things yesterday. She wouldn't have been in that park alone if it hadn't been for me messing up. Besides we don't even know if she's dead and we certainly don't know if she has been taken by your serial killer."

"What about me? I should have waited on her and walked her home?"

"We've got to do something."

"Do what?"

"I don't know."

Me either…"

"Missing," repeated Dale.

"Puff, gone, vanished," expressed Ted, snapping his fingers.

"My mother is missing too."

"Serial killer, I knew it. He got her too. He's after all the females."

Dale thought he should report his mother's disappearance to the police too. He should go by the hospital and check on his dad and tell him she was missing. He should find Debra. He should do a lot of things. He had too many choices and even more unsolved mysteries. He didn't like making decisions. His brain in overdrive, he could not concentrate. His head ached.

The last bell rang, signaling the start of homeroom. Dale just sat there and did nothing. He had a fleeting thought looking over at Jake, Stoner and Mack. He wondered if they had anything to do with this. None made serious eye contact with him except for Mack. He grinned and made the cut throat sign, his trade mark threat. Mack sure hated his guts. He wondered if Mack hated Debra's enough to do something to her. He shrugged it off. None of them were kidnappers or killers, just bullies.

What was he supposed to do about Debra, about his mother and about his father? He shouldn't be facing such things at sixteen. He had no one to talk to except Ted. At least he was now talking to him.

The teacher made a brief announcement about Debra Floyd but no details. First the other girl, Cassie had been killed and now his girl, Debra, was missing. It sounded funny, if only in his head, referring to her as his girl. This was bad on so many levels.

This particular school day must have been the longest one in Dale's short life. He timed his exit at the sounding of the final bell and sprinted for the exit, first to leave history class. Attempting to blend in with the kids pouring into the hallway, his plan appeared to be working until someone snagged him by the collar from behind.

Stoner had a firm grasp on his shirt collar. Jake stepped in front of him. "Where's your girlfriend?" asked Jake, smiling like the Cheshire cat.

Dale did what he does best and shrugged. Jake didn't appreciate the gesture and slugged him in the gut. Those who witnessed the assault did nothing, relieved it was Dale instead of them.

"Did you do her?" asked Stoner, chuckling loudly.

Dale never saw it coming. He never really visualized such a response. He balled his hand into a fist and simply swung with all his might. He delivered a right handed, round house blow, glancing harmlessly off Stoner's cheek. Stoner reached up and felt his cheek. His blood shot eyes were blazing in pure rage. Dale knew he had crossed the proverbial line and was in deep trouble. A skinny kid like him should know better than to instigate an altercation with a much larger, tougher and meaner adversary. Who would have ever believed Dale Thomas Jackson could have mustered up the guts to defend a girl's honor? Something definitely had to be in the water here.

"You got spunk, Jackson-hole, but spunk will just get your butt kicked," commented Jake.

"And you have a death wish," added Stoner, still rubbing his hand along his reddening cheek.

Just like the blow Dale had delivered, he never saw the second one coming either. Stoner landed a solid blow square to Dale's nose sending him reeling backwards and on his back. The back of his head hit the tile floor so violently that everything went black.

When he came to, he was in the grasp of pitch darkness. Panicked and disoriented, he began flailing his arms at the nothingness. His hand struck something solid, prompting a noisy crash. He then felt water on his pant's legs and shoes. The wetness unnerved him even more. Worse still, he wasn't wearing his glasses.

He could see just a glimmer of hope, light spilling under a doorway. He ran his hand along the wall until he located a light switch. He covered his eyes, the exploding florescent illumination temporarily blinding him. Assessing his surroundings, he saw the mop and bucket overturned and murky water staining the floor. He was in the janitor's closet. They had locked him in after Stoner had punched his clock. He steadied his breathing once the florescent light recharged his confidence.

He felt his nose. It hurt very badly and his nostrils and upper lip was caked with dried blood. It didn't feel broken but then again he wasn't sure how broken was supposed to feel. Making a fist and holding it up to his face, he mustered up a little smile, recalling how he had actually stood up to them, two of them. Outmanned and outnumbered, he had taken them on any way. His knuckles were swollen and bruised. His throbbing nose confirmed he had come up on the wrong end of it. It didn't matter. He had completed another first. He beamed with delight. He located his glasses hanging from his shirt collar. He hadn't remembered placing them there.

More urgent on his agenda, he had to escape his imprisonment then find Debra. He looked around for something he could use as a pry bar but saw nothing in the janitor's arsenal that might work. He reached over and jiggled the door knob. It turned and the door opened freely. He could not fathom that they hadn't locked him in the closet. Cautiously cracking the door just enough to peek outside, he realized the hallways were empty. How long had he been unconscious he wondered, now feeling the lump on the back of his head.

He saw a wall clock at the end of the hall. He had only been out for about thirty minutes. Passing the bathroom, he started to stop and clean up but opted against it. Sporting his wounds and bloody shirt made him feel like a mighty warrior returning from battle. He began his quest for his sanctuary, home. The walk home served to be uneventful. The few people he did meet gave him wide birth and strange looks. None asked him what happened or if they could help.

Ted Parker sat patiently on Dale's porch, waiting to greet the returning warrior. Dale, using his newly discovered talents, snuck up on his unwary friend and tapped him on the shoulder, sending him bounding for higher ground.

Dale smiled and said, "If it would have been them, your butt would have been history."

"What happened to you? It looks like they finally nailed you?"

Dale grinned. "I actually stood up to them…just before they put me down for the count."

"No way!"

Dale held up his fist to show Ted the results of the not so deadly blow. He recounted the events proudly, captivating Ted's undivided attention. He embellished it a tad to sound more like an actual fight.

"You do realize that this will only make matters worse."

"How could it be any worse? Their kind is going to do what they always do whether we retaliate or not. We may as well get in a lick or two along the way."

"You're crazy. You're just asking for it."

"We never ask for it. They do it because they can get away with it. Why make it so easy for them? Why not wear them down?"

"Right, like how many times can they enjoy knocking us on our butts until the thrill is gone or they're too tired?"

"Something like that, and sooner or later they'll seek out easier targets."

"I think you underestimate them. I think a good fight is what they enjoy and you didn't exactly offer up a good one. Bam, one lick and you were out cold and stuffed in a closet. That really sounds like more fun than usual to me."

"Has there been any more news on Debra?"

"Nope, they haven't found her yet."

"I'm really worried, Ted."

"Me too, and you think the same serial killer got your mom?"

Dale shrugged. He really thought his mom had skipped out on them, unable to face the fact that his dad was in such bad shape. If she could have just seen what he had seen at the hospital, she would have changed her tune. Dale still decided not to report her missing. He had heard the tales about Social Services. With one parent in the hospital and the other missing, Social Services would surely try to haul him away if they found out. What choice did he have? He would take his chances alone for now.

67

"Our Mister Jackson is quite disturbed about Debra Floyd," commented Everett Graham to his assembled team.

"I don't understand what he sees in her," stated Chris Herndon. "She's such a psycho babbler."

"Chris, keep your personal opinion in check please. She's technically one of us, as defined in our creed."

"Right, like you really care."

"Chris," warned Everett.

She pretended to zip up her lip, wondering what the big deal about Debra Floyd was. Her disappearance simply served as bait to lure Dale into their fold.

"Any new observations to report?" asked Everett.

"Jake and Stoner encountered our Mister Jackson after school," spoke up Butch Harmon.

"And…"

"Jackson struck Stoner and Stoner didn't take that too well. Stoner KO-ed Jackson and then they locked him in the supply closet. I made sure I checked on him afterwards and unlocked the door so he could escape easily."

"Was he hurt?" asked Chris.

"Just a bloody nose it appeared," replied Butch.

"Very impressive," smiled Everett. "He continues to surprise me. Is their anything else to report?"

"The gang met at their usual afternoon spot after school. I wasn't close enough to overhear their conversation."

"Do the police have any suspects in the Floyd case?"

"If they do, they're not reporting it," answered Kit.

"Excellent, then is our other situation under control?"

"Ronny and Greg are on top of it," answered Kit. "They'll text us if anything breaks."

"What about Mack?"

"We tailed him as requested and discovered where he hides the gun when he comes to school," reported Kit.

"Good work…"

"Do you still think he is responsible for Cassie's death?" asked Chris.

"Given the circumstances, I don't think there is any doubt; at least not as far as I'm concerned," answered Everett.

"He's such a slug."

"Are we still on schedule?" asked Kit.

"It all hinges on Dale Jackson," answered Everett. "And Chris, you know your assignment."

"On top of it, but I really hate not telling him the truth."

"Stop being so smitten. There's no wiggle room for mistakes and really no cause for you to fall for him. Worst case scenario, it would just be a waste of your time and his, and it certainly doesn't contribute to the greater cause."

"Are we really sure about Jackson?" asked Butch.

"Affirmative," responded Everett.

"And Ted Parker?" asked Butch.

"Negative…we only need Jackson. If there's nothing else to discuss then this meeting is adjourned. Butch, text Greg and Ronny and report anything out of the ordinary to me."

"Aye, Aye, sir." Butch simulated a salute.

"Everyone, let's stay low profile and communicate via text. Keep me posted if circumstances change," Everett advised his team.

68

Brenda, now sporting a black eye and bloodied lower lip, had been removed from the holding cell, provided medical attention, and had been placed in another cell with two less intimidating females. She had not asked about making a phone call, more embarrassed than ever about her condition. She continued to suffer from withdrawal symptoms and really craved a drink and her pills. She just couldn't seem to focus beyond her immediate situation. Desperately needing to make bail, she couldn't initiate the process.

The once crowned beauty queen holder, and up until now, faithful wife, had taken a mighty tumble. She had experienced bullying first hand. The climb back would be difficult at best. Brenda didn't seem inspired to even try. Brenda Jackson was lost in a world of her own making. Without her alcohol and narcotics as a crutch, her journey seemed futile.

She could not focus on Dale or Darby, even though deep down she knew she should. She stared at her cellmates, a very robust white woman with stringy blonde hair, sitting with her knees under her chin. She was gazing into space, oblivious to her surroundings. The second, a petite Hispanic, very frail with numerous scars and bruises up and down her arms, was fidgeting nervously, pacing back and forth. She pegged the white lady as being in her fifties, almost grandmother looking in appearance but she wasn't sure what had landed her in here. The other lady couldn't be much older than twenty or so but it was hard to really tell in her obvious frazzled state. Tracks on her arm indicated she used needles.

Neither of the women seemed to care about the others in the cell. The ladies shared no conversation. At least here thought Brenda, no one threatened or attacked her. She would have probably ended up dead if she hadn't been removed from the holding cell. Former beauty queens could be ruthless, sneaky and underhanded but rarely did any of it lead to physical blows. Their cat fights resulted more in tongue lashings, each lady understanding that scars and bruises affected their livelihood and honored that code. Only once had she ever witnessed a real cat fight among contestants and that had resulted in minimal hair pulling and tossing of make-up. Those days were behind her now. What might be ahead scared her more.

Doctor Fitzgerald examined Darby Jackson, very pleased with his sudden turn around. Although he had only minimal movement, his eyes were open and he no longer lay in a comatose state. Speech still eluded him but he could communicate with the hand squeezes. Fitzgerald could not diagnose whether the paralysis might be permanent or only temporary or how much mobility he may regain.

He hoped Darby's son and wife would return. Their presence had worked miracles or at least the young man had made an impact. He wasn't sure if his wife would stimulate the same results in his recovery. He thought it had been very peculiar that she had not visited lately. Perhaps their relationship was strained. That was not uncommon when this sort of thing happened to a spouse.

Darby's thought process remained sharp. He just lacked articulation capabilities and he had to rely on doctors and nurses asking the questions. They never asked the questions that he wanted to answer. Sadly he had no recollection of being trapped in the darkness. His aspiration for knocking the medical profession on its butt had vanished when he had awakened. He didn't remember his experiences from the other side and how he had heard and felt all the sensations from his comatose state.

He wished he could inquire about Brenda and Dale but he could not will the words to form no matter how hard he tried. They should be here and it wasn't like them not to have been here by now. Surely Dale would have wanted to return after yesterday's breakthrough. Subconsciously he could still feel his son's touch then realized Doctor Fitzgerald held his hand.

Fitzgerald instructed Darby, "Squeeze once for yes if you hear me."

Darby did just that.

"Wonderful…are you in any pain?"

Darby squeezed twice for no.

"Are you hungry?"

Darby squeezed twice. He so wished he could direct the doctor to ask him the questions he wanted him to ask. Looking deeply into the doctors dark brown eyes he strained to make the words form on his lips but to no avail, his mouth remained closed.

"Mister Jackson, you do realize that this is quite the miracle that you are back among us. Sometimes God's intervention defies our medical know-how."

Darby squeezed his hand once and wished he could smile.

"I'll be honest with you. I don't know to what extent you will recover and what mechanics you may regain but you have already exceeded my expectations. Frankly, before yesterday's visit by your son, your situation didn't look so promising. He's a fine young lad."

Darby squeezed once.

"Is there anything I can get you before I leave?"

Darby wanted to scream, yes my wife, my son, my life but simply did all he could do and squeezed once instead.

"I certainly opened that can of worms didn't I so how can we solve this hand signal dilemma? It requires me to ask the correct questions, doesn't it?"

Darby squeezed once then strained with all his might to make his mouth work. It didn't.

"Here goes my version of twenty questions. Are you thirsty?"

He squeezed twice.

"All right, so we covered the gamut, food, water and pain. What's next?"

Darby closed his eyes and concentrated. He attempted to transfer all his energy to his vocals. Doctor Fitzgerald watched intensely, sensing Darby's anguish. To his amazement he detected lip movement; not much at first but movement just the same.

"That's the spirit."

His lips began to form a word even though he emitted no sound. Fitzgerald could make out the letter B. He can definitely envision "bra or bro".

"Brother?"

Two squeezes

"Bravery…"

Two squeezes…

"So frustrating," spoke the exasperated doctor, thumping his fingers on the clipboard resting on the edge of Darby's bed, causing it to fall to the floor and papers to flitter loose. Retrieving the papers and clipping them back to the board he shouted "Bingo!"

Darby squeezed twice.

Fitzgerald laughed. "No, I didn't mean the word BINGO. I guess I should have shouted eureka instead. Brenda, you're asking for you wife. Her name jumped out at me from the paperwork I retrieved from the floor."

Darby squeezed the doctor's hand once and opened his eyes.

"I'm not sure why she hasn't visited but I will try to reach her if that's what you wish?"

Darby squeezed once.

"I'll call immediately. Do you require anything else?"

Darby locked eyes with Fitzgerald and squeezed twice.

"Rest now, Mister Jackson, and I'll let you know what I find out."

Darby squeezed once to confirm.

69

Like Holmes and Watson, Dale and Ted had decided to conduct their own investigation into Debra Floyd's disappearance. They began by visiting the park where the police had already searched. They even checked their secret hiding place inside the tree line but no Debra. Walking back into the clearing, Dale stopped at the edge of the lake.

"You don't think she's in there, do you?" asked Ted, picking up on Dale's body language.

Dale shrugged then said, "I hope not."

"Wouldn't the police have sent divers in there if they thought she might have drowned? They would have dragged it with those hooks."

"Guess they don't think so then," said a hopeful Dale. "Or maybe it's just too soon for them to think that way."

"Debra wouldn't have gone in that lake by herself. She didn't have a swimsuit. Besides she's an excellent swimmer; much better than me." Ted tried to convince both of them it was impossible.

"Then where is she? Did she just run away?"

"Debra wouldn't do that either, even to teach you a lesson."

"Even if she was pissed at me…"

"Even if she was pissed off at you," repeated Ted. "Besides, she had already decided to make up with you. We both had."

"So we're back to your serial killer theory then?"

"Well, think about it; first Cassie and now Debra and what about your mom? It could be one person doing all of it."

"Isn't there somewhere she likes to go?"

"Not that I can come up with."

A group of figures had gathered near the bathrooms. Ted saw them first and nodded to Dale. At first they couldn't make out who they were then they began walking towards them. "It's Jake and them," whispered Ted.

"Are you sure?" asked Dale, then he picked out the shaggy headed Stoner from the approaching group

"Let's get out of here," shouted Ted.

Dale pointed. "The woods…"

When they turned and sprinted toward the woods, so moved the horde. Dale and Ted picked up their pace. The horde sped up too. Dale yelled, "Run…"

Once in the cover of the woods, Dale told Ted, "We've got to split up."

"No way, we've got to stick together."

"Two against them, that's not good odds."

"Better than one against them," answered Ted, terrified of receiving another beating.

"If we split up, maybe one of us can reach help."

"Help from whom? And the one who doesn't make it gets his butt kicked. You're a runner. I'm too slow. I'm the one they'll catch."

There was no time to discuss or debate this further. Dale took off in the opposite direction. Ted, caught off guard, just stood there in disbelief. Dale had deserted him and he knew how fast he could run. He made his decision. He followed him.

After a couple of minutes of running, Dale hesitated to catch his breath. He heard approaching foot steps and prepared for the worst. Ted stumbled into view, holding his side and wheezing.

"I thought…" but before Dale could complete his sentence they both heard the rustling in the brush behind them. Dale froze then grabbed Ted by the arm and shushed him. The bushes exploded with footfalls. Dale pushed Ted forcing him flat on his stomach. He hit the ground beside him. Jake and the others scurried past, way too close.

Both prey lay there until the woods became silent. Dale eased to his feet first then motioned for Ted to stand. The two slipped to the edge of the clearing, eyeing the street on the opposite side of the park's expansive lawn. They had to run for it. They really had no other choice. Dale couldn't wait there for dark.

Running, Dale quickly outdistanced Ted by twenty five yards. Ted was already running out of gas. Luckily neither Jake nor any of the others were anywhere to be seen. The street lay less than fifty yards away.

Mack stepped from behind the restrooms. He had what looked like a gun in his hand. He was less than thirty paces away and to their right. Dale could see the sneer on his face. He intended to shoot them for sure.

"Going somewhere, girls," yelled Mack.

Dale came to a screeching halt. It took a few seconds for Ted to catch up with him, bent over and holding onto his knees. Finally standing upright, he saw Mack waving the gun. "We're dead."

Dale stared at Mack, contemplating his next move. Mack twirled the gun on his finger like a Wild West gunslinger. That's when Dale made his decision. "Run!" He screamed, calling Mack's bluff

Ted, still winded, followed. Both braced for the gun shots that were never fired. Reaching the street and the safety of people and traffic they slowed their pace. Neither of them looked back. Eventually they arrived at the intersection where they would go their separate ways.

"Where do you suppose Mack got that gun?' asked Ted.

Dale shook his head and shrugged.

"Do you think it was loaded?"

Again Dale shrugged.

"What are we going to do now that they have guns?"

Dale didn't answer.

"Do you think they're the ones who killed Debra?"

Angered by that remark, Dale spoke up. "We don't know if she's dead. She's just missing."

"I'm sorry. I shouldn't have said that."

"Go home, Ted."

"Tomorrow should be interesting."

"Today already has been."

70

Brenda perched on the edge of her bunk. She seemed to do a lot of perching lately. The big blonde and little Hispanic woman had been released on bail. She shared her cell with no one at the moment. Solitude offered few answers for her dilemma. Layering the seat with sheets of tissue, she could at least conjure up the nerve to sit on the toilet in the cell she had all to herself, except for the intrusions by guards. So far they had all been female.

As if on cue, an officer materialized just as she stood to pull her pants back up. The brunette Amazon motioned her over to the cell door where she slipped a food tray though an opening. She spoke not a word and performed the task almost too robotic. Her face was weathered. She wore hardly any makeup and could have been on the cast call for every prison movie ever made.

"I would like to make my phone call now," Brenda requested in such a quite tone that she almost startled the guard.

"Very well, I will bring you a phone," she replied in a very petite and eloquent voice. Brenda had expected to hear a guff, raspy, manly voice and she too was surprised by the response.

"Enjoy your meal. I'll return in about twenty minutes with a phone. Do you need anything else?"

"A get out of jail free card would be nice," Brenda replied, receiving a warm smile from the Amazon, an officer Robinson by her name tag.

Okay, thought Brenda, so who am I going to call? She ran through her options. I can't call Darby. I could call Dale but he can't post my bail but at least I could see how he's doing. I could call Ed, Darby's boss but what would that do for Darby's career if he lived to have one. I don't know Ed's number so that is out anyway. That leaves my parents in Florida. They could wire the money. How could she ever explain this to them? She had been nothing but perfect all her life. Pacing the cell she could come up with no answer.

She recounted the charges against her. They had booked her for driving while impaired, no driver's license, parking in or in front of a no parking zone, not wearing a seat belt, public urination or something like that, and she believed they mentioned she had somewhat resisted arrest. Sadly she remembered little of the transgressions but nevertheless, her reputation of perfection had been tarnished big time. They could probably tack on child abandonment and plotting to be unfaithful. She heard the footsteps of the returning officer.

"Your phone, Mrs. Jackson," spoke Officer Robinson. "You have ten minutes."

"How long have I been here?"

"Make your phone call, hon. I'll be back in ten."

Brenda stared at the phone in her hand as if it were an alien object then she began to cry. She didn't know who to call. She was lost in a world of her own making; one she did not know how to escape.

71

The final bell rang signaling the start of another school day. Dale and Ted had avoided any conflicts from their ruthless peers, however, Jake, Mack and Stoner watched them with weary eyes from the back of the class. Dale mentally prepared for the next inevitable encounter. Ted just squirmed uncontrollably, worrying about the beating they would surely receive sooner or later. Debra Floyd remained missing a second day.

Mack licked his chops, anticipating an encounter with his next victim. He suffered withdrawal symptoms from not having his Colt but he would retrieve it after school. The monster within him had been unleashed recently. Years of abuse had programmed him to become this cruel beast. Like the mythical vampire craving blood, Mack's hunger gnawed at him relentlessly. Already having taken it to that next level, he wanted more.

Everett Graham and his assortment of ears and eyes kept tabs on the abusers and their potential victims. No one but Dale knew that their secret society existed. Pieces of their puzzle were falling in place. Soon the world would know The Shadow Men by name and the world would forever be changed in their wake.

The school now rested on a powder keg, fuse lit, poised for the explosion that would soon be delivered. The scenario screamed for heroic intervention. One appeared unlikely. Sometimes things just have to run their course and in the aftermath a better world evolves. The Shadow Men banked on that theory, slightly manipulated of course. .

Without the support from his family, Darby continued to reclaim his life. Still unable to speak, he and Doctor Fitzgerald had perfected their questions and answers technique to minimize the number of questions required. The doctor had been unable to contact Brenda Jackson but had left several voice messages. He had received no return calls, unaware that Dale avoided them because he had no way to reach the hospital. He wasn't prepared to tell anyone his mother had deserted them. He still feared social services and potential foster care.

Bail had been set for Brenda but she had not completed that phone call yet. She held firm to her decision not to call her parents and that left her with no plan B. She should have at least called Dale or checked on Darby's condition while she had the phone, but panic stricken, she could no longer think with clarity. She could barely function at all. She had plummeted to a new low.

The judge had informed her that he would appoint her a lawyer. She had refused but afterwards could not rationalize why she had abruptly made that decision. Depression had her in its firm grasp. Brenda gave in to its demands and sank deeper into the pity pit. She justified it as her punishment for being an unfit mother and almost an unfaithful wife. She seemed to remember something about the judge suggesting a psychiatric evaluation. That was just what she needed for the final nail in her coffin, a fitted straight jacket.

She had always been in control of her life and those of her family. Look how the mighty had fallen. Brenda could not fathom why she had become this pathetic excuse for a human being. She had given up and she had never been a quitter. She should have made that phone call. She should have accepted that offer for a lawyer. She curled up on the cot and cried instead.

The worst possible news had hit the air waves. Police in the South Carolina border town of Rock Hill, about twenty six miles from Charlotte, had discovered a young female's body dumped on a secluded rural road. Details were sketchy at best from the neighboring state but Charlotte police were interested in the case. The reporter had mentioned the Debra Floyd disappearance in conjunction with the late breaking news report. Implications too often came true.

Dale and Ted had thwarted one brief encounter with Jake and the gang. A strategic show of numbers by Everett and the others had deterred the potential attack, too many witnesses. Dale now sat in the middle of their secret hideaway in the park's forest. Ted sat beside him, trying to console his friend. Both were distraught over the news report and held onto the hope that it wasn't her.

"First Cassie and now this," mumbled Ted. He started to mention Dale's mom and the serial killer but decided against it after seeing the worried expression on his friend's face.

This drew no response from Dale. Elbows on his knees and chin in his hands, he could have passed for a stone figure if not for the eye blinking and an occasional deep breathing. Dale almost regretted ever having made friends with Debra and Ted. He had been so much better off being a loner. He had not had to face such grief before. He could see how people were driven to suicide. He wasn't sure how close he teetered on the edge of it himself.

"Maybe it's not her," said Ted again breaking the deathly silence. "The discovery was made in another state. People are killed elsewhere all the time. It doesn't have to be her."

Dale vaguely heard Ted mumbling. He had shut out the world as only he could. No shrugs, no nods, he just wanted to be left alone. He didn't want to discuss it and wished he could stop thinking about it. He would have asked Ted to just get lost but that would have required dialog, and he didn't feel like talking.

"I wonder how long it will take for them to identify the body?" asked Ted. "Not knowing is almost as bad as knowing the truth."

Dale could almost hear that snorting laugh of hers. He even missed her constant questioning and nonstop jabbering. How had he grown so close to her in such a very short time? Why had he allowed himself to? His sorrow boiled like a slow simmering pot, on the brink of boiling over. Even deeper, a rage gained momentum. Both were firsts for him. He had never experienced this emotional spectrum and the thoughts racing through his head scared the crap out of him. He ping ponged between revenge and suicide and everything in between. None of these were good feelings.

Finally he could bear it no longer. He had to do something, right or wrong. He stood up and started heading for the park clearing. He didn't have a plan yet but he had a target.

"Where are you going?" asked Ted, jumping to his feet and tagging along.

"Trust me. You don't want to know," he spoke quite deliberately.

"What are you going to do?" asked a now panic stricken Ted, seeing the look on Dale's face.

"Go home, Ted."

"You don't want me to come along? Remember, I'm your protector."

Dale stopped in mid-stride. "Go home," he warned his friend, placing a finger on his chest.

"I don't know what you're up to but maybe I can help," replied Ted, undaunted by the threat.

"Absolutely not, Ted. Please go home. I mean it."

Ted had never known that such a skinny little fart like Dale could be so intimidating. His eyes were just plain scary looking, almost evil. He was about to do something either very dangerous or very bad or both. How could he allow him to go it alone?

Dale pushed him and yelled, "Go." These antics reminded Ted of how someone tries to prevent their dog from following them. Why was Dale treating him this way? They were supposed to practice the buddy system. There was no safety in traveling alone.

Dale soon realized that Ted didn't think he was serious. He clinched his fist and did the unthinkable. He struck Ted in the gut. He regretted this action almost immediately but it had to be done. Unlike his attempt to strike Stoner, this one had landed on the button. Ted doubled over in pain, sucking air and in shock by Dale's actions. Dale didn't apologize. He just turned and walked away.

Ted stood there trying to regain his composure. He didn't try to follow, more hurt by the action than by the actual delivery. In his heart he knew Dale hadn't meant it. Whatever he was determined to do, he was determined to do it alone. For now Ted would live with that, whether he wanted to or not. He just hoped Dale didn't get hurt or do something he would regret.

Dale rambled the streets over the next hour and finally saw what he had been searching for; Jake inside the arcade, not a care in the world. Rich and David stood nearby. None had apparently seen him staring at them from outside the arcade store front window. Like a bull, he charged the trio, his horns set on taking out Jake. Rich caught sight of him at the last possible second and hooked an arm under Dale's chin, sending him sprawling on his back, lungs deflated like a punctured balloon.

Jake rested his foot squarely on Dale's chest while his two cohorts kneeled down and subdued him by his arms. Dale, still too stunned by Rich's defensive maneuver, had not regained his breath.

"You're getting just a little too damned cocky for you own good, Jackson-hole," snapped Jake. "This lesson has been coming for a long time." He continued to grind his heel into Dale's chest. "It's time to show your scrawny butt who's the boss around here. Take him outside, boys."

By the time they had dragged Dale into a secluded loading dock between buildings, he had regained his composure. He yelled, "Why did you do it?"

Confused by the question, Jake answered, "Do what, hit you in the gut?"

"Murder Debra," screamed Dale at the top of his now inflated lungs, his voice echoing off the walls.

"Hold it down. You're friggin crazy!"

"Hold it down," Dale continued to yell. "So the world won't know what you and your band of crazies have done."

Jake buried another fist into Dale's gut to hush him up. It worked. "What makes you think she's dead and we had anything to do with it?"

Dale couldn't answer. He was gasping for air.

"We don't murder people, at least not yet. You could be our first though. What makes you ask such an idiotic question?"

"The news," Dale managed to spit out. "They found a body, a girl's body."

"We've been here all afternoon. We haven't seen the news. If I have the boys set you free, will you behave yourself?"

Dale nodded he would. "Rock Hill police found a body. Charlotte police think it might be her. You didn't have to kill her."

"There you go accusing us again. Haven't you wised up by now?"

Dale clinched his fists, readied himself for another assault. He decided he would beat a confession out of Jake. He took one step forward.

Observing his actions, Jake held up his hand to signal stop, then said, "We haven't harmed her, not that we didn't want to, but I promise you we haven't and we certainly wouldn't have killed her if we had. That's not our style."

"Liar!" yelled Dale and then Jake buried a third fist in his now tender mid section.

"Stop your screaming. I'm telling you we didn't do her."

"Listen to him," chimed in David.

"We're not killers," added Rich. "And we don't appreciate you spreading those sorts of rumors."

"Then who killed her?"

"How should we know? Do you think we have Mafia connections?"

"I wouldn't doubt it." Dale was still slightly bent over but held eye contact with Jake.

"Look, I'm going to have them turn you loose one more time and if you persist in this silly-ass crap we're going to really have to mess you up, understand?"

Dale nodded. He still didn't believe or trust any of them but this wasn't getting him anywhere. He unclenched his fists. They were doing him little good clenched anyway. He hadn't landed a single punch.

"Okay, so you saw this on the news," repeated Jake. "And they didn't actually say it was her so why get so worked up?"

Dale didn't answer. He just stared Jake down, looking for answers.

"How did she die?" asked Rich.

"They haven't said. What about Cassie, did you kill her?"

"Boy, you just don't have any manners and even less sense. Get out of here before we do something all of us might regret."

Dale took another step towards Jake. "Don't even think about," warned Jake. "I'm giving you a chance to walk away."

Dale delivered his own warning. "I'm going to get to the bottom of this and you better hope it doesn't lead me back here." He turned and walked away.

"Hey Jackson-hole, I hope it isn't her. I mean it."

"You got that right and you better hope I don't find out that you had anything to do with it if it is. This isn't over, Jake. I'm not backing down from you anymore. That is a promise."

Cutting the corner and rubbing his aching stomach, he was immediately flanked by Kit Argo and Chris Herndon. "Everett wants to see you," advised Chris, seeing the pain on his face.

"Leave me alone," snapped Dale, pulling away from her.

"It's about Debra Floyd.'

"What about her?"

"It's a game changer and should help you make up your mind," said Kit.

"Come with us," encouraged Chris. "He'll explain."

Dale followed, almost zombie like, the ordeal and the beating having taken its toll. Chris had coupled her arm under his. Touching him gave her a tingle. She blushed at the feeling. Dale felt nothing. She led him along like a little puppy dog, saddened how troubled he appeared to be. For the first time she regretted her involvement and her decision to become one of the Shadow Men. Too late to turn back now, she sighed. She texted Everett to let him know they were bringing Dale.

Soon they had delivered Dale to their leader. Dale eyed him with apprehension. Everett was really no better than Jake. They both had an agenda and used people. Dale had grown tired of being used and abused. His life belonged to him. His decisions counted.

"We have heard about Debra Floyd," stated Everett Graham. "It is such a terrible tragedy."

Dale stood motionless. He had heard this speech already, sort of. He didn't trust Everett anymore then he did Jake. He subconsciously clenched his right fist. He was ready to take his frustration out on someone, anyone.

"We know who did it," Everett confessed.

"Who?" yelled Dale, snapping out of his stupor, "Who killed her?" He couldn't believe he had just said that. She couldn't be dead.

"Please keep your voice down," pleaded Everett, scanning the patrons of the mall's food court.

"Don't play games with me. I'm not a good gamesman. Who did it?"

"Who do you think?"

"It was Jake, wasn't it?"

"They tend to do what they want, like they're above the law, don't they? It's like they think they are untouchable," stated Butch.

"I confronted Jake. He said he didn't do it."

"Maybe he didn't or maybe he did, or just maybe he's protecting the one who did. They tend to stick together."

Dale maintained stern eye contact with Everett, thinking he wasn't any better. "You're saying another of their kind is responsible."

"Their kind, I like that analogy. Seems obvious given the circumstances wouldn't you agree?"

Dale, fuming now, started to leave but Butch and Greg grabbed him by his arms, stopping him in his tracks. He was growing tired of being subdued and jerked his arms free. "What are you going to do, take them on by yourself?" asked Everett.

"I'll turn them in to the police."

"Where's your proof?"

"Wise up. You have no evidence," added Kit.

"The police can find it once I put them onto the trail."

"And if they can't find proof that they did it then you're next," warned Chris. "You do realize that they don't like you?"

"Your call," advised Everett, "or you could join us."

Dale hated making decisions. His track record sucked. He certainly didn't trust this Everett kid.

"Do you want the killers or not?' asked Kit.

"What's in this for all of you? Why am I so important in this stupid tug of war?"

"We have been assaulted by them relentlessly forever just like you have," explained Everett, "and forever stops now."

"So if I say I'm in then what?"

"It's not quite as simple as that," stated Everett. "You must pass one test. Call it your initiation so that we know you're trustworthy."

"I want to know who did this so what do I have to do?"

"Chris will walk you home. She'll provide you with your task. We must be sure you're with us to the end."

"The end?" questioned Dale. "That sounds so final."

"Let's go," motioned Chris.

"The meek shall inherit the world," boasted Kit, snapping a photo of Dale and Chris with his cell phone as they walked away.

"Victory," added Ronny, high fiving Kit.

He had no doubt now. This place was indeed something out of the Twilight Zone. Crazies were running rampant. It was infectious. Debra Floyd was most likely dead just like that Cassie girl. He couldn't bring her back and he wasn't sure if he wanted to live without her. Fact he would avenge her murder. Obsession devoured his mortal soul. The pimply faced skinny ass recluse had purpose and a death wish. He pushed his glasses up.

"Are you all right?" asked Chris.

"Anything but…and stop asking me questions. For once, just shut your damn mouth for a change, how about it?"

That stung her like a slap in the face. Dale had been pushed too far and it scared her. She wanted to tell him the truth but did as he had asked. She stopped talking for now.

72

Brenda Jackson, still in her familiar surroundings, sat on her bunk, sober as a judge and contemplating her options one more time. She really had only one option and knew she had to bite the bullet and do it; call her parents. She couldn't stay in here forever. Her son and husband needed her and she needed them. Standing, she knew she had to call for the guard and this time make that phone call, if they didn't think she was crying wolf again.

Another woman had just been placed in the cell with her. The heavy set black woman with short braided hair had seemed highly agitated from the time they had locked her in but she had said nothing. She had begun pounding her fist on her bunk and had just thrown her pillow toward the bars. Tears were rolling down her cheeks.

Brenda had been there already and thought maybe she could console her. At the sound of her voice the woman leapt from her bunk and began yelling, "You, you're the one that reported me, aren't you?"

"Me, reported you for what?"

"Yeah, it was you. I'm sure of it. I saw you haul my children off. You were that white woman in that van. Now you're in here to spy on me so you can tell them not to give my children back to me."

"I've been in here the whole time. I assure you I know nothing about your children."

"Don't you mention my children, I'm warning you. You did it. I know you did it. I hate liars and you're a liar and don't even try to lie about it."

"I'm sorry. You're not making any sense. Let me get the guard for you."

"So now you're going to call in your help. You're not getting off that easy," the woman yelled as she charged Brenda, grabbing her by her hair and slamming her face against the concrete wall.

Dazed, Brenda fell to her knees. The wild woman, still holding her by a handful of hair dragged her toward her bunk, then flipped her on her back and began slamming the back of her head against the floor. Brenda, the former beauty queen and faithful wife and mother, floundered around like a rag doll unable to scream, blood filling her mouth and throat.

The woman let her head drop to the floor and reached for a pillow on the bunk. "Try to take my children will you and make them think I'm unfit." She covered Brenda's face with the pillow and held it there until Brenda went totally limp. She removed the pillow and spat on Brenda's pale lifeless body, then returned and sat on her own bunk as if nothing had just transpired. There would be no phone call.

Darby Jackson wiggled his fingers on command. Doctor Fitzgerald smiled. "You're progressing nicely, Mister Jackson. I'm sorry we still haven't had any luck contacting your family."

Darby regretted this also. He feared something terrible had happened. He concentrated, willing his lips to move. He longed to talk, to be able to phone his home and contact his family. He wondered if Brenda was intentionally staying away, possibly protecting Dale, worried how seeing him in a coma might scar him for life. That had to be it, he thought. More determined than ever, he would lick this and reunite with his family.

"Do you wish for me to send the police to check on your family?" asked the doctor.

Darby squeezed his hand twice. He didn't want to traumatize them. In good time he would be back in their loving arms.

"Very well, rest then," advised Doctor Fitzgerald.

73

"So that's it?" asked Dale.

"Yes, complete the task and once we confirm you have completed it, you're in," verified Chris.

"*In*, what's that supposed to mean?"

"You'll be one of us."

"And just exactly what are you?"

"Shadow Men," she answered, knowing she wasn't supposed to utter those words until he had completed his initiation.

"Shadow Men," he repeated. "Catchy."

"Please keep that to yourself. I wasn't supposed to tell you that yet."

"So I do it tomorrow and then I'm a Shadow Man, just that simple."

"Yes, it's just that simple."

"Then what…"

"We initiate our plan," she told him as she kissed him on the cheek.

He wasn't moved by her kiss nor did he appreciate it. "So I guess I'll know the plan tomorrow."

"Yes. Don't look now. It appears you have company." She pointed to Ted Parker perched on his porch. "Remember, you can't tell him anything. You're our last recruit."

"Sounds like I'm enlisting for life."

"Something like that," she replied. "See you tomorrow. Please do what's expected of you." She headed back up the street.

Dale ambled down his walkway. Ted threw up a hand and greeted him as if nothing had happened earlier. Dale nodded.

"So why were you with her again?"

"Never mind her, Ted…why are you here? I told you to go home."

"I did and now I'm back. What did she want?"

"She's concerned about Debra just like we are. Is there anymore news?"

"You're not going to like it. That's why I'm here."

"Spill it."

"They haven't been able to identify her body yet. The Rock Hill police said parts of her were missing."

"Parts were missing. What do you mean parts were missing, Ted?"

"She had been decapitated. Her hands, feet along with her head were missing. They only have her torso. The serial killer cut her up into a bunch of pieces."

"Mack the knife," cursed Dale under his breath, clinching his fists.

"What?"

"Nothing," replied Dale, remembering that Mack had that knife and now a gun.

"You didn't have any run-ins with Jake and that crowd of his, did you?"

Dale shook his head no. "Thanks Ted. Now please go home."

"Are you going to be all right?"

"No, are you?"

"No word on your mom?"

Dale shook his head no.

"You still think she skipped out?"

Dale shrugged.

"How's your dad?"

Dale shrugged again.

"You want me to stay here with you tonight?"

"No, I want you to go home."

"All right then, I'll head home. See you tomorrow at school."

Dale nodded and tried to smile.

"Meet you at our usual place?"

"I'll see you in class."

"Don't do anything stupid. I'm running out of friends."

Dale turned and walked into the house, turning on the lights as he passed through each room. He heard the answering machine beeping, indicating that there were new messages. He walked into the kitchen where the machine was located on the bar and watched the blinking light while he poured a glass of juice. Sitting at the bar he continued to watch the blinking red light, undecided whether he really wanted to listen to them or not.

Taking a swig of the orange juice, he assessed his situation. After all, he had choices. Everything in his world came with choices now, like it or not and he didn't. Good news or bad news, he wondered. If his dad had gotten worse, what could he do about it? If he had gotten better, he faced the same dilemma. He had no transportation and no mother. He could probably overcome the transportation obstacle but how could he possibly explain his mother's absence again? Why had she run out on them at a time like this?

Dale took another swallow of the juice. The bitter taste caused him to smack his lips but drew him no closer to making a decision. In some ways he felt like he had grown up in the last few weeks and in other ways he felt smaller and more vulnerable than ever. With neither parent around he had definitely had to step up to the plate but Dark Thirty still held him prisoner. Some things were impossible to overcome.

Dale had actually stood up to bullies more than once. He had discovered he liked girls. He had made friends. He had ridden a bike and driven a car. He had learned to prepare his own meals and stay by himself. Staying by himself hadn't always been successful in the battle against Dark Thirty but still he had done it.

Dale's presence had helped his dad return from the dead. He had learned to make decisions and had discovered that making them didn't always result in a happy ending. Dale smiled thinking how he had even experienced an adult situation in that shower. That had been both scary and invigorating until he figured out nothing was broken. Yep, he had surely come a long way in a very short time.

The beeping and blinking machine jolted him out of his trip down memory lane and his assessment of his accomplishments. Choices, to listen or not, what was a man to do? He downed the last of the juice and set the glass on the bar then slid the answering machine directly in front of him. The display indicated three messages. Dale pressed the delete button three times and immediately questioned had he made the correct decision. That was the flaw in having choices. You were never really sure.

Darkness began rearing its ugly head but he had an uglier monster eating away at him right now, tomorrow's task. He removed the note from his pocket and unfolded it. He read it wondering if Chris had written it or one of the others. He suspected it didn't really matter. He read it a second time then a third. It was quite direct and to the point.

What sort of games were these Shadow Men playing? How ironic, he thought, if he completed the task and passed his initiation, he too would be a Shadow Man. He, one who is terrified of the dark and the ominous shadows lurking within its evil core, could soon be a Shadow Man. And why was Chris the only girl in a guy's game?

He chuckled out loud thinking how he had so often criticized Debra for asking him all those questions. Boy, he sure had his fair share of them lately. Maybe she had possessed him. He didn't want to think that thought because if she had, that meant she was dead. How brutal, to dismember someone like that. Had they raped her like that Cassie girl before they killed her? Revenge, there would definitely be revenge. Thinking about a passage from a bible study, Dale altered the version and whispered, "Vengeance is mine saith the Shadow Men." He folded the note and slid it back in his pocket. Who was the real monster now?

Chris used her cell phone and called Everett on her walk home. Like a general, he expected his troops to report in and to keep him posted. She didn't feel much like a soldier.

"What does your instinct tell you?" Everett asked her. "Is he on board with us or not?"

"He's a tough read but I think you've pushed all the right buttons. He's a nice guy and I hate what we're doing to him."

"Nice guys always finish last or at least until we alter the game. I warned you to not let this become too personal."

"Do you really think we can do this?" she asked, shrugging off his accusations that she felt something for Dale Jackson.

"It will end tomorrow night one way or the other. Are you prepared for either outcome?"

Chris expelled a ton of breath then answered, "We swore to it, didn't we?"

"That's not what I'm asking you," pressed Everett, attempting to read the tone in her voice.

"Am I prepared to be a martyr? Are you?"

"Perfectly, long live the Shadow Men and forever we will change the world."

Chris ended the call. Her faithful leader was sounding scary. She began to have regrets, questioning what she had gotten herself into and if there was a way out. Everett made it perfectly clear that once in, you were in. She sighed. She no longer embraced her new found cult.

74

Jake had assembled them in his backyard. His folks were attending some sort of social event at his father's law firm so meeting here had seemed to be the logical place for him and his boys. Still disturbed by Jackson-hole's accusations and sudden bravado, Jake had decided something had to be done to put a halt to all this talk of kidnappings and murders. He wanted no part of it and certainly had no intention of having his name being thrown into the suspect pool.

"What do you make of his finger pointing?"

"His honey is missing," spoke up Stoner, toking on a joint. "He's just grasping at straws. He has nothing. We've done nothing, so end of that story."

"Man, put that thing out," he warned Stoner. "Don't be doing that crap in my back yard. I have neighbors."

Stoner licked his fingers then pinched out the smoldering joint and placed it behind his ear. He had burned one before arriving so he had a good buzz going already and didn't need it. Eyelids heavy, he tried to focus on the conversation.

"I knew we should have done him a long time ago," stated Mack.

"We've done him several times already, once knocking him out cold and putting him in that closet. I pounded him today and he doesn't care."

That wasn't exactly what Mack had in mind when he said, *do him*. He thought best not to clarify his real implications. Obviously Jake was copping out and dragging these other guys down with him. He was no real leader by a long shot, thought Mack. Jake couldn't afford to muddy up the water too much with his parents being so prominent and upstanding in the community. Mack didn't have those sort of family pressures. He should have taken over long ago but still, Jake could serve as their scapegoat if things really went wrong. They surely seemed to be heading down that path.

"Guess everyone has heard by now," continued Jake. "They hacked her up and apparently scattered the body parts."

"Do you think the same one that did the retard did motor mouth?" asked Stoner.

Ray looked over at Mack. He thought better of commenting after he saw Mack fondling the Colt hidden in his belt under his shirt. Mack returned the evil eye. He had no doubts that Mack could be capable of carving her up. He didn't carry that buck knife for the hell of it and he was just plain crazy to boot.

"I was wondering that too," said David.

"Don't killers usually kill people the same way?" asked Rich. "Cassie wasn't chopped up."

"I don't know; think about those *Friday the 13th* movies. Jason killed those camp kids every kind of way," said Stoner.

"That's just a movie," Jake pointed out to his blurry-eyed, stoned friend. Getting ripped was Stoner's talent.

Stoner was unfazed by the comment. "What about the *Texas Chainsaw Massacre*?"

"Cool movie," snickered David. "Leather Face was a hoot."

"Does anyone have any idea who might be doing this?" asked Jake.

Again Ray glanced over at Mack but said nothing. Ray worried that if Mack did go down, would they be deemed his accomplices. Actually, only he and Buddy could be tied to Cassie. Their DNA would most certainly spell doom for both of them if it got that far. Planning ahead, he figured he could testify against Mack and bargain for his own life if it came down to it. Right now he could say nothing while Mack was on the loose. Mack the knife wouldn't hesitate slicing and dicing him.

All conveyed that they had no idea who was perpetrating the crimes. Even Mack chimed in saying he had not heard anything on the streets. Ray thought how convincing he had sounded. As long as Mack had the gun, he could say anything he wanted.

"All right then, we've got to defuse Jackson. Does anyone have any ideas besides beating the snot out of him? I don't think that will work on him anymore."

Mack spoke up. "What if we can come up with a way to make him look like he was involved in the killings? With the heat on him, he would have to leave us alone."

Jake asked, "How could we possibly pull that off? We have nothing tangible to link him to them."

"I have that other pistol we swiped from the pawn shop," answered Mack. "We could plant it somewhere and then tip off the police saying we had seen him threaten both girls with it. Think about it. He's new in town and the killings happened after he arrived and the gun is stolen. We can make the cops think he was in out the pawn shop thing."

"That's good," exclaimed Stoner.

"What if he's really the murderer?" asked David. "He sort of looks like a younger Norman Bates. What do we really know about him?"

"He does act sort of weird now that I think of it," added Rich.

"Has anyone ever seen his parents?' asked Mack stirring the pot.

"No, I don't believe we have," replied Jake, buying into Mack's theory.

"What if he's already done them and stashed them in the freezer or something?" asked Stoner. "And he enjoys doing girls. He can handle them better than guys."

"Think about it," continued Mack. "First we're told that his old man is a police detective then we hear he's a vegetable in the hospital. Doesn't that alone seem a little hokey?"

"And where's his old lady?" asked Stoner. "No one takes or picks him up at school or anything. He's iced them already for sure."

"Crap," exclaimed Jake. "We might just be on to something."

Mack smiled. This was just way too easy. "Where can we plant the gun and get the ball rolling?"

"Why don't we just call the cops and snitch on him?" asked Stoner.

"The gun plant serves two purposes," rationalized Mack. "It takes any potential heat off of us."

"You mean you," Jake corrected him.

"Jealous Jake," snapped Mack. "Remember, you have that stupid picture of the race car driver? You had your chance to take something worthwhile but you didn't."

Jack stared down Mack, but quickly lost the stare down. He suddenly realized he feared him. The Colt probably reinforced his feelings. For a fleeting moment he wondered if Mack could be the killer. He sure hoped not. Their association with him would only incriminate all of them. Finally he turned his back on Mack, his only way to show the others that he hadn't rattled him. He wasn't so sure the others were buying it.

75

The homeroom bell had rung and Ted saw no sign of his friend, Dale. He had either overslept or skipped school. Ted opted for the latter. He had smelled something fishy yesterday in his demeanor. Hindsight, he should have never given in to Dale's demands and should have camped out there. He couldn't be searching for Debra now. They had found her body, pending the positive ID. This stunk. His pal could be in trouble.

Trying to rationalize the situation, Ted thought maybe he had to go to the hospital or possibly his mom had returned home. What if she had returned and whisked him away? She had taken him somewhere and he would never see him again. Not knowing was driving Ted squirrelly.

His absence did not go unnoticed by Jake, Mack or even Stoner. Jake wondered what had prompted Jackson to skip today. Had he gone to the cops already? He had not counted on him not being here. Geeks like him always came to school. It was like some sort of unwritten law, a code of the nerds. Yep, he was up to something for sure.

Mack sat there and fumed. This screwed up everything. He had stashed the pistol with his Colt, and he had planned to retrieve it and covertly sneak it in during gym class and plant it in Jackson's locker. While the others were playing baseball, he could sneak to the hiding place and bring it in where there were no detectors or surveillance cameras. Well, he didn't really need him here to do that, he thought. Maybe with him not being at school today would play into their favor. They could point out his strange behavior just before the gun had been found by school officials and the cops.

Stoner wondered where the little possible murderer had disappeared. He smiled, visualizing him off somewhere killing somebody else. You had to watch those quiet types for sure. They were the ones capable of doing crap like this. Stoner's imagination went wild, thinking of the possibility of Jackson leaving a string of corpses state to state. How cool would it be to say he had known a real killer and had helped capture him? He needed to burn one badly.

Ronny Templeton of the Shadow Men, also shared homeroom. He surmised that the plan had been set in motion when he spotted the empty seat. Dale Jackson had come through for them. Everett had been absolutely right in his conviction to bring Jackson into the fold. Something bothered him. Jake and the two others were acting suspicious like they were up to something. Surely they were not the reason that Dale wasn't here? Could they have headed him off and done something, preventing him from completing his mission? He tried to dismiss this thought but how would he know for sure?

Chris Herndon sat three doors down, directly behind Ray. She too stressed out about the unfolding events. She had Dale's locker under surveillance until the bell rang, prompting her to go to class. Dale had not shown his face. A part of her wished he had chickened out but she knew everything depended on him doing what had been asked. She had a bad feeling about today. She wasn't a hundred percent sure she was prepared for the outcome. Once you're in, you're in for life. She didn't like the premise.

Everett Graham sat in his class across the breezeway, calm, cool and collected. He had long ago prepared for this day. Selection of the right mix of recruits had been meticulously calculated. The plan had been orchestrated flawlessly, at least up until now. Dale Jackson was the wild card. The Shadow Men had a lot riding on him. He looked over at Kit Argo and nodded. Kit touched the side of his nose in response. That signaled that no one had seen Jackson this morning. He had taken the bait. Everett looked over at those poor unsuspecting bullies, Rich and David, and felt a sense of pride.

Dale had never cut school, had hardly ever missed a day, yet here he stood outside, while class commenced without him. He felt too much like a fish flopping around on the shore. This was supposed to be called playing hooky so maybe he should pay homage to Carl O'Conner and go wet a hook or drown a worm. Best to stick to his assigned task, he figured.

Dale ensured class had begun first then he followed the directions provided to him by Chris Herndon. He liked Chris but not nearly as much as he had liked Debra Floyd. They were so different. He trusted Debra but no longer trusted Chris. What did either of them see in him? No girl had ever seen anything in him before he had arrived in Charlotte. He figured they had lower standards here. Whatever the reason, he soaked it in and thoroughly, enjoying the attention or had until now. He so missed Debra. This was for her.

Okay, he should be close now and just like magic he had found it. To his surprise, he had entered the bonus round. It had been so easy. He wondered why it necessitated him missing an entire day of school. Homeroom wasn't even over yet. He could still make it in time to get in a full day. He thought long and hard but his assignment did not include attending school today.

Besides, he would see Jake and the others. He wasn't sure if he could contain his hatred towards them and as Everett had pointed out, he couldn't take them on alone. He didn't think he could count on the Shadow Men coming to his defense, not at school. They had displayed no evidence of aggression or violence. They apparently depended on wit and safety in numbers instead. Ted, Debra and he had used that same strategy. Debra was now gone. He couldn't visualize them defeating Jake and the others in a fair fight. They didn't have much of a chance in an unfair fight either.

With the first part of his mission completed, Dale had the day to kill until the others joined him. He was not accustomed to having this much time on his hands, not during these hours in late August. He had to keep a low profile for sure. He would stand out like a sore thumb. Although he had plenty of time to go to the park, he decided it was best not to because he would be too much in the open getting there.

Dale came up with a plan. He could cut over to the library then through the back streets to the cemetery, the same cemetery where he had been locked in that crypt. He had a sandwich and bottle of water so he was good to go. The sunny summer morning would make the graveyard much less intimidating. Hurry up and wait as they say. He would join the Shadow Men at five PM, almost nine hours from now. This would be the longest day of his life.

Mack waited inside the boy's shower until the others had exited for the baseball field for forty five minutes of warm sunshine and national pastime bliss. This would allow him more than enough time to covertly slip off the school grounds and to his hiding place to retrieve the extra pistol. He had already breached an opening in the fence the night before. All that remained was for him to successfully get out and back in undetected by human eyes. He would plant the gun during one of the last class changes. He already knew Jackson's lock combination having observed him numerous times as he accessed his locker. He relished every moment leading to Jackson's demise.

The officials and police should have a field day with this one, especially after he and the others anonymously planted the seed that Jackson could be the killer of both girls. One problem stymied the plan. Jackson's DNA would not match those deposited by Buddy and Ray. That would possibly absolve him from Cassie's murder but his reputation should forever be tarnished just the same. He would never be able to explain the gun and soon it would link him to the pawn shop break in. Either way, he would be out of the picture and suspicion would be drawn away from the rest of them.

Mack completed the first leg of his journey, making it through the fence unobserved as best he could tell. He would have rather taken care of Jackson by other means but he had no choice but to stick to this plan. After all, he had been the one to suggest fueling the fire in this manner. Planting the pistol would fan the flames. Either way, Jackson would be history.

He soon arrived at his hiding place and set his book satchel down to retrieve the pistol. Cursing an oath under his breath, he reeled, seeing that the extra pistol was gone and so was his precious Colt. Someone had found them and had taken them. Mack looked around quickly fearful that the cops might have his hiding place staked out and him under surveillance. He saw no one but that didn't mean they weren't there. Too late either way, he had been caught with his britches down, guilty as charged if they wanted to take him.

Worse still, his finger prints were all over both guns. He had planned to wipe the extra pistol clean before planting it in Jackson's locker. Now, he was the one screwed. At least neither gun linked him to the other crimes, only to the pawn shop robbery which still spelled trouble. Struggling somewhere between rage and panic, Mack stood there like a deer caught in the crosshairs of a rifle. He wasn't sure what to do next. He had lost control of the situation and the risks were high that he might not get out of it unscathed. Then he saw the folded piece of paper where the guns had been stashed.

Dale Jackson stashed the two confiscated guns along with his lunch in a hedge row and began strolling among the tombstones. He ran his fingers along the top of one weathered by time and tilted slightly backwards. Francis A. Lewis, born January 22, 1879; died September 12, 1927, Loved to Farm, Died from a Kick from his Favorite Mule, Pappy. Dale enjoyed reading the names, dates and especially the inscriptions on many of the ancient ones. It helped kill time until his scheduled rendezvous with the Shadow Men.

Robbie Grimes, born July 4, 1853, died December 25 1859. We brought you into this world with a bang on the 4th and buried you on Christ's birthday. We enjoyed you for six short years. We love you, Mom and Dad. With that, Dale thought about his own parents. If he would have had his driver's license and a car, he could have spent this time checking on his father or searching for his wayward mother. He didn't even own a bicycle.

Walking deeper into the graveyard, he caught movement from the corner of his eye and ducked behind a huge granite stone. Two men were erecting a canopy tent near a freshly dug grave. A third was unloading folding chairs from a flatbed truck. Luckily none of them had seen him. Staying low, he altered directions, only standing when he had lost sight of them after going down a slope.

Dale soon found himself in familiar territory. The crypt where Cassie's body had been found and the same one that had imprisoned him loomed straight ahead no more than twenty yards. Something drew him toward it like a powerful magnet. It beckoned for his return. He resisted its lure, more concerned that the police may still be watching it in hopes of capturing Cassie's killer. He had already experienced the crime scene and had no desire to return yet it tugged at him. The hairs on the back of his neck tingled, standing on end.

He took a couple more steps in the direction of the crypt then suddenly felt the Siren's call. He could almost imagine faint voices whispering his name. He wondered if Cassie's spirit was trying to reach out to him. Maybe she needed closure to move on and he played a key roll in bringing her peace. He shivered, suddenly feeling chilled. As much as the supernatural and the unknown intrigued him, the crypt struck fear in his heart. Still the uncanny sensation persisted.

Before he could give in to the temptation of once again exploring the inner sanctum, he heard some sort of engine approaching and again ducked behind nearby tombstones. A caretaker riding a four wheeler pulling a utility cart appeared to be heading too close to his current location. He back peddled until he heard the engine fading. Once he put some distance between himself and the crypt, he no longer felt compelled to visit it. The spell had evidently been broken.

He found an old oak near where he had stashed the guns and flopped down at its base. He leaned against the old trunk and soaked in the rays. The late morning summer sun toasted his outsides. Soon he entered the world of head bobbing, drifting in and out of dream world. As bad as things were, he had no horrific nightmares. He experienced only good thoughts and visions, at least at first. His dreams were filled with better times with his parents and he saw Debra Floyd, smiling and snorting that laugh. She seemed more animated than ever.

One particular image depicted Debra sitting on her bike and motioning him to follow her. He was on foot and trying to keep up. She shouted for him to hurry. He was losing ground fast even though the scene seemed to be occurring in slow motion. She pointed somewhere ahead but his eyes were in a blinding fogginess. He could not focus on whatever she wanted him to see. Suddenly she vanished ahead in the thick fog bank. He asked where she was and he could hear her shouting but try as he might, he could not find her. She was lost but her voice eventually became weaker and weaker until it faded all together.

Dale woke feeling defeated. He envisioned somehow that it was his fault that she had become lost and he had not been able to find and rescue her from that engulfing fog. It had all felt so real and he so helpless. Suicide nudged its way into his thoughts. His death could reunite them possibly but taking one's own life supposedly cursed you to a life in hell so there were no guarantees that he would ever see her again if he followed through on this.

Finally returning to the world of the present, the position of the sun now alerted him that it must be late afternoon. He had thought he had only just napped for a few minutes but it appeared he had been out for hours. The great outdoors apparently had a calming effect on him. He did his best sleeping outside in the daylight. He reached in his pocket and retrieved his band-less wrist watch and sure enough, it was just past four PM. He had just enough time to make the rendezvous zone by five. He gathered up the guns and whiffed down his sandwich along the way.

The afternoon streets were a buzz with rush hour tragic. Every hour seemed like rush hour in Charlotte. Dale, keeping a steady pace, headed towards the rendezvous spot. He had paid little attention to the guns, handling them only once when he placed them inside his bag. He wondered what Everett wanted with them. Surely he didn't plan to use them. He assumed he would soon find out.

Earlier, Mack had retuned to the gym class one pissed off and concerned puppy. He had shown the computer generated note to Jake before the start of their next class. Their plan now foiled; they were at the mercy of the one who had stolen the guns. Adding insult to injury, the note had been signed by Dale Thomas Jackson. The little weasel had skipped school to perpetrate this travesty against them. Mack had never wanted his hands on someone so badly in his life.

Jake more than ever was convinced that Jackson was the killer. He had large balls for such a little skinny nerd and now he had the guns. This made him doubly dangerous. What they had no way of knowing was that Dale hadn't been instructed to sign the note; only to take the guns and leave the anonymous instructions. Dale had decided to sign it at the last minute to antagonize them. It had worked.

To further complicate Everett Graham's original scheme, Mack was not supposed to have discovered the missing weapons and note until after school, leaving them very little time to react and work a counter plan. Now the bullies had almost a six hour heads-up but the Shadow Men didn't know this fact. While Jake's plan had come unglued, so had Everett's and now Dale had inserted his own agenda into the mix.

After the last bell, Jake assembled his cronies to fill everyone in on the missing guns and note. Mack, still fuming could hardly contain himself. He wouldn't rest until he got his hands on the brazen little bastard. Jake, while more calm, was ready to make him pay too.

He read the note out loud.
YOUR WEAPONS ARE IN SAFE HANDS.
IF YOU WANT THEM, COME TO THE
VACANT TEXTILE WAREHOUSE ON
SEVENTH AND ELM. WE NEED TO
TALK. JAKE, MACK, STONER, RICH,
RAY, DAVID PLAN TO BE THERE AT
10 PM. THIS IS OF THE UTMOST
IMPORTANCE.
IT'S TIME TO BURY THE HACHET.
Dale Thomas Jackson

"Does he have a death wish, stealing my Colt?" shouted Mack.

"Like I said, he's got balls," added Jake.

"What do you really think he's up to?" asked Ray.

"Maybe he just wants to bring an end to us picking on him," said David.

"Stealing my Colt won't buy him any bonus points."

"I don't like it," commented Stoner. "This stinks. I think it's a set up."

"What do you think he's going to do, bring Parker along and ambush us?" asked Jake. "He has no other friends except for Debra Floyd and she's dead."

"He's got Mack's guns," Rich reminded them. "That equals out the playing field."

"I can't imagine Jackson-hole stooping that low, to shoot us."

"Hey, we wouldn't have believed he would stand up to us at all," said Stoner, feeling his face where Dale had struck him.

"I think we should go there now and stake the place out," stated Mack.

"So we're going to camp out there for six hours," commented Jake.

"Well, it is all the way across town," Ray reminded them, "and why so late on a school night."

"He laid out of school so he's had all day to get there," said Rich.

"That blows," stated David. "We don't have wheels today."

"I can't believe Jackson picked way over there," snapped Mack.

"I tell you, it stinks," repeated Stoner. "We need to get our hands on some more guns."

"I'm not robbing another pawn shop," vowed Jake. "Do any of your folks have any we could sort of borrow?"

"My dad hunts and he has a shotgun and rifle but he keeps them under lock and key," said Rich.

"My old man has a military pistol but I think it's just for looks," said David.

"Only the Colt has bullets," spoke up Mack. "And that little prick can't be a good shot."

"It would probably land him on his butt if he fired it," laughed Stoner. "But just the same I don't trust him. He's been showing off his ass too often lately."

"Might be that Jackson-hole just wants to build up a little reputation," stated Jake.

"Oh, he'll have a reputation all right, one for being dead," fussed Mack.

"Here's the deal," said their leader, Jake. "Everyone check in. Call your folks or whatever and we meet at the mall food court in thirty minutes. We grab us a bite then we head to that mill. Hopefully, we'll be there before Jackson-hole and nab him and the guns when he shows up. I can't see him being there now."

"Then we make him pay," added Mack, and he wasn't thinking a mere ass kicking.

"I'm with Mack," added Stoner. "We owe him something real special."

"Sounds like you have something in mind," said Jake.

"If he hasn't, I have," answered Mack for both of them. "He's good as dead."

Jake looked into Mack's eyes and believed he meant just that. He was losing control of him and wasn't sure how far Mack would push things and if he could stop him if he had to. Jake saw this getting out of control but didn't know how to derail it without looking like a wimp. He had always been the leader. For the first time he wished he wasn't.

76

Dale Thomas Jackson stood inside the dugout on the third base line. From the height of the grass in the outfield and weeds growing in the infield baselines, the baseball field had not been used in a very long time. He figured Everett had chosen this spot for that very reason. He was about fifteen minutes early but saw Chris Herndon approaching from the dilapidated first base side bleachers. She was alone.

Dale watched as she made her way along the perimeter fence passing behind homeplate. She waved, her full mouth of pearly whites, reflecting off the sunshine. She wore a red blouse and cut off jeans that didn't do much for her spindly white legs. That's why Dale hated to wear shorts. He always thought he had bird legs.

"Well, did you find them?"

"Right here," he patted his bag. "Where are the others?"

"It will just be me and you."

"So are we going to that mill to meet them?"

That had been the original plan but Chris didn't tell Dale that. Instead she said, "You've passed your initiation. You are now a full-fledged Shadow Man."

"Just like that…"

"Just like that…" she repeated.

She had been instructed to escort Dale and the guns to the mill where he would participate in the final ceremony, cleansing the world and making it a better place. She had opted to deviate from plan. She had also decided she didn't want to be part of it either. She stood firm on her decision.

"I thought we were going to be there when the others arrived."

"Change of plans, we're to hide the guns and then go to your house and wait for further instructions. Everett will text me later."

"What are they going to do when Jake and the others show up?"

"Convince them to stop their bullying ways."

"Their kind won't listen to our kind. Everett should know that by now."

"Everett does not believe in or follow those preconceived rules. He thinks the time has come to change things."

"Jake won't compromise with them. They'll probably just end up getting their butts kicked."

"Another reason why we shouldn't be there," Chris smiled, touching Dale on his cheek. "Bruises look so nasty on me. Purple is not my best color. Let's stash these guns and go to your house and wait."

Dale tried to conceal his disappointment. He wanted to be there. He deserved to be there. He owed Debra. He thought about going anyway but he didn't know exactly where this mill was located. Sure, the note spelled out an address but still, this was a big city and he was a little fish in a huge bowl. He sighed and decided best to follow their instructions. After all, he was now a Shadow Man but was low in the pecking order.

They decided to hide the guns under a pile of weather worn lumber behind a graffiti laden restroom. They made one additional stop by a McDonalds for a soda and fries on Chris. Dale had no money. She convinced him it was part of his little welcome party to the Shadow men.

It was almost seven-thirty by the time they headed down Dale's street. Conversation had been scarce. Dale still brooding about the turn of events, felt a little guilty for spending time with Chris. He almost felt like he was cheating on Debra, another first, feeling this way. He tried to corral his anger, thinking about what they had done to her. He shouldn't be here. His thoughts were disrupted by a familiar figure. Ted sat on the front porch steps like a statue.

"Why are you here?" Dale asked angrily.

"You weren't at school. I got worried."

"I'm fine."

"And you're with her again," Ted said, displaying a little anger of his own.

"Go home, Ted."

"You say that a lot lately."

"He means it," chimed in Chris.

"What have you done? Have you used witchcraft on him?"

"Yeah and if you don't do what you're told I'll turn you into a frog."

"Ted, please go. This doesn't concern you," said Dale trying to tone it down.

"Oh, what's the matter, you two want to be alone?"

"Matter of a fact, we do," Dale answered, shocked by what he had just said.

Chris smiled and crossed her arms, not believing what he had just said either. She liked it but it still shocked her just the same. Guilt showed its ugly head. She should tell him but not now. She would milk the moment and see where it might go.

"You heard him. Three's a crowd and you're number three."

"You're both messing up. I just know it." Shaking his head, he walked away. Dale just didn't get it. He was his protector and Dale sure needed protecting. This wasn't over yet. He wouldn't allow it to be.

Dale watched his friend make the turn at the end of the block and drift out of sight. Ted didn't understand but he was trying to protect him. It was screwed up all right.

"Let's go inside and you can tell me more about the Shadow Men."

"I suppose since you are now one of us, why not?"

"I'm not sure if I should feel honored or be leery."

"Yes," replied Chris to both.

Chris began by explaining it should be no mystery to Dale that bullies had ruled the earth since day one. They preyed on the weak, those least likely to retaliate or resist their wrath, because the bullies were spineless yet ruthless. Dale required no history lesson because he had already filled in too many chapters. He encouraged her to skip that part and get to the formation of the Shadow Men.

Everett Graham had also been bullied by Jake and his band of tormentors. He had suffered abuse since the first grade until now at the hands of Jake Tyler. He had always considered Everett to be an easy mark. Everett, even to this day, had never stood up to him or any of them. He had taken what they had dished out like so many of the weak.

During the past summer Everett had decided that he had had enough of being the butt of their jokes and a source of their income. Too often he had to fork over what wealth he had in his pockets or face a beating or worse at their hands. Their MO was to have their victims strip down and run them naked or in only their underwear through a public arena. Now as a teenager this exercise had gotten to be much more embarrassing especially for those not endowed anatomically. The family jewels paraded in front of peers both male and female could leave lasting emotional scars and had for Everett Graham.

Everett, realizing that organizing a resistance to fight them was futile and down right moronic, had explored other alternatives for deterring or at least curbing their appetite for relentless attacks. He came up with the name Shadow Men, not to sound threatening and menacing, but rather to stand for those who remain in the shadows, covertly taking care of business while remaining anonymous and out of the limelight.

His intent wasn't to protect all of the less fortunate from the bullies. That was not an obtainable goal and, he decided, a very unrealistic one. Hindsight, Chris now admitted Everett's creation of the Shadow Men had been more to CYA, protect his own ass. She, as had the others, been naïve to this fact. She had at least seen it for what is was way too late but the others still believed in the cause. Everett was quite the snake charmer, not so unlike his counterpart, Jake.

Everett was very selective in his recruiting process. He had a method to his madness but only he knew the formula. He personally had handpicked everyone. Dale had been the final pick. Everett had this fixation about the number seven. He often referred to the western cult classic, The Magnificent Seven. He portrayed himself as the movie's main character, played originally by *Yul Brynner*.

Dale interrupted, "So, is what we have here his brand of *Revenge of the Nerds*?" asked Dale, thinking Debra would be proud of him being talkative and actually asking questions.

"Much more evil and devious that those movie nerds," Chris quickly responded.

"I thought battling it out wasn't his intent?"

"No battle, no fight, no war; just total annihilation I'm afraid, but then I'm getting ahead of myself."

"Annihilation, but they're still here?"

"Not for long…"

"Okay, finish it, Chris…now."

She did just that, telling Dale how Everett first recruited his right-hand man, Kit Argo. Poor Kit had moved here last year, two months into the school year so he had no chance of blending in and as luck would have it, he shared PE with the entire Jake clan. One look at Kit and there was no mistaking he wasn't the athletic type. To make matters worse, Kit avoided taking showers in front of his peers, which is a hygiene requirement for PE, not to mention it just stirred the pot of the tormentors. They love making fools of the less fortunate.

Surrounding him at the conclusion of PE, they ordered him to shed his jockey shorts and head to the shower. Kit did the unthinkable. He flatly refused. They assisted him in the removal process. They pounced on him and stripped him down, planning to parade him around the locker room and eventually into the shower.

Chris explained that the rest was just secondhand information of course, confessing never having seen Kit in the buff, but to their disappointment, Kit was manlier than they had anticipated. Their plan had backfired. This infuriated Jake and the gang to be upstaged by such a puny little runt like Kit. Surprises often come in small packages. Kit had always been ashamed thinking he was a freak for being different.

"They abused him in other ways, unthinkable things. Kit won't talk about it. I think he hates them worse than Everett if that is possible and he never reported the abuse."

"Would you have?"

"Probably not," admitted Chris.

She continued. Everett had his dad pull some strings with school officials this year to excuse Kit from having to take gym class. It was explained as medical reasons and it really wasn't that far from the truth. Indebted, Kit became the first pawn on Everett's chessboard. Rumors are that there might be more to their friendship, she elaborated and winked.

Chris recounted how Butch Harmon, Ronny Templeton and Greg Rollins each overcame their demons with Everett's help and fell under Everett's control for one reason or another. While each story varied, the theme remained the same. They had all experienced extreme abuse, more so than others, at the hands of Jake and his demented followers. Everett had been their great savior.

"So that leaves you and you can spare yourself the embarrassment, I get the picture."

"Aren't you even curious as to why I'm the only female Shadow Man?"

"Not in the least," he lied but still feared too much sexual content might cause his own uncomfortable awareness.

"Suit yourself."

"You want a soda?"

"Sure," she answered.

"Then you can tell me what the Shadow Men are up to tonight and why we are not participating."

Sitting at a circular table in the mall's food court, the combatants chomped away at their preferred fast foods, everyone except Mack. He just slurped on a large root beer eyeing the rest and resenting them all. He could have taken care of Jackson without their help after he retrieved his Colt. They were just cramping his style, especially Jake.

He especially loathed the faithful leader, having been given everything on a silver platter. Mack had never really accepted Jake as one of them. He could have so easily blended in with the snobbish jocks and Beta Club crowd if he had wanted to but for some reason he had chosen to be the rebel. Mack just wasn't sure of the cause.

"Did anyone talk to Ray after we split up?" asked Jake.

"He said he had to go home first," acknowledged Rich.

"Maybe he's just running a little late," added David. "Give him a few more minutes."

Gutless wonder, thought Mack. Ray was no better than that other little dip, Buddy. At least Buddy realized it and had bailed out quickly. Ray on the other hand had pretended to be still in. Mack had seen through that charade from the beginning. He had absolutely no guts and Mack could easily envision Ray being Jackson and Parker's third wheel, worthless fagots all of them. He would personally take care of Ray after they finished with Jackson. It would be his pleasure to eliminate the potential squealer before he had a chance to tell what he knew about that Cassie retard.

"Let's go," commanded Jake. "We want to be there before Jackson-hole arrives."

"It better not take long," advised Rich. "I have an eleven o'clock curfew on school nights."

"You'll be cutting it close getting home in time from that mill," warned David.

Stoner had not muttered a word. He sat leaning against a post, eyes closed and zoned out. He had gotten hold of some powerful Columbian reefer from a cousin and it was promptly kicking his butt. All conversation sounded far away and muffled.

Rich began waffling. He had just gotten off probation with his dad recently and didn't cherish being back on it. His dad still believed in governing with a thick leather belt and the back of his hand. He could still feel the stinging effects from both of them.

Jake stood to signal their departure. David and Rich both stood up too, David nudging Stoner back to life. Mack took his time about standing, his way of protesting Jake's authority. Jake took note of it immediately and knew they were closer than ever to a head on encounter. While Jake was larger and much more athletic than Mack, he wasn't so sure he could take the little bulldog on in a one on one.

Mack carried his buck knife everywhere except on school grounds and he wasn't afraid to use it, Jake suspected. He didn't know where he stashed it before entering school each morning. Obviously it wasn't the same place as the guns or he would have bitched about Jackson-hole having gotten it too.

"I've got to take a dump," announced Rich. "I'll catch up with you guys in a few minutes." He rushed off like he was about to drop the load in his pants. Mack, suspicious of Rich's behavior, told Jake he had to take a leak but would meet them outside Belk. Trailing just twenty paces behind Rich, he saw him hang a right just before the restroom and towards another mall exit.

Closing in quickly, he grabbed Rich by the arm and spun him around. "Little Richard, the john is back that way."

Rich, caught like a rat in a trap, couldn't utter a response. Mack had his arm in a vise-like grip. Rich could see the fury blazing in his eyes and almost pissed his pants.

"Come," advised Mack. "I've got to take a leak. I'll walk with you."

Rich did the only thing he could do and accompanied Mack back to the restroom. He had expected to pay hell tomorrow for chickening out but at least he would have had all night to come up with an excuse. Now he had none and Mack knew exactly what he had been planning to do. He could have probably smoothed this over with Jake, but not with Mack.

Once inside the restroom, Mack forced him into an empty stall and clicked the lock behind them. He pulled out his buck knife and held it up in front of Rich. The knife's blade reflected off the florescent lights temporarily blinding Rich. "I'll come along, I promise," whined Rich.

"I couldn't give a rat's ass whether you come or not. Here's what I want from you. Tomorrow, you align your butt with me as the new leader. Jake's rein is over. In return I don't stick that pretty face of yours with my knife. I'll tell Jake you had a bad case of the runs and won't be joining us. You got it," he asked nicking the side of his nose with the point of the blade.

Trembling and now in dire need of the john, Rich whispered he understood and agreed. After Mack exited the stall, Rich dropped his pants and unleashed his bowels. Mack at least wouldn't be lying to Jake about the runs part.

Mack joined the others outside and informed them about Rich's little problem. Jake shrugged, figuring the four of them were more than enough to take care of Jackson. Mack thought there were three too many. He wished the rest would be suddenly stricken with diarrhea, with the exception of Jake. He wanted to pound him, almost as much as he did Jackson.

77

The Shadow Men arrived at the ball field but did not see Dale Jackson as expected. This perturbed Everett. He demanded perfection from his chosen followers.

"Maybe he's just running late," stated Butch.

"He's had all day to not be late. This is unacceptable; totally unacceptable."

"Perhaps we misjudged Jackson," said Kit.

"Could be that he had cold feet," added Ronny.

"No, I don't think so. He wanted revenge for Debra Floyd. I saw it in his eyes. He believed we could deliver the guilty party to him and assist in this revenge plot."

"Then what could have possibly derailed him?" asked Greg.

"Chris," stated an enraged Everett Graham.

"You really think Chris would have betrayed us?" asked Kit, "For the likes of Jackson?"

"I do and she has. I tried texting her earlier and she ignored me. We'll not worry with that now. I am convinced Jackson completed his directives so we shall stay our course. We'll give our guest a warm welcome as scheduled. I'll discuss this unforgivable betrayal with Chris tomorrow, face to face."

"If we have a tomorrow," added Kit.

"Tomorrow is forever. It's our future, our destiny," stated Everett with a deranged gleam in his eyes.

Kit was thinking that Chris might have been the intelligent one. Even if they pulled their plan off flawlessly, would there be a future for any of them, he wondered. He owed Everett a lot but was the price too high. Hadn't he more than repaid the favor? Past, present and future all seemed one big blur.

"Shadow Men, our destiny awaits," Everett spoke with his influential smile. "The meek shall forever dominate the earth."

"And God forgive us, for we know not what we are about to do," whispered Kit. "Or at least that will be our plea."

"Shadow Men," they screamed in unison.

78

"So tell me, Chris Herndon, why the Shadow Men didn't want me there? They told me who killed Debra. I owe it to her to be there."

"You tell me. Are you prepared to be a murderer?"

"Eye for an eye, isn't that how it is supposed to go.'

"You've certainly become quite vocal."

"And one who has choices and I have learned to be quite decisive."

"Did Debra Floyd bring you out of your shell?"

He almost shrugged but instead answered, "Yes, I believe she did. Why did they involve me?"

"I told you. Everett believed in the power of seven and you are the seventh."

"Then why am I not with them or you? Without us they are only five."

"Because I decided not to take you there..."

"So they are expecting us..."

"They arc."

"Then why are we not there?"

"Because what they are going to do is wrong and until you, I saw things their way."

"So I impacted your decision."

"I had choices, too. I decided I no longer wanted to be a Shadow Man."

"You still haven't told me what they plan to do."

"Eradicate their tormentors."

"You mean they plan to kill Jake and the others. I thought they didn't believe in violence."

"No, they would never think of taking them on in a fair fight. Trust me, they aren't planning anything fair."

"I don't understand."

"You took Mack's weapons and left the note. They'll go to that old factory building seeking the writer of the note, set on revenge, intending to reclaim their prize. Everett plans to trap them inside and torch the building and burn them up inside."

"And you went along with this?"

She nodded. "I'm no better than them."

"But you're here and not with them."

"It doesn't change a thing. I'm still part of it. I'll be just as guilty as they are if their plan works."

"And so will I. I signed my name to that note. They're seeking revenge on me. I planned to do the same to at least one of them but you screwed up my plan too.

"But not Everett's, I'm afraid."

"We should stop them."

"You, me…how can we possibly do that?"

"I've got a new plan."

"Count me in then," she smiled.

Dale so consumed by her revelations had lost track of time and his keen senses. Dark Thirty had managed to sneak up on him. Dusk knocked on the door. Dale scrambled to switch on the lights. Chris stood there not knowing what to make of this sudden transformation. Finally she asked, "What's gotten into you?"

Dale paid her no attention as he ran the gamut, switching on every light. Chris thought he looked like a madman. She witnessed Jeckle and Hyde, Dale oblivious to her presence, sprinted up the stairs.

"What's happening to you?" she screamed. "Are you on drugs or something?"

79

"Creepy place," said David looking around the huge emptiness of the textile mill.

"Easy enough to get in here through all the broken windows," commented Stoner. "Those sure were wild looking machines in that other section back there."

"Guess they're like dinosaurs now," said Jake. "The textile business has died around here says my dad. He says America sold out and let it go to other countries."

Mack mockingly clapped his hands. "History class a second time today. Are you planning on being a teacher, Jake?"

"Bite me."

"So where do you think Jackson will come in this place?" asked David.

"So many possibilities," responded Jake. "We'll have to fan out and each stake out a different direction."

"Good plan, Jake," smarted off Mack. "That's why you're our faithful leader, I suppose."

Mack was playing him, thought Jake. What was he up to and why now, he wondered. "All right then, we'll do the north, south, east, west lookout points."

"Oh, please let me be north," Mack raised his hand figuring that to be the logical entry way from the street.

"Which way is east?" asked Stoner.

Jake pointed.

"I'll do west," said David.

"That leaves south for me," stated Jake. "Take your positions."

"Hey bright guy, what do we do when we spot him?" asked Mack.

"What else...jump him then bring him to this location and yell for the rest," instructed Jake.

Right, thought Mack. If I see him first I get my Colt, then I test it. They can follow the sound of the shot. Then, I'll take care of my old buddy, Jake.

"Well, there it is," said Butch, pointing towards the old brick building.

"Shadow Men, check your lighters," commanded Everett.

"Testing completed and exits are prepped and ready," answered Kit. "We're a go."

"Remember, we don't engage until all are inside section bravo and I'll be the solo rabbit with Chris AWOL. Kit, that means you pull double duty with our Mister Jackson AWOL too," verified Everett. "No witnesses, an arson attempt gone badly by our horde of worthless bullies."

"And if they nab you?" asked Ronny.

"Proceed as planned," ordered Everett. "I'll accept the consequences. Sadly, Chris apparently did not share our dream."

"Don't let it come to that," said Kit, placing his hand on Everett's shoulder.

"Shadow Men forever," shouted Everett.

"Forever," the others repeated.

Mack heard voices. Had Jackson brought others? The door creaked open just to the left of his position, nearly two hours ahead of Jackson's note's instructions. Whoever these people were, they were screwing up everything. He hoped they would leave before ten o'clock. He recognized them. All attended his school and all were worthless little turds.

The one called Graham began barking some sort of instructions to the others and pointing. They began spreading out as if taking strategic positions. Mack didn't like what he was witnessing. It stunk to high heaven but for now he could do nothing but watch.

Chris ascending the stairs, watched as Dale frantically entered and exited rooms, flipping wall switches and lamps on, oblivious to her. He looked like a woodland creature bounding just ahead of the blazing fire. She could do nothing to intervene. Eventually he slowed. His breathing returned to normal. He looked her directly in the eyes. "It's okay. It's okay. Really, it's okay."

"What brought that on?"

"Dark Thirty is here," he whispered.

"Are you afraid of the dark or something? You speak of it as if it something real."

"Dark Thirty is more than just darkness. It's the purest evil. It lives to steal your soul, my soul...."

"Have you always been like this? I mean...does it happen every night."

Dale shrugged. "You've got to stop the slaughter. The blood will be on our hands if you don't. You've got to go to that mill and stop the Shadow Men."

"We'll both go. I thought that was the plan."

"You don't understand. I can't. It waits for me out there and would never allow me. You've got to do it."

"Are you crazy? I can't stop them by myself."

"Call the police."

"And what, have them all arrested? I can't do that."

"Then you must stop them. You have time if you go now. You told me about where it was and you can make it there before they do it."

Chris rubbed both hands through her hair. She should tell him. He deserves to know but now wasn't the right time, not while he was in this state of mind.

"All right, I'll try but I think it's futile. I know Everett. He is determined to see this to the end. He's obsessed with it. He's almost as crazy as that bunch that messes with us."

"Go,'" he yelled and she did.

"Stupid, stupid, stupid...stupid" Dale shouted. "I should be there. I signed the note. I stole the guns. He killed Debra. I owe Debra. Mack is evil. He killed Cassie. Mack is a demon. He killed because he likes killing. Mack is the Anti-Christ, a murderer. Mack...Mack...Mack is Dark Thirty...he is Dark Thirty...Dark Thirty killed Cassie...Dark Thirty killed Debra...Dark Thirty must be stopped."

Ted Parker sat on the edge of the porch listening to the rants of a madman, his friend, the madman. He was the self appointed protector of the madman. Dale Thomas Jackson needed him whether he knew it or not. Just try to make me go home this time, he mumbled, as he entered the house, poised to fight if he had to.

80

Mack found it difficult to hold his position and remain hidden. He had no way of signaling any of the others and really had no intentions of doing it in the first place. He thought it best to just observe and try to figure just why they were here. He had identified all five of them and despised each and every one. Of course Mack wasn't really keen on people in general. Those little dips always seemed to travel in packs lately and that alone made it difficult to cull one from the rest and have a little dishonest fun.

Darkness approached and this made it difficult for Mack to monitor their movement. All five appeared to still be in this massive factory room but he wasn't completely sure until he spotted a series of lights. It was cell phones. They were texting one another. He counted five locations. They were setting up camp in this room for some reason. Why, he still wasn't sure and where was Jackson with his beloved Colt? Mack felt naked without it. He still had his buck knife but it just wasn't the same.

Jake sat in the diminishing light, struggling with what to do about Mack. He had obviously lost control of his primary henchman and wasn't sure what he might pull next. He wondered if the others were preparing to back him. There would be a showdown soon with Mack, of that he had no doubt.

First things first, teach Jackson a valuable lesson and by doing so maybe save face with the others. His was concerned about Mack getting his hands on that Colt 45 again, so it might just be prudent that he laid claim to it first. The Colt could be the ultimate game changer. The owner could hold the winning hand. Jake had never been a loser. He didn't intend to start that trend now.

Everett Graham, founder of the Shadow Men, wiped sweat from his forehead. It must be at least 100 degrees inside the old mill. Summer still had its foothold and the mill, without much air circulation, held the heat in its grip. The back of his tee shirt clung to him as if he had just climbed out of a swimming pool. Even in the oppressive heat his skin tingled, anticipating the forthcoming events and the ultimate end for his tormentors. He still fumed about Chris Herndon bailing out on them. She had apparently prevented Jackson from showing. He should have known better; inviting a female into the fold.

He played out the events in his head. If they pulled this off without a hitch and he had no doubt that they would, he still had the other situation to deal with. His options were narrowing. Ultimately he knew what must be done to tidy up all loose ends but he dreaded it just the same. The others would have to be dealt with for jumping ship.

Kit still agonized over following through with this. Sugar it up and justify all you wanted. It was still murder and premeditated at that. He wasn't sure of the penalty for it but figured it could be severe if caught and convicted. He had not disclosed his feelings to the others but wondered if they were thinking the same thing.

At Everett's persistence and justification, they were in over their heads but it wasn't too late or was it? Chris had been the smart one. She probably had a conscience. Would his allow him the same escape and what would be the consequences if he chickened out; not as bad as the consequences if he completed the task.

Still there was that other thing hanging over their heads and he wasn't sure what Everett planned to do about it. Kit figured if he somehow got over this hurdle, he may have to draw the line if bad turned uglier with the other situation. The darkness and ticking of the wristwatch didn't help. Both seemed to magnify his concerns. Waiting allowed too much time to ponder.

The oppressive heat sucked the life out of him like a tick on a dog. Perspiration formed puddles at his feet. He glanced at the time on his phone; less than fifty minutes until the designated show time. Reckoning time approached. He had to resolve this soon. Could he really live with himself if he went through with the plan? The act seemed so senseless now that it was near.

Five minutes before ten…

Mack could smell his own body odor. His confinement had offered no relief from the relentless heat. Even darkness had not impacted a significant temperature drop. This stupid waiting had gotten to him. What were they doing? Then it struck him like a lightening bolt. Glancing at his waterproof diver's watch he knew what they were up to. They were waiting on them to arrive.

This had been a set-up. The theft of his guns by Jackson, the note had only one purpose, to bring them here and not to hook up with Jackson but instead for some sort of ambush. But what did they plan to do? He had seen them bring in no weapons and surely they weren't so stupid as to take them on in a fair fight. Where was Jackson?

Mack wondered. Possibly they already had weapons concealed at each one of their hiding places. What did they have, baseball bats and hockey sticks? Even with those, the little farts couldn't think they could stand up to them. No, they had his Colt and even if they didn't know how to aim and fire it, it still gave them a decisive advantage. But he had one thing up on them. They didn't know that their prey was already in the building. Sadly, neither Jake nor the others knew what he knew.

Everett figured it was just about show time. He sponged the perspiration from his face with his tee shirt. His job, lure them center stage then the Shadow Men could ignite the strategically staged combustibles. The fire would trap them inside. They would perish in the fire. He would be rid of Jake and his horrible horde. Everett texted the Shadow Men stating it was time. He stepped from his hiding place, his flash light aimed at the floor as each stride took him closer to the middle of the room near the plant's main entrance.

Kit watched the flashlight dance along, realizing it had begun. He still had time to stop this. The others had not yet arrived. No blood stained their hands yet. He still wondered whether Ronny, Butch or Greg possessed the guts to put a halt to it too. He doubted any of them had the backbone to do it even if they were so inclined. None of them would defy Everett because he had them too brainwashed.

Only he could stop it now and he wasn't so sure that he could muster up the courage to do what needed to be done. What would it take to buck Everett? If he was going to do it, he better act quickly. Too late, the main entrance door creaked open and the patter of footsteps indicated their guests had arrived.

Everett held the flashlight up to his face and it illuminated it like some ghoulish freak. It was imperative that they saw him and advanced to his central position. "Welcome," he offered his greeting, his voice echoing in the cavernous room.

"Stifle it, Everett," spoke a familiar voice.

"What is this, a cameo appearance?" asked Everett now redirecting his flashlight in the direction of the speaker.

"We can't go through with this," warned Chris Herndon.

"Sure we can if you will be so kind as to hide your pretty little ass, or better still, assume your assigned location. Remember, you are a Shadow Man and you swore to an oath."

"Well, I'm recanting my sworn duty and if you don't halt these proceedings…"

"You will do what, my dear Chris," he finished.

"I'll report it to the authorities."

"But you forget…you are part of this too."

"I don't really care how terrible these scumbags are, this is nothing but cold-blooded murder. You can't just burn them to ashes."

"And can't we? Think of all the obscene things they have subjected us to and especially what they did to you. You can still stand there and tell me they don't deserve it."

"That's exactly what she said," replied Mack, stepping from his hiding place, grabbing then twisting Chris's arm behind her back with the buck knife against her throat.

"No RSVP, how rude," exclaimed Everett, "and where are your pals?"

Mack didn't respond to his question. "Tell your nerdy buddies to come out of their hiding places before I slit her throat from ear to ear. I know where they are. I saw you texting one another."

"Not until yours show their faces," countered Everett.

Mack could not deliver on that request because Jake and the other two were in different sections of the textile plant. He doubted they would hear him if he yelled for them. "I'm telling you a second time, you sneaky little queer, order them front and center along with you. You and your band of spineless faggots were going to torch us, weren't you? Don't even think about lying. I heard what you two said."

Everett knew, one quick text and the Shadow Men would ignite the fires but his plan could not be implemented until the others were in here with Mack. He had to call Mack's bluff. "Slit her throat and then you'll be the murderer. Oops, I forgot, you're already a murderer, aren't you? She's a female, so there you go, the perfect scenario, except, there are witnesses this time."

"I haven't killed anybody, not yet." Mack didn't take kindly to being backed into a corner. It left a bitter and vile taste in his mouth, coming from the likes of one of them. Time to up the ante, he penetrated Chris's throat with the point of the knife, just enough to produce a trickle of blood. There was no turning back now. All was being laid on the line, do or die literally, and Mack didn't intend on being the one dying. He could easily slit her throat then nail Graham but the other four were poised to start their fires. The question, could he escape if they did.

He decided to spell it out. "So here's what we have. I do her, then you. Your little buddies might or might not have the balls to start those fires. Either way, you won't know if they did or didn't, will you? I believe they call this a Mexican standoff, don't they my little faggot friend?"

"Oh, they'll set the fires, I assure you and then you'll join me in hell, won't you? Either way, it ends here."

"And this accomplishes exactly what? We'll all be dead. Jake and the boys will just pick them off one by one."

Kit Argo, sweating bullets, didn't like where this was headed. No good would come out of them setting the fires now just to rid the world of Mack. Chris certainly didn't deserve to die at his hands.

With lightening fingers, Everett keyed in, *Butch, engage.* After a slight pause, fire blazed from the south exit.

Kit dropped his head at the sight of the fire. Mack's mouth dropped open, disbelieving that they intended to go through with this. They had never reacted like this, ever.

"You got a death wish, don't you?" asked Mack.

"How did you ever guess?" replied a smiling Everett Graham. He keyed, *Greg, engage.* A second fire ignited to the right and quickly traveled along the expanse of all the windows.

"Okay, you started it, I'll finish it. Her death is on your hands."

The thunderous echo of the gunshot was a game changer indeed. "Drop that knife, you murdering son of a bitch," yelled Dale, now standing in the main entrance way. The recoil almost dislodged the Colt from his hands.

Still clutching Chris, Mack spun around to face Jackson fearlessly. Mack couldn't believe it. There stood Jackson, pointing his very own Colt 45 directly at him with his right hand. He held the other gun in his left. He looked like a deranged Gumby.

Mack laughed out loud. "You don't know who you're screwing with do you, Jackson?"

"A cowardly girl killer," replied Dale. "And I'm here to even that score. Fess up and I might spare you but I doubt it."

"You really think you can hit something with that Colt. You best stick with that other little pea shooter. It's more your style. It doesn't pack the punch that's going to knock you on your ass."

Everett texted, *Kit, engage.* Nothing happened. *Kit, engage.* Nothing happened. He then yelled, "Shadow Men engage."

Kit flicked on his flash light and closed the distance just behind Dale. Dale tried to keep check on Kit while covering Mack and Everett. Gun slinging was not his forte. Mack had been dead on with his allegation that he probably couldn't hit any of them unless they were leaning against the end of the Colt's barrel.

The smoke from the other fires was already enveloping the room, prompting Chris to cough. And with each cough, came another trickle of blood because Mack still held the point firmly against her neck.

"It's over," yelled Kit.

"Not quite," responded a voice from behind.

Kit turned and was caught by a right cross from Stoner. Jake and David stood three feet back, Butch held between them. They had heard the gun shot then saw the smoke smoldering out the windows and blocking access from the rear of the facility. The trio had crossed paths with Butch as he tried to exit. He had a bloody nose and a swollen left eye. Greg and Ronny had witnessed his capture and had already left the premises, fearing the worse and not wanting to be part of it.

This had turned into quite a cluster, thought Everett, choking back tears from the snaking smoke. He wished Kit had completed his assignment and set those other two fires. "My counterpart," he greeted Jake.

"What going on here, Everett?" asked Jake.

Mack answered, "Jackson baited us here and the rest of these spineless wonders had planned to torch the place with us inside. It's getting rather toasty already, don't you think?"

"Everett Graham, you were going to kill us just like that," barked Jake, snapping his fingers. "We never killed any of you?"

"What you did to us was worse than a slow tortured death."

"We're talking murder here and we don't do murder."

"I suppose Cassie Richards doesn't count."

"You're crazy. I've been down this road with Jackson-hole already. We didn't kill Debra either."

"Ask Mack to deny it. Look at him with that knife to Chris's throat. He's poised to do again. I think he gets off on it."

Jake eyed Mack. He believed Everett Graham. Mack had killed Cassie. He could see the truth in his eyes. "You did it, didn't you?"

"He did," echoed Everett.

"I told you I didn't kill anybody." Mack turned to face Everett, blood in his eyes now. His body stiffened. Chris prepared for the inevitable, her throat was about to be slashed and she was going to die.

"Mack," yelled Stoner. "Why, man? We don't kill people."

"He suffers from *little man syndrome*," commented Everett. "Runts like him always want to be the big man."

Mack found it difficult to focus. All the accusations and the smothering smoke were getting to him. He turned one way then the other. Everett inched closer. Tears ran down Chris's cheeks. Jake spouted obscenities as did Stoner. David feared they were all about to die in the fire. They had set Ronny free and he had scrambled towards the door.

"Reckoning day," shouted Everett.

"Shut the hell up," yelled Mack as he felt the barrel of the gun to the back of his head. Dale had managed to sneak up on him.

"This is for Debra Floyd," shouted Dale Thomas Jackson, pulling the trigger.

"Noooooooo," screamed Chris. "Debra isn't dead!"

The gun clicked. Mack fell to his knees, squalling like a baby past its feeding time. Dale had fired the gun in his left hand, not the Colt 45. No bullets, Dale was spared from another first.

Jake and Stoner rushed Mack and snatched the buck knife from his hands then shoved him face first onto the concrete floor. "We've got to get out of here," yelled Jake.

Everyone made it to the safety of the front lawn. Jake and Stoner still restrained Mack. Everett and Kit kept their distance, standing side by side with David.

Dale finally managed to ask Chris, "Alive, what did you mean by that?"

"Mack did try to kill her, roughed her up real bad, and then dumped her body in the cemetery in a crypt. He left her for dead. Kit and Butch had been tailing him. They checked on her and she was still barely breathing."

"I felt her when I was in the cemetery earlier, at the same crypt they locked me inside."

"She's still there," said Chris. "Still in bad shape but alive."

"Why didn't someone take her to the hospital?"

"Everett didn't want her to be found until he used her alleged death to bait you in becoming a Shadow Man. I wanted to tell you when we were at your house but you were acting so crazy."

Dale pointed the Colt at Everett then at Mack. He didn't know which one to shoot first. He hated them both. Sirens broke the silence.

"Fire trucks are on the way," said Stoner. "We better get the hell out of here."

"Nope, police," said Dale. "And everyone stay put. I told Ted that if I wasn't back within an hour to call 911. It's been about an hour."

"Damned fool," spouted Everett.

"Yep, that would be me and proud of it," smiled Dale.

"Let's go," commanded Jake.

"You're going nowhere," stated Dale, aiming the Colt with both hands now, "It stops here. The abuse, the beatings, the murders, the lies…it all stops now. Jake, Everett you're too much alike and we don't need either kind to be among us. I figure we have plenty of stuff to assist the police in putting every last one of you away in juvenile detention. Arson charges and attempted murder should help. And real murder by Mack is the clincher."

Dale made them sit down against a wall, blue lights were exiting interstate 85 and were just a couple of minutes away. He gave Chris the Colt. "Shoot the first one that moves. I'm going to the cemetery."

"The pleasure is mine," she said, kissing him on the cheek. "You know, Everett would have killed her next if this fire thing had worked out. He planned to blame it on Mack."

Dale adjusted his glasses on his nose, nodded and then ran like the wind.

81

Dale sat outside the emergency room waiting for news, any news. Debra's parents had arrived and Dale explained the best he could to bring them up to speed. A reporter snapped photographs, flashes temporarily blinding Dale.

"Young man, how does it feel to be a hero?" asked the reporter.

Dale shrugged.

"You saved this young lady and have solved a murder and most likely prevented others. Your heroics prevented those teenagers from committing possibly the worse mistake of their young lives. You are indeed a remarkable lad. Would you like to make a statement for our readers?"

Dale almost shrugged but then he did another first. He actually reflected and spoke from the heart, "Most of the shadows of life are caused by standing in our own sunshine. There is a light at the end of the tunnel but first you have to find the light switch and then change the bulb before switching it on. No one can make you feel inferior without your consent. Bullies are such cowards and the dark is just the opposite of light and neither should ever be feared. I'm no hero, sir. I'm a survivor who has finally seen the light. Don't quote me. I surf the internet."

The reporter smiled then reached and proudly shook Dale Thomas Jackson's hand. "Son, it has been my honor to have made your acquaintance. You take care."

Mister Floyd nodded to the reporter and then asked, "Isn't this the hospital where you father is recovering?"

"Yes sir," replied Dale.

"Go check on him, son. We'll let you know when they bring her out and thank you for saving our little girl. You are the true friend she said you were."

"I like Debra. She sure talks a lot but she is my friend too." He then headed to the elevator. He beamed, now adding hero to his list of firsts. A friendly face greeted him ahead.

"Good job, Ted," said Dale.

"You're not going to send me home again, are you?"

Dale smiled. "You know I never meant any of that, don't you?"

"I'm here. What do you think?

"Let's go find my dad."

"The police detective," grinned Ted.

"Nope, just my plain old dad,' answered Dale.

Exiting the elevator, he walked down the hallway toward his dad's room. The hallway felt like the walkway of shame. He had let his dad down. He hoped he would forgive him. He paused at the closed door and glanced at the room number. He pushed the door open but his dad's bed was empty. He was too late.

A voice from behind startled him. "Dale Thomas, you're okay!" said Darby sitting in a wheel chair.

"You can talk."

"I can talk," replied Darby as Dale fell into his arms.

Dale didn't know where to start so he just blurted out, "I don't know where mom is. She hasn't been home in days."

"Push me down the hallway," Darby told him. "I need some air. Who's your friend?"

"Meet Ted Parker, my devoted protector and loyal friend."

"It's a pleasure to meet any friend of Dale's."

"I'm one of two but I'm probably his best."

Darby liked this Ted Parker. "How about helping Dale wheel me down the hallway?" They had only traveled the distance of three doorways when Darby asked them to stop. He motioned through the open doorway.

"Mom," yelled Dale. Brenda Jackson was lying on her back black, blue and bandaged. She opened her right eye. The left was completely covered with gauze. Even with the swollen and cracked lips, Dale recognized her smile. Darby smiled too. He had his family back and would never let them go again.

As Dale hugged her, it suddenly dawned on him. He had finally licked Dark Thirty, forever. He still had no concrete answers why it had terrified him so but felt it was somehow associated with bullies. Debra's shrink would probably agree with him. Dark Thirty was but a name, nyctophobia, but he no longer feared it, phobia conquered. Bullies would always be bullies but from this day forward he would tackle their kind head on. Dale Thomas Jackson would no longer be a submissive bottom feeder. Evolution, the meek had moved up the food chain. It was time to go wet that hook.

I read this posted on line just after completing Dark Thirty and it summed up what I had envisioned in writing this novel. Heather had it right.

The Call for Help

Posted: 12/30/2011

This poem come from my heart because i have been bullied since i was in pre-k and i'm a freshman now.

With in my life i see a light of joy and everyday it keeps fading into darkness. So i wish the light would come back. Also i fear what will happen once i'm in the darkness, i really hope my life can be bright once again. My friends i hope you'll help me out of darkness and into light, so will they be there for me or will i stay in darkness? At the start of my life i was only a little into darkness and mostly in light. Then when i started going to public schools i started to trail off into the darkness everyday. Some times i her the light calling me back, but the darkness always comes back. I just feel like an outsider, but always living in darkness. I just wish someone out there would come and help me back to the light. Then i can start over in the light and stay away from darkness. So if someone is out there please help me out of darkness. I beg you if anyone is out there once and help me and the others whom have walked this path of darkness. Til then we are still going deeper and deeper into darkness.

By: Heather

From the author for I have been there...

Say It

Kids have a knack for being cruel to other kids. I should know. I've lived both sides of cruel street. Until you've journeyed down both paths, you should be prepared to reap what you sow. Can you dish it out and then take what is dished? It's not so easy for everyone.

1966, having progressed with the same peers my first six years of school, I now found myself in junior high where three grammar schools had merged to establish one seventh grade class. Welcome to Abbeville High. New faces, new territory, and now having to re-establish my place in the primal food chain, growing up isn't what I had envisioned. Such is the life of the teenager.

At least for me back in the day, I didn't have to fret about being murdered by a peer like is common in today's schools. Worse thing I might have gotten a bloodied nose, a black eye or have been labeled as a loser or social outcast. Verbal abuse can often be worse than a good old fashioned butt whipping. So the question, how does one ensure they are accepted by "the in crowd", the click, the social elite, and avoid being labeled a book worm or geek or just plain loser?

Answer, study hard, excel in sports, become the class clown or take the low road, identify those worse than you and make sure you profile, highlight them as the targets of abuse. Sadly, I chose the low road. Boy was I stupid but what did I really know other than survival mode. Lesson learned, path chosen. I would achieve class clown status later in my quest. First I would experience the meaning of humble and I must confess that kids don't particularly embrace humble. We were so not into that.

Who remembers the classic cartoon, *Milton the Monster*? It was a classic in my day. *The Milton the Monster Show* graced Saturday mornings on ABC from 1965 to 1968.

Milton, the *Frankenstein's* monster looking character was anything but frightening. Always smiling and extremely good natured, he was just a big sap with a goofy good hearted demeanor and silly voice to match; bull's-eye on his back for bullies.

Like any cartoon series, it came with its own theme and musical lyrics. I'll spare you the entire song but it ended in "I'm Milton, your brand new son," as the square headed goof ball monster greeted his new daddy and creator, Professor Weirdo and side kick, Count Kook. Corny I know, so where am going with this, you ask?

Let's fast forward one year to 1967, having somehow survived my first year in junior high, managing to more or less fly below the radar screen. Fresh meat, a new crop of seventh graders had arrived on the scene, and they were fair game for our taunting and prime bait for diverting any attention to those of us that were potential bottom feeders.

One particular kid was big for his age, even larger than most of the seventh graders and had this oversized square head that so resembled Milton character's. Wearing huge black rim glasses didn't help his cause and his buzzed crew cut only drew more attention to the resemblance. A small group of upperclassmen, ninth graders sharing the same gym class with us picked up on this remarkable resemblance to Milton the Monster and so the games began.

Quickly they pointed out to junior that he looked just like the cartoon character then they asked him to sing the Milton the Monster song to validate their suspicions. The Milton clone willingly accommodated the older boys, not realizing his error, hoping to avoid conflict and deter further abuse. He knew the song by heart, every stinking word which led to his downfall and the relentless onslaught to come.

Thereafter, every day during gym class he was tormented by his persecutors and the taunt was for him to say it, say it! Instead of the entire song, he was only expected to repeat the last line; 'I'm Milton, your brand new son' followed by two toots mimicking cartoon Milton's ability to blow his stack.

In an attempt to be socially accepted by the upperclassmen, several of us eight graders joined in on the ritual taunting, all in good fun, of course, or so we justified it. It surely was better than being picked on or beat up on a regular basis by those same upperclassmen.

This progressed quite well for many weeks. We alternated turns pinning our victim to a gym matt or cornering him in the locker room and demanding that he say it and he always did. It was almost as if he embraced his role. We even attacked other wimpy seventh graders making them say it. Life was good. We were in the click and at the top of our game. We had our outlet, the diversion in place.

Then we suddenly had a new player, this renegade ninth grader, not of elite status, one we definitely called a bully back in those days. Apparently he had observed these antics and decided it was time for him to join in and flex his muscles. Ah, but he knew not how to play the game and he very aggressively targeted none other than me for the Milton role. I had never performed as Milton and I didn't embrace the opportunity. This wasn't going to be good.

Obviously I was being outgunned by a much older, larger and stronger adversary. One particular day he made his play. I had been launched into a most uncomfortable compromise in the locker room setting with the entire gym class as a captive audience. I had stubbornness on my side, something that my attacker had not anticipated.

Relentlessly, he chanted at me to say it. I refused. He pushed me and repeated, 'Say it!' Undaunted, I stuck to my guns and said nothing. Pinning me against the lockers very forcefully he commanded for me to 'Say it!' Six simple little words to a familiar melody, 'I'm Milton, your brand new son', would have ended the attack but I would rather take a beating than utter those words. I figured that was next on his agenda.

I scanned the onlookers for any signs of help but obviously there would be no rescue launched on my behalf; cowards! I was on my own. Now more frustrated than ever and losing face with his peers, he pushed me into a corner and delivered several more non-life-threatening blows to my shoulder and upper torso, 'SAY IT!' He repeated loudly. He lowered his voice and said, 'You've got to say it!' I shook my head no. I prepared for the beating I was sure I was about to receive for not playing the game and utterly disgracing the bully to boot.

He leaned in close and pleaded, 'Come on now. You've got to stay it. Say it. I said say it.' I stared into his eyes and I knew at that very moment, finally, my tormentor had realized he had met his match. He could not force me into saying it by threats or by inflicted pain. He could still settle for just kicking my butt but instead, he pushed me away, unleashed a few choice four letter words for good measure and one final blow, then allowed me to live another day.

Life lesson, from that point on, I no longer targeted the Milton look alike or any of his cronies. Saying it had lost its appeal. I had walked a mile in his shoes and my feet were blistered and hurting. To those I so unfairly treated, I do apologize, especially Douglas. I didn't say it to him then but I should have.

And to those other Milton's out there, stand your ground and don't say it or do anything that compromises your pride and belief. If you're not the physical fight back type and I certainly wasn't, then it's best to take a butt whipping and refuse to give in to the real bottom feeders. They're the ones eventually humbled. You might eventually wear them down but unfortunately they'll only target others.

Oh yeah, I'd rather be a live snitch than just another statistic. Look around. There are more of you than there are of them. Talk about it among yourselves and please don't bottle it up inside. Easier said than done and times are different now, I'm sure. CYA, do what feels right and by all means live to see another day! Whatever you do, do not become one of them and taking a life, theirs or yours, is not the right path. I don't have all the answers now just like I didn't have them then but I was certainly part of the problem, when times were much simpler than today.

PROSE PRESS

The origin of the word prose is Latin, *prosa oratio,* meaning straightforward discourse.
Prose Press is looking for stories with strong plots.
We offer an affordable, quality publishing option with guaranteed worldwide distribution.

Queries: E-mail only.
proseNcons@live.com

www.ingramcontent.com/pod-product-compliance
Lightning Source LLC
Chambersburg PA
CBHW061549100726
47898CB00002B/302